DARK SIDE OF TIME

DARK SIDE OF TIME

A Novel by
Vladimir Chernozemsky

Triumvirate Publications
Los Angeles, California

Dark Side of Time
by Vladimir Chernozemsky

Published by: Triumvirate Publications
497 West Avenue 44
Los Angeles, CA 90065-3917
Phone/Fax: (818) 340-6770
E-Mail: Triumpub@aol.com
Web: www.Triumpub.com
SAN: 255-6480

This is a work of fiction. All incidents and dialogue, and all names and characters with the exception of some well-known historical and public figures, are products of the author's imagination and are not to be construed as real. Where real-life historical and public figures appear, the situations, incidents, and dialogues concerning those persons are entirely fictional and are not intended to depict actual events or to change the entirely fictional nature of the work. In all other respects, any resemblance to persons living or dead is entirely coincidental.

ISBN: 1-932656-02-2

Library of Congress Control Number: 2004112526

First Edition. Printed in the United States of America
0 9 8 7 6 5 4 3 2 1

Cover and Page Design by Carolyn Porter
One-On-One Book Production, West Hills, California
Production: Nancy Gadney
Editing: Carolyn Porter, Steve Hobson

DEDICATION

With All My Love

to

Jesus of Nazareth

TO MY READERS

The *Dark Side of Time* had been simmering in my mind since I first read the Bible's New Testament. "Wow!" I thought. "What a novel this could be!" About the same time, a traveling Kabuki troupe introduced me to the ancient Japanese Noh Dramas, with their strange chants and stylized movements. They scared the daylights out of me!

Then an idea formed in my ever-plotting brain...what a marvelous combination those two would make — elements of the New Testament written as a Noh Play.

Years later, as a young actor in Paris I participated in "Theater of the Absurd," which was a virtual reproduction of what I had encountered in Kabuki Theater. Jean Cocteau and Ionesco did their best work there, so did actor, Jean-Louis Barrault, in such plays as *Waiting for Godot* — which to me is the perennial Noh Drama, minus the Japanese religious connotations.

And so I spun a tale out of these sources — Theater of the Absurd, Noh Plays, the New Testament — a novel about the various reincarnations of Christ and his coexistence with the Anti-Christ.

Theater of the Absurd could more rightly be called "Theater of the Abstract" — in broad lines: The Absolute. Reality is only a negligible part of it. Most of the characters in my story live in our adopted reality; however, some of them travel back and forth in time between realities. Their transit-stage is the theater, which of course, is merely pretend-reality.

Actors in a Kabuki play wear masks and heavy makeup. Characters in the Testaments do not. Yet this doesn't necessarily make them more believable because they were committed to parchment in ancient times as literal fact. The point is that we must choose not to blindly believe, not to surrender our right to examine history and to doubt all the dogma and rhetoric presented us.

In the early 1970s I met, by chance, a person in Rome who gave me access to important confidential information buried in the vaults of the Vatican Library. During my research, I came to find that in certain Scriptures of the New Testament, because of many individuals repeatedly hand copying these sacred writings through the years, there had been numerous distortions of the original texts. Essential parts had been replaced with material absolutely unrelated to the actual historical events recorded in the ancient biblical documents I was reading. I began to see links between the teachings of Aton of Amarna and Jesus of Nazareth, and the appearance of Christ during the Catholic Inquisition.

And when I read this inscription written in the margin of one of those early New Testament manuscripts by its scribe, a Monk:

"Lord, forgive me. I was ordered to do it."

...I began to suspect that beyond mere human errors in the transcription process, there were also changes to those formative versions of the Scriptures dictated by their overseers in the Church. This is supported by a generally known letter from a Medieval Abbot to his Bishop, expressing the Abbot's concerns about being forced to make certain modifications to the Scriptures on orders from his higher-ups. The Abbot was gravely concerned about what would happen to his immortal soul for changing the Scriptures. (Unfortunately, there is no record of the Bishop's response...)

Thus, according to history as I now understand it from those old manuscripts, in my story, the first appearance of Jesus was not in Judea, but earlier, as Lord Aton in ancient Egypt. And his current coming is long overdue. Recent global turmoil indicates that the Anti-Christ may have returned in new and terrifying forms — but as before, he still seeks world domination and a total destruction of our civilization so he can rule over the ruins.

However, as you read on, you may begin get wind of something new to come...

Vladimir Chernozemsky

PART ONE

THE CRIME

THE CRIME

KNOWING ALL, WE SO MAY DIE,
OR FLEEING DEATH AND DOOM,
WE MAY ESCAPE.
Homer — *The Odyssey*

In the eyes of a 9:00 to 5:00 worker, the life of a drifter might seem adventurous. At the same time, a drifter is looked upon as a subject of deprecation. It takes a certain amount of courage to drift in the void, but this simultaneously appears as a mindless act perhaps triggered by an obsession to avoid roots or attachments. In such case a life becomes sour and sooner or later leads to despair. First of all, one would have to cut his original roots and then bury the memories. Gordon Bates gradually followed such a path without really intending to. Then it turned into a habit and the habit took possession of him.

He never finished his archaeology classes in college. After he had left for college, his parents decided to start a new life and simply left him and the country to do so. Gordon decided to assume the Aristotelian logic, which, according to his Webster Collegiate Dictionary, was the doctrine of syllogism, to emphasize the empirical and particular, or to be scientific rather than metaphysical. As his roots disappeared, he let everything Platonian be purged out of his system.

He left college behind him and became a day laborer, going from job to job. The South American wetbacks hated him for taking the jobs they might have had and made his existence quite difficult. Thanks to some knowledge of martial arts he had very few fights — still he had to watch his back. Because of his darker complexion, one could agree that the presence of some African blood ran through his veins. He couldn't care less, but not claiming to be a minority deprived him of any chances for better paying jobs. He just made the most of what he had. It wasn't much, but there was very little he tried to do about improving it. He simply did not care.

Gordon's love life wasn't particularly tidy. Desiring to remain unattached, he simply turned to chance meetings void of responsibility for either party. Prostitutes were repulsive to him, especially those with sad stories. He harbored a hostility toward men, which he never tried to understand. He didn't try to make friends and no one tried to befriend him. Feelings of loneliness never bothered Gordon and he was simply contented to be left alone. Music to him was just background noise and books, at their best, okay but an unnecessary pastime. Movies were downright boring to him, and dreams about the future practically absent from his life. He had a natural aversion to boozing. Because he was a born athlete, sports was his one interest — they gave him a good sense of timing and coordination. His brush with religion in school had only strengthened his long-held suspicion about something unclear and mysterious and had never been attractive to him.

Now, in the last days of the old millennium and the coming of the new, a final denouement was generally expected. To Gordon, it meant nothing. The year 2000 was just another number.

He had learned neither to hate nor to love — he was a complete bystander.

Even bystanders have to eat, especially after a day of hard labor. He was familiar with the little plump black waitress in the hot-cafe kitty-cornered from the building where he rented a dirty, furnished efficiency. In Memphis, Tennessee, a tenement of this kind didn't cost much. The long hot summer combined with the steady humidity of the mighty Mississippi made all faces depressed and sweaty. Even the black waitress, with her forgotten African ancestry, peered at him mournfully. He stirred in her nothing more than a mild interest.

"The same as usual?" she asked.

"Same as usual." Gordon drawled.

Her low-drawn voice cracked as she looked toward the hot grill with the eyes of a martyr and asked, "A cold beer?"

"Make it two. You need to cool off too."

The girl sighed and wiped her fleshy face with a musty kerchief. "Gawd's my witness I do."

She marched toward the kitchen dragging her feet and her extra large buttocks stuck to the wet fabric of her skirt provocatively. Gordon, mildly interested, wondered how old she was. He pondered her heavy bosom, her full lips always half open, the corners pointing down like a tragic mask from a Greek play. He had never seen her smile. Maybe she wasn't young at all, or perhaps age didn't matter to her — a timeless wench, straight from another millennium. She watched him eat as she sipped from her beer. Gordon's labor-toughened hands stopped with knife and fork dug into the tough meat. He had never asked her name. Did it matter? As their eyes locked sluggishly, she seemed to read his thoughts. "I'm finishing my shift in half an hour," she flatly proposed.

Without seeming to react, Gordon went on with his overdone beefsteak, washing it down with the cheap beer. Thank God it was icy. "It's a damn hot evening," he finally observed after a long silence.

"So it is. It might get cooler after midnight," the waitress responded coyly.

Gordon pushed his plate back, nibbling on the last French fries. "No... it won't. It may get even more stuffy."

The waitress made a try for a smile. It failed. "You don't look like a white man, but the sun will kill you, college boy."

His thick dark eyebrows knotted over his large nose. "I'm no college boy. I dropped out long ago. What is your name?"

"Steffy," she giggled.

"Don't you have an African name?" Gordon pushed.

She looked at him slightly shocked. "What are you talking about? My family's name is Steward."

Gordon glanced at the bill and left ten dollars in the little tray. "Too bad... I thought you'd have an exotic name, like Mouamba, Luanda or something like that."

She took the bank note and put it between the impressive swelling of her breasts.

"Why?... I don't even know anybody that's been to Africa. Now, tell me, what's your name?"

Gordon had a nice set of pearly-white teeth. His smile made up for some of his other shortcomings. He brushed a few crumbs from his lips, "You can call me Bates — like the guys on the job."

Gordon continued to probe Steffy. "You dislike your race?"

Her voice became brisk and defensive, "Well, it is said that I'm from Egyptian stock. My people served the pharaohs. Some of them in a high capacity."

Gordon fought a belch and lost the battle. "Pardon me... By the way, Egypt is in Africa."

The young waitress picked up his dirty plates and silverware with great clatter. "You're a very boring person."

He caught her wrist at the moment she was ready to leave. "I'm sorry...I didn't..."

She pulled her wrist without much verve. "I don't care what you think of me."

"Can we make peace?" Gordon cajoled.

"Why?" Steffy sniffed.

Gordon consulted his watch and commented suggestively, "You'll be out in a few minutes."

"Soo-o-o?"

"Damn... I told you... I'm sorry," he said a little louder than he meant to.

Steffy, looked at him more closely, then with a slightly exaggerated sigh said, "You live around the corner?"

Gordon pushed a toothpick between his front teeth and nodded curtly.

The girl pondered a bit, then, "Just for a short time. I don't like boring men."

She did like boring men.

Chapter 1

PETER MOUGHABEE

The next day was Saturday and Gordon slept in late. The night before was rather a blur. He had passed most of it with that so called Nubian Egyptian. It didn't matter one way or the other. At least it passed the time. The telephone rang several times but went unanswered. Someone seemed desperate to get in touch with him or more than likely it was for the guy in the next room. They shared the same line. Gordon stayed in bed for another half-hour celebrating the fact that he was still a young man with a healthy, able body and a whole free day ahead of him. As usual, there was nothing planned in his mind, but there were no unpaid loans or poor relatives in need, no love affairs or binding friendships. He neither liked nor disliked himself and his conscience wasn't anything he gave much thought to. He would have made a good marine or something in the military line, but his sense of discipline wasn't up to that level. Besides, he didn't like to be commandeered around even on the construction job, which, for the time being was still tolerable. There was nothing that held him — he was his own king.

Gordon rose from the bed and faced the full length mirror. As usual he had slept in the nude. On Saturday mornings he was the last to stir. As he stood in front of the wide-open window, it didn't occur to him that his nakedness would offend his neighbors. His neighbors thought that hedonism was his only stimulus in life. The powerful sunlight played over the smoothness of his tight skin. His heavy-boned, large-muscled body had no fault. Though a little bit heavy for his height, a careful inspection showed no trace of fat. The same auburn hair, curly and unruly over his head, sprinkled his well-sculpted body. He flexed his back and pectoral muscles for awhile, then his biceps, hunched his mighty shoulders and admired his beautiful bodybuilder's figure.

Last he looked at his face — that part of the show he didn't like a bit.

Under dark brows, two brown eyes glared at his reflection with a certain amount of cruelty and suspicion. The nose was large and not quite straight over a full sensuous mouth. The wide cheekbones, seemingly much too large in proportion to the face, tried to harmonize with the girth of the neck.

His rested body craved some vigorous action. The best thing he could think of on a hot summer day like this was running to the river for some splash diving and swimming with the other guys.

The telephone rang again. Gordon hesitated. Another wrong number? The ringing was insistent. Oh, well, what the hell...

"Hallo!" he shouted into the receiver.

The voice on the other side was neither friendly nor disagreeable, "My name is Dr. Peter Moughabee."

Gordon waited but nothing more was forthcoming.

"What can I do for you, Dr. Moughabee? Mo-ga-be — is that how you say it?" Gordon was becoming impatient.

The silence at the other end was interrupted by breathing and a little coughing as of an addicted smoker. Then the voice came back again, "Steffy didn't tell you?"

"Steffy? Oh, yes, the waitress, well she might have been telling me things, but I'm afraid I didn't pay much attention. I'm not used to smoking pot and she insisted. I'm really sorry, Dr. Moughabee. Wait a minute...something's coming back to me...it was about some kind of a job."

"Archaeology," Dr. Moughabee stated blandly.

Suddenly, Gordon felt a burning thirst. He looked longingly at the refrigerator. Vague questions whirled through his mind. "What are you talking about? Archeology? In college, I did nothing that amounted to much. I mostly dug trenches on minor projects."

Dr. Moughabee laughed softly in his well-cultivated voice. Gordon recognized a strong British accent as the Doctor askeed, "You haven't quite fallen in love with Cleopatra then."

"Never got back that far — only short affairs on the campus," Gordon joked.

Dr. Moughabee laughed some more then asked, ""Why did you take up archaeology to begin with?"

"I don't really know, I think it was my mother's idea. I couldn't find anything more interesting. Besides, it was outdoors. See, I love the great outdoors."

"Why did you quit?"

"I simply ran out of money and incentive."

"You mean out of parental support," Dr. Moughabee suggested.

"How do you know about that? Steffy couldn't have told you. We didn't get that chummy."

His answer jolted Gordon. "Coincidently, I knew your father some time ago. I invested some money in his research."

Gordon sat down heavily on the bed and groped for a cigarette on the side table. He wondered if Dr. Moughabee knew where either of his parents were. But then again, did he really care? After all, they never seemed to have cared about him. This unexpected call and conversation was beginning to make his head spin. Finally, Gordon asked, "Are you a banker? When and where did you meet my father?"

"No, not quite, but I am independently quite wealthy, if I may say so. When and where I met your father is unimportant at the moment."

There was a lengthy pause, then Gordon spoke, "Well, you may be right. I'm sorry to disappoint you, Dr. Moughabee, but I am not a practicing archaeologist by any means. Not even as a student."

"Then what are you going to do with your life?" queried the doctor.

"Do I have to do something in particular? I was going to do some swimming. It's very hot, you know?" Gordon became sarcastic at this point.

The doctor followed suit, "Yes, I know, Mr. Bates. I happen to live in the same area at the moment. It's too hot for tennis, even golf, but I can offer you my swimming pool if you care to come and see me."

Gordon stretched himself over the damp bed. Perspiring heavily, he answered rudely, "See you...hell...I don't know anything about you or what you really want from me."

Dr. Moughabee coughed some more. "We have to start somewhere, don't we? Unless you have something more important on your mind, I'll send my chauffeur to pick you up. His name is Ouloulangha."

Gordon Bates had nothing more important to do.

The chauffeur was very deferential, the car a vintage Packard. After a smooth drive, they came to a rambling old mansion built in the early twenties but lovingly maintained. It was situated in an English type park with trees even older than the residence, all overlooking a panoramic view of the mighty river that seemed to go on forever. Tennis courts and a large swimming pool were hidden from view, though Gordon had a glimpse of them as they drove up the drive to the entrance. Inside the old mansion, it was soothing and cool.

The man at the large bay window seemed entirely transfixed by the majestic flow of the Mississippi. Though he felt the presence of his guest, he still couldn't part from the enthralling view.

"It's so much like the Nile in her glory days," mused Dr. Peter Moughabee.

Gordon wasn't quite sure if that had been addressed to him. "Isn't it still glorious?"

The man didn't budge. "Not in the sense I see it," he sighed.

Dr. Moughabee was one of a kind. A simple description didn't do him enough credit. He was elderly yet ageless, corpulent without being fat. The inscrutable face revealed a pair of sharp eyes that were seeing far beyond the river.

"Have you seen the Nile, Mr. Bates?" Moughabee finally asked.

"On TV, if that counts," a nervous Gordon responded.

The man smiled without any malice. "No, It doesn't."

"Are you from Egypt?" inquired Gordon.

Dr. Moughabee cut his eyes from the window and looked at Gordon.

"I am a Nubian. In a way, our destiny has always been attached to Egypt. A sense of belonging developed as millions of Coptic Nubians left their bones in the sands of Egypt." He moved to his desk with the step of a hunter, "May I offer you a cigar, something to drink? I'll take you to the swimming pool as I promised."

Gordon was becoming more and more bewildered — he wondered what his role was in this play. Everything around him looked so theatrical — a simple wooden cross amidst African war-masks and Egyptian artifacts spread around the room. Even the old Mississippi River looked somehow different through that window. The whole encounter seemed surrealistic.

"I've really stopped smoking, Dr. Moughabee, and I don't drink much and never before swimming — though I suppose a little bit of gin and tonic won't kill me."

The Nubian chuckled humorously and went to the large bar in the corner.

"All I drink is a glass of wine now and then."

He brought the drinks to a coffee table and invited his guest to sit in a deep stuffed chair as he commented jovially, "Business before pleasure."

Gordon followed the hefty gentleman with his eyes as he sat on the sofa and raised his glass. "To your health, young man. Cheers!"

"Cheers!" Gordon downed his drink — they finished at the same time.

The host smiled benevolently. "I've been watching you for quite sometime, Mr. Bates."

"Watching? What in hell do you mean — how and why would you be watching me?"

"Oh...I have some people that I can trust. Money can buy many things, and I have my reasons — we will get to that..."

Gordon leaned forward in his chair, "This is getting nuts — I want to know what's going on."

The man shrugged his heavy shoulders. "First of all, I knew you were in Memphis. In fact I made it happen."

"And, how could you do that?" asked the bewildered Gordon.

"I own the construction company where you are working." Dr. Moughabee cut a cigar and lit it carefully.

Gordon put down his empty glass and tried to gather his thoughts. "But why...because once upon a time you knew my father?"

"I knew your mother too. Oh my, she was a beautiful Creole," Moughabee mused.

Suddenly, Gordon felt a headache coming on. "Beautiful, she couldn't have been — I look like her...but why did you say 'was'?"

"I thought you knew, Gordon." Dr. Moughabee seemed sincerely surprised.

"Knew what?"

"She was bitten by a poisonous insect in the vicinity of Cairo. She's buried there."

"Where?" demanded Gordon.

"Tell el Amarna," informed Moughabee

"The new capital of Amenhotep IV?" wondered Gordon vaguely remembering what he had read long ago.

"Also known as Ikhnaton," added Moughabee.

Cold sweat ran down Gordon's face. "And my father?"

"He just disappeared," the doctor sighed.

The young man pushed his empty glass toward his host. "Forget swimming. I'll have another drink."

Gordon had loved his mother. He was never sure of what she felt toward him. Maybe something akin to love. Gordon gulped the refill and as the alcohol went down he felt a little calmer. Dr. Moughabee shook his large head. "I am sorry to be the bearer of bad news."

"Well, it has been a very long time and it always seemed my parents were more interested in ancient myths and legends than in me...that much I remember."

"The fact is, your dad worked for me," Moughabee continued with his surprising revelations.

"Here in Memphis?"

"Not here. There, in Egypt."

Gordon suddenly put down his glass and stood up from the chair. He was almost mumbling when he said, "Anyway...thanks for telling me — although, I don't know why or what it means..."

"Where are you going?" demanded Moughabee.

"Actually...I don't know. I find all of this quite unsettling — what is really going on?"

Dr. Moughabee let the smoke of his cigar go in a wide stream. His eyes had a strange opaque quality. "I want to make an offer to you."

Gordon smiled skeptically — "Here it comes — another job?"

"You can take it as you wish. I think I'm offering more than that."

Gordon suddenly felt spun around and empty...come to think of it, he was all alone. All alone in the whole wide world. He had never thought along that line before.

"Do you know anything more about me — do I have any relatives?" he beseeched Dr. Moughabee.

Who answered with a question of his own, "Have you noticed that you are not quite a 'white boy'?"

"It has been brought to my attention," Gordon answered matter-of-factly.

"But not enough..." Moughabee dropped the bomb, "I am your great-grandfather."

Gordon looked at him in open-mouthed disbelief.

"You can't be that old."

"And that is only your presumption, son. De facto, I am very, very old. Maybe the most descriptive word for it is ancient."

Gordon shook his head. His world was spinning. It couldn't have been the gin...unless his drinks were laced — maybe it was all the weed he had smoked the night before.

The final push down the rabbit hole came from the voice of Dr. Moughabee — "Your true name is Ikhnaton."

From that moment things happened rapidly, like a blur whirling through Gordon's mind. Being so swiftly placed in Egypt, a land so full of the ancient mystery, the contemporary land didn't yet seem a reality to Gordon. He was ill-prepared to meet the scope of existence in this charged dimension. He had lost contact with his own persona before becoming another one. Gordon was faced with a plethora of "whys and whens" with no hint of what was coming next. The "now" (at the moment) was in El Uqsor in a comfortable hotel room with a view of an ancient temple and the great Nile. He had made very few contacts. People left him respectfully alone. Dr. Peter Moughabee wasn't present. He had given him a couple of credit cards and some cash, then put him on a flight to Cairo. Mr. Ouloulangha was waiting for him at the airport. He wasn't just a chauffeur but the secretary of Gordon's newfound great-grandfather and as closed mouthed as he was in Memphis. Gordon felt he was being treated as an object.

For the time being Gordon Bates felt completely estranged from all that he had known — he hardly saw any other guests. However, his bills were paid, his meals generous, in the large leather case and in the closet of his room, he found everything he could think of...though his mind was scattered all over and totally helpless to even put two and two together. He did enjoy the Olympic size swimming pool.

The only information vaguely given to Gordon by his great-grandfather — at least what he could recall through the haze of the mind-boggling events — was something about searching for a mummy. A mummy buried somewhere in the hot sands of Nubia, untouched by time and of such importance that it could change history as we know it. He couldn't recall anything else he was told — he would just have to wait.

The bed was comfortable and the air-conditioner purred monotonously. Feeling a little on edge, he got up from the bed. He had slept in his swimming briefs so he didn't have to change to go to the pool. His jump from the springboard was nearly perfect. He swam automatically, lap after lap, thinking about the little waitress Steffy with her large bosom and provocative hind parts. He was horny, but he had yet to meet a replacement in the new environment. "Those Sheltering Skies" were overheating, like in a Bertolucci film. But this was the real Africa, and a feeling of *déjà vu* came over him. Gordon tried to purge his thoughts, concentrating on the methodical work of his muscles. It felt good. A fool's luck had been bestowed on him and he aimed to stretch it as far as he could. He was simply chosen for an unknown reason. Why him, of all people, was still the great mystery.

His credits in archaeology were practically nonexistent and this was the first time he had traveled abroad. It was ridiculous to think that he could qualify for this job. Why then? His parents had traveled quite often, but they always left him behind. Egypt was often mentioned in family conversations, though vaguely and he wasn't part of the conversations. When it came time for him to attend college, his mother had suggested he study archaeology. His father never fought his hard-headed wife. His interest in the future of his son seemed minimal.

Suddenly Gordon was brought out of his chrysalis state. He had been sent to this strange country almost like a package. His mother had enigmatically died here, or so he was told. Gordon was twenty-two and attending college when a formal letter from an agency in New York notified him about the disappearance of his parents. There was also a check for five thousand dollars included. He had seen them so little, so he didn't miss them. His homecomings from boarding school were few and far between, he simply didn't have any sentiments. He soon drifted apart from his past, with neither photo albums nor memorabilia of any kind, his memories just faded into oblivion. Still, it hurt to be abandoned like an unwanted house-pet.

How did his mother look?

Certainly not like a mother. More like a very intelligent and stilted aunt who was baffled by his complete absence of interests and vocation in life. She didn't like to pose for snapshots, because she thought herself unphotogenic. His father was a complete introvert. They tried to do things together and nothing came out of it. It wasn't Gordon's fault; neither one of them was a talker. They didn't know how to converse with one another. His father had a light complexion with dark blue eyes and thinning light chestnut hair. Gordon's father was much older than his mother and kept a moustache that was most distasteful to his son — thin, slightly covering his upper lip, hiding a scar from a boyhood accident. It was almost impossible to look into his eyes. He always found a way to escape eye-to-eye contact. Secretive by nature, he seldom confided anything to anyone. His one redeeming feature was he was fit as a fiddle and never sick. Another thing in his favor was that he could perform magic with his hands. Gordon never knew how his father performed his tricks. Some of them were truly amazing.

And now his great-grandfather! Where was he all this time? Gordon had never heard about any relatives in Africa or anywhere else for that matter. If Moughabee had picked him at random, why was he piling up all these expenditures for a nobody, a simple misfit?

And who in the hell was Ikhnaton?

Didn't his newly-found great-grandfather claim that Gordon's real name is Ikhnaton? Surely that's a mistake. He vaguely remembered something about an Egyptian king with a nickname like that. Someone from the Eighteenth Dynasty or there about. Someone whose name had been scratched from all monuments.

Gordon shook his head and laughed loudly, thinking to himself that anyone who was unimportant enough to be forgotten was a likely candidate to be a relative of his.

The hotel seemed abandoned. There did not seem to be a living creature around. The balconies and the lounge chairs around the pool were empty. So much the better. He was not attracted to people and never had a pet. But there was something in the skies above, turning and turning in the dry scintillating air. A bird like those in the illustrations in his text books. The Pharaoh's bird...he couldn't remember its name. Something like the scarabs and the tiger's tail. Ah...the Golden Horus...yes, that's it!

Suddenly he sensed the presence of someone in the vicinity of the pool. He looked up to see a woman covering a chair with a bath towel. There was something strange about her. She looked somehow familiar to him. He stopped swimming and started treading water on the deep side of the pool. When the woman turned her face toward him, he had no doubt whatsoever. It was his mother spraying some kind of lotion over herself.

"Hi, Gordon," she said quite casually, "you can go on swimming. It's only old me. Do you think the color of my bathing suit is too loud? Shocking, isn't it? I was unable to find anything even halfway decent in the local stores."

Gordon almost drowned, spitting out the chemically treated water, swimming to the edge of the pool and taking a hold of the slippery tiles. He tried to lift himself out but his hands kept on sliding. Finally he gave up and just hung at the edge trying to clear his vision blurred by the excessive amount of chlorine. He thought perhaps he was hallucinating.

"Am I seeing things? Or is that really you — my mother? Are you staying at this hotel?"

She laughed a bit, made herself cozy in the chair and puffed on her ever-present cigarette.

"Don't tell me you don't know." She blew a stream of smoke in his direction, adjusting her sunglasses over the ridge of her nose. "Yes, silly. Since your arrival. You better get out of the water and let me spray some repellant over you. The air is full of gnats. Come to me and keep me company for a change, like a real gentleman. I ordered drinks for us."

"Drinks?"

"Drinks. Don't tell me you wouldn't enjoy a drink after swimming."

Gordon swam to the ladder and pulled himself up. He shook off the water like a wet dog, still rubbing his eyes, trying to quit dreaming. But she was there, looking at him with a funny expression on her face. Gordon felt weak, so he sat by the edge of the pool.

"Honest to God, I hadn't the foggiest idea you were here until now."

"You haven't changed a bit; dumb like a piece of wood. Come here and I'll rub you off with my towel. You never thought of bringing a towel with you, did you?"

"I don't need a towel. I like to dry in the sun. For heavens' sake, it's already hot as an oven. Why do you shudder? You haven't even touched the water."

"It's my nerves, son. I'm vibrating, not shaking. Do you want a cigarette?" she said offering him the pack.

Gordon didn't want anything from her. He still felt he was hallucinating. "Is father somewhere around too?"

"Your father? Oh, you mean my husband. No, I haven't seen him for years, and I don't want to. I wrote to you about our legal separation, didn't I?"

"No, you did not. I have never gotten a line from you, or my father for that matter."

She seemed slightly annoyed. "Oh, the mail nowadays...Can't you think of something else?"

"I can think about you and my father working for Dr. Moughabee." Gordon found it difficult to believe this conversation was taking place.

"He was our client." She was curt.

"Your client or your boss?"

His mother shrugged her shoulders. "A client is always a sort of a boss. Especially somebody with the wealth and power of that man."

Gordon slit his eyes against the sun. "And he isn't related to you or my father?"

"Certainly not to me, and your father had no relatives whatsoever," she huffed indignantly.

"Weren't you close to your boss for awhile in New York?" Gordon continued to probe.

"That didn't mean a thing. Now you see him, now you don't." She seemed to become more annoyed.

Gordon was becoming impatient with this strange encounter. "And you prefer not to see him at all?"

"What for? If you want to be a puppet in his crafty hands that's your own business. Don't blame me later." This she stated rather cryptically.

Gordon closed his eyes and said in a hushed voice: "I wouldn't think of it."

When he opened them again she was gone. In the air hung a very slight whiff of bug repellent. Gordon's body had dried to a point that he felt his skin burning. He headed for the door and stopped.

He was almost completely alone except for the royal hawk in the sky. The Man-Falcon.

Dr. Moughabee listened patiently to Gordon's tale. He didn't tell it very well. The young man was a disastrous storyteller. He didn't seem able to control his train of thought and the whole soliloquy finally ended with a sudden mental block. The old gentleman smiled very politely and not once averting his gaze through the jet's window. It was a four-seater military plane. The indispensable Mr. Ouloulangha sat up front with the pilot.

Dr. Moughabee broke his silence with his hypnotic voice, "Do not let your odd experience trouble you for the moment. Sometimes only events in the future can answer the enigmas of the present."

Gordon's eyes were fixed on the strange golden ring on Dr. Moughabee's middle finger. It seemed to the ex-student of archaeology that it was very ancient but well preserved, and the intricate work of art might date back to the New Kingdom. The symbols, however, were unfamiliar to him. The name Ikhnaton still gave him problems. Gordon thought to himself that something was changing within him.

Dr. Moughabee smiled as if he knew his thoughts. "Ikhnaton is the missing link in a chain of enigmas — a period of Egyptian history fallen in the hands of certain people with great power and influence."

"Are you one of them?" asked Gordon.

"Yes. By the Will of God, I am. There are no secrets between me and the unhappy King, Amenhotep IV."

"What do you expect of me? So far I have gone along with your game. Now, I have every right to know my part in it."

"And you'll know all of it in the course of the 'game' as you call it. That woman from the Land of the Dead shouldn't have interfered with your destiny," Moughabee sneered.

"Shouldn't a mother care for her son even from beyond?"

"Of course, of course. I feel responsible too." Moughabee seemed to become uneasy.

"Does that go for my father as well?"

"Your father? What about him?"

"Is he still alive?" Gordon asked, almost wistfully.

Dr. Moughabee hesitated. "Yes, he is. And you will meet him in time. Do you know the meaning of the symbols on my ring?" He held out his hand.

Gordon looked at it carefully. "I think it means 'Father,' though I never have been good at deciphering these things."

“But you’re right,” exclaimed Moughabee, “that’s exactly what it means, though, in a larger sense, it also could signify God. This word between the ‘Flower’ and the ‘Ankh” form the sacred Trinity.”

Gordon pulled himself away. “What does this Trinity have to do with me?”

“More than you can imagine, son. You’ll see in the monastery…” His voice faded out and Dr. Moughabee didn’t say anything for the rest of their journey.

After landing at a military base, they were greeted by a group of seemingly high officials, some of them in uniforms. Dr. Moughabee was met with pomp and deference reserved for heads of state. After a few cryptic remarks spoken in Nubian dialect, Gordon was introduced to each of the gentlemen in such a way that he didn’t catch any name except his own. He shook hands with them and received some light bows during the exchange. The whole entourage boarded two army jeeps and left the base on a narrow road that lead to the interior desert. Gordon was hungry, but nobody mentioned anything about food. Their faces were somber and not a word was spoken.

The scenery subtly changed. Hills at first, then rocks and palm trees. A lonely fort appeared as did signs announcing a frontier crossing. The flag was Ethiopian. A small group was awaiting them. After an exchange of greetings, Dr. Moughabee, his secretary Ouloulangha and Gordon boarded a small helicopter that was sitting behind the fort. Gordon’s hunger was demanding attention, but he felt constrained to bring the question up. It was awfully hot and uncomfortable. After awhile, bottles of Coke were passed around, though the drink brought little refreshment. It was unpleasantly warm and left a disagreeable aftertaste in Gordon’s mouth. Moughabee didn't show any signs of hunger or fatigue. There was not a drop of perspiration on his broad, ebony face.

Gordon had no choice but to be patient. He simply slept for the rest of the afternoon.

Shortly after a magnificent sunset, the chopper started to descend. There, barely discernible in the thickening dusk, Gordon saw an oasis and a temple of some kind still visible in the dusk and nearby a circle of small bonfires indicated a heliport. The men waiting for them were not wearing the robes usually worn in a monastery. Most were half naked and barefoot. Hanging around their scrawny necks were beads and other trinkets, the sign of the Ankh mostly. Flowers, wilted from the heat, covered their partially shaven heads. Here and there beards were visible.

The one who seemed to be the head priest had, by far, the best and the fullest beard. Beneath the flickering flames of the smoking torches, he looked like an ancient prophet. He studied the faces of the newcomers with a degree of suspicion. It was obvious he knew Moughabee and Ouloulangha, so he paid special attention to Gordon and the pilot, then shifted his piercing eyes back to the young American.

"Is this The Man?" he asked.

Dr. Moughabee gave him one of his best smiles. "That's The Man," he answered, "I hope you approve of him, Excellency. He came from far away to find his blood and kin amidst the friends of his Great Father."

"Is it true, young man?"

Gordon looked at his mentor, then back to the priest. "It may be the truth, though everything seems a mystery to me."

The priest obviously didn't know what to make of his answer. He turned toward Dr. Moughabee for enlightenment.

"For safety measures, a man with royal blood has to be kept in darkness, Your Lordship," Moughabee improvised.

The priest shook his head sadly. "That shouldn't be shocking to me. It is a reflection of the times we live in."

He led the way to the temple. The darkness had swallowed most of the landscape and the moon had its dark side toward the planet Earth. The priest stopped at the top step to the entrance, as though he had changed his mind. "You must be hungry and tired."

"My great-grandson and I are hungry to see Him," announced Moughabee.

The priest abruptly faced his guests. For the first time Gordon saw how old and decrepit the man was, but his eyes exuded power and vigilance; his voice was quiet but imperative.

"You can see him only when your eyes can penetrate through the darkness enveloping our world. For that to happen, you must first step into His dimension. I'm not so sure that you're fit to be in His presence."

Dr. Moughabee was running out of patience. Gordon had never seen him angry before now. His anger grew as did the throbbing veins on his forehead. He suddenly blew out of control. "I knew it. Don't even for a moment think that you can patronize me. You're just an unclean mortal, and you will do whatever I ask!"

The priest recoiled as if he had been whipped. A cold, unfriendly chill passed over the gathering, as he stated, "Since the last moon, the stars have changed their position. The familiar constellations have moved from their eternal beds. We must follow the signs of Heaven."

The other men closed ranks around the priest. Dr. Moughabee's rage rose to the surface. "Have you old goats changed the location of the Master without my consent?"

The priest pressed his thin bluish lips together and squeezed out his answer through his tightly clenched teeth. "We do whatever is the best for Him according to our knowledge."

The powerful, bass voice of Moughabee exploded with a force unknown to Gordon. "You double crossing jackal! You dared to disregard my will!!!"

The Ethiopian priest took a firm hold of his amulet and pointed it at Moughabee. Instantly, lightening ran backward through the Ankh and burned the old priest to ashes. His men, as if in a trance, fell on their knees and hit the rocky ground with their foreheads. Moughabee was merciless. "Where is the mummy of the everlasting Aton?" He roared.

Then they all opened their mouths. Everyone of them had had their tongues cut out so they could not unwittingly betray their Master. Furiously, Moughabee, closely followed by Gordon, went to the poorly constructed temple. In front of the horrified men, he took one of the burning torches and set the ramshackle building on fire. It caught instantly and spread with incredible speed.

With angry hisses, three large cobras abandoned their nest hidden somewhere in the foundation. Moughabee centered his fiery eyes on the pale face of his great-grandson. "Now only you, Ikhnaton, can lead me to the whereabouts of our Father."

And Ikhnaton knew but didn't share it with Gordon. He still had to make up his mind.

The Ka of Ikhnaton needed some time to find his bearings in the mortal world on this moonless night. It flew through the Celestial Kingdom, to the Valley of the Dead and to the tip of the Great Pyramid. The tiny, birdlike creature rested there. It felt the mighty presence of the Great Cataracts and listened to their strange moans. In the vibration coming from them, Ikhnaton's Ka detected a certain irregularity. It became one with their wave-lengths and floated over the desert for a long distance. The oasis and the burning monastery shone from afar, but didn't come into focus. What was attracting the senses of his Ka were the anonymous dunes of the Great Mother Desert. There was the Beginning and the End and there was where Aton resided again. The cowardly monks had returned Him to what they thought was his element.

Then the Ka of Ikhnaton thought about that strange young man, Gordon. He liked his body. It had some great potential, but his mind fell far short of being acceptable. What abominable ignorance! And the face. Until now, it didn't matter that much. To be asleep in the personality of someone else, there was no need to care about the outside look, nor did the inner counterpart have to bear responsibility for any impression left on the public. But this guy was worse than ugly. He was impersonal, just one of the crowd, not withstanding the unaligned nose. It was easy to change the intellect, but the physical infringement had to be done gradually. Moughabee will be helpful. It was small wonder that in spite of his sexy body only third-class prostitutes were receptive to Gordon. And that was unacceptable to a pharaoh. Of course Ikhnaton didn't mind a handsome youth thrown in now and then, but that could be a problem with a fellow like "macho" Gordon. Ikhnaton had little time to study the character of his soon-to-be host, though it wasn't difficult to perceive a mind like Gordon's. Lord Aton wouldn't have permitted any liberties with morality. That was forbidden territory.

Far below, in the still, warm sand slithered the three cobras evicted from their home. Were they on a mission of their own? They were heading in the same direction as the Ka of Ikhnaton.

Ikhnaton's Ka sensed the nearness of the burial site. The monks had left no signs of any kind, and it was in the middle of nowhere. A gargantuan task for any human to find it!

But it must be found for the sake of history and perhaps serve up the truth of one human being whose history was riddled with mistakes through time. Alas, living within the mediocrity of a twentieth-century human mind had tainted the lexicon of an ancient Pharaonical Ka.

In the morning, Gordon awoke ravenously hungry and alone. The pilot and Ouloulangha had slept in the helicopter for security reasons. Gordon's great-grandfather had left the bungalow at the landing site. Moughabee had been restless all night, spending most of the time sitting in a chair. But Gordon's youth and overloaded senses succumbed to the excitement of the day, and he fell into the sleep of the dead. Or was it something else? Pieces of his vision came together in his still-deluded mind: being on the top of a pyramid, watching from afar the burning temple, the fugitive cobras, looking for something in the desert. It was one of those convoluted dreams that besieged him more and more often these days. The entrance of his great-grandfather snapped Gordon from his desultory thoughts.

"Get ready and come for a quick breakfast. We have to start early," ordered his great-grandfather.

"What about the monks? You burned their monastery. It still stinks of charred timber."

"I paid them well. What difference does it make?" He suddenly stopped and looked closely into Gordon's face, "Say, what happened to your face overnight?"

Gordon felt his face which was wet from perspiration.

"I don't know. I haven't been in any fights recently. Maybe mosquito bites?"

The old man shook his head passively, "No, it...doesn't matter. Let's go. This place isn't safe. We've got to find the mummy before something else happens."

As they spoke, Gordon took care of the sleeping bags and water canteens.

"Now that the old priest is dead, who is going to tell us where to find what you are looking for?" Gordon asked.

Dr. Moughabee paused, then pointed a finger at Gordon, "You!" he said, and headed out the door.

Chapter 2

FROM THE KA OF IKHNATON

Even from the noisy, ill-smelling machine called a helicopter, I was able to see the tracks of the sacred cobras leading to the hiding place of Lord Aton. As yet, I have not decided if I want to disturb Lord Aton's peace or leave him alone. Does it make any difference to me if Aton was part of something greater than our friendship? I, the Pharaoh of the Two Kingdoms of Egypt and Son of Ra, who had befriended Aton, an unknown boy who knew how to create miracles and win without forcing an issue — why did, I, Amenhotep IV, the ruler of all people on both sides of The Mighty Nile, change my destiny forever? Was it my mother that brought Aton to Thebes? Had she helped my wife Queen Nefertiti establish a new religion? At that time we didn't trust the Old Gods anymore. They sent us pestilence and an extreme drought. Aton promised us wealth and prosperity for the price of a handful of flowers. He promised no more blood and violence, just peace and an abundance of livestock, grain, fruits and vegetables for everyone.

I heard about it from the High Priest of Ra and I laughed. Yet the priest didn't laugh. He advised me to quell those rumors amidst the poor and punish the instigator.

"And who is the instigator?" I asked. The priest looked up at me from his low chair. His rat-like face puckered with venality, "A peasant boy!" he hissed.

Curiosity made me order my attendants to bring the peasant boy, Aton, to the palace, and I fell in love with him.

I treated Aton like a God and made him Messenger of the Only One!

After a quick breakfast, the small company took to the air in the helicopter to start the search over the desert. Gordon looked straight into the face of Moughabee and he studied his bottomless dark eyes. "Why do you want that mummy so desperately?"

Moughabee didn't flinch. "Because He is my Lord. The Messenger of God!"

"Aton?"

"Aton."

"And who do you want me to be?"

"You cannot be anybody else but Ikhnaton."

The rotor blades of the helicopter made the words vibrate and everything felt absurdly unreal to Gordon who paled under his dark tan.

"I'm feeling nervous about that name. Dr. Moughabee. In fact, I'm feeling more unsure about everything — let me out of this."

"I'm sorry, now this is impossible. Have you looked at yourself in a mirror?"

"Not since that morning in the hotel after the nightmare. I did look kinda strange," Gordon admitted

"Do you think everyone can see the spirits of the dead?"

A nameless horror passed through Gordon's mind.

"I'm not dead yet," he whispered almost to himself. "We are at the threshold of the twenty-first century. Things like that don't happen."

Moughabee took Gordon's cold hands in the warmth of his own.

"Things like this will keep on happening forever."

"What's going on with me?" a frightened Gordon beseeched Moughabee.

"For a while, you maintained a double Ka. Now it's just one," Moughabee explained.

Gordon closed his eyes and tried to pray but didn't know how. When he opened them, it was with a pair of new, serene eyes. He looked quietly at the Nubian.

"It's alright...great-grandfather. Somehow, I feel what is happening is meant to be."

THEATER OF THE ABSURD: IKHNATON, CLAD IN GORDON'S CLOTHES BUT STILL WEARING HIS PHARONIC SYMBOLS

I'm feeling comfortable in the body of this guy, Gordon. He let his guard down from the very beginning, so I didn't have to force myself. I can use his body to my content, but it must be with my face. He is too ugly for my taste. His age is fine, but his thinking is short-sighted and primitive, though in this century of technology, I don't quite understand mankind. What has man been doing through all these centuries besides dreaming and playing with mechanical toys? My biggest problem was penetrating Gordon's wall of passiveness. Now, he is all mine. The only thing I have to remember is his stupid name, Gordon. I must be careful, though, especially about my need of his body. I think I desire him more than Aton. He was different. I knew that He was much stronger than I, and I didn't even try to make passes. But this commoner is the kind of man I can handle any time. His brain is mush, typical of the modern world. In my century, I was thought of as a passive character. Nowadays, I'm a volcano, a boiling passion, a fountain of desires. I had one hundred beautiful women at my disposal...as well as my Queen. I've been given a man who has no notion about my sentiments. Maybe Aton knew me through and through, using me for His cause. I have to talk again to Him, to unlock His Ka from the power of His divinity. A conversation, man to man. Alas, He isn't a man. I should know better than anyone else. I died for Him and His cause. My only God till the end of time!

BACK TO NOW

Gordon became aware that his eyesight was much sharper. Now he was able to see not only the appearance of things, but their profundity. Cause and effect, into all four stars racing away through the infinite. It appeared strange that Gordon had never thought about it before...just drifting from one thing to another without really thinking at all.

The cobras had done well, their senses were much stronger than his, but he could put two and two together. His mind was far ahead of them, already in the dune where Aton's mummy was buried.

THEATER OF THE ABSURD: A CONVERSATION IN THE ABSOLUTE

"Hey, Aton, wake up! I'm coming to see You. Your devout disciple Ikhnaton is flying in the sky like a great blue heron, across time and distances, a divine creature worthy of You, the Greatest of all gods."

"Modesty has never been one of your virtues, Ikhnaton. I am just the shadow of a god who is yet to come. The reason for your coming is no secret. It follows the designs of the Almighty, so I'll let it happen."

"You don't trust me anymore, My Lord?"

"I never fully trusted you, Ikhnaton, but I love you as I love even my enemies."

"I stood by You to the bitter end. My family was slaughtered, and I lost all the riches of the world. Then, for some reason, You didn't open the Golden Doors to the Celestial Kingdom for me."

"Did you ever ask yourself why?"

"Of course not, I count on Your explanation, my Lord."

"I don't owe you anything, Ikhnaton, or shall I say Amenhotep? You shouldn't have made any sacrifices for me. Your destiny was always in your own hands. You made a choice..."

"Yes, my Lord, I've paid dearly," interrupted Ikhnaton. "At that time, when the soldiers broke through the walls of my palace, we cried out Your name for Your help, holding our Ankhs high."

"And I'm telling you again: I'm just the foreshadow of the Almighty. Nothing is done without His Will. By myself I am nothing!"

IN THE NOW

"Here is the *Place*," said Gordon, unemotionally. "Right beneath us, in the middle of nowhere."

Moughabee gave instructions to the pilot, and soon the helicopter landed not far from the spot pointed out by Gordon. Tools were unloaded and Ouloulangha and the pilot started digging at the site with great care. After ten minutes of digging, they went down on their knees and pushed the sand away with their hands. At first, there were just patches of dirty clothing, later, a form, and at the last brush stroke, the "face" was uncovered. It was beautifully preserved. A large face with high cheekbones and eyebrows coming together over a slightly aquiline nose. A large sensual mouth peeked through a drooping moustache, and an almost square beard. A light breeze played through the thick forelock of hair. The broad chest gave an impression of breathing and something like a sigh...

Gordon looked at Him in a state of transfixion, then shouted, "Why, this is the face from the Shroud of Turin! I'm sure of it. I even did a paper on it. It's Jesus Christ!"

The pilot and Ouloulangha were frozen with gaping mouths. Only Dr. Moughabee disagreed, and uttered through his teeth, "It's Lord Aton. From roughly thirty-five hundred years ago."

PROSCENIUM OF THE STAGE: IKHNATON, DRESSED AS PHARAOH

As Amenhotep IV, I was impregnable. Then Aton came. I remember His face when He was brought to me for the first time in my palace in the heart of Thebes. His was radiant, beautiful face, full of spiritual power.

I knew, by intuition, that we needed a completely new environment, a brand new capital city with a palace full of light and freedom and a great temple dedicated solely to the One and Only God, creator of all the gifts of nature. We would be a nation of happy people without miseries, violence or hate. A land of total harmony. Alas, how little did I know you then, Lord Aton!

A realm such as this simply cannot exist here on earth. Human nature sets its own priorities, sadly in absolute disregard of natural resources and universal rules. Mankind considers itself the centerpiece of creation and nothing else matters.

What did I know about my own subjects. Nothing. I didn't care. As long as they performed their duties, they could stay. I had taxes to maintain my court, my wealth, my army and to buy the loyalty of the innumerable priests. Did I know about suffering and deprivation, the corruption of judges, the starvation and the agony of slavery? Of course, I did. But then, I considered it normal. Who would think otherwise?

Lord Aton seemed to understand. He was infinitely patient with me. It took years before I recognized that He was my master — I was not His. My illicit love for Him made me blind — After all, I was the Pharaoh.

The realization of what was happening took me a long time. When Queen Nefertiti gave birth to a son, Tutankhaton, later known as Tutankhamon, truth appeared on the scene. I realized I was only a dumb spectator.

BACK TO PRESENT

In the helicopter, Gordon rode next to the mummy. He felt compelled to study every feature of Aton's face, as if he'd never see him again. Contrary to the rules imposed by Moughabee, Gordon had unveiled Aton's face and tried to sniff the scent of it like a dog. It had dried up, every hint of a scent had disappeared.

"I love you, Aton...I love you..." he whispered in his ear. The mummy had no answer to this.

THE STATE OF ISRAEL

In the High Office of the Pope's Prelate in Jerusalem, a man in a white cassock looked through the tall French windows out into the garden. His eyes were partly invisible behind the thick eyeglasses that dominated his dour, aesthetic face. He was soft spoken so his secretary had a problem hearing him and was afraid to ask him to repeat. He wrote in a thick ledger whatever he was able to catch.

Not far from the Prelate's Residence, in past centuries, Pontius Pilate had held court over Jesus of Nazareth. It was barely two thousand years ago.

As far as the Prelate was concerned, little had changed. "This is an act of blasphemy, but it cannot be publicized in any way. I officially recommend a policy of total disregard; unofficially, we must use any means to stop it immediately. This mummy has to be destroyed as soon as possible. It is not an historical artifact and it is of no value whatsoever except to a handful of arrogant Copts in the Upper Nile district. A certain American citizen with Nubian roots has provided ample funds, which attracted a few high officials in the Nubian Army. This man is not supported openly by the Egyptian government, but a number of politicians are ready to support this fictitious story, this blasphemy, in order to gain glory for themselves. Naturally the Holy Church and the Vatican cannot seem to be involved in any way. We must count on certain 'Special Forces' to prevent this foolish enterprise from going any further.

"In a situation of this kind, all decisions have to be made by a civil leader, paid for by a civic organization. Our Office cannot be tied to this in any way. The people we need in this action should be of pure Arabian extraction. The role of the much younger American is not quite clear. Rumors from a small Ethiopian monastery, report violence and black magic on the part of Dr. Moughabee, who apparently assumed the rights of succession. Rumor further has it that the spirit of a shadow Pharaoh from the Eighteenth Dynasty has been unleashed back onto the earth."

The secretary looked up at his master for more. The Prelate took off his glasses and rubbed his small inflamed eyes. "That's all for today. Make it presentable and leave it on my desk for signature. I don't have to remind you that total discretion is absolute. Only I can choose and approve of persons reliable in this action."

The secretary arose and coughed uneasily. From the door he ventured to ask, "Doesn't any involvement on our part give certain credence to those absurd adventurers?"

The Prelate carefully placed his eyeglasses over the bridge of his royal nose and sighed, "Not if the reincarnation of Christ is in the equation."

BORDER BETWEEN EGYPT AND ETHIOPIA

Late in the afternoon, the Commander of the Nubian fort came to visit Dr. Moughabee. Ouloulangha and Gordon were asleep by the mummy at the back of a low-ceilinged room. For the second day a nasty sandstorm blew over the region, hindering communications and making travel impossible. The wind howled like a pack of hyenas over the roof and whistled through the ill-fitting window frames. Though men had scarves on their faces, the sand still found its way into their mouths, noses, eyes and ears. Worst of all, the sand inundated the food supply.

The officer was in a bad mood. "It seems that the sirocco winds are mightier than at any other time. My soldiers think that the mummy has brought on the ill winds. They saw three unusually large cobras in one of the storage rooms. That's an evil omen."

Moughabee was upset about the weather more than anyone else, but answered with feigned indifference, "You don't believe that, Colonel, do you? We have to wait at the border for authentication by a team of specialists. A purely bureaucratic matter. Otherwise, we would've been out of here by now."

"I haven't received permission to let you go. We want you out of here more than you know. Everyone is in a foul mood. The sirocco is doing it. How am I supposed to restrain my soldiers?"

"You want more money? You'll have more. Now go and tell them that if they don't behave well, I'll unleash the curse of the cobras. I have them right here, in this room. They faithfully guard their Pharaoh," Moughabee answered vehemently.

The colonel stepped back and looked around in the murky light. In the background, the wind spoke with many voices — the voices of the dead.

"I hope we have a quiet night, sir," he stuttered, clicked his heel with a curt bow and left the room hurriedly.

Gordon had a dream.

A dream about the only time his father took him fishing in the Blue Ridge Mountains. For several days and nights they hiked and camped together. They never caught anything. Neither had any idea that the inhabitants of the fish ponds knew in advance about their coming. The best result was that a rather uneasy relationship grew warmer in the cool nights. They actually had conversations and a bond of attachment began to grow between them. Gordon remembered a number of funny stories that his father told him. When other boys bragged about what their fathers did, Gordon had no idea what his father did for a living, so he had to make it up. He told his classmates that his parents were private detectives, which as it turns out wasn't that far from the truth. They were paid to do historical research — that of course, he learned much later.

In this particular dream, he was fishing with his father, trying not to look at his distasteful pencil-like moustache. Finally, he mustered the courage to ask, "What kind of work do you do, dad?"

His father shrugged his shoulders. "Nothing much. I simply do whatever your mom wants me to do."

"And that's all?"

"That's all, son...and sometimes it's more than I can take," his dad said with a certain amount of sadness.

This was the closest Gordon had ever felt to his father. He wanted to help him out of his misery.

"Isn't there something we can do, dad?"

His father threw the butt of his cigarette in the pond and smiled forlornly. "Just live your own life, son. Never leave it to a woman to tell you how to live it."

"Can't you try and live your life in your own way?"

"No I can't...it's too late. I am tired, and it doesn't matter anymore."

"It matters to me. Won't you do it for me?" His father lit another cigarette. Even then he didn't look at Gordon. "For you?...Why? I hardly know you, son."

"Have you ever loved somebody?" Gordon asked.

Then the stranger — his father looked at the young boy with a certain curiosity. "It's weird that you, of all people, should ask me a question about love." He thought for awhile and shaking his head said very quietly, "No...I don't know exactly what love is...it might be one of many things that passed me by." He sighed, "I don't think we will catch any fish today."

Gordon wanted to ask the father in his dream why everyone was calling him Ikhnaton, when that wasn't his real name, but the man who had never been a father figure to him wasn't there anymore. Gordon wondered if he had ever existed.

Anyway, to Gordon, that dream meant nothing. At least that's what he kept telling himself.

Moughabee hadn't slept for the last forty-eight hours. Some say he never sleeps. Coffee was his only sustenance in the morning. He very seldom had a glass of wine and certainly never anything stronger. The pilot hadn't been around since their arrival. For the first time, Moughabee felt that money couldn't buy everything, especially in a God forsaken country like this. He had no power over the sirocco either.

He woke up Gordon. "I need to talk with you."

Gordon sat on a bench at the crude table. It was getting dark, as a smoky gas lamp was burning down to its last. In the heavy darkness, Moughabee's face was almost invisible. Only the whites of his eyes signaled his presence. He sat down heavily at the table.

The wailing and screaming of the wind was horrendous. Gordon felt his throat dry and gritty.

Moughabee's voice cut through the windstorm, somber and dusky as from the very heart of night.

"If anything happens to me, son, I want you to know a few things that might be helpful in the long run."

Gordon tried to visualize the ebony face against the raven darkness, but failed.

"What makes you think that I'll stick around with this affair to the bitter end?"

"What makes you think that there will be a bitter end?"

Gordon shrugged his shoulders, so the old man went on.

"With me or without, this is just a beginning, there is no end, at least not on the horizon. Even so, the end is just the beginning of something else. And He must come again to sit to the right side of His Father, to judge us all, risen from the depth of times, to the very last minute of Creation."

Gordon looked in the direction of the mummy but heard only the wind and the snoring of Ouloulangha. Nothing was discernable in the darkness. 'To the last minute of Creation...' Gordon thought and felt some fear creeping into him. "I'm listening to you, great-grandfather."

Moughabee didn't speak for awhile, then started again. "You recognize me as the great-grandfather of the past. I'm aware of your personal tribulations. They are Godsends. You must be proud to be chosen. Ikhnaton was a great man in a very human way. He had his faults but died with dignity and courage. His restless spirit wasn't accepted in Heaven, nor was it sent to the Netherworld. He had to find his own way through the primeval darkness, back to this dimension of our time. His son, King Tut, didn't suffer through the same ordeals, though his glory was given to him by humanity alone, he lived long enough to crack open the Door of the memory of his forgotten father. Now Ikhnaton has his last chance. Let him be within you?"

Gordon took his time before answering. "I haven't talked to him yet. He already has taken certain advantages of me. Can you grant me the opportunity to talk to Ikhnaton, man to man?"

"Yes, I will. You have every right to agree or disagree with him. I'm going to receive him now, and you can talk to his entity through me."

From the dark emptiness across the table rose a small shapeless light. It grew and thickened until the outline of a man took its place.

"The Ka of a dead Pharaoh salutes you!"

"What do you want of me?" asked Gordon, in awe, trying to maintain his sanity.

"I beg for a temporary home within you so the truth may live. I'll leave you in peace once I finish my mission."

"What is your mission? What is the 'truth'?" begged Gordon, beginning to relent — feeling more drawn into the circumstances compelling him.

"I want to connect the chain of events...the missing link."

"The existence of Aton?" questioned Gordon.

"To prove the existence of the One and Only God."

"We have just one God..."

"No. Your God is torn to pieces. A piece for everyone: Catholics, Protestants, Jews, Hindus...too many to name. They all pretend to have the whole of Him when all they have is a piece."

"What do you have?"

"The whole Truth," the spirit repeated

For a minute Gordon listened to the screams of the wind and the thousand voices of the desert. Then he uttered sadly, "Why choose me? I'm only twenty-five years old, and I haven't lived yet. I don't even know what love is all about. I'm unwanted and alone."

"So was the Christ...because he was Love itself."

Gordon experienced a last wave of hesitation, then asked, "When will you leave me?"

"The moment I'm pardoned and The Door to Heaven is open to me.

The young man closed his eyes and spoke resignedly, “Then God let it be Thy Will. You may enter into me!”

It wasn’t until the early morning that the storm abated. Dr. Moughabee had his eyes closed, as if asleep. Suddenly, the distant sound of the rotor of the helicopter got him up to his feet. During the storm, it had been locked in a hangar. He walked to the window and peered through. The helicopter was taking off. He swore under his breath and pushed the window open to see better. Their room was guarded by two armed soldiers. Moughabee moved slowly to the back of the room. Gordon was sleeping calmly by the mummy, three royal cobras coiled at his feet like faithful guards. Ouloulangha sat up on his haunches and looked at them in silent terror. Moughabee smiled.

“Fear not, Ouloulangha, they will never do any harm to us.”

The secretary got up nervously and stepped behind his master.

“Are they his?” he asked.

“Yes, they are. They are a symbol of his pharaonic power.”

“In this situation we need more than symbols. Obviously the pilot was instructed to abandon us. I’m sure we are closely watched even now.”

“God is with us, Ouloulangha.”

“What can God do for us, Sir?”

“More than you can think of. I can buy the jeep of the commander.”

“Bah...he’d be arrested,” said Ouloulangha, shaking his head.

“He’ll cross the border into Ethiopia. He’s half Ethiopian anyway.”

“How far can we go in that jeep?”

"They're a sturdy vehicle. We can reach the nearest port and take a boat up the Nile. Listen, our host is coming. Let's have a little fun with the cobras."

Ouloulangha chuckled as he agreed with his master.

Half an hour later they were in the jeep, cobras and all. It wasn't quite pharaonic but far better than waiting for their doom in the sand-covered fort. The great Nile lay ahead, or, at least they thought so.

After driving two hours under a merciless sun, a police chopper appeared and started hovering overhead. A crackling loudspeaker demanded that they halt. Two automatic machine guns hung threateningly out of both sides of the chopper.

Ouloulangha stepped on the brakes.

The jeep was too small to hide a mummy. It was covered, but it was still obvious for anyone seeking it.

"Leave it to me," commanded Dr. Moughabee. He got out and walked toward the landing helicopter. Through a cloud of dust and sand, two men, dressed in police uniform, approached Moughabee briskly. One of them kept an evil looking police dog on a short leash.

Moughabee sighed with relief as he recognized the uniforms.

"Thanks be to God, you were sent by Hussney El Barrack all the way from Beirut?"

"You are Dr. Moughabee? We do need to see credentials, sir," commanded the senior of the two officers.

"Certainly," said Moughabee as he handed over his papers.

After verifying Moughabee's credentials, the officer looked at him and in a polite manner asked, "Dr. Moughabee, one more question — do you know the password?"

"Uraeus," Moughabee quickly answered.

The two officers saluted and smiled, then became serious again as the senior officer told Moughabee, "We must move quickly, you are in danger. Get everyone aboard our chopper at once."

As they moved swiftly to load the mummy on the helicopter, the guard dog sensed the Pharaoh's cobras. Hearing their low, threatening rattle, the dog pulled his handler all the way back to the helicopter.

The three royal cobras uncoiled majestically, straightened up to their tails and listened intently to the rotors of the vanishing chopper, until the silence of the desert buried all sounds.

Chapter 3

EL BARRACK MEETS ATON

The residence of Hussney El Barrack was outside of Beirut high in the mountains. It had no central architectural style. An Arabian castle was the best description. The compound had been built into the rocks with whatever material had been at hand. Made up of different size blocks, these buildings were connected to each other through empty inner courts. There were a few palm and olive trees here and there and a pond surrounded by willow trees that were filled with different species of birds. The whole compound was surrounded by a thick wall the same beige color as the rocks and that melted into the mountain becoming a part of it.

The heliport was on the flat roof of the largest block, and a narrow staircase led to a small oblong court. A large double door opened to an enormous hall decorated with everything the Near East had to offer in luxury. Sheik Hussney El Barrack was sitting oriental style in an almost empty room. A bubbling water pipe was his only company. He was dressed and shod in the best France and Italy had to offer, and he had just the outline of a beard on his face. His features were all drawn in straight lines and angles, though the eyes, hooded by heavy eyelashes, had remarkable strength and intelligence. It was difficult to tell his age, but he was certainly not an old man.

Only Moughabee was ushered into this apartment through a narrow door. For him, sitting on an ornamented camel saddle wasn't a problem. He had known this kind of environment since the birth of history.

"Is He with you?" asked the Sheik.

"Yes. Both of them. It happened as if different forces had become united in focus: the Eye of Wisdom."

"Praised be Allah! Problems are to be expected when the human element gets involved, there are plots and intrigues badgering the martyrs of this world. As the Prophet said, 'If you want to see yourself, don't look into the bottom of a well, look into your heart'."

"Tell me, what came to your ears, my noble friend?"

"Whatever has come to my ears, Peter, you have seen. I am faced with deception and ploys, even in my own home. Who do I trust with my life? However, to the point, the tentacles of the Roman Prelate are very long."

"The shadow of Rome," mused Moughabee.

"The Pope only knows what he wants to know — closes his eyes to the rest."

Moughabee lit one of his black Egyptian cigarettes and blew smoke toward the high ceiling. The master of the house clapped his hands. Servants brought a low, round table covered with sweets, fruits and freshly brewed green tea. The silence grew deeper when they left. Only bird-songs were heard from the inner court. The evening arrived unnoticed. After a time, the sheik pointed out a distant star through the small window. It was Sirius.

"Tonight I would like to speak to the Master of the Underworld and the Pharaoh," the sheik spoke softly.

The Nubian nodded slowly.

After being served a good meal, Gordon's body cried out for physical exercise. He went to one of the courtyards and started with some stretches, then practiced some karate chops and kicks. He wished for a long swim, but there was only the small fish pond. So he methodically followed his training session. A voice from within advised him that very soon he would need his fighting techniques. Suddenly he felt someone's eyes watching his every move.

It was a young man, sinewy and slim. Gordon smiled a bit forcibly. "Who are you?" he asked. "Are you a son of the Sheik's?"

The youth didn't return his smile. He kept on watching him carefully as if making mental notes about Gordon's strong points and shortcomings. "Yes, stranger, I'm his only legitimate son, Aldan. And who are you?"

His English was impeccable. The American sensed some animosity. It set him on alert.

"My name is Gordon Bates. I'm a guest of your father."

They continued watching each other, like two animals sniffing out each other's weakness.

"I'm practicing the same moves," said Aldan, "Maybe we can try something together."

Gordon paused then nodded curtly. "Why not? We might be able to learn something new from each other." He took off his shirt. Aldan followed suit, and they faced off. They started feigning a fight, then the blows and the kicks became real, hard and malicious. Blood spattered on both their swarthy faces. Aldan fought adamantly but soon began losing ground to Gordon. Gordon resisted the neck hold and the blows to his midriff, then suddenly Aldan's tripping leg sent Gordon to the sandy ground. Aldan jumped on top of him, viciously punching his face. Gordon, becoming very angry, caught hold of Aldan's right hand and twisted it to a breaking point. The youth tried to kick his way out to no avail. The young American twisted even harder.

"I could break your arm. Give up!"

The youth was biting his bloodied lips to prevent himself from crying.

"Break it, if you can! " he gasped almost indistinctly.

At that moment, a female voice broke the intensity. "That's enough, Aldan!"

Both fighters looked up at the resolute young woman standing before them. She seemed to have a magic affect on the fiery youth.

"O.K., sis, don't get huffy. We're just practicing." He then hissed under his breath to Gordon, "we'll finish this some other time."

Gordon let him go and looked around for his shirt. He found it and wiped off the sweat and blood from his face. The youth started to followed his example, but then tossed aside his stained silk blouse. Gordon had to save the day.

"It was a fair game, lady. Your brother is pretty good in this discipline."

"Fighting?" she said sarcastically.

Gordon shrugged his shoulders. "Fighting. A man has to know how to defend himself."

"Do you have a clean shirt?" she addressed Gordon.

"No, I'll have to wash this one."

"And have you washed bloody shirts before?" the young woman asked Gordon.

"Well, yes, but it doesn't always come out very well."

She smiled as she commented, "You're damn right, it doesn't."

Gordon was slightly shocked by the language of the sheik's daughter. She turned to her brother, "Take care, Aldan, help your new friend."

Her brother smiled for the first time since Gordon met him.

"I'll take Mister Bates for a bath, find him a clean shirt and tuck him into bed."

The young lady smiled too. "Don't be so patronizing, Aldan, I saw who won. I'm glad Mr. Bates gave you a good spanking. You badly needed it." Then to Gordon, "My kid brother thinks himself invincible."

Aldan wasn't pleased. "That was just some sparring, Helena. The real fights are ahead."

"Well then, be sure to keep enough spare shirts handy, brother. Good night, you two." And she left. Gordon looked after her with a mixture of feelings that he didn't care to sort out immediately. "Helena?" he said to himself.

"Yes, Helena. Sounds Russian, doesn't it?" remarked Aldan.

"It sounds good to me."

"Let's go to the baths. It's too cold to stay outside half naked...unless you want to do some more 'sparring'."

Gordon looked at his adversary with some degree of surprise. He sounded quite friendly.

"No, Aldan. I've had enough exercise for an evening. Let's go to the bathes."

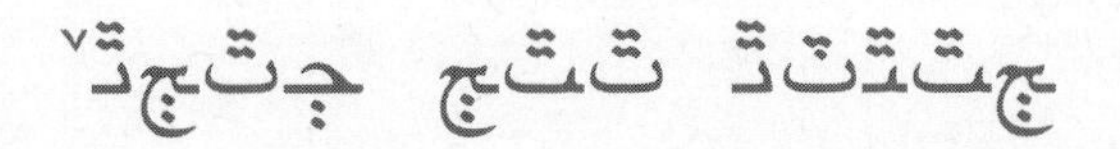

Dr. Moughabee glanced at his great-grandson from head to toe. "I've been looking for you. Where did you find that change of clothes?"

"Oh, they were given to me by Aldan, one of the sheik's sons."

"I might have guessed."

"Why did you say that?" asked Gordon.

"He left his signature on your face."

"No teeth lost," shrugged Gordon

Moughabee shook his large ebony head. "Well, if you two share the same wardrobe, you cannot be enemies. He's the Sheik's favorite son."

"A quite volatile young chap, though; I hope his father is in better command of himself."

"He is...Aldan isn't his only son, but the only one that counts. Let me clean you up a bit. You have to meet the master of the house tonight and a lot depends on the outcome of that meeting."

"As you say, sir. But with a face like mine it won't make much difference."

The old man put his hand on Gordon's massive shoulder.

"Have you seen your face lately, son?"

"I still haven't looked in a mirror since I left the hotel in El Uqsor, though I have felt some changes. Could that be *him*?"

Moughabee nodded. "Ikhnaton was a rather handsome man. And still is, judging by your face. He was quite vain, you know. He wouldn't like his borrowed property smashed by fisticuffs. You have become much leaner, too. Get used to the changes, son."

Gordon passed the tips of his fingers over his face and threw a quick look at the mirror behind his grandfather. His body build wasn't the same as he knew it, and the face...the face was striking.

"Yes, I'll get used to it," Gordon assured Dr. Moughabee..

About midnight the three men were seated around a low round table. Gordon, in spite of the masterful repair of his face, didn't feel quite comfortable. So far he had been lucky, but for how long? He imagined how Anubis had ushered the ex-pharaoh into him, his own personality disposed of as an old unmatched shoe. Did he have anything to be sorry about? Not as far as leaving his aimless, drifting life behind. Had the master of the house noticed the bruises and cuts on his favored son's pretty face? They were considerably more noticeable than on Gordon's. Maybe great-grandpa should have taken care of him, too. And the sister — Helena, a real beauty. It was somehow pleasant to remember her and the way she had disciplined her brother. Would Gordon have actually broken Aldan's arm without her intervention? Very possibly, he had been that mad. He had committed senseless brutalities before when anger overwhelmed him. In this case, that would've been a great mistake. Aldan's father, the sheik, might've taken it out, not only on him, but on the whole affair. What might happen then? Musing on, Gordon wondered if he would be able to keep the fair looks of the pharaoh even after this all ended? Not likely, as stories of this kind never have a good end, except in Hollywood.

The star, Sirius, twinkled in the dark frame of the small window. A single lamp of fine engraved glass caused the darkness outside to appear even thicker. The faces of the two older men were quite inscrutable. It was as if they had all the patience in the world. The mummy in the corner was as hard as granite and could last forever. The sixty-thousand-dollar question in the young man's mind was, how long would *he* last?

The air around them became extremely chilly. The mountain air or the mummy's spirit? Suddenly Gordon felt very tired and sleepy. Gordon's consciousness melted into nothingness, and the youthful pharaoh now within him awoke and shook off the cobwebs of antiquity.

"Finally, we can talk," said Ikhnaton impatiently, "I'm tired of silence. Do we have to wait for Lord Aton?"

Moughabee sighed from the depth of his enormous chest. "No problem...we can talk with Your Majesty. As far as Lord Aton is concerned, He comes and goes of his own volition. Nobody has power over Him. We can only pray for His coming."

Ikhnaton seemed irritated by the lack of attention toward him.

"Then let's pray. My face is swollen and painful, my hands, too...what has happened to me? Have I been in a fight, or is it Gordon, the bearer of my Ka taking advantage of my passivity?"

"We cannot reveal the presence of your Pharaonic Majesty to the household," said Moughabee placatingly, trying to hide a thin ironic smile. "You have to remember that you're only borrowing this body."

The Pharaoh brooded, "These are ridiculous clothes. Not a single jewel."

"Alas, Your Majesty, everything on earth is transient."

Ikhnaton looked around himself with a short sigh. "You're right, Moughabee. I should remember that. Who's that man?"

"The owner of this house Your..."

"Quit the formalities, Moughabee, and call me lkhnaton. Is this man somebody that I have to talk to?"

"Absolutely, Ikhnaton," said Moughabee, as to a naughty child. "Sheik Hussney El Barrack is the Master of this region."

Ikhnaton, for the first time since his arrival, paid real attention to the third man in the room. "Hussney El Barrack? It doesn't sound familiar to me. Is he from our land?"

"He is from the present time, Ikhnaton," explained Moughabee

"Then he has never met Lord Aton."

"Never, but he wants to meet Him."

Ikhnaton pondered this proposal in momentary silence then, "I see. Does he know about our times?"

"You can ask him in person, Ikhnaton, just talk to him."

"Is he able to hear me?"

"Of course he is. Talk to him directly," suggested Moughabee.

With a mixture of curiosity and suspicion, Ikhnaton turned his large, piercing eyes toward the host.

"Are you the master of this house?" he demanded to know.

Hussney El Barrack was uncomfortable and glanced at Moughabee, who gave him a little encouragement with his eyes. Then Hussney made a slight bow with his head toward the Pharaoh.

"I'm flattered to have Your Majesty under my roof — you are most welcome."

"There are so many things to remember," Ikhnaton mused. "And so little time."

At that moment a radiant light came from the corner. The strong, square face of Lord Aton came in full view. His body wasn't very well outlined, but it didn't matter. The eyes were soft and full of compassion, but penetrating at the same time. He looked much younger than the face of the mummy.

"We have an eternity to remember, Ikhnaton," he said in a mellow, joyful voice. "The end is near, and so is the beginning. I expect to, in the near future, return for the last judgment, so before my third coming, you must restore the truth as it was in the beginning."

"You mean tell about your life as a peasant?" said Ikhnaton slightly shocked.

"Yes, Ikhnaton. You have to tell the story as it is. The whole of it."

The Pharaoh felt quite uncomfortable. "But it was so...unimportant, My Lord."

"The second time, I was reincarnated in a manger," continued Aton.

"It wasn't a manger," objected the Pharaoh.

"How do you know? You were not there!" contradicted Aton sternly.

"I was taught that by my tutors. I'm ten years older than you, though, now, we appear closer in age."

"I have worked in the fields since I was taken out of the cradle," Aton stated calmly.

"You were beautiful!" exclaimed the Pharaoh.

Aton spoke again rather sternly to Amenhotep, attempting to make his point. "Work made me beautiful and prematurely wise, I didn't have tutors."

"The Only God taught you," retorted the Pharaoh, trying for one-upmanship.

"The Only God taught all of us," smiled Aton.

"As far as I know He was not as successful with the rest."

"It was not a mistake on His part."

After a long pause, Ikhnaton asked, "Where shall I start?"

"How about with the beginning."

"It was very dreary," remembered Ikhnaton.

"The Truth, Ikhnaton, the Truth!" commanded Aton.

The Pharaoh looked beseechingly at Aton, then at his waiting audience. "I was told that the country suffered one of its worst famines. Children died. My tutor-priest explained that Amon-Ra was angry with humankind for not offering enough sacrifices. Little was bestowed upon the temples and the priesthood. People were interested only in their own well-being, in spite of the pontifical warnings."

"The Truth, Ikhnaton, the Truth!" interrupted Aton.

After a certain hesitation, Ikhnaton went on with his tale. "The Truth was different. The Ramses of the Old Kingdom had squandered its treasures, spending too much in building their gigantic palaces, temples and pyramids. The wars, even the victorious ones, were expensive and unprofitable. They invited pestilence and divested fields of grain tended by slaves who didn't care about the land. Hatred and corruption grew everywhere. The rich despised the poor for their poverty; the poor coveted the life of their masters. But in spite of the pomp of the royal ceremonies and military parades, life was far from wonderful anyplace. Even the high and mighty felt that there must be more to life than greed. A compassionate Pharaoh could've changed things. The pharaohs, however, were intimidated by the powers of the high priests, who fiercely protected the wisdom of the Past; their secrets were never shared with anyone. People trembled when confronted by the arrogant might of the gods. It was believed that only the priesthood knew how to appease them. It seemed as if nothing would change. My father and great-grandfather built the Colossus of Memnon and many of the temples of Luxor. Lower and Upper Egypt were completely raped. Even the Cataracts were sighing. The whole land moaned.

"Then tales were heard from the very bosom of Mother-Earth. A Man will be born at the end of the Eighteenth Dynasty. He will proclaim loud and clear the coming of the One and Only God. I felt the end of my rule was at hand, and wondered how to save the throne of the Kingdom for my son. Without notifying the priests, I sent my trusted servants to look for the *Man*. Years passed with no favorable news. I was ready to give up the search, though my own mother and my wife, Nefertiti, insisted I continue. They believed in the New Man, sight unseen. I didn't want to displease them. For the sake of my unborn son, I had to give one last look! The very High Priest told me that a new star had just been discovered in the sky. He believed it was heralding the end to the calamities. My interpretation was somehow different. The name of the star was Aton."

At that time, I was not known as Ikhnaton but as Amenhotep IV.

TIME WARP IN THE THEATER: CURTAIN OPENS ON PHARAOH'S GARDEN

Amenhotep IV studied the captivating face of Lord Aton in front of him. His eyes, deep in their sockets, were shrouded in mystery, dreamlike in a way, but strong and fanatic at the same time. His nose was perfectly straight, the mouth and the jaw a bit heavier, though in harmony with his body build.

They had met in the garden full of exotic birds. The Pharaoh had ordered his guards away and pretended to smell the blossoms of a colorful bush. Giant cypress cast their shadows — swords pointed at an invisible enemy. The youth waited for the older man to speak. The Pharaoh inhaled the bittersweet fragrance of the blossoms. "Welcome, stranger," he said kindly. "You're younger than I thought. Your blue eyes and golden hair are so unusual for an Egyptian. How old are you?"

"Sixteen, Majesty," replied Aton.

"As you're obviously not overwhelmed with the presence of a Pharaoh, don't feel bound to fall prostrate at my feet, though I am a God."

Aton wasn't intimidated at all. He even smiled. "There is only one God in Heaven and none on Earth. To be a leader of men is a responsibility, not a privilege."

"Well, how am I fulfilling my duty, young stranger?"

"I don't judge. I'm only the voice of my Teacher."

Amenhotep took a few steps toward Aton, physically attracted to this wonderful specimen. He wanted to kiss the rose-like lips, to zestfully embrace his vigorous body, to take him to the privacy of his fabulous apartments. Instead, he struck the boy's shoulder with the knot of his tiger tail. "Your God, I believe. And where do I fit in the picture, for heavens sake?"

"In His Temple, Majesty."

The Pharaoh moved to Aton's side. They were almost of the same stature and build. "In the temple, hey? Well, well, well...where is His Temple then?" the Pharaoh asked in an almost joking manner.

Aton held him with his compassionate eyes, "In your heart if you open it to Him."

"Is that so easy?"

"It's easier than building a temple with stones and marble or sacrificing bloody flesh to His likeness."

Amenhotep put his arm around Aton's warm, muscular back. "I disagree, a true God would enjoy sacrifices. What shall I give him?"

The youth freed himself from the Pharaoh's greedy arm and caressed the fragrant blossoms blooming beside them.

"A twig of this bush will be enough for Him."

The Pharaoh was frustrated. He knitted his eyebrows into a frown and tapped the young man again with the tiger's tail. His face became crimson with desire for this intriguing young man. "Enough of this silliness! I'm only ten years older than you and just as handsome," he removed his dark blue wig and some of his jewels. "I want to wrestle you, and you must obey me!"

The strange youth smiled again. His smile maddened the strapping, young Pharaoh, who launched himself at the his young visitor. In the next moment he found himself tossed down on the golden sand, head over heels. He looked up in dismay. "You can't be that strong. I'll have to try another hold."

Aton shook his head. "Don't humiliate yourself, Majesty. You'll be on your back again." He extended his large, firm hand to Amenhotep, who took it and got to his feet sobered and shamefaced.

"I've been working in the fields since I remember. That's my strength," explained Aton kindly.

The Pharaoh came up close to Aton, as if to smell him. "This can't be true," he uttered through his clenched teeth, "I won't tolerate it! I've been trained all my life, put to hardships as a warrior so that no one could stand up to me."

"Your mentors deceived you," said Aton softly, "they never matched you up with a stronger man."

The Pharaoh drew back and examined Aton from head to toe. "Just who are you?" he asked.

"I am Aton," he answered simply.

"Like the star?"

"Like the star."

"You seem like a young god to me," exclaimed Amenhotep.

"I'm just a simple peasant boy," Aton replied.

"You don't talk nor act like a peasant," retorted the Pharaoh.

The Pharaoh knelt down, hands embracing the small of Aton's back, resting his head on his sinewy midriff. "You'll be My Lord, now and forever," he claimed reverently.

"I know. That's why I'm giving you a new name — Ikhnaton," said the youth sadly, "but we won't die together."

"You cannot die, Aton!"

"Yes, I can and I will. My Only God is not going to resurrect me. The next time He'll take me into His Kingdom. Then, only my heart will remain on Earth until the final judgment."

Ikhnaton looked up with pain in his eyes. "Will you save me, Lord Aton?"

The youth put his hand over the head of the Pharaoh and answered quietly, "I'll try to save everyone."

RETURN TO PRESENT

Aton became aware of Hussney who, awestricken by the appearance of Aton, had been trying to say something but had failed in the attempt. Then Ikhnaton intervened.

"Let me introduce our host, My Lord."

Aton acknowledged Hussney with a question, "What does he know?"

"Lord, he knows only what Moughabee has told him."

Hussney fell from his seat and prostrated himself on the floor. "Forgive me, Lord, I didn't believe in You until now."

"Many people don't believe in resurrection. I come to make myself known again."

Hussney came slowly up to his knees, all his arrogance and great self-determination now brought to humility. "I'll serve You as I can, Lord Aton. My position in this world is a lowly one, but you have my love and obedience until the end of my time."

TIME WARP: IKHMET AT THEATER'S CURTAIN

The child Aton was found one morning, sleeping on the doorstep of a hovel nestled in a cluster of poor homes called Amarna. My parents already had three sons and a daughter of their own, but they gladly took him in. In those days poverty was shared more easily. This new adopted family member needed to grow up as soon as possible, so that he could pull his share working in the fields. The sons in my family didn't have names. They were called son One, son Two and son Three. Only the little daughter had a name — Oumana. But the young child my family took in knew his own name to be Aton. The priest-collector of taxes laughed about it. There was already a star in the sky with the same name, though, no one was able to explain how that tiny boy knew about it.

The boy simply announced, "I'm not a number, my name is Aton."

Aton was different from the rest of my family. He had golden hair and blue eyes, and his adoptive parents let him keep his name. We, his step-brothers, were disgruntled about this. At every opportunity we ganged up on him, but Aton stood his ground firmly. He even beat up one of my brothers two years older than he. Number Two, who was Aton's age, was defeated even more soundly. Number three, me, a year younger than Aton, gave him more problems than expected, but later I became Aton's best friend and follower.

Oumana kept away from her rowdy brothers, but she wasn't afraid of Aton. She even offered herself to him, but he shook his head resolutely, "That isn't right, sister."

"I'm not your sister," she protested.

"But you are in the eyes of God," admonished Aton kindly.

Hands on her hips, Oumana demanded, "Ha...which of the gods?"

"The Only One."

"How can that be?"

"I simply know."

I, as Number Three, lusted after Oumana more than my brothers did. I had hidden myself to listen to Oumana and Aton's conversation. When I heard that brief exchange I decided to join them.

"Ha, ha...Aton is lying. Who has ever heard of worshipping only one God?" I taunted.

Aton didn't get angry, he merely said, "You have heard it now."

"But that's a lie," I shouted.

"No, it is the truth I speak," Aton insisted.

I bristled up and started to argue with him, but Oumana stepped between us.

"Don't argue with my kid brother, Aton. I believe you."

I, as Number Three, now had more than one reason to be mad. "You keep out of it, sister. Just because he is handsome, doesn't mean that he's always right. He's so conceited, he treats us as if we have the plague. I'm sick and tired of your preaching, Aton! I almost vanquished you before, remember? I'll flatten you down again. If you know everything, wise guy, why don't you give *me* a name?"

Young Aton smiled in his charming way. "From myself I can give you nothing, but God has names for everyone."

"Then ask Him, please, I'm holding my breath!" I mocked angrily.

Aton put his hands together, looked toward the sky and whispered something, then calmly faced my rage. "Your name is Ikhmet. You have the heart of a warrior."

My mouth fell open. "Son of Sekhmet, the goddess of war? Isn't that a blasphemy?"

"Of course, it isn't. It's just a name. The goddess should be honored, if anything," Aton offered me assurance.

Oumana turned to her younger brother. "Ikhmet. I love that name, it sounds so much like you."

I, as the newly baptized, shrugged my wiry shoulders, a bit confused, then flexed my muscles and clenched my fists . "Let it be so. I am Ikhmet. Who dares not to believe it?"

IN EL BARRACK'S CASTLE

Moughabee caught the Pharaoh's shifting eyes. "Do you remember Ikhmet, Majesty?

"Yes, I do. He became my best general," said Ikhnaton. "Then he betrayed me to the priests. He kidnapped Prince Tut, sent him to the priests for protection and guidance, then engaged me in a gruesome combat to the death."

Lord Aton peered straight ahead, as if there was something written in the darkness. "I wish I knew why he did it."

"Because he never really believed in you. When I ordered the statues and the temples of the old gods destroyed and their fabulous treasures confiscated in favor of the state, all commoners turned against me. Even Nefertiti was horrified. Mother was the sole living member of the Dynasty that backed me up."

"Did you do it for the Love of me?" Aton asked.

The Pharaoh, in the remolded body of Gordon, was silent for awhile.

"I did it for you, at least in the beginning. The rest was done for my own glory."

"Explain it!" demanded Aton.

Ikhnaton started reluctantly, and then, gradually, he was able to control himself. "After everything was crushed it didn't matter any more. In my boyhood, it was quite different. When I was tutored by the priests, I really believed that my Father was Amon and that I was born for greatness not of this world. The Sun God meant everything to me! I never took a challenge that I could not win. A competition meant only victory to me. I wanted Amon to be a Sole-God and unique in the whole universe and then, you entered the scene. Well, even you did not survive in the end." A cynical smile played across Ikhnaton's lips. "At least my son is a central attraction in a museum," quipped Ikhnaton.

"Is that where I'm headed?"

"I truly don't know, my Lord. Maybe our host can tell us."

Hussney El Barrack had to escape the empty stares of eternity. He tried to find his voice, but it was lost. Instead, he shook his head. Probably nobody in the whole creation knew, except Allah...and He wasn't talkative.

TALE OF QUEEN NEFERTITI, ACCORDING TO A SALVAGED SCRIPTURE

As a woman, Nefertiti, in her time, was a wonder.

She would've been a better man than her husband. Her fine education and intelligence were surpassed only by her beauty. In the whole wide world there was not another pair of eyes that even came close to hers. Amenhotep was guided only by his impulses, his behavior based solely on instinct. He seldom regretted anything. In his mind, nothing was his mistake. Wasn't he a God!?! Nefertiti encouraged him to look for Aton, because he had to be found. He had to give people something that they were missing — goodness. He had to plant that seed in them.

Nefertiti fell in love with Aton from the very first moment she saw Him.

She wanted to bear His child. Amenhotep had a lot of children from his secondary wives, but none from Nefertiti. And he wanted this son more than anything in the world! His instinct told him that only a son from Nefertiti would make a great Pharaoh — the Pharaoh Egypt needed desperately. For a change, his instinct was right, but only a god would be able to help. Why not Lord Aton? No matter how lordly He was, Nefertiti burned in His Heart. He was a Man after all!

She knew the right time. It was during the intensely violet twilight hours that happen only on the shores of the Nile. The silhouettes of the royal palms seemed to be cut out of the very heart of night. Thousands of creatures provided the background music. Her husband, the Pharaoh had gone to Thebes on some pharaonic business. He had given up on trying to seduce Aton. What he got from Him was only his name — lkhnaton.

Lord Aton came to Nefertiti out of the scintillating waters of the Nile. He had been swimming in them for hours. The beasts never harmed Him. They knew who He was. The water drops covering His perfect body glittered like fireflies in the darkness, as if the bright stars had nested on Him. They were His only clothing.

Aton saw Nefertiti on the terrace and stopped. His luminous eyes examined her seductive curves as if she was the statue of a goddess. She noticed His large member growing. He came up the steps and took her in His arms.

"Welcome to Amarna, Queen Nefertiti," He whispered. The marble floor became the best bed in the world.

Chapter 4

THE ESCAPE

A DREAM IN THE DREAM

Gordon woke up on the floor. Through a small window with no frame or glass, he could see a piece of cloudless, blue sky. The bird chirping was loud and clear, coming either from a branch or ivy near the window. His head was aching. He was naked and experiencing dull pain in certain muscle groups. Strange pieces of conversations and images of unknown origin clouded his head. One of his front teeth was kind of wobbly. Then he remembered the fight with the young son of the sheik. And the young woman! Under her thin, long dress Gordon had seen the rounded silhouette of a shapely body. He felt aroused just thinking of her. He only hoped there would be a chance of seeing her again.

Helena!

That was it! La belle Hellaine. Gordon looked around the room for his clothes — no clothes, there was only an earthen water jug. He realized he was feeling very hungry.

Helena! He had to find a way to see her again. And he needed to find some clothes. The morning was cold, but it was warm under the thick coverlet. He dozed until he heard footsteps on the tiles of his room.

It was Aldan. He was scantily clad and obviously shaking from the cold. "I'm freezing."

Gordon lifted up the covers, and Aldan crawled under to get warm. He was cold as ice. His teeth were chattering sporadically.

"Where have you been to get so cold?" asked Gordon

"I discovered a very important secret, even though I had to spend most of the night freezing. I was crouched on a rock under the window of the highest turret of our house. And then climbing down I fell into the pond."

"You're crazy, Aldan and too old for pranks like that. But tell me, what's so secret?"

"It's about you, and that strange Nubian, and my dad, too."

"Your dad?" Gordon asked surprised.

"Yes. The mummy was there also."

"Why were you spying?"

"Because I wanted to see what you were up to, and I heard everything."

"What did you hear?" prodded Gordon.

"What do you mean? You were there, too."

"Yes, but I fell asleep."

"You did not...unless you were talking in your sleep."

"I don't talk in my sleep," Gordon snapped.

"But you do...sleepwalking too," protested Aldan.

Now Gordon got mad. He climbed on top of Aldan, sat on his chest and slapped him twice across his face.

"One of those slaps is for my wobbly tooth and the other is for your cockamamie story."

The youth wiggled vigorously under him, and blood spurted from his nose.

"Listen, I'm telling the truth," gasped the struggling youth.

Gordon released Aldan and sat back flexing his muscles. Aldan, now free from Gordon's grip, was still angry, feeling insulted by the slaps. He struck out at Gordon.

The anger overtaking both the young men seemed as though it pulsed from another being. Gordon, again pushed Aldan down on the bed and held him with arms of steel. Then, suddenly, with the voice of Ikhnaton, claimed, "I know you are Ikhmet, the general who betrayed me — not only me, but Lord Aton and my son Prince Tut!"

"He wasn't your son," hissed the youth under the vice-like hold. "Aton fathered him!"

Ikhnaton shook his head so violently that drops of sweat sprayed over his perennial foe.

"No-o-o-o-ooo! ! !"

"Yes, you crazy Pharaoh! And Nefertiti is my sister. And you'll never have her! Never, ever!"

Gordon awoke bathed in cold sweat. He had slept straight through the morning. The sun was blazing everywhere and the small window of the cubicle was its mirror.

The clothes he had borrowed from Aldan were lying on a heap in the middle of the cubicle.

Hussney El Barrack paced up and down the largest courtyard. Aldan stood up against the wall, hands crossed over his chest.

"Did you spy on us last night?" asked El Barrack as he stopped in front of his son.

"No, I didn't," Aldan answered a little too quickly.

His father stopped close to him and looked into his eyes. "That's not what Moughabee told me."

"Who? You mean the wealthy Nubian? He doesn't know what he's talking about. Somebody lied about me and I'll find out who. I'll kill him with my bare hands."

"You'll kill your own sister?" his father asked.

"No. But I will get the person whispering in her ear," promised Aldan

Hussney took up his pacing again, then once more confronted Aldan. "Are you going to betray me?"

"No. I'm going to save you."

"Fool! You are already lying to me. Your sister will hate you."

For the first time a baffled look came into the greenish eyes of the youth.

"Helena doesn't know a thing. After she broke up the fight between Gordon and me, she went to the women's quarters."

His father interrupted, "Helena was unable to fall asleep. She brought me your discarded wet clothes. After finding them she checked your room. You were not there."

"I fell asleep on Gordon's bed."

"Why?"

He dropped his head. "I was hoping to finish off our fight, but he didn't come back."

His father's eyes closed tiredly.

"Were you planning to kill our young guest?"

"Not exactly…we already fought, and I wanted a rematch."

"Enough of that, look in my eyes, son. Stop lying to me, I want the truth from you before giving you into the hands of Moughabee. He knows black magic, and he'll penetrate down to your truant heart."

Aldan drove a fiery look straight in his father's eyes. "You'll let him do that to me?"

"You leave me no choice. You'll be locked behind bars for the duration."

A cruel smile distorted Aldan's lips. "Then kill me. I won't stay in your dungeon."

"Son, I love you, but you have disappointed me terribly and I intend to keep a close eye on you. By the way, you have been spending a lot of money in Beirut's bordellos and striptease parlors. Who paid for these escapades?"

Aldan bit his lips. "Everybody knows, as your number one son, some day I'll inherit your riches, they bet on me in fights."

"You haven't fought publicly. You're under age. Now tell me, where did you get the money?" demanded his father.

"I got a loan," Aldan finally admitted.

"From whom?"

"Someone that I don't want to mention," he answered quietly.

"The emissary to the Prelate in Jerusalem, that cursed Frenchman?" El Barrack surmised immediately.

"He wanted a couple of our guards for a special mission," Aldan confessed.

"Did they ask you not to tell me?"

Aldan shook his curly head no.

"What then?"

"I said you wouldn't mind."

"Did you think I wouldn't mind your betrayal of my guests, too?" El Barrack's anger mounted.

Aldan's face was on fire. "I thought you loved me more than you would a couple of strangers and their loot. Besides, they are Christians."

"So they're dispensable?"

The youth shrugged his shoulders. "What do I care?"

Bitterness turned down the corners of Hussney El Barrack's lips.

"As long as there are people like you, there will be no peace on earth. You'll be locked away until I change my mind."

Aldan fell to his knees. "Won't you let me kiss your hand before sending me to die? For the sake of my dead mother, give me your pardon so I can go through the Gates of Paradise!"

The sheik was silent for a long time. Then he looked down at his handsome son.

"I cannot, Aldan, Allah won't let me do it. You broke one of the basic laws of His Prophet. You were ready to sell our guests. Do you think Helena will understand your double play? You know she's a Christian, too."

"Are you going to tell her, Father?"

"I don't know yet. Greed and jealousy possess you. Go away from my sight, Aldan. There is not a drop of repentance in you."

The youth came up to his feet like a panther and, before Hussney had any chance to stop him, he was at the terrace's end over the canyon.

"A word from you, and I'll jump to my death!" exclaimed Aldan.

The sheik looked at him squarely and intoned firmly, "Aton!"

His son became deathly pale.

"Try to sell him another time, Ikhmet!"

Aldan, visibly shaken, stepped back to the safety of the terrace.

"Who told you about Ikhmet?" he stammered.

"Lord Aton," replied his father.

By noontime, the house attendant reported to his master that a few friends of Aldan's had set him free.

"Everyone involved should be captured and punished," ordered the Sheik, "let my agents look for Aldan. I want him under close control."

The attendant made a short bow and hurried away.

Dr. Moughabee came out of a shady spot and joined the Sheik. "What's on your mind, Hussney?"

"As you can see, we are a house divided. I cannot trust anyone. Even my first son is disloyal to me. We have to move Lord Aton's mummy to a smaller place that can be kept under surveillance, or to a large city where it's possible to live in anonymity. In Damascus I have some powerful friends. For the time being any travel by air is impossible. The helicopter was disabled during the night. It will take a lengthy time to be overhauled."

Moughabee listened to him silently. There was no doubt that his friend was in a state of shock. He was unable to think properly. Aldan meant more to him than he was willing to admit, and the situation had come to a very dangerous point. The Egyptian

Government could issue warrants for arrest. Everyone involved in this affair could be arrested on sight as a common thief. A major archeological artifact had been stolen. They had to disappear for awhile.

"I have an idea, Dr. Moughabee," El Barrack spoke up. There is a tunnel under the building, deep inside the mountain. It's manmade, but empties into an unexplored cave. My family have used it as a hideout for centuries. It has been used for many purposes, even for mining. Aldan only knows how to get to the entrance, but the tunnel itself is heavily booby trapped. I'm the only one that knows how to defuse the explosives. Aldan doesn't know the code. Since he was a child, the fear of tales about people held in the cave until their death kept him away from any exploration. He feared I would lock him there. To me it was an escape route in case of emergency. At the opening on the other side of the cave, there is a well-hidden military truck, its fuel tank filled to the brim and all maintenance done only by me. During our bloodthirsty war of attrition, that made great sense."

Moughabee sighed deeply. "It makes sense to me as well. But is there something you are not sharing with me?"

The Sheik was uneasy. "At a certain point the tunnel forks. One of the roads, as I told you, leads into a huge cavern. It's absolutely unexplored. For all I know it may be going to the center of Earth. The other leads to the exit. I have never been past this place."

"Who put in the mines — how did know where the exit was?"

"Professionals laid the mines. They were killed later in Beirut. The situation in our country is still volatile — corruption everywhere. My own private army is divided into different factions."

"How did you maintain the truck?"

"Driving to the back. I know the exit from the people that worked on the tunnel. They took the correct fork and made it all the way through, though I never had, because of my fear."

"I hope my magic works underground, never tried that before. Where is my grandson?"

"He is with my daughter Helena. She's a Christian. We cannot leave her behind. I haven't thought yet what we will do if we make it safely through."

Moughabee was becoming impatient with the Sheik. "We'll drive to the coast and hire a speedboat to Cypress. I can count on important people there."

The Sheik hesitated for a moment, then said, "Do we have even a remote chance of making it, Moughabee?"

"We have many chances if we act immediately," he answered the Sheik.

"Then let be it Allah's Will! I have emergency knapsacks with food and water rations for the whole household in storage. I'll find two dependable soldiers to carry the mummy. Let us hurry!

Moughabee smiled for the first time since the events of that morning. "Don't forget, Hussney, Lord Aton is with us."

Within the hour the group gathered at the bottom of a spiral staircase in front of a vault in the rock. A large, fortified door was outfitted with a modern electronic locking system. The soldiers made it just in time.

Outside, a helicopter had disgorged a company of Syrians. They were searching the compound, and it was only a matter of time before they reached the underground vault.

Hussney punched in the code and the massive door slid to the side. When the last member of the group passed through, it closed behind them and locked automatically. Led by the Sheik, they went single file through the tunnels. Light was inadequate. The impression was that they were criss-crossing a great pyramid. Gordon walked right behind the leader, Moughabee followed, then Helena, Ouloulangha and the two robust soldiers carrying the well-packed mummy firmly strapped to an army stretcher. Everyone was armed. At first the pace was brisk, but it gradually slackened due to the extra weight on their backs. Helena carried nothing except an over-the-shoulder first-aid kit. Breathing was difficult and the lack of fresh air made them feel increasingly tired.

Gordon approached the Sheik. "What will happen if someone tries to open the door?"

"The system is activated. Aldan is not stupid. He won't tell the Syrians about the tunnel. He knows that anyone who tries to follow us would be buried under tons of debris. My son is a show off, but easily frightened. While quick to be melodramatic, when the real action starts he's always somewhere else, out of danger and well protected. Most people think of him as a hero. He's a good actor, but I can read through him. For him life is a stage. But that doesn't make him less dangerous."

"How about the electric lights? He wouldn't forget them."

"If he cuts them off, there is a twenty-four hour battery back-up," explained El Barrack.

The tunnel suddenly turned down. For a while, walking seemed easier, but the floor wasn't smooth as before. It was slippery, and unexpected potholes appeared here and there, dug up and torn by forces of nature. Their progress was slowed even more by the necessity of finding and diffusing the mines, then, once safely past, setting them again. Oddly, everyone's watches had stopped at the same time — eleven a.m.

Before long, the small group of fugitives arrived at a spot where the tunnel split into the two passages. Hussney El Barrack looked helplessly at the rest.

"I have never been further than this. Very few have. I tried from the other side, where the truck is camouflaged, but it was even more confusing. One consolation though, there are no more mines beyond this point."

As he feared, Moughabee's magic powers had waned. The thin air bothered him more than anybody else. Lord Aton's Mummy was incommunicado. What was left?

"You're not a fool, Hussney. How could you plan on a quick exit without exploring the full length of the tunnel? Now you have led all of us into this trap."

The Sheik shook his head. "I warned you, didn't I?"

Dr. Peter Moughabee sat down on a pile of rocks.

"Yes, you did, Hussney. But somehow we have to make a choice — which path will lead us out."

Hussney sat down next to him. He was getting edgy. He wanted a smoke, but the effect of smoking in oxygen deprived air was unpredictable. He drank some water from his canteen. The small group looked to the two men to lead them to safety, but time and air were running out.

Suddenly, hideous laughter, magnified ten times, echoed in the high vault over their heads.

Ikhnaton's "Ka" was hanging in the air looking scornfully at the bunch of fugitives. He broadcast his thoughts, tossing them throughout the chamber.

"Do I really want to save them? Maybe I do, maybe not. Did Aton ever help me? I believed in Him like no other person on earth. Yet, at the disappearance of Prince Tut, His own child...He did nothing—He did not help me either. What am I to do with the bearers of His mummy?"

Moughabee was the only one that understood his words. He addressed him in his mind. "Cut the histrionics, Ikhnaton. You stole Prince Tut. You delivered him into the hands of the priests in a desperate attempt to appease them."

The Pharaoh was silent for a long time. Just when Moughabee thought him gone, he suddenly came back to life. "One of those roads leads to the Egypt of my time, and the second one leads to that ugly contraption you call a *truck*." He then flew in a rage back to the Absolute.

THEATER OF THE ABSURD: IKHNATON STEPS UP TO PROSCENIUM

There was an ode dedicated to me:

Oh, Ikhnaton that came from the glorious Amenhotep,
You lead us to the fountain of knowledge
To drink from the everlasting wisdom
Of the One and Only God!"

Why did I, the Pharaoh of Upper and Lower Egypt, complete master of the greatest kingdom on earth, steal my sole inheritor and deliver him into the hands of my worst enemies? Because I truly loved my wife Nefertiti, and she used me, humiliated me. She presented me with a bastard instead of a son.

How did I get to know the truth about Prince Tut's birth?

Tutankhaton looked and acted like his biological father. I had no doubt that the priests would kill Prince Tut. Therefore, I dispossessed them of their foolish temples, took their riches into the state treasury, and reapportioned their fertile lands to the peasants who had worked them for centuries. Those priests had every reason to kill "my son."

But they didn't. They only changed his name from Tutankhaton to Tutankhamon. The rest is history.

Ikhmet, as General Harremhab, assaulted my palace. Officially, that shameless act was executed in the name of my son. Unwittingly, I had made this arrogant peasant leader, head of the army. He had performed some special services for me and Aton thought highly of him. Later, I learned what a rascal this lowborn peasant was — and I tried to alert Lord Aton. I was too late. His faith in Ikhmet Harremhab had grown unshakable. The general now hated my guts, and his ambitions were lofty. Between him and the pharaoh's throne stood only me…and Prince Tut. For Ikhmet, usurping the Pharaonship was just a matter of time. Lord Aton resisted my idea to arrest him for treason. If he had failed with his foster brother, he said it was entirely his own mistake. The One and Only God wanted it that way, and His will would prevail. I think Aton wanted to be tortured and put to death. He had chosen to be a Martyr.

NEFERTITI ENTERS CENTERSTAGE

Nefertiti believed otherwise. She stormed into my room, not as a Queen of Egypt, but as an angry wife of a fish merchant. "You stole my son just to humiliate me!"

"We all have to learn one day how to be humble, Nefertiti. Especially with the army surrounding the Palace," I reminded her.

Nefertiti's face expressed utter deprecation. "And you're doing nothing!?!"

"No less and no more than the father of your beloved son."

"My son is a Demigod."

"Your son is not even a man yet. From now on Prince Tut must prove his Divine Rights."

"You hate him! You always have!" hissed the Queen.

"You're only partially right. I loved the boy for years, and hated him only for a day or so. Then it didn't matter anymore if I formally stayed on the throne. I had spent all available resources to attract more adherents to our cause...I mean...the cause of your lover."

Nefertiti wouldn't back down, "How do you dare to say that!?!"

"Why not? What more can I lose except my life? Tell General Harremhab that I'll be alone and unarmed in the little room of the corner turret and not altogether ready to surrender. Let him come to me, man to man. Do you think he'll find enough courage?"

"Oh, yes, and he will kill you with his bare hands," she warned.

"That still won't make him a Pharaoh — not as long as Prince Tut lives. Though in due time, I'm sure he'll take care of him too."

"Over my dead body," sneered the Queen.

"Yes, over your dead body, Nefertiti," I agreed.

FLASH TO PRESENT

Moughabee guessed right. In the truck they found a whole chest full of military uniforms. Hussney had at least been very thorough at this end — I.D. tags, papers, even some medals. The water supply and food rations were sufficient and in perfect condition. So far everything seemed almost too good to be true after all they had just been through. Hussney El Barrack, more relieved than anyone, turned to Dr. Moughabee and asked if it was time to load up and move on to the coast as planned.

Moughabee had become very still, silently looking out toward the east, as if he saw or heard something.

He turned to El Barrack and said, "I have a feeling the theological winds have changed in our favor. We won't have to go far on our own. In my mind's eye I see what is happening now that we are free from the cave. The Prelate in Jerusalem didn't follow up on the instructions from Rome. To stop us at any price means to be bought, if possible, but not to stir things up politically. Your son Aldan got it wrong and acted precipitously. When the Prelate learned about Aldan's betrayals, which led to some reckless decisions by the government, he decided to try and find us. I sense we will meet him soon."

Hussney was open-mouthed at this disclosure and asked, "But how could he?"

Moughabee told him that the Prelate was well versed with this territory. He could show the way to the driver of a four-wheel-drive vehicle.

Hussney didn't like the last bit at all. "Why not hire a helicopter?"

"Because the helicopter is noisy and attracts too much attention. You underestimate the astuteness of Rome, Hussney. I hope that this time I am on the right track."

Hussney El Barrack coughed discretely. "Since I met you some twenty years ago, Peter, I have only deep respect for your unusual endowments. Sadly, I'm afraid times have changed and not exactly changed in our favor."

"Perhaps. According to my inner eye, at this very moment, the Prelate and his secretary are making their way to this place. They abhor publicity. Understandably, that's a peg in our favor. So lets head out now. We can still offer our guests a couple of military rations."

Chapter 5

THE PRELATE MEETS THE MUMMY

About 45 minutes later, Moughabee called a halt under a rather high rock formation. They didn't have to wait long.

The Pontifical Prelate and his secretary came along the rocky path unaccompanied, However, they were linked by a short wave radio to a protection squad stationed at a reasonable distance.

Dr. Moughabee waited at the base of the path with an unexpectedly meek and polite face. "What a pleasant surprise, Monsignor!"

The Prelate didn't return the smile. He pushed his metallic eyeglasses up his thin curved nose and said a bit vitriolically, "I wish I could share the same sentiments, gentlemen, but I am not here for pleasure. I'm here on a mission bestowed upon me by a higher authority."

Moughabee enjoyed the situation enormously. "I'm sorry to discover that there are some differences of opinions within the Mother Church unintentionally triggered by us. May I be of some help?"

The Prelate coughed, more to gain time than, to relieve himself. "You certainly may, Dr. Moughabee. I don't need any introduction to your company, if not in person, I know them quite well by description, and of course Sheik El Barrack has been my guest on several occasions. What I'd like to do, before anything else, is to see the mummy in your possession.

Dr. Moughabee nodded politely and led the guests to the covered stretcher in the back of the truck. The Prelate looked fixedly at the unveiled face of Aton with no more emotion than some slight paling.

His secretary demonstrated undisguised surprise. After a moment of hesitation, he crossed himself with a visible tremor in his fingers.

There was a significant change in the Prelate's voice, "The Pope was right," he muttered almost to himself, "it is extremely upsetting. The resemblance is uncanny..." then in his normal voice, "Is it true, Dr. Moughabee, that you can establish vocal contact with the...the...person in this mummy?"

"This mummy has a name, Monsignor...Lord Aton. You have to talk about Him with great respect."

The Prelate nodded slowly without removing his eyes from the Exalted Face in front of him, then stated with dignity, "He'll be treated as a Prince of Princes. Under your escort He'll be taken to a palatial villa on the outskirts of Jerusalem. Until establishing His true identity, we have to treat this affair with utter discretion. The impact over the populace of a discovery of such magnitude cannot be predictable. As for the...uhm...reincarnation of Amenhotep IV or Ikhnaton, this kind of mysticism is quite different from the Doctrine of The Holy Church. Processing this claim must be even more rigorous and path finding, though I solemnly swear in God's name, that everything will be done properly and with the due respect."

Gordon couldn't help but think how strange the ways of God are sometimes and how much stranger they become when interpreted by men.

The villa on the outskirts of Jerusalem had a large swimming pool, something that Gordon was most happy to enjoy. For him water was like a shelter, a protection of his privacy; it gave him concentration and internal peace. The evening was quiet and the water clear and cool. Gordon thought about Helena. She was staying on with them as a secretary to her father. So far they hadn't had a chance to be alone. He didn't want to harbor any hopes. Helena was a lady by all standards. Was she attracted by his new looks? If that was the case, how long could he count on the pharaoh's wizardry? He sensed that she had seen in him more than what was really there. How long would he be useful sheltering the "Ka" of Ikhnaton? Would he be kicked back to the good old USA and a life of total obscurity?

He saw Helena coming down the steps. She didn't try to play any game of coincidence. She wanted to talk to him and did it straightforwardly. Dressed in simple elegance, her beauty was electrifying to him. He got out of the pool and looked for his bath towel. She had it. "Let me help you, Gordon."

He put himself in her hands. Before long, they were embracing each other. Then, they were kissing with fervor and abandonment.

"I'm nobody, Helena…just nobody. I don't have a dollar to my name," Gordon announced, coming up for breath.

"Neither do I, Gordon…everything belongs to my father, not counting a small inheritance from my mother's side. That's why my brother Aldan is ready to do anything for a handful of money no matter what."

"I have no grudge against him, Helena. All I want to think about right now is you — you and me together."

They spent the night in the small pool house. No one missed them.

After dinner, Dr. Peter Moughabee and the Prelate secluded themselves in the room with the mummy. The Nubian reached for a cigar, but the expression of silent disapproval on the thin lips of his host forced him to change his mind. He had already had some wine and the lucid precision of his line of reasoning had suffered a bit. The large room languished in darkness and the spare Victorian furniture looked unaccommodating and hostile. The Roman Prelate didn't seem to be bothered by the surroundings.

"Have you read, Dostoevsky, Dr. Moughabee?" inquired the Prelate as they settled in.

Moughabee tried to make himself as comfortable as he could. His excessive body weight always cried for more support. "Yes. I have read some of his writings."

"*Crime and Punishment*?"

"Yes and also the predicaments of Prince Mishkin in the human menagerie."

"You have done surprisingly well," the Prelate commented dryly.

Dr. Moughabee smiled, "You mean...for a Nubian?"

"No...of course not. Please, try to think of me as an intelligent priest. If we both somehow get rid of our mutual animosity, we might be able to reach beneficial results. I don't like to preach, though I make, from time to time, some efforts to explain myself through literary images.

Dr. Moughabee stifled a sigh and tried to adjust his large buttocks over the narrow chair. "That calls for a cigar...if your Eminence doesn't mind?"

"I guess, we both agreed to become more amenable."

The Nubian took his time cutting and lighting the cigar, then pulled deeply from it with obvious relaxation. "By all means. You have my undivided attention."

In the gathering dusk, the slim, straight figure across from him looked even more rigid than the chairs. "I presume you haven't read 'The Legend of the Great Inquisitor'?"

"A novel?"

"No, just part of a novel, though it's a story by itself, not incorporating any of the known characters from the rest of the book."

"Are we talking about Lord Aton?" Moughabee guessed.

The Prelate hesitated for a moment then nodded slightly. "In a certain way…yes."

"I'm listening."

"It was in the darkest period of the Spanish-Catholic Inquisition. An enormous *auto de fé* was in preparation. The Great Inquisitor wanted to see for himself all the heretics to be put to death. The scene described by the author is quite reminiscent of the 'Christians to the lions' in ancient Rome. No one was spared because of age, even the babies had to go. I, personally cannot picture extreme cruelties of this kind committed by the Church of Christ. Numbers have been greatly exaggerated and the babies…added for a dramatic effect. Some well informed sources insist, that this Great Inquisitor was totally blind, so his inspection of the victims is a grotesque lie."

The Prelate switched on a large table lamp, which spread very little light for its size. Obviously the diocese was saving money.

Moughabee fidgeted with impatience.

The Prelate noted this and continued, "I'd better hurry to the point. The Inquisitor wanted to meet the condemned the night before. The prison, according to the author, had a funnel like shape, so the journey of the Great Inquisitor was much like Dante Alighieri's travel through the Inferno. Reaching the very bottom floor, he found only one prisoner. It was Jesus Christ. It was pitch-dark in the dungeon, therefore, the would-be blindness of the Great Inquisitor is not of any matter."

"Maybe he lost his eyesight after the fact," commented Moughabee.

"I have no idea…does the story come back to you?"

"Yes, now I remember. The Great Inquisitor asked the Savior, what in hell was He doing there? Jesus answered, 'I came to be crucified one more time!' 'No!' exclaimed the Great Inquisitor. But the Inquisitor had no chance to spare Him. The Holy Church, as an entity, had far too much power in those times. Can't you see it?"

"And now?"

"Now..." The Prelate looked in the general direction of the mummy, "...Maybe we can spare him."

THEATER OF THE ABSURD: IKHNATON APPEARS AGAIN

Those stupid clowns seriously think that they can get rid of me! I, the real force in this tragedy, Amenhotep IV, the only Pharaoh that stood daringly against the priesthood for an unknown God! Of course, I made my share of mistakes, who doesn't? But to ignore me completely...! Even that snotty boy whose body I dwell in and have improved, is using me for lovesick purposes. If that Arab girl, Helena, intends to let in the spirit of Queen Nefertiti, she should go through me. For goodness sake, Nefertiti was my wife!

And Aton, of them all! He owes me something in the final count. Why lavish all attention on Him? He only acted in a legend. I made it happen for real.

PRESENT TIME

Helena pressed her vibrant body into what used to be the man Gordon, and questioned him, "Somehow you seem different, darling. Who are you?"

Gordon smiled with bitterness. "If I say...will you believe me?"

"Just level with me, I love you."

"I can't level with you any more frankly than I have in our past hour together. I tried to 'invest' into you the last of what I think is the real me," Gordon tried to explain.

Helena strained her large eyes to see his expression in the darkness. "I don't understand. I like what I see and feel of you."

Gordon luxuriated in her tenderly, possessive hands. "But it isn't me, Helena. It's another guy that died thousands of years ago. Now he has possessed me. He's locked out of Heaven and his eternal peace. I guess he committed an act of betrayal that follows him throughout eternity."

Helena drove her will into him even more forcefully.

"I believe you. I think my brother is possessed too. I think it's Satan himself."

Suddenly the charismatic man in her embrace laughed huskily. "He's worse than Satan. He's been my worst enemy since I knew him as a boy."

Helena felt the sudden change in him.

"But you hardly know Aldan," she protested.

"His name is Ikhmet, and he has the heart of a cobra. Find him, tell him to come and see me here. I will finish him off with my bare hands. I'll take care of him once and for all."

Helena was horrified. "Why do you hate each other so much?"

Gordon, now Ikhnaton, laced his strong arms around her and burned her with his fiery eyes. "Because of you, Nefertiti."

Ouloulangha knocked discretely on the door of the apartment occupied by Sheik El Barrack and his daughter. Helena opened the door and invited him into their small living room.

"My father will be with you in a few minutes. Make yourself comfortable. You can smoke if you like. I'm going to make some coffee and tea, a drink perhaps?" She tried to make him comfortable.

Mr. Ouloulangha offered his strong Egyptian cigarettes to the young lady.

"Just for yourself, I don't indulge. May I ask you a question?" The Nubian's secretary let out a stream of smoke through his large nostrils exactly like his master, nodding at her almost imperceptibly. Helena took a couple of steps toward him, then stopped to check in the direction of her father's door, "How well do you know Mr. Bates?"

Ouloulangha hesitated only for a moment. His voice came to her softly with a degree of confidentiality. " I have my personal impressions of Mr. Bates. Why do you ask?"

"Could he murder someone in cold blood?" Helena blurted out.

Ouloulangha wasn't too taken aback, "He does have a hot temper, but are you thinking about your brother?"

"Yes."

"Well, I am quite sure I can set your mind at peace. Dr. Moughabee asked me to keep an eye on Gordon. Your brother has been in Jerusalem for some time now and seems to have an excellent rapport with Gordon. Myself and others have witnessed them spending most of the day together in various entertainment houses where female customers are forbidden. They drink and enjoy watching the entertainment. They were also seen meeting with the Russian Consul together."

"Are you serious!?!" Helena found it difficult to believe what she was hearing.

"I'm afraid it's true. I didn't like it any more than you. The Consul was waiting for them in one of those Karate training places. He is a regular there. They had a low key but animated conversation. The whole thing lasted for about half an hour...give or take."

"Are you going to share this with my father?" Helena took another tact.

"Only if I'm asked, which is not likely," Ouloulangha assured her.

"I'll be quite grateful if you don't. Father doesn't trust Aldan on any terms, especially political." Helena stopped speaking when Hussney El Barrack entered the room in a businesslike manner.

"I see Helena kept you company in my absence. Tend to the refreshments, my dear, I think we'll need them."

Helena left the room with an empty smile. The Sheik sat close to his guest.

"To what do I owe this visit? Is anything wrong?"

"Tonight Moughabee is going to entertain the Prelate. He wanted your presence too, but the Roman didn't buy it," Ouloulangha announced.

The Sheik knitted his thick eyebrows. "I didn't think he would. My son, Aldan, for his own selfish purposes, has spread the news about the mummy all over. A number of foreign diplomats have tried to reach me. I paid a visit to the Russian Orthodox Church. The Bishop happened to be there and he's of course very close to the Russian Embassy and wanted to know if I'm withholding something. Reporters pressed around us and we were photographed several times. I tried to be evasive, but I had to give out some kind of information about the new archeological find. What I told him he already knew. The Protestants had already released their version to Associated Press and *Taggeblat*. Even my barber told me in confidence about it. I have no idea what Dr. Moughabee is going to do. A lot of money is ready to change hands. The Chinese and the Indian governments are unusually generous. The Leading Rabbi believes that we have to level with them as well. Egyptians insist that a property of theirs has been stolen. They could be very nasty. My bank account in Cairo is blocked, but that had to be expected. I had already transferred the main body of my funds to safe havens. My son is just profiting from a tricky situation. Does Gordon have anything to do with the latest developments?" El Barrack asked Ouloulangha.

"I think it may be possible, Excellency, that he is doing a favor for Aldan."

"That's a surprise, why would he do that?" gasped El Barrack.

"One cannot be so sure when dealing with a split personality. Gordon can be after something absolutely different."

"You mean the Ikhnaton side of him?"

"I don't know what I really mean, Excellency. It's beyond my scope," Ouloulangha shrugged.

"You paid the Egyptians with Moughabee's funds. I'm quite sure that you paid yourself handsomely."

Ouloulangha was a little insulted by El Barrack's insinuation. "My master has always been more than generous to me," he answered huffily. "But the deal with Associated Press was his own. He had to protect himself."

Hussney El Barrack lost his temper. "The price of Lord Aton can be staggering, not to mention the powers that desire him that are involved. Even my daughter isn't safe. After all, she could be kidnapped and Gordon as well for that matter."

"Sir, do you think your son Aldan is in back of this mess?"

The Sheik wiped his forehead. "I don't know for sure, but I think he has gotten into things way over his head."

"Do you think his life is in jeopardy as well?"

"Yes, it is...don't forget, he has a name in the panopticum too as Ikhmet or whatever." The Sheik took some deep breaths before he went on, "I guess I'll have to abduct my own son in order to save him. To put it simply, we're in the hands of the Pope, so we might as well move to the Vatican."

Ouloulangha thought briefly. "You may be right. I'll discuss all this with Dr. Moughabee. Actually only Dr. Moughabee can keep the Genie in the bottle to a certain point. I hope that he has enough good sense to destroy the mummy if the situation gets out of hand."

Hussney shook his head. "He cannot do that. We're already in the second phase of the ordained chain of events. Allah be merciful! In Jerusalem, Lord Aton had his second reincarnation as Jesus. He's being kept away from the Gates of Heaven also. The New Millennium is knocking at our door. Will that be the Kingdom come and the end of civilization as we know it?"

"Perhaps we are at the end of the world, sir. Through my master's magical powers, tonight's meeting will be held in the power fields of Sirius — the home of all dead sinners. Lord Aton is in charge of it."

Hussney El Barrack suddenly felt a chilling wind rising around him, leaving him sapped of energy. "In a way," he uttered tiredly, "I'm glad to miss that journey. I wish I didn't know even this much. Knowledge such as this isn't made for the human mind."

The view from the top of the residence stretched far and wide under the brilliant stars over Jerusalem. The distance of the city lights made stargazing possible without their interference. It was a moonless night, and everything else except for the glow behind Mount Zion was in darkness.

Standing with the Roman Prelate, Dr. Moughabee pointed out the constellation of Sirius. "The third star from the center is the home of Lord Aton."

The Roman Prelate tried to focus his rimless glasses on the star. "I think I can see it, though I was expecting something closer and bigger."

The ebony face of the Nubian was hard to see in the darkness, but his voice was loud and clear. "I won't disappoint you, Eminence. We can start any time you're ready."

Some perplexity showed on the normally stony face of the lanky Prelate. "I thought you were going to demonstrate the transfiguration of the mummy in front of me."

In the darkness the teeth of Dr. Moughabee were clearly visible in a wide grin. "If you're not afraid, I can show you something far more impressive. A voyage to the very Seat of the Lord."

A slight breeze from the Dead Sea came to the Prelate like a touch from another world. "How can this be accomplished, Dr. Moughabee. Are you a hypnotist?" questioned the skeptical Prelate.

"No, Eminence, I'm only a medium. In this particular case, I'm fulfilling the wish of my Teacher."

"Your Teacher? I am not sure I see a connection here. You call yourself great-grandfather of the young American, Gordon Bates. Is there something more about your family that I don't know?"

To the surprise of the Prelate, Moughabee admitted, "I'm actually Gordon's father." Then he added, "In a way, the rest of my folks are up on Lord Aton's constellation."

"The Isle of the Dead?"

Dr. Moughabee shrugged his massive shoulders. "You can call it that. For me, it's the Isle of Eternal Life."

The cool breeze became even stronger. The wail of a strange animal came on its wings.

"Aren't you tempted to stay on that isle, Dr. Moughabee? The Isle of Eternal Life?"

"I am. But I am here to fulfill the will of My Lord."

"One last question. Is He the Jesus of our times?"

"Yes, Eminence. Before, now and forever."

Gordon and Helena were swimming together in the cool waters of the pool. Their strong and rhythmic breast stroke was taking them almost effortlessly from one side to the other.

After several laps they came to rest at the deep end of the pool.

"Do you still hate my brother, Gordon?" Helena asked after she caught her breath.

"No, of course not. I even like him in a way."

"Didn't you tell me the other night, that you want to meet him, one on one in the bathhouse for a deadly combat?"

Gordon laughed huskily. "Battling with Aldan to the death, why would I do or say a thing like that?

"Because, you said he did it to you in another life. It was a matter of betrayal," Helena continued.

Gordon shook some water out of his eyes. "I hardly know your brother, Helena. We fought once. It was more a test of strength than anything else."

"It's not what I saw, Gordon. It looked like you were trying to kill each other."

"Fights look bizarre and dangerous in the eyes of some women. A spurt of blood, a wobbly tooth, or a black eye — I know it looks murderous. Many male friendships start with a free-for-all-melee."

"I hope so. Let's get out. I'm not used to night swimming. It's getting cold."

Hussney El Barrack was restless.

He was pacing around the small room with powerful zeal and purpose. He suddenly stopped in front of his son, sat down with his legs crossed and inhaled deeply from his water pipe.

"This is the last time I put up with your shenanigans, Aldan. No more gallivanting around the country and plotting behind my back. You're too young to know how to work a power play, and how to stay on top. There are too many things at stake for your selfish and childish attempts for power. Our family fortune, our religious canons call on us to do good for the world's society.

There are far too many people on this planet. Millions of the less fortunate expect progress to automatically raise their living standards. This simply won't happen. Instead, millions will be dispossessed even of what they have already. Brother will turn against brother; only the fittest will survive. The world leaders have no illusions, but there's little one can do under the present circumstances. Now is the time that we need a strong and just God. It doesn't matter the color of His skin or His background. What matters is that He be unshakable and pitiless.

In the depth of this night, two beings are traveling billions of light years in the hope of bringing the God we need down to Earth. And you my son, only think short-sighted of your own destiny."

"That's for you to believe, Babba. I can wait, my time is tomorrow."

A derisive smile turned up the lips of Hussney. "Your time is tomorrow…are you so cocksure that you have time left in Allah's hourglass? Maybe the last grains are running out; how are you going to stop it?"

"I'm young and strong, Babba, think about your own last grains of sand," stated Aldan brashly.

"Foolish is the word for you, my son…and I don't have another," El Barrack answered somewhat dejectedly.

"Tell me what to do, Babba. Do you want me to kill that young Christian, Gordon Bates? Piece of cake. I could do it with my bare hands. I could even kill Helena, no matter how much I love her. What do you expect me to do? Ikhnaton fucks her in the darkness of the bathhouse. Right now, this minute. They fuck each other like they did thousands of years ago. The same way he fucked me as a boy. You think Ikhmet could swallow the humiliation for the sake of your social harmony, brotherhood or religious tolerance? Never! NEVER!!! What is mine is mine!"

Was it Aldan speaking or Ikhmet, thought El Barrack, "You, fool…don't allow yourself to be ordered by that crazy old general of the Egyptian past. Don't let him in! Think about surviving, my son! Do you want to end up on the dark side of time? They don't even have graves there. Where is the Soviet Empire? They are sharing the same oblivion with the Nazis…and the Romans…and the Egyptian Dynasties in the same mountain of trash called History."

"Where do you think you're going, Babba?"

The Sheik pulled hungrily on his water pipe. "On Judgment Day, I'll be sitting next to God."

Chapter 6

A VISIT TO SIRIUS

When Moughabee transcendentally took the Roman Prelate to Sirius, the transference was beyond belief. It was neither day, or night. There was something iridescent in the air that caused the unseen to be visible. A prevailing color, violet, shining through shimmering streams of light reminded one of Aurora Borealis. This was created by the leading star Alderbaran. There were no clouds and the horizon seemed endless. The two terrestrials walked over a substance that seemed made out of silver dust. Visibility was painfully unlimited yet there was nothing to be seen save the great expanse of infinity.

"Is everything made of emptiness?" exclaimed the Prelate.

Peter Moughabee laughed quietly. "We never see everything, Eminence, only what we want to."

"Then what we want to see is near nothing."

"Out of our world, yes. It's near nothing. Yet hidden in the potential of near emptiness, there is more to see than any place on Earth," mused Moughabee.

The Roman Prelate looked at Moughabee quizzically, "You've lost me."

Moughabee sighed patiently and slowed down. "During their war with the giants, the gods were pursued into Egypt by Typhoon.

To escape, each god was forced to change shape, to morph into a jackal or a falcon. Pan, leaped into the Nile and turned the upper part of his body into a goat and the lower into a fish. That was worthy of commemoration in the heavens."

"I never understood that ancient gibberish," complained the Prelate.

Moughabee looked at the indignant priest the way the real Pan would have in his time — with a little humor. "The goat made a giant leap, Eminence. From a poor excuse for an animal, to an immortal constellation in the universe."

The Prelate kept a puzzled, ponderous look on his face.

Moughabee continued, "The simplicity, Eminence, the simplicity is deceiving. Man wanted to worship a god they could see or imagine. The one and only God remains invisible to us until our faith reveals the truth. He is the greatest enigma in the universe."

"Can we ever dare to look at God!?!"

"Why not? If we're created in His image, we should be proud, not scared to look in His Face. He is the enormity of the whole Creation, and His Soul is, filled with the never ending fires of the giant stars, then we are too lowly even to think of Him. That's why he sent us a Man-God so we could listen to him and follow Him. And what did we make out of it? We threw Him in a bonfire, as we did Joan of Arc, and Galileo, and countless others. And Earth, our Earth, in spite of everything, keeps on turning. The only questions is: for how long?"

The Prelate stopped and turned deadly pale. "And now, you want to throw the Holy Church into the bonfire?"

Moughabee looked at him with pity. "Our Lord doesn't throw anybody in the fire. That's Satan's department. Don't ever confuse the two. They are the two ends that never meet."

At that moment, pregnant with all the bitterness born in the world and all the promised joy of Heaven, He stood in front of them, leaning upon His golden staff.

Moughabee fell upon his knees. "Master!"

Aton smiled broadly. “Yes, it is I. Did you expect me to send Anubis to you? I was watching both of you coming from the very bottom of the swirl that brought you here. Something in your appearance made me believe that it must be you, Moughabee a sage among men.”

“I hope it’s not my corpulence, Lord Aton,” Moughabee laughed.

Aton laughed softly. “Something in your stride, perhaps. That very characteristic stride of a man born free. You have never been a slave, Moughabee,” intoned Lord Aton.

“Thank You kindly, My Lord. I think You project yourself very distinctly, too.”

“Not as a Saint I hope. I always had a zest for life and didn’t miss any human frailty. I have never been overly proud of myself, but never ashamed either. I miss my body for the love it inspired in me. I’m deeply grateful to the women that made a man of me and gave me the joy of having sons and daughters. It’s not a sin to be in love with every part of your body and being. It’s the only reason for blessing and celebrating human life. By the way, do you like my garden, gentlemen?”

Moughabee and the Prelate looked around, astonished. It was the Garden of Gethsemane, and Lord Aton seemed quite at home. “Will you sit down with me for awhile?” He asked invitingly.

Moughabee was paralyzed with fear. “Do You think it’s reasonable, Teacher?”

The Man-God laughed faintly again. “Of course it’s reasonable. I know what you mean, but it just doesn’t matter anymore.”

Moughabee was unable to believe what he just heard. “Did I hear You right? Caution doesn’t matter anymore in Jerusalem?”

“Not for me,” Aton replied.

“I’m afraid I…”

“It’s very simple, Peter. I’m going to be arrested, so where better than in this olive garden, among my friends. Aren’t you my truest disciple, Judas?”

The Prelate's face became deadly pale. "They were listening to us all the time, I'm sure. Your voice carries..."

Peter Moughabee shook the frail shoulders of the Prelate. "Do you mean they are here?"

"Don't panic, Peter, they are everywhere. Are you afraid?" asked Aton.

"Yes, Lord. I'm afraid," admitted Moughabee.

"I think you'll make up a fine pretext. Tell the Romans you fell in with the wrong company."

The broad, dark face was bathed in tears. "No, My Lord, I won't do it again. I'll die with You!"

Aton looked at him with sadness and love, then quickly embraced him.

"It doesn't matter how many times you'll do it, Peter. I'll always love you, as I love Judas and my brothers, my mother and my wife. Let Our Father's Will prevail, now and forever!"

"It seemed strange that You consented so easily to meet us, especially out in the open."

"I wanted to meet you as a free man, that's all."

"But You know that Judas had sold You out. You'll pay dearly for that. You'll be taken away any moment now. I know this place like the palm of my hand. We can escape, it's easy in the night!"

The Lord patted Moughabee's head of thick dark hair.

"Now, now, you know very well that we cannot change history."

"But this way, You're losing Your freedom...Your life!" protested Moughabee.

"That's correct, too, Peter. I'm just tired of being afraid. Fear is worse than any prison. I continued being afraid as long as it was good for my flock. Now You and the others will take care of it. To run away is a selfish instinct born by the fear of not surviving. It is humiliating, Peter."

"I'm scared myself, My Lord. Honestly, I'm scared to death. Won't You ask Your Father to save us all?"

"But He will save us all at the end, Peter. Don't be afraid of the Romans," coaxed Aton.

"No...not anymore of them, but for You..."

The Lord placed His finger very lightly between the eyes of Peter. "For me? Thank you, my good friend. It's a big thing to be concerned for someone that you don't really know."

"I know all about Your life and sufferings. I shared them as much as I could — the persecutions, the human ingratitude, the insolence of the High Priests, the mockery with the Divine Law and the desperate struggle to stay alive," contradicted Peter.

"It's not my life that counts now, Peter. I know you're physically very strong. You must fight your ignorance. Promise me!"

Peter embraced the knees of His Master with deep, religious fervor and pleaded one last time, "They are coming! Let's run away, please!"

"Will you stay with me this time, my friend?"

The large, powerful body was shuddering with devotion and dedication. "Yes, I will, My Lord. Now and forever!!!"

MOUGHABEE STEPS UP TO PROSCENIUM

Yes, I was Peter the Fisherman and that picture is still engraved in my mind. The powerful figure of Lord Aton, whom they now call Jesus of Nazareth, in the custody of shameless Roman Guards. "Do you know this man?" they asked me.

"Noo-o-oo," I denied Him. "I've never seen him in my life!"

"And you?" they turned toward Judas, who quickly approached the Master and kissed Him on His mouth. "This is the seditious person you're looking for and the other one is a disciple of his."

I hid amidst the stubby olive trees. And the earth didn't scream to God! I had so many questions to ask Him which now He'll never be able to answer, and the group was already facing away in the melting eddy of a ghostly moonlight.

Many centuries later the great Russian prophet Dostoevsky launched an enigmatic observation, "Beauty will save the world." It didn't save it then, so why now twenty centuries later? The world is dying. Why doesn't beauty save it?

And, if in one part of the world, under persecutions not inferior to those of the Romans, hundreds of thousands of silent Christians sacrifice their lives for the love of God, what then? Does the terror abate? Is the evil arrested and righteousness praised?

When a certain madman speeds across the desert to desecrate everything we believe in, does it matter if his name is Sadam Hussein? It was the Russians and the Chinese that stood behind him, ready to finish the fallen angels with a thrust of steel. They simply measured us according to their personal scale of values. Death to the enemies, glory to the new masters of the world! Where are the real values? Are we doomed forever to rebuild the Tower of Babel? Where is our deliverance from the likes of Hitler and Stalin, our protection from false prophets like Marx and Lenin?

Maybe there is no deliverance at all until the last Day of Judgment.

CURTAIN OPENS ON ANCIENT JERUSALEM

For three days in a row, an enormous crowd besieged the palace of Pontius Pilate. The Pharisees were waiting impatiently in the corridor. A group of Roman Soldiers were torturing the Man-God, hollering at Him amidst taunting laughter: “Why doesn’t your daddy save the precious life of his bastard son? Aren’t you the Judean King?”

STAGE REVOLVES TO REVEAL A SCENE FROM PHARAONIC TIMES

The elite Egyptian Guard broke through the palace door in the new capital city of Amarna.

There was no panic inside. People were down on their knees praying to the Only God, before piles of flowers and fresh fruits heaped at the base of the marble obelisk. They didn’t know that God didn’t have a mouth with which to eat, a face or a body. He is Infinity, an ever-growing, gigantic mind.

“Where is the man called Aton?” the young General Ikhmet Haremhab asked in a thundering voice. When there was no reply from the crowd he threatened, “You’ll be killed to the last man, if you don’t answer me, minions of the fallen pharaoh!”

Ikhnaton stepped out boldly. "First you have to take me down, peasant boy."

The young man disarmed himself. "I'll do that with my bare hands in the privacy of your tower."

BACK TO NOW

A half moon hung over the swimming pool. To Gordon, the night was dark and hostile. His Ka was taking over. He pulled off his briefs slowly, watching the half-open door to the shower room, then glanced at the back of the residence. — not a light.

The sport complex was well secluded. Eerily, the loud cricket's chirping stopped suddenly, as if in anticipation of something.

Then Gordon saw Aldan standing at the open door. He was completely nude and his skin glistened softly under the moonbeams. An electric current went through both their tense, muscular bodies, arousing their senses as if lovemaking was forthcoming, not a mortal combat.

Ikhmet bared his perfectly matched teeth. The moonlight made them stand out in his handsomely dark face. The voice was low and husky, "Hail, Great Pharaoh! Your Chief General salutes you. I'll wrestle to win you over once and forever or die in the course of our dispute. There is no room for both of us on this planet."

The metallic voice of the other man stepped over the last words of Ikhmet.

"Hail, General! I am only too willing to accept your challenge — a fight to the death with bare hands. Let's do it."

They walked silently to the large grassy spot behind the bathhouse. In the middle of it, they faced each other, hands outstretched, dodging left and right, with every single move of their limbs. Swiftly the two combatants fell into a tight grip, their deep, hard chests clashing with a dull thud, sinewy hands grasping feverishly for a vulnerable spot.

Like a rapacious beast covered with the blood of his prey, Gordon dragged the nude body of Aldan over the marble tiles, from the bathhouse's back door to the deep end of the swimming pool. After the disposing of the muscular body of his defeated foe, with great rage, he threw the bloody genitals that he had torn from the crotch of the youth into the foliage.

"I paid you back, Ikhmet! Nobody can escape destiny even after thirty-five hundred years of transfigurations. There is no salvation for Nefertiti, either. It's only a matter of time."

The night had no answer for him.

THEATER OF THE ABSTRACT

Lord Aton had turned his face with repugnance.

"Human beings forget that simple common sense should act as a restraint, that even when faced with lawlessness or great acts of evil, one must be aware of the line beyond which a man becomes a wild beast."

The crowd in front of the Pontius Pilate residence raged, choked with venom and hatred;

"To death! Death to, the blasphemous traitor. Give us Barnabas instead!"

PRESENT DAY JERUSALEM

The next morning, the usually quiet residence of the Roman Prelate in Jerusalem was at the center of a storm. TV trucks were stopped at the entrance gate and low flying helicopters circled overhead. The square in front of the building was filled with emergency vehicles and cars belonging to Special Forces. Reporters and a gaggle of noisy paparazzi were trying to find an entrance to the large swimming pool behind the palatial home. The naked body of a young man was found floating there. Everyone wanted to question the Prelate, but he was nowhere to be found. Nobody had seen him since dinnertime the night before. Dr. Peter Moughabee was unaccounted for as well.

About noon, another news flash electrified the crowd of onlookers: the Roman Prelate was found hanging from a tree in the Gethsemane Garden. He had taken his own life.

The Holy City was stunned. So was the rest of the world. A persistent rumor spread across the world: Christ had come again and Judgment Day could not be far off.

Diplomatic missions and heads of states were silent. Too silent.

PREVIOUS NIGHT'S END

There was a knock at Helena's door.

At first she didn't know if she was dreaming or if she had just awakened. The day was beginning to dawn, it was almost five.

"Who is it?" she croaked.

"It's me..." whispered a voice on the other side of the door.

"Gordon!"

"Let me in, please," he begged.

Something in his voice was broken, hopelessly broken. She slept naked but a light negligee was at hand. Shakily, she pulled it on.

Gordon was naked, water dripping down his swarthy skin. His face was bloodied and swollen. There were deep scratches across his chest and a blue-black mouse had formed under his left eye. He had reddish marks at his throat and a front tooth missing. He threw himself onto her bed and covered his head with a large pillow.

"I spent the night with you, here, all night!"

Helena closed the door and locked it, then stood over Gordon and asked, "Is he dead?"

"Yes, he put on a grand fight for his life. One of us had to go. We both knew it from the very start. I had to avenge myself."

Helena sat at the end of the bed, then she put her trembling fingers on his hairy thigh, "You didn't have to do it, though I never loved him, I'm just sorry for his wasted life."

The young man cast the pillow away and pierced her with Ikhnaton's eyes, "But you shared the throne with him. You knew only too well what he had done to me in that little room at the top of the tower. He threw my body at your feet. The soldiers shouted acclaim, and you said nothing, even when my torn genitals splashed blood over your golden sandals. The very instrument that had given you ecstasy and pleasure for so many nights."

"But not a son," hissed Helena with the voice of Nefertiti.

The man shrieked with rage, "You double crossing wench! You sold me for a son!?!"

The young woman kept her cool. "No, for a real man."

"A God!"

"You can put it that way. Will you now kill me to appease your revenge?"

Gordon was devastated by the knowledge that Ikhnaton was only the shadow of a God. He dug his bruised face into the bed. "I can't kill you. You wanted to save the throne for Prince Tut. It was a desire stronger than you. But after Ikhmet murdered him cold-bloodedly from behind, with a statue of Osiris, without giving him any chance to defend himself, even then you went to his bed and made him a Pharaoh."

She caressed the strong heavy thigh. "I did it for Egypt, Ikhnaton, so that Egypt wouldn't fall into the hands of the High Priests. They were afraid of that handsome peasant."

"Did you know?"

"Of course I did. When Aton refused you, you had to find somebody to replace him. Ikhmet was more than willing. He was ready to give anything in this world to become a General. His ambition served him well. You thought he'd be only yours, as a lowborn always belongs to the highest bidder. You knew little about people, and that was your downfall. Now, I'll swear in court that I spent the night with an American called Gordon. Let me attend to your bruises. They have to look as if I made them."

From: *The Office of the Roman Prelate in Jerusalem*
To: *His Holiness, the Pope Most Holy Father*

Holy Father,

My name has never been used, so I remain nameless.

This is my last report to you, and I allow myself some freedom from the pomp and decorum accepted as a way of life by the Mother Church. The worst of your expectations are accurate. Aton from Amarna and Jesus from Nazareth are the same Man. I repeat, the same Man. The fifteen centuries in between their lives are of little import. Time, as we all know, is unfathomable. I sold Him then, as I've been ready to sell Him in present times, when everything will come to its logical end. I'm sure that you'll feel extremely embarrassed by my drastic exit. Short changed, too. Though you've lavished on me all sorts of honors, I have betrayed you. Your counselors, the cardinals, will be capable, as usual, of finding a way out. It had been done in the past. My last advice to you is to put the mummy behind the walls of Vatican City as soon as possible, and keep it there with great Honors. Make it a Holy Taboo of the Papal Court that will be uncovered in time. Though there is almost no time left, believe me. I saw Him, and I don't want to see Him at the Day of the Last Judgment. After so many years with the Holy Church, I am still shamed. I hope you fare better than I. Perhaps there are a few more tricks left up your sleeve.

I'm sorry to be such a bad sport, but I never felt quite comfortable in the Big League.

Truly Yours,
Judas Iscariot

Hussney El Barrack walked nervously back and forth, as was his habit. Moughabee followed him with his large opaque eyes. Finally the Sheik closed the door to the terrace and approached the Nubian.

"O. K., I'm not going to press any charges against your protégée Gordon, but the mummy cannot go behind the walls of Vatican City. Everyone has the right to see it. The pressure from all sides is tremendous. The Russians want to have it, even if they have to start a thermo-nuclear war. The Americans are ready to pay the Egyptians any price, so the government must proceed in the High Court and get the mummy back on Egyptian soil. The Abyssinians are pressing us too. Pakistan is backing them, but I don't know why. Japan, France and Great Britain make strange bedfellows, but they support an Armenian claim. They don't want to admit the Coptics to the club. If the mummy talks, it will name the oldest Christians. Spontaneous manifestations have erupted in a number of cities and some Catholic missionaries have been set on fire. People want to know the truth!"

Moughabee cut himself a cigar, lit it and started puffing, arching his thick eyebrows, "Do they?"

"Yes, they do. And neither tanks nor police cordons will stop them. We're sitting on a keg of dynamite."

"One more reason to hide under the cassock of the Holy Father. He's granting us asylum. Nobody will dare shoot nuclear rockets at the Vatican," said Moughabee.

"You can't be serious, Peter."

"Oh, but I am. Only a papal aircraft and his helicopter with His markings can get us out of this place."

"So, then, you're going to surrender the mummy to the Pope?"

"I didn't say that. Are you going to surrender your daughter to Mr. Bates?"

The Sheik dropped his head. For the first time Moughabee saw tears in his eyes. "I don't know. This afternoon is certainly one of the worst in my life. I have no other valid son. By wedding my eldest daughter, Gordon Bates, will in due time, inherit the family fortune. Children by secondary wives don't count much."

"Certainly, he is a better man than your rightful heir who is dead."

Hussney pressed his hands to both sides of his head in total desperation, "I have no idea who Gordon Bates really is."

"He is a decent fellow, I know him," comforted Moughabee.

"You know him? Do you also know the guy who murdered Aldan so fiendishly?"

"No, I don't know him as well, but the crime was done for revenge."

"And are you going to share your knowledge with me?" begged the Sheik.

"Some day after the marriage. Gordon's my only heir, too. Helena couldn't dream of anything better."

The Sheik resumed his aimless pacing. "I'm not that sure about it, but you've got me cornered. I like Gordon. The question is how long will he stay one and the same?"

"I can say the same about Helena."

The heat became unbearable. Hussney opened the door to the terrace again. "Anyway, our conversation is being recorded for sure. What I don't know is by whom. Who's getting the tapes?"

"Does it matter?"

After a short pause, the Sheik stopped pacing and looked helplessly in Moughabee's eyes, "No. Nothing matters anymore."

Chapter 7

THE MONASTERY

The secretary of the dead Prelate had a long conversation with the Vatican. The cardinals wanted him to keep on stalling until a special emissary arrived on the spot. Unfortunately, the trouble had spread and none of the bishops were able (or willing) to leave their assigned posts. Finally, someone was to fly from Malta, but that took time. The crowd around the residence grew, and its restlessness was threatening.

Peter Moughabee had sent Ouloulangha for the keys to the vault. Everyone in the residence was afraid of the strange Nubian, especially because of his political and media contacts. It was much better for him to be with the mummy than with the crowd outside. Right after lunch he was taken downstairs and the heavy door to the vault opened. Moughabee walked inside and made a sign to his faithful Ouloulangha to close the heavy door behind him and wait in the anti-chamber. His faithful servant paled, but he obeyed. It wasn't up to him to make decisions.

The lighting along those empty corridors was quite bright. The keys to gain access to the large platform where the body of Lord Aton lay, were steady in Moughabee's big hand. He was the guardian of his Master's properties. The plate slid away smoothly, and Moughabee removed the linen shroud as if his own beloved child was lying there. Tears filled his eyes and found their way down the mahogany cheeks. He placed his large greying head lightly over Aton's cold breast.

"I'm here, Master, and I don't know what to do. It's a different world from what we knew. Our miracles wouldn't impress even a first grader. Mankind is so polarized that a simple misunderstanding could bring the dreaded Armageddon upon us. Who is there to save? The arrogance is the same as before but much more powerful, the methods more sophisticated. Nobody is ashamed of lying, even in Your Name. Your Second Coming, as described by the best of Your disciples, has been changed to a point that even I can't recognize it. Your Family has been denied veracity, there are no brothers, no sisters. Your virile and strong father, who You helped for so many years, is depicted as a decrepit old man. The voyage toward the east and Your stay with the Great Sages of the Sun is merely spoken of as a walk in the desert, competing with Satan in wizardry. Nothing about Your marriage and the jealousy that tormented our souls. You told us: I have no time to share with my wife but on the road. Then Your brother James said: All that follow You left wives and children behind. Sorrow darkened Your eyes, You chose my road, not I yours. I would never come back as a man and this woman has every right to have me until the last. If you miss your families go back to them. That kind of Love is blessed by God but, please, don't begrudge me the brief joy I can give to Mary of Magdala. Every one of us felt a searing pain in his heart, as if we knew that we'd have nothing more than a few months with You. What awaited us from that point on was to make our own shining path throughout the darkness of this world. Perhaps we tried to do our best with Your blessing, perhaps we failed You. Who knows? Now even God is depicted as an old man. I'm tired My Lord, not by serving You, but by serving You justly. It's not for my puny strength to compete with today's wizards. I need Your Hand to guide me."

The Lord didn't answer.

"Where is Gordon, Father?" Helena demanded to know.

Hussney El Barrack didn't look up from the newspaper. "On the Isle of Malta."

"Why?"

"Why? Why? You're an intelligent lady. Gordon Bates murdered my son and your brother."

"Gordon killed him to protect himself. My half-brother had been on his tail from day one. He was jealous of him and simply hated his guts," protested Helena.

"I thought they were friends. They certainly went together to all the ill-famed places in town. I don't even know who paid their bills."

"Aldan was a blackmailer. He was involved in dubious enterprises as well; narcotics, laundering dirty money."

The Sheik sighed dejectedly, took off his glasses and cleaned them methodically, "So what? He's dead now. You could say a good word about him for a change."

"He was a handsome youth…but what a waste! I wish I could say something better."

"You used to mother him when he was a young boy. I think you loved him in a way. Everything changed when Mr. Bates came around. I don't blame you. He's handsome as well, but he has no money whatsoever. Correct me if I am wrong."

"Money doesn't happen to mean the same thing to me as to you father. He told me he was just drifting from job to job — no relatives — a drifter until he met Dr. Moughabee."

"You said it all," the Sheik threw the newspaper aside. " I have no sympathy for people of this kind."

"He's a human being," said Helena.

"Are you sure? I didn't press charges against him, so many gentlemen at the club think that I killed my son, Allah be merciful. As far as I'm concerned, Bates might be a schizophrenic with some homosexual tendencies. So stay away from him. This young man is bad news," the Sheik warned.

"Aldan had the homo tendencies, but drugs were his downfall. His brain was shot. He wanted Gordon badly."

The Sheik crossed to the window, "I haven't slept much lately. My premonitions are driving me crazy."

Helena joined him at the window. "I'm going to Malta," Helena suddenly announced to her father.

"You believe Gordon is a scapegoat. It might be better for you abroad but not in Malta."

"Father, I love him. If he wants me, I'd marry him tomorrow."

The Sheik smiled with dark irony. "Is Dr. Moughabee going to take care of you too?"

"I don't count on him, nor on you. I have my own little savings," she responded.

"You're talking about your mother's money? Anyway, you're of age, and I can't stop you from going. I think Gordon has a split personality, too. How are you going to cope with it?" the Sheik questioned her.

"Nowadays, everybody seems to have a split personality, including me," she confessed.

The phone rang. Helena answered. She put a hand to the mouthpiece.

"The Russian cultural attaché. Do you want to talk to him?"

The Sheik shook his head.

"He's not available right now..." she listened impatiently to a long tirade, "Yes, I'm his secretary. I'll tell him to call you back as soon as possible."

Hussney shook his head again, "They are crazy. I have no idea how the mummy can help with their internal affairs. But with the Russians one never knows. When are you leaving, Helena?"

"As soon as I'm able to secure a reservation," she answered.

"Make two. I don't think I want to stick around under the circumstances. You need a chaperon."

Helena smiled for the first time in many days. "You're welcome. I can keep my money in the bank."

"You may need it soon, with your strange liking of drifters. As a matter of fact, I like Gordon. Basically, he's a good fellow, though a terrible Pharaoh. I'll miss Aldan's chicaneries, also. I was relieved to see them getting chummy, but what an ugly outcome. I guess my perceptions leave a lot to be desired. After all, Aldan was my son and heir."

"If you fail, try, try again."

"Not at my age. Officially, Aldan's death is accidental, so Gordon may not be such a bad son-in-law if he stays out of trouble...if we all manage to stay out of trouble. But the mummy seems to be coming with us. The Vatican won't offer asylum to a pagan, so the monastery in Malta is a matter of convenience."

Helena flashed another furtive smile, "Nowadays all roads seems to lead away from Rome. At least I see why Gordon is in Malta — a matter of convenience."

The Sheik lit a cigarette. "To Malta, then."

"To Malta. Say, Dad, when did you resume your 'bad habit'?"

"Smoking 'grass?' The morning after Aldan's 'accidental death.' It hurt me more than I expected, perhaps a sense of guilt. I should've done something for him."

Suddenly Helena felt very warm toward her father. "I wish I had done more for him, too, but we're only mortals and our destinies playthings to the gods. One hardly knows for whom the bells toll. Now I'm talking like a literary almanac. By the way, where is everybody?"

"At a press conference. I ducked out, said I was 'under the weather'..." After a pause of uneasiness between them, the Sheik spoke tensely, "I've been having dreams lately."

"What dreams?"

"About some sort of tragedy, a conflict of extreme proportion."

"The Armageddon?"

"You can call it that...though it seems so incongruous when I look at the palm trees bathed in morning light." He drew on his hookah, hungrily inhaling the smoke deep into his lungs.

The conference room had poor ventilation and it was hot as hell. The attendance was tremendous. Everyone wanted answers about the death of the Prelate and Aldan, son of the Sheik. It seemed as if every newspaper, magazine and TV station had sent a representative. The news agencies tried to dominate the independent guys with little success. It was a free for all. Ouloulangha and the public relation's man from the Vatican had to bear the whole load. Dr. Moughabee hadn't said a word. A barrage of questions came about specific unanswered details. They remained unanswered. Then the reporters tried an indirect approach. *Chicago Tribune* wanted to know if the absence of Sheik El Barrack was due to the sudden death of his son.

"Very likely," Ouloulangha said suavely, "Next."

The *Globe* man asked about Gordon Bates' whereabouts.

Ouloulangha shook his narrow head as if an impertinent fly bugged him, " Mr. Bates has nothing to do with all this, he is an American citizen who was working with Dr. Moughabee. Mr. Bates can go where he pleases."

The same reporter had a follow up question, "Is he the same Gordon Bates whose parents disappeared?"

"That's my understanding."

"Do you know if they are dead or alive?"

"So far nobody has found them, dead or alive," replied Ouloulangha.

The *Figareau* representative came up even closer. "Were they under contract from a company controlled by Dr. Moughabee?"

Ouloulangha repeated the same movement with his head, "At that time, I wasn't employed by Dr. Moughabee."

A Russian agency was next. "But, do you think Mr. Bates Sr. is still alive?"

Dr. Moughabee stepped up to the mike and spoke emphatically, "Frankly, we don't know, and I don't care. But I care about Gordon, and I want him out of this."

"Do you mean the murderer of Aldan El Barrack or 'the curse of the mummy'?" asked another reporter.

"None of this is the sordid affair you suggest. Aldan and Gordon were seen all over the city on very friendly terms," Dr. Moughabee expressed himself with a wave of his hand.

Moughabee continued, "Besides, this is supposed to be a Press Conference not an investigation."

"Then why all this mystery about the mummy?" someone shouted.

The whole crowd was hushed, while the Nubian regained his composure.

"Because it is not ready to be revealed to the public — the project needs to be analyzed further to know what we are dealing with for the sake of humanity."

"Don't you think people have a right to know the truth?" The audience was persistent.

"No…because truth is a commodity that doesn't fare well these days. It will be distorted and used for other purposes. Humanity is at the brink of a chasm."

The Pope's representative got to his feet. "Enough, Dr. Moughabee. A tragedy in the making…a doomsday…that's what all of them want to hear. I think the purpose of this conference has been lost. We'll call for another as soon as the new Prelate is here. Ladies and gentlemen, I hope we meet again very soon."

Someone that had been introduced as a press agent of NBC laughed out loud. "After the fact?"

"What fact?"

"The fact that the mummy is leaving Jerusalem."

There was a gasp and an outcry from those present.

The man from NBC went on, "Whose mummy are you hiding from us? We've had enough mummies through this century."

The sole representative of the Pope crossed himself. "Let's go home ladies and gentlemen…with our faith in the morrow."

Strangely depressed the gathering broke in silence.

A few hours later all the media announced a hypothetical: IS IT *CORPUS DEI*???

∠٦٧ ٥ټ

Gordon Bates was restricted only to the grounds of a monastery. He saw nothing of Malta, though there was little curiosity in him. Mostly apathetic, he seldom ate and lost weight. There was no swimming pool in the monastery so, almost mechanically, he started doing calisthenics. Several monks tried to engage him in conversation. He declined politely. They left him alone, but there was no peace inside him. He had strange visions and sensations. The bruises from the fight, attended to by a monk, were generally gone; the inner wounds persisted. Finally, he slept, long and deep, without dreaming. He woke up strangely relieved and asked for some food. It was brought almost immediately. The tray had been waiting by the door. The monk stood in attendance. Gordon ate hungrily and asked for more. Once again the food was served quickly.

"What day is it?" he asked.

"Thursday, the 7th of November, 1999...Five in the afternoon."

"It's almost dark," Gordon observed.

"The days are shorter," replied the monk.

Gordon pushed the food tray back. "I have slept long...Say, you're very young. What's your name?"

"Aldano. I'm a novice."

Gordon stiffened, his alarmed eyes studied the face in front of him.

"I see...Aldano. I knew an Aldan."

Gordon Bates became quiet and thoughtful. The youth took the tray and made for the door.

"For heaven's sake Aldano, don't go. Could you spare some of your time to talk with me, please?" Gordon begged.

The youth was only too willing. A handsome smile lit up his face. "I have nothing to do until vespers."

The room was a white cubicle with a crucifix, a bed, bed stand and a small prayer bench. A single round open window, high up out of reach, hung over them like a violet moon. In the distance, the choir was rehearsing Bach's *Aria*. Gordon looked for his clothes.

"Don't worry," the lad said, smiling, "Your clothes have been taken for washing. In my family everybody was used to nakedness. I have five brothers. Now most of them have found jobs in the military. One of them is a prizefighter. We used to share the same bed in our altogether. So don't worry about having no clothes for the moment."

"Take the bench, Aldano, and sit down so I can see your face."

The youngster obeyed, then he took from his robe a box of matches and lit the candle on the stand. Now they looked in each other's faces with a certain curiosity.

"I miss my brothers very much…we use to roughhouse, but all in good fun. Our Irish dad ruled us well. We were very poor but ate well…you have brothers and sisters?"

Gordon shook his head. "Not that I know of…how old are you?"

"Sixteen going on seventeen. How about you, what's your name?"

"Gordon Bates…twenty-five." They spent the next hour becoming acquainted.

"Your dad must've taught all his brood English," Gordon remarked.

"Yes, sir…all of us. A very nice present, isn't it? But you cannot be twenty-five. I saw you exercising…you can't be more than a couple of years older than me. We're of the same size. I bet you I can take you down for a fiver! I wrestled you already in my mind. It wasn't easy, but I won."

Gordon came up on his elbows piercing the novice with deeply set eyes. "You can't be him…can you?"

"Who're you talking about?" puzzled Aldano.

With a moan, Gordon fell back on his pillow. "I don't know, there are so many things I don't understand recently…"

The boy walked toward the door with his head down.

"...please, don't go...whoever you are. Don't leave me alone!" Was Ikhnaton taking over with his Egyptian lust?

The youth stopped, turned around and looked at him with his luminous eyes.

"Do you really need me?"

"I do."

Aldano came back, took the chair and wedged it under the doorknob. Then, as he went over to the bed, he kicked off his sandals and pulled off his cassock. His voice was a mellow rich baritone. "Move over, brother."

He was a big boy! His warm juvenile body felt good against Gordon's skin. Their strong, well rounded thighs interlaced under the cover, and both became sexually aroused. Their hands explored each other's stoutly built abdomens and backs in a sexual frenzy. Gordon recognized the velvety, low voice of Ikhmet, who announced, "I won't leave you ever, my worthy adversary. Now I'll be part of you."

From the Maltese airport Hussney El Barrack called the monastery repeatedly. Nobody had any idea who Gordon Bates was. Helena phoned the Residential Vatican Office on the isle. No luck there either. The phone line cracked and went dead.

A limousine took them to the best hotel in town. Their reservations were lost. The manager was desperate. He had no vacancies. There were other hotels, but no vacancies. He worked on the computer for half an hour looking for a room to no avail. There was some kind of Euro-Seminar on forensics being held and all rooms were occupied. Maybe the Sheik and his daughter could be booked in a countryside motel.

In the cozy limousine interior, the two of them commented on all mishaps of the morning. Were they coincidental?

The chauffeur, an old gentleman, addressed them in fluent English spoken with an Irish brogue: If the lady and her father weren't fussy, he could house them at his own place. His sons had left the nest, so he had plenty of room.

Hussney and Helena were speechless. Then Helena answered quickly, of course they weren't fussy. Under the circumstances anything was better than sleeping in a park.

The house was in the oldest part of the city, very small, but tidy and comfortable. The boy's room now had a double bed, a large wardrobe, and an old-fashioned washstand. A wall against the window offered a display of framed photos.

Helena clapped her hands. "What a handsome family!"

The old man's face flushed with the compliment. "All six of them...a noisy bunch. That's their mom, let her have Peace in Heaven."

The Sheik smiled. "I don't see your picture."

"My picture? Why? I'm still here. Perhaps a year or so from now. My name is Michael Brandon, call me Brandon, or Mike if you want. You must be tired and hungry. It's almost lunchtime. Now everyone needs some privacy. The bathroom is right here, Ms. Helena. Follow me if you will, Mr. El Barrack."

Helena couldn't tear her eyes from the handsome bunch. The one before the last took her aback.

"Wait a minute, look at him, Dad. Isn't he, minus the blond hair, a replica of my brother?"

Hussney El Barrack's mouth hung open. "Allah Almighty!...A carbon copy!"

The amiable host followed their eyes and smiled broadly. "Ah...the prizefighter! I'm his trainer and manager. He'll be very happy to know that there's a look-alike of him in a foreign land."

Sheik El Barrack was still unable to assimilate that incredible likeness. "What's his name?"

"Marko Brandon. That one next to him is the youngest of them all, Aldano. Their mother was of Italian descent."

The limo had some problems negotiating the entrance to the monastery, but once inside, there was plenty of room to park. The guests were quickly ushered into the main office, where the Abbot was sorting out papers on his huge desk. Mr. Brandon introduced his charges, though it was difficult to say if the cleric was impressed with the Sheik's title or the beauty of his daughter.

"Yes, Aldano, of course you can see him right now…I'll bring him up, in person, though you can't see him for more than a quarter of an hour. I'll trust your judgment, Mr. Brandon."

"What's the matter? Is he a prisoner?" asked his father.

"Nobody is imprisoned here. Everyone must be his own jailer. Aldano's personal discipline has a lot to be desired. I don't think he's the right material for a monk. Yesterday he missed the rehearsal of the choir and vespers. One with true vocation doesn't forget about things of this kind."

"Very well, then, I personally never approved of his 'Vocation'…it was Aldano's idea. He has too much temper for this kind of life. I'll be glad to hear his version of the story."

The Abbot lifted his eyebrows, interlacing his thin bony fingers. "As you wish, Mr. Brandon. His fate is in your hands. Now, will you excuse me? I'll bring him to you."

When the Abbot left, the visitors exchanged glances.

"What in the world was that?" exclaimed the Sheik. "It sounds very fishy to me."

"And fishy it is. I'd be glad to take my boy back home!"

Helena said nothing, but moved over to the Abbot's desk. With the knowledgeable hand of a secretary, she perused the papers. "There is a message from the mission in Jerusalem. It reads: He doesn't exist."

Mr. Brandon seemed to suffer the same bad temper as his son. "Who doesn't exist…Aldano? Why from Jerusalem?"

Hussney moved quickly to the shoulder of his daughter and read the message himself.

"We came from Jerusalem, Mr. Brandon. It pertains to someone we know."

Hearing the sounds of steps coming from the corridor, Helena and her father returned to their previous spots. The door opened, and the Abbot ushered in his delinquent novice.

"I think your father has come to take you home, Aldano," said the Abbot.

Mr. Brandon exploded, "What do you think of that, son?"

Surprisingly Aldano appeared with his head hung down, breathing heavily as if coming straight from the athletic field.

"Not right now, dad. I'm not quite sure if I want to leave yet."

His father looked as if someone had just hit him in the face. "You…don't…want to…leave…yet!?!"

"You heard it from him," said the Abbot triumphantly, "I better send him out. We don't want to influence his decisions one way or the other."

Tears ran down the old man's cheeks. "My son…Aldano… What's the matter with you? You turned the other cheek!?!"

The youth said nothing. He kept his eyes firmly down.

Then suddenly the Sheik said gently, "Will you give a message to Gordon, that Mr. And Ms. El Barrack are waiting for him, here?"

Aldano's head came up like a 'jack-in-the-box'." "Do you know him?"

The Abbot went deadly pale, trying to say something, but Helena beat him to it, "Of course, we know him. We flew to Malta just to see Gordon. Is he O.K.?"

Aldano's eyes, blue as cornflowers, traveled with lightning speed from face to face.

"Yes, he's O.K. I'll tell him immediately, if THEY will let me see him."

Sheik El Barrack looked at the Abbot imperatively, pointing at the large crucifix over the desk.

"You won't lie in front of your Lord, will you?"

The Abbot said forcefully, "I don't know...if the young man wants to see you."

"All right then, let's go and ask him together."

The Abbot jumped up, "No-o-ooo, you don't understand. It's not in my powers..."

"Whose powers then...the Pope's? Let's call and ask him."

"I...I can't just call him direct."

"You can't, but I can," asserted the Sheik, "I can talk straight to him and he has to listen. I'm sure he'll be very unhappy with you for bungling this affair."

The Abbot tried several times to say something, but nothing came out. Finally he whispered harshly, "It's not only my responsibility...His Holiness has many important things on his mind." The Abbot was finished. He shook like a leaf, his bluish lips trying to form some imaginary words into sentences. With trembling hands he took off his Abbot's ring and gave it to Aldano. "Go...and fetch him...I can't move. Show my ring to the brothers.

Aldano grabbed it quickly. "If Gordon's leaving, I'm leaving too!"

The Abbot just nodded his skeletal head. Mr. Brandon brought him a chair, passing an arm around Aldano's waist. "That's my boy! Speed it up!"

Aldano didn't wait for more invitations. He left the room.

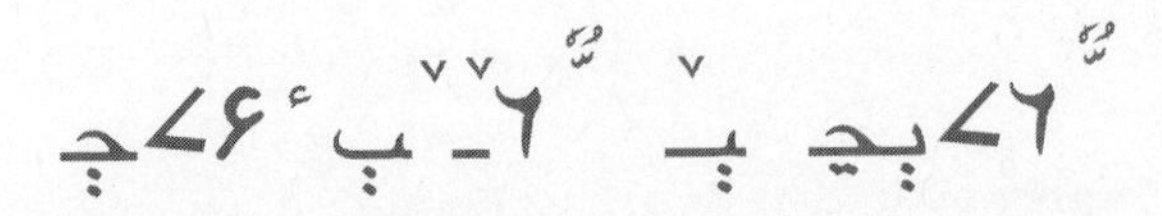

That same evening, the Hotel manager called, very apologetically, about the delay. There was a cancellation, and now one of their best suites was ready for Sheik El Barrack and his daughter. Gordon stayed with Mr. Brandon and shared the double bed in the boys' room with Aldano.

Helena moved with her father to the hotel's suite, though deep within herself she felt that something was dead wrong.

"Pray to God," her father advised, "He'll help you."

"I can't ask God for anything. He owes me nothing."

"Then quit worrying yourself. Nothing will happen to Gordon."

"Are you sure?"

The Sheik licked his dry lips. "You don't mean Aldano, do you?"

The almond-shaped eyes of Helena looked sharply at her dad. "I mean many things that only a woman in love feels."

"You think Ikhmet has entered Aldan and is looking for revenge."

"In a way."

"Allah Acbar! That boy is still a child."

"Not quite. My half-brother was only a couple of years older. What bothers me most is that Gordon hasn't come to see me at all."

The telephone in the living room rang. Helena answered. "Ouloulangha asks for hotel accommodations. The situation in Jerusalem is unbearable."

"Let me talk to Moughabee," demanded the Sheik.

Helena gave him the phone. "He's on the second line."

She went to the window and opened it. Her face was burning. In a few minutes Hussney joined her.

"I suggested Palermo. He agreed. We'll be leaving tonight. Call Gordon."

"I have to get a drink. Do you want something?"

Helena went to the bar and came back with a cocktail in her hand. Hussney was smoking at the open window.

"Do you feel Ikhnaton is in him?"

Helena drank thirstily. "Yes and he killed my brother."

Hussney puffed on his cigarette. "You're right. We have to be honest. Is that boy in danger if he shares accommodations with Gordon?"

Helena smiled bitterly, "Even if Gordon wanted to, he couldn't possibly leave Malta without him. The youngster is fascinated with everything he says and does. Let's hope that's due to the unusual situation in the family. All those rowdy boys thrown together in such a small place."

"There is no time for debate. We can't leave Malta and abandon Gordon on his own recognizance. If anything happens to Aldano, the old man would be stricken dead. I like him very much. However, Aldano Brandon has to be protected from his own naiveté. I don't want anything bad happening to him. His father cannot control a situation of which he's absolutely unaware."

Hussney blew out a long stream of smoke and pondered the dilemma, then went on, "We might be taking a chance, but we don't seem to have any choice. We have to take young Brandon to Sicily."

Helena felt depressed, even though she wholeheartedly agreed. She dialed the Brandon's phone number. No answer. That really scared her. She whirled around and got dressed, then asked the switchboard operator to secure a taxi cab."

"Wait a minute, Lady Helena. I think I saw your limo at the entrance to the hotel. "

Helena waited, with her heart pounding in her throat. Soon the operator returned. "Yes, Milady, Mr. Brandon and two young men just boarded the elevator."

Helena found a few words to thank him. Then, she ran to her father's bedroom. He was resting in bed.

"They are on the way to our room. All three of them!"

"Allah knows His job, my child. You better meet them at the door." His voice was strangely cracked, "I'll join you later."

"Father, you're not well," Helena protested.

"Nonsense, I'll be with you in a few minutes. Go."

The doorbell rang. Helena went to open the door. Old man Brandon had a basket with a beautiful arrangement of flowers. Helena, embarrassed, took the basket.

"Mr. Brandon, you may not believe it, but this is the first time in my life I've received flowers. I don't know how to thank you," Helena gushed, face beaming.

Mr. Brandon smiled gallantly. "That is a mistake that has to be corrected."

She invited them into the comfortable living room. The old man was unsettled. "Where is your father?"

"Resting in the bedroom. I'm worried about him," Helena responded.

Mr. Brandon smiled broadly. "I'll take care of that, old people know their maladies."

Helena took him to her father's bedroom then came back. Gordon had borrowed a suit of formal clothes from the wardrobe of Aldano's older brothers, including a tie and white handkerchief. Helena had never seen him dressed up, and to her he looked more like a fashion model than the boy next door. Aldano also wore his best, and the difference and the likeness were striking. They both looked like mannequins: one handsomely dark, the other blond and blue-eyed.

"Sit down, gentlemen, make yourself comfortable, smoke if you wish. What will you drink?"

Gordon coughed a bit to clear his voice. Another mannerism that he never had before.

"Thanks. I'll take scotch on the rocks. A double please."

Helena looked at the youngster.

"Me, too. On ice, if you have any," said Aldano.

"A double, as well?"

"I always take a double, when its affordable."

Helena couldn't help smiling. "Well, it is affordable. Actually it's on the house."

She went to the bar, while Aldano Brandon whispered to Gordon, "This young lady is fantastically beautiful and rich. Are you sure, she's considering you seriously?"

Gordon smiled with newly found cockiness, disdainfully shrugging his massive shoulders. "It's very possible. You don't expect me to ask, do you?"

"You'd better do it before she changes her mind. I know Americans are straightforward and blunt, but you seem to go overboard. She won't take that kind of treatment," said Aldano.

"Well, my boy, I don't think of myself as a typical American. I'm kind of a stranger in my own land."

"What's the big deal? You simply ask her if she really digs you — yes or no. It's only a question."

"You don't get it, kiddo. It's embarrassing."

Aldano shook his head disapprovingly. "If you say so. Aa-ttention, she's coming with the drinks."

Helena disbursed the large servings. She didn't feel the presence of Gordon at all. This person was behaving rather childishly. She lifted up her glass, "Cheers, gentlemen, to your health."

Aldano grinned widely, "I'll drink to that and to your beauty, Lady Helena."

The hostess blushed a bit. She would've loved that compliment from Gordon, but he was silent. For quite a while, they drank silently. Then Helena, a bit tipsy, tried to break the ice.

"Say, Aldano, how come you entered the monastery? You don't look the type."

"You're completely right, Lady Helena, I do not."

The stranger in Gordon didn't like the intended direction of the conversation. "Helena, please."

Aldano Brandon coughed a bit, and said in his low, fully matured voice.

"Yes, Helena, I am the athletic type. I thought the monastery would be something like a free school — they have a gym and a track for running, even a soccer field. A lot of the men there are very athletic, weight lifters too. But then they treat novices like army recruits. No fun, no games. Most of the monks there don't talk. I'm quite religious, but I wouldn't go that far for all the tea in China. It turned out to be a lifelong obligation. That's way too much. I'd like to get married, have children. Then we can all watch TV. I mean to have a normal life. Father warned me, but he'd never been religious. I don't think I ever saw him crossing himself. I see you wear a large golden cross around your neck. That's pretty...Will you marry me?" he joked.

Helena choked on her drink. Gordon was taken by surprise. "Stop drinking that whisky like water, or I'll beat the shit out of you. I swear to God, I'll do it! Don't make yourself obnoxious, hear me? I'm quite serious."

Aldano finished his drink as if nothing had been said to him, smacked his lips and resolutely put the empty glass on the coffee table.

"I can take another drink." He became belligerently challenging, asking for a fight.

Gordon hissed at him, angry beyond belief. "Stop you dunce. If you can't hold your liquor, don't drink. I love this lady as I have never loved anyone in my whole life. I truly love her, understand? So don't talk like that!" At least he sounded like himself.

Finally, the door to the Sheik's bedroom opened, and Mr. Brandon helped Hussney El Barrack to a stuffed chair. Then he faced the feisty young men, accustomed to solving situations of this kind.

"Now...now...what's the matter? It's very bad taste to start a fight in a grand hotel. Hold your horses, and I'll find another place where you can settle your differences. What's this drunken brawl about, Aldano?"

Young Aldano struggled with his words — Ikhmet trying to speak within him, "This asshole thinks he can marry Lady Helena just like that. Only over my dead body. If Helena marries anyone, it's gonna be me!"

Gordon shook his head angrily, "Those are my words. You can't even remember something that was said a minute ago. He's just had too much to drink," he tried to explain.

Helena began to laugh, like she hadn't laughed in months, maybe years. Even the Sheik laughed, but broke off coughing.

Old man Brandon didn't laugh. He simply wasn't impressed with the performance. "You're making yourselves a laughing stock, boys. If I were Helena, I would've kicked you out on your pretty arses, never to see you again. She's a real lady and what are you? A couple of street punks."

Finally Helena stopped laughing, tears streaming down her face. "I needed that laugh, Mr. Brandon...honest to God, I needed it desperately."

"Very well then...at least that farce served a purpose. I'm glad to know. Years ago, I would've spanked both of you boys. Shame on you, behaving like idiots. Now if the childish tussling is over, I have a very serious matter to discuss with you young people."

At this, even Aldano sobered up.

"Tonight, all three of you are taking a flight to Palermo. I made the reservations while you were arguing. You'll have valid credit cards, and once in Palermo, you will wait for the party from Jerusalem. It's dangerous for them even to stop over here, so they're taking a direct flight to Sicily. His Excellency, Sheik El Barrack, is in no condition to fly. I'll take care of him. Any questions?"

Aldano raised his hand as if in school. "Do I have to go along with Gordon?"

"No. Unless you make up your mind to let him fly alone with Lady Helena."

"Over my dead body. Eat your heart out, Gordon, I'm coming."

Brandon put his hand on the tousled hair of his son, "No fights, sonny! You'll be on a serious mission and you have to behave like soldiers."

Helena gave him a warning look that said *don't treat them like children*.

Old Brandon spoke like a referee, "Come on, shake hands."

Gordon and Aldano shook hands without looking at each other. Brandon went to the Sheik and said in a low voice, "They'll work together fine. Aldano is jealous, but he doesn't know the real reason. If he stays back here, he might talk. Gordon has blurted out almost everything to him. Enraged, Aldano is capable of any sort of harm, but Helena can watch them."

"She wasn't able to control her own brother," Hussney observed.

Obviously, Brandon was well oriented on the subject. He pondered a bit, then suggested, "Now that she knows the deadly consequences, she'll act differently. She's a very clever girl, and she's in love with Gordon."

Sheik El Barrack spoke loudly so that the three young people could hear him. "Buy everything you need in Palermo. Helena will get my instructions. Listen to her. Mr. Brandon and I will join you as soon as I can take a flight. Be blessed! So long."

In the limo, Helena tried to remember her father's instructions. She had to verify all hotel reservations and have the rooms in readiness. Contact had to be made with a certain retired professor of oriental science in another city on the island. The rough spots in the relations between Gordon and Aldano had to be smoothed out before they resulted in altercations. She had to keep her feelings for Gordon in check so the temperamental youth wouldn't have any reason to start up the rivalry again. Do men need a reason for jealousy? Two strong and capable young men coupled with a single female is already one too many. It was the basic law of the jungle, and humanity hadn't moved that far away from the jungle. Both of them born athletes, they'd be subconsciously looking for competition. And if her brother had found a way into his volatile namesake, Aldano, danger would be spelled with capital letters. He'd look for revenge. For the time being they were silent but with muscles flexing. Obviously, any amount of alcohol made Aldano hyper. She had to watch out for this. A grave problem was how to address their ancient counterparts. Right now she wished for the authority and strength of Dr. Moughabee, though he hadn't done anything to prevent the fatal confrontation in Jerusalem. Perhaps, he wanted it to happen. More likely it was the great number of problems he had had to confront. Maybe he's quite close to the limits of his own endurance, and he has to be watched, too. On another hand, Helena was aware of her own limitations and frailties. She had to grope mostly in the dark. It would be a close call.

The Abbot was waiting for them at the airport of Valetta. He was going with the young people to Palermo. Now, that was a surprise. Did her father know about it? Was it by his arrangement?

If that were true, on whose side was the Abbot?

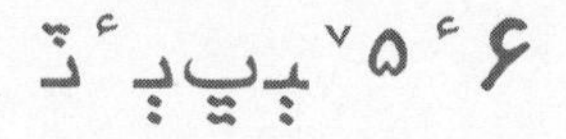

At the airport in Jerusalem, Dr. Moughabee checked the flight sheets of the small chartered jet. One flight was to Cairo and the other to Palermo. The Palermo flight had been chartered at the last minute. It was canceling the previous one given *proforma* to the authorities. Ouloulangha had spent some time with the young flyer while loading their baggage on the plane. He thought the world of him. Moughabee wasn't that sure. (He could be a plant.) There was a mob of foreign correspondents, diplomats, reporters and numerous paparazzi in the main lobby.

Now they all were watching intensely through the glass. For a moment, Dr. Moughabee thought he spotted the long, pale face of the dead roman prelate in the crowd. Was it possible that he wasn't dead and was still pulling the strings? A replacement hadn't come yet. Then again, it could've been anyone.

Dr. Moughabee waved a hand informally and boarded the plane.

Chapter 8

PALERMO AND PROFESSOR MIDHAD

The youngsters' flight to Palermo wasn't crowded and the seat next to Helena was not occupied. With her permission, the Abbot sat next to her. His name was Paul Le Gogguen and he was fluent in several languages, some of them dead. (That, of course, they learned much later.) For the time being, his presence was an embarrassment to the three young people, especially to Gordon. He stopped talking, pretending to sleep. Actually, he was trying not to miss any part of the conversation. Unfortunately, much of it was covered by the monotonous noise of the jet's engines. Le Gogguen explained that he received orders from the Vatican to facilitate their mission.

"How do you know what our mission is, Le Gogguen?" asked Helena.

"Don't kid yourself," Le Gogguen answered. "By now anyone interested in the story of the mummy knows it in intricate detail. The media took care of that, going overboard with trivia and ignoring the essentials. First you're going to see Professor Midhad. I know him from college. We helped each other several times in a number of affairs, and he came to see me in the monastery. He thought of it as a restful place, especially when Aldano wasn't around."

Nobody seemed to pay attention to his little barb so he went on, trying to keep his voice above engines' noise, "Professor Midhad considers himself a citizen of the world. I have a gut feeling he's an atheist. God and religion had never been discussed in our conversations. Professor Midhad is a very private person and doesn't appreciate young company. He might refuse to see you if I don't ask him personally. Consulting him about the basics of your 'mission' is necessary. His intimate knowledge of the oddities in the ancient world is vast. His main interest is the immortal Ka, and the transplantation of it in present times."

Helena was impressed by Le Gogguen's sincerity. "I don't quite understand how Professor Midhad can believe in something so outlandish as the Egyptian Ka, while denying the very existence of God. As a man of the cloth, do you believe in this myth?"

"Yes, I most definitely do believe in this phenomenon. I was aware of the process of...shall I say substitution, in Aldano and later, upon the arrival of Mr. Bates, his own possession. It's not a split personality, it's a total eclipse. I didn't interfere, because this kind of power is extremely complicated and any nonprofessional intervention could lead to serious consequences."

"I wonder how much you know about the most recent events."

"The Vatican has very trustworthy intelligence, Lady Helena. I was under consideration for a promotion, so I was given a briefing. It might sound unbelievable to you, but cannibalism and carnage is still practiced even in the most developed countries on the globe."

Helena looked straight into his eyes. He reminded her of the Prelate in Jerusalem, minus his steel rimmed glasses, though she was convinced that he had them in one of his pockets. "I read books and magazines, padre."

The Abbot nodded noncommittally, "I'm not patronizing you, Lady Helena. Aldano's behavior under my tutelage wasn't Mr. Bates' fault, nor were the strange events on the grounds of the Residence in Jerusalem and the monastery that I call my home."

Gordon opened his eyes widely, then closed them hurriedly, "Mr. Bates won't lose his virility because of a temporary possession by an ancient Ka, although the bisexuality has to be isolated as soon as possible."

"My God!" shouted Aldano, "How can you stop something of this kind, Le Gogguen? Soldiers, monks and sailors, in spite of their close controls, find a way to appease themselves. And I'm not talking about masturbation."

The Abbot flushed but he kept his composure. Helena's curiosity was piqued. "How might a thing like that be dealt with?"

"Only God knows. This is something you have to discuss with Professor Midhad. He might have an answer."

"Exorcism?" suggested Helena.

"I don't know."

Helena looked at Gordon. He seemed to be much younger than his actual age. Compared to their first encounter, age-wise, he appeared much closer to Aldano Brandon than to her. And all of it had happened in the two months since she met him. His boyishness was so natural that sometimes it was hard to tell the difference between him and Aldano. In his eyes, she probably looked much older. A terrible trick on the part of Mother Nature, or someone else.

Gordon probably had guessed her thoughts. Without opening his eyes he said, "I like you as you are, Helena."

Helena suddenly felt hopelessly out of place.

Helena and the Abbot met eye to eye. The man of the cloth shrugged his bony shoulders. She had the pressing need to talk to someone, anyone. "I haven't asked for a confession, padre, mainly because I didn't approve of father's closeness to my brother Aldan. I guess I was painfully jealous. Sometimes I downright hated my brother. I'll never miss him..." she confessed.

"This is an attitude problem." the Abbot concluded. "No one is immune to it. Remember Jesus and his brothers, more to the point, his favored enemy, James? Young James must've been the same roguish lad like Aldan, always looking for mischief. He was jealous of his half-brother and they fought not only with words.

There were indications that they fell in love with the same woman, which started a bitter rivalry between them. As a result, Jesus left his native country for many years. He knew how to read, but writing He never learned. James excelled with his writing skill. As the leader of what was left of the followers of John the Baptist, Jesus needed a secretary. Before taking the road to Golgotha, he advocated celibacy and total abdication from family ties. Mother Mary, under the pressure of his brothers, filed a petition in Jerusalem asking the authorities to hold her 'demented' son in an asylum. Christ had to go into hiding. Then quite suddenly He veered off and asked His brother to act as a go-between for him and Maria of Magdala. James brought them together half-heartedly but openly criticized the shameless manifestations of love by the newlywed. Most of Jesus' disciples were critical of his ficklish changes of mind. I think they all loved Him, not for His miracles, but for His extreme spiritual beauty and charm."

The Abbot went on, "My own faults are mine only. Don't begrudge the frolicking of this young man, Helena, because it won't last long. Nothing does on earth, except regrets and constant dissipation. Don't blame yourself for what you hold against your family. If Christ was prone to preconceptions and faults, why should you be above reproach? You don't pretend to be a saint."

Helena looked at the young men who were dressed in the same combination of dark blue blazers and light gray slacks like college boys. She herself felt prematurely aged and paralyzed by her own indecision. Deep within herself she craved luxury and elegant parties. All her schoolmates were from the upper crust. After graduation, her life had become drab. No jewels, no colors, she became quite haphazard in her manner of dress. That had to change. She made a mental note to look for something colorful in the stores of Palermo. When Gordon and Aldano went to the toilet, Helena moved even closer to the Abbot.

She had to put some feathers in her bonnet, or she'd slowly turn into an old maid. Damn the ancient Ka, she had to live her own life! "You speak so freely, Padre. Aren't you restricted by the Catholic Dogmas?"

The man lifted his hands toward the sky. "Dogmas live and prosper behind the walls of convents and churches. Millions of people won't part with them overnight, but the Christian Intelligentsia is well into the avant-garde. We cannot afford to leave discoveries only in the hands of heretics. The original Gospels have been lovingly preserved in the secret library of the Vatican. One can still find in them the sweet primal sin dominating over the warnings of the prophets, a precious hope, that even without a future, we have at least a remarkable present. Away from the monastery, I belong wholeheartedly to my own free thinking."

IN THE PRIVATE, RENTAL JET

Dr. Moughabee was sitting next to the pilot carefully reading his mind.

At first, there were no traces of any significant thoughts, then he felt an awareness about the sorry state of the engine which was a cause for some concern. The pumps in the hydraulic parts were responding unevenly. The fuel injection could fail in the blink of an eye. The pilot had filed all the forms for an inspection, but so far, nothing had been done. A Lebanon company held ownership of the plane. It had to pay the Jerusalem authorities for an inspection. Maintenance and parts were costly. So the small chartered planes were run with mideast nonchalance. Everything was placed in the hands of Allah, and a prayer to Him would prevent danger from evolving into catastrophe. The pilot had said all his prayers, and "what will be, will be."

Dr. Moughabee was alarmed enough so that he set his mind on the engines. There were quite a few problems, though none of them lethal. His mind explored all of the plane's functions and mechanisms. God be praised! No immediate danger. Dr. Moughabee returned to the pilot's mind, and found that his name was Ayram. Ayram also had quite a few household problems, the mortgage on his house and the insurance of the Mercedes, his two wives and their children, all of which cost a lot of money. This flight was a blessing. It paid top dollar. He had taken a number of bribes but didn't know how to proceed. Ayram had no loyalty but to himself.

The young man began perspiring.

If he lands in Palermo, he has to confess his double game to the Italians, and beg for asylum because he would have betrayed the Egyptians. His family...Allah will take care of them. They are innocent. If the Egyptians threaten to kill them...it would be a tragedy, but he was young enough to start anew. Anyway he was sick and tired of the situation in the Near East. And "the curse of the mummy" was something to think about.

Moughabee stopped reading the confusing thoughts of their pilot and tried to contact Lord Aton.

MOUGHABEE'S INNER SELF: DIALOG WITH ATON'S MUMMY

"I'm sorry to bother You, My Lord, but the situation is a bit above my own powers. If You don't want to be bothered say so. I'm afraid we're in the hands of a pilot with an unbalanced way of thinking. What am I to do? It seems to be a dangerous situation — we could end up back in Egypt."

"Living is a dangerous state, Doctor Moughabee. You should know that."

"Are You belittling me, Lord Aton? Perhaps you're angry with me. If that's the case, what can I do to placate You?"

"No, my friend, you didn't transgress against me. You forget that in my embryonic state I can't be harmed. You have to worry only about yourself and your companion. You're supposed to help that fellow Ayram. He's absolutely confused and doesn't even know it. That's really dangerous. You have to change the thoughts in his head."

"How?"

"Give him a sense of security. Make him pray to God with you. That should restore the peace in his mind."

"But he already said all his prayers and nothing comes of it."

"Praying with somebody else is different. You could not betray a man that has shared a prayer with you, could you?"

Moughabee scratched his head. "Lord Aton, times have changed since your last time around. People betray without any remorse. They simply empty their heads as this fellow does, and then curse the Devil. That 'the Devil made me do it' explains everything. People even lament themselves as victims. These victims don't deserve a prayer. Anything done by them is completely obliterated; what's done to them is never forgotten. Good deeds are taken as a token of stupidity, and they will accept anything but looking stupid in their own eyes. Their own good deeds are always questionable, and seldom appreciated. By the way, this morning I saw the 'dead' Prelate in flesh and blood."

Lord Aton laughed out loud for the first time. "Did you really believe, even for a moment, that he hung himself on the same tree as Judas?"

Moughabee felt most embarrassed, "It was announced by very responsible sources."

"What do you qualify as responsible sources? Newspapers, radio, TV? An official speaker at a press conference? A close friend of yours? Where did he get it? I don't know life on Earth as well as you do, but I don't believe news from the 'horse's mouth'."

"Like Doubting Thomas?"

"Now you've got me! Like Doubting Thomas, exactly! He would've been quite at home nowadays. I'll bet he'd fare and prosper well because of his lack of faith. In present times, even angels cannot afford to be naive, Moughabee."

"Then, what shall I do?" pleaded Moughabee.

"Well, let me see…it won't be a big loss one way or the other. History wouldn't change course because of people like Ayram."

"How about Ouloulangha, Teacher."

"No great loss either. My mummy will go back to obscurity on the bottom of the sea. As for yourself, you only have to part ways with this small, insignificant planet lost in the Great Milky Way, which, on its own, is a speck compared to the Universe."

Moughabee shuddered at the thought of leaving this small, insignificant planet. In the relatively short course of his stay, he learned to love it, in a way. He knew that the end was near, but, on the other hand, he couldn't cold-bloodedly disband his mission and confess that he had fooled just about everybody into a false sense of hope. It wasn't only a question of repentance. People, as bad as they were, had a bright side, too. Many had created divine works. Surely, even Jesus listened to a melody of Mozart for one. Perhaps the hoi polloi didn't matter, but Moughabee liked them for being able to put up with their anonymous lives and continue to propagate. Some of them had gone through more predicaments than any of the known great heroes. It's just that no one knew about it, and that was quite valuable in the eyes of Moughabee. Especially, their making of larger and larger wholes, greater than the sum of their parts. A homestead as a prototype of a whole state and further…an appropriately comfortable, homey world. There were not that many in the known universe. One doesn't have to hate existence just because it has a dark side…

Aton broke into his thoughts, "You're daydreaming, Moughabee…or shall I call you, Peter? We've known each other for such a long time that we can tolerate our differences."

Then Aton asked Moughabee, "Are you satisfied?"

"To start with I wasn't dissatisfied…only looking for justice."

"And justice will be done. This pilot will deposit you safely in Palermo, so the show must go on: the Pope will make a pilgrimage to you…with your approval…of course."

"It's not to satisfy my vanity, Lord Aton. It's to merely try to save the planet Earth and my beloved Humanity from extinction."

"You'll never change Peter."

"But I did. Now I'm Doctor Moughabee from Nubia."

"And I, Lord Aton, am residing on a dead planet."

"I know You as Jesus of Nazareth."

"And I know you as the Fisherman of human souls."

THEATER OF THE ABSURD: IKHMET (ENTER STAGE)

I am General Haremhab, though I'm known as Ikhmet, the mighty one that overthrew the Eighteenth Dynasty and restored the city of Thebes as the capital of Upper and Lower Egypt. Sculptors were sent throughout the country to repair the shrines of the ancient gods, which had been defaced by Amenhotep IV. I sat on the throne and the grateful priesthood proclaimed me the Pharaoh. Order was restored in the land. Monuments, names and temples mutilated by Amenhotep came back into existence. I defeated him in a fight to the death, a hand-to-hand combat. It happened in a small room on the top of a tower in Amarna with no witnesses whatsoever. After my victory, I threw his broken body from the tower, down to the feet of the crowd below. All new temples dedicated to the One God were completely destroyed. Everywhere, the name Ikhnaton and his reliefs were chiseled out. His nobles' tombs were hidden. The ruins of Amarna were left to the elements. Even the whereabouts of Tutankhamon's tomb remained unknown. Everyone that participated in the speedy preparation and the funeral met his death. Dead people don't talk.

Many, including the Pharaoh's wife and mother, thought that I killed the eighteen-year-old Tut. I didn't have the courage to murder Aton's only son. I love Aton more than anything in the world, I owe everything to him...but I don't consider him a god. The Chief Priest took care of the murder. He personally killed the young Pharaoh, poisoned his wife and was going after Nefertiti, when I put a stop to the murders.

Since early childhood I was a scrappy kid and had a natural knack for free-for-all wrestling. I had many matches and defeated all my elder brothers. Aton was only a year my senior. He was stubborn as a mule. We fought each other to a state of total exhaustion.

One day, Aton and I had to take our few goats to a distant, grassy meadow. The moment they started to graze, we went at each other. It was a couple of hours before noon and no one around to pull us apart. That morning we had decided to have it all out to the finish. When we tumbled in the muddy stream and Aton rolled on top of me, he said haltingly: "Listen, Ikhmet, I don't mind if you kill me, but this time around we have to find which one of us is going to live. Your existence will be a danger to the future, therefore, I'll kill you if I can."

I didn't need any additional incentive. Not me! I was eager to have a fight to the death with him. Then suddenly, we realized the reason for our wild behavior. We were two highly competitive boys who thought we hated each other's guts and strove to kill each other. At the same time we came to the conclusion that the deep emotion we felt was admiration and love. We were absolutely sure that we wouldn't fight each other again to the end of our days.

STAGE LEFT: ALDAN EL BARRACK STANDS SILENTLY AT A DISTANCE FROM IKHMET

After his debacle and death, Ikhmet found a contact for his own Ka, on the isle of Malta, I, as myself, followed him. Now I'm sitting in a tiny corner of the brain belonging to that vigorous boy Aldano. my section of Aldano is right across from Ikhmet's. He watches me, I watch him. Because of his seniority, I cannot act without his permission. We haven't said a word to each other, but we read each other's minds. Now I see Ikhmet is ready to talk.

"Won't you give me a little chance, Master Ikhmet," I pleaded. "I did my utmost for you? Now I crave my revenge."

"You want to destroy Aldano?" Ikhmet mused. "With Moughabee around Aldano cannot be empowered by you. Aldano has sto engage Gordon in a one-on-one, honest fight. You have been discovered already, and if you do something outlandish, they'll kick us both out. What will that get you?"

"Who are 'they'?"

"Moughabee, his secretary and a professor in Messina. I wouldn't write off the old Irishman, Brandon, and even that raggedy crow, the Abbot. Your sister, Helena, has Nefertiti on her side. It's almost like a new Trojan War. All the heroes have a helping god," explained Ikhmet.

"I didn't know so many of them were involved," grunted Aldan. "In the hustle and bustle, I was buried without my genitals.

My prick still lays in the bushes. After that grizzly event, nobody cares for a swim in that pool. The water is murky, but who's going to change it? The new master from Rome is miserly and superstitious. He won't ever go near those bushes. Besided, swimming isn't his passion."

"Don't be ridiculous, my friend. It would be of little help even if your crotch was intact."

"Don't you want to have all your parts, ancient man?"

"I am wholesome, with or without those body parts."

"Why is Amenhotep's Ka making Gordon look younger and younger every day?" Aldan continued. "Let's set Gordon and Aldano against each other! I'll bet against the mixed blood."

"They are both of mixed blood. Very few purebreds have survived the modern world."

"Come on! Where is your warrior's spirit, Master? Risk it all! I'm betting on the Blond Maltese. What's your bet? The Memphis Raven? They'll be ready to come out soon. *Fet vous jeu, messieurs*!"

"Quit that boyish gibberish, Aldan! Let's put our heads together for something more essential."

"O.K., boss! Anything you say."

IN PALERMO, SICILY

Professor Midhad didn't look like a typical Turk.

But, how does the typical Turk look? The man behind the desk could've been any nationality. He probably had difficulty classifying his young guests, as well. Blond, ruddy cheeked Aldano could've been taken for an Aryan. Helena had a light complexion too, maybe a Russian. One thing was clear to the professor, the third visitor was an Egyptian. The letter from the Honorable Sheik Hussney El Barrack didn't mention who they were. He simply asked him to hear their stories, then come to his own conclusion. "It's pertaining to your main scientific field, Professor," said the note. Still, that didn't help much. He had no intention of following up this case. The phone call from his long-time friend, Le Gogguen was also evasive. He said it was worthwhile spending time with these characters, and that he would appear later, so his presence wouldn't intimidate his young guests.

In the note there was a little more information. Gordon has lost about fifteen pounds in the last three months, his age had been reversed and his face refined to a dramatic point. Changes had also happened to the blond youth and the young lady. Perhaps the good professor could advise how to cope with these changes.

"Strange, very strange..." said the professor finishing his second glance at the letter, "All people change with age, and some more than others. I don't see how this pertains to my field?"

Helena knew that neither one of her companions would answer the question, so she had to take the initiative. "I think my father refers to your interest in the Ka, according to Egyptian beliefs in ancient times."

Professor Midhad laughed condescendingly, "What does Sheik El Barrack know about Egyptian Kas?"

"Not very much. Something in the three of us led him to believe that a strange occurrence has taken place, taking over our personalities to a dangerous point."

The professor rearranged the stuff on the top of his desk, then asked, "Who gave you the name of Helena?"

"My mother," she replied.

"Why?"

"Because she liked it. Erroneously, she thought it Russian."

"Why did it have to be a foreign name?" the professor pursued.

"Oh, I see...let me think about it. I didn't expect the questioning to go in this direction. Her name was Nefertiti. I remember calling her 'Titi.' She was born and raised in Alexandria. She might have wanted to save me from a curse that caused her to die quite young."

"How did she die?"

"Sleepwalking. The roof terrace of my father's castle in the mountains of Lebanon didn't have any railing so it could be used as a helicopter pad. The canyon at the front part is actually a vertical fall. Very little was found of her," Helena explained sadly.

"I'm sorry to hear that. Did she have any reason to commit suicide?"

"No. I don't think so...though she was often depressed."

"Did the foreign name lead the curse astray?"

Helena's head dropped a notch, but she still looked straight into the professor's eyes.

"I don't think so, "Helena mused.

"Do you sleepwalk?"

"I don't know. It is more like daydreaming."

"Is the top terrace of your father's castle your favorite spot?" asked the professor.

"It has a breathtaking view."

"Do you know how Queen Nefertiti of the Eighteenth Dynasty died?"

"I know she remarried out of the Dynasty, to a young man from a peasant family. After the murder of Tutankhaton, he was proclaimed the Pharaoh of the Two Egypts."

"You mean, Tutankhamon?"

"She never called him that."

"Why did Queen Nefertiti marry General Haremhab? Was it because he saved her life."

"She wanted to kill Ikhmet," interrupted Helena.

"Did she?"

"Well, no, she didn't. According to my mother, after the first night, she fell in love with him. He was extremely sexy. Ikhmet loved her ever since he saw her when he came to the palace with Aton, another handsome man she fell for."

"Aton sired her beloved Prince Tut. Why not her husband, the Pharaoh of the land, who was young and sexy in his own right."

"Amenhotep was bisexual and Ikhmet, to further his own personal ambitions, became his lover. Then Ikhmet killed him with his bare hands."

"Is that according to your mother, too? Did Nefertiti ever try to revenge the fall of the Eighteenth Dynasty?"

Helena put a trembling hand over her forehead. " Now I see. Ikhmet was forever damned with his devastating, unsatiated love for her. He became morose and lost interest in sex. He never begot a son to inherit the Kingdom. He died the way he was born — a peasant. Haremhav was denied a Pharaoh's burial."

"Why? Haremhab was a good Pharaoh."

"Mother said the priests had no other choice but the general. A peasant on the throne of Ra! They called him the Good-Giver, though never forgave his peasantry."

"Did your mother tell you this story?"

"No, she didn't. It is the other Nefertiti speaking directly through me."

"Are you fascinated by chasms?"

"Nefertiti tempts me. Night after night, I walk to the end of the terrace.

"In your dreams?"

"I don't know. The entrance into the other dimension is never clear. Sometimes, I think the Queen had nested within me and the entrance into the other dimension is only through her."

"Have you tried to address her?"

Helena shook her head. "We don't talk to each other. It's either all me, or all her."

"Who's talking now?"

"I'm not sure, Professor Midhad. I'm never fully conscious when she takes over. She's not afraid of you."

The old man walked around the desk with a silver stick and placed his bony hand protectively on Helena's shoulder. "I'm not afraid of her either."

"I don't like you," Queen Nefertiti revealed suddenly, jerking away.

"I don't care. Do you want revenge over Ikhmet?"

"Amenhotep has already avenged himself. There will be no more peasants in the family."

"I thought you loved Ikhmet," pushed the professor.

"Of course, I loved my second husband. I told you already."

"Have you visited your brother?"

"I never had a brother! Who told you that?" The queen was taken by surprise.

"Paul Le Gogguen."

"Helena's half-brother, maybe. Nowadays, no one knows who's real and who's just imagined."

"I know."

Helena as Nefertiti laughed huskily. "You don't know the truth. You're just imagined through me."

"And these young men, are they imagined too?"

The Queen looked in the direction he pointed. "There is no one there. But I smell the loins of young, sexy males. They'll fight each other for my love!"

"If they don't exist outside of your imagination, they can't fight. How can nobody fight nobody?"

Nefertiti moaned with lust, her bare arms lacing behind his neck, "Oh, you, ancient trickster, you know better than that. I'm talking about my husband and the peasant boy."

"You told me, they fought already."

"They'll fight for me again and again, till the end of time."

Then, where is Aton in the picture?"

"Aton is a god. One can love him for his divine mission on earth."

"Malarkey. He sired your son," accused the professor.

"I wanted a Divine Son for the throne of Heaven on Earth. Egypt had enough peasants and slaves. Amenhotep was the son of a Jew boy. Amenhotep's mother used to set her champ against her husband's and every time he won for her, she gave herself as a prize to him. The Eighteenth Dynasty had expired long ago. It happened sometime during the reign of Ramses' sons. Aton was the Only God, and we killed Him!"

Chapter 9

MOUGHABEE'S DREAM

At the airport in Palermo, Dr. Moughabee didn't see his advance party. It was eight in the morning and Christmas decorations made the modern structure even uglier than it was. The weather was the same as in Jerusalem, so was the building…or at least, comparable.

It almost seemed to Moughabee that they were back in Israel, until a loudspeaker announced in Italian, "Welcome to Palermo."

Suddenly, in the sea of faces, he glimpsed one he expected least of all to see — the Roman Prelate from the Holy Land. God Almighty! It wasn't an illusion. The man, smartly dressed in a dark business suit, made his way through the mob straight to the Nubian. The church official seemed glad to see him.

"I'm sorry. My flight was late. I should've met you at your arrival time. Paul Midhad is in Messina with the youngsters. Professor Midhad had to postpone his visit to Spain, but it is urgent, and he is in a hurry. How was your flight?"

"Uneventful. Pardon my indiscretion, but are you allowed to wear civilian clothes? You look different without the vestments of your rank — almost human," laughed Moughabee. "Come to think of it, I've never known your name. It wasn't in the newspapers. Is it possible that you were not baptized?"

The Prelate actually cracked a smile. "Unbelievable but true. I have a name that I seldom use. My friends call me Marvel. It sounds like a magician's sobriquet, but I'm used to it. Marvel is a nickname from my college days. My true name is the same as the name of Pope Pius. My parents believed one day I'd reach that far. I had told them about my dreams of being the High Priest of Egypt."

"In the times of Amenhotep IV?"

"Around that time, I'd guess," the Prelate confessed.

"After the messy situation in Jerusalem, what shall I call you?" asked Moughabee.

"Mister Marvel or just Marvel." There was a short beeping, and the Prelate took a phone from his pocket. "Sorry, I'll be right back with you." He said a few words, listened, then said to Moughabee, "The limo belonging to the local Diocese is at your disposal."

"Remarkable. I don't seem to use any other type of vehicles lately." Moughabee took out his own pocket phone, "You don't mind if I call Ouloulangha? We hired a van for our baggage. The pilot is loading it. He's a strong fellow. I have a feeling that he's in no hurry to go back."

Moughabee ordered his secretary to come out on the front ramp and follow the limo, then he walked with his escort toward the exit. The Roman Prelate presented him with one of his rare lukewarm smiles. "You can stay in the Diocese. That way your 'trustee' will be protected."

"I hope so. My reservation at the hotel could be used by Mr. Ayram."

"Of course, of course. The pilot. He's an Armenian converted to Islam. That doesn't happen very often. I wouldn't advise him to return. There was a lot of publicity about the mummy and the tragic happenings in Israel."

"Omitting your well organized death..."

"Oh, that's forgotten..." laughed the man, "the sources have been punished. Did you really believe that I could do something so melodramatic?"

"The Testaments are full of melodramas. People like them. In fact, I'm a man prone to serious melodramas myself."

The Prelate hesitated for a moment, then said, "I have a child, Dr. Moughabee, the result of a little love affair that terminated my aspirations. I really hope that in time you'll see me as a human being. Actually, Judas didn't betray his Teacher solely for thirty silver coins. That's the official Church version. In truth, it was a crime of passion. He loved Jesus so much, that he was unable to share Him with the others. The marriage was the last straw. His treason was a revenge to an unfaithful Master."

"The Kiss?"

"Yes, the Kiss."

"Is that the reason you wanted to see Lord Aton in person before fully committing the Church?"

"Yes, it is. And I want to see Him again."

"Will you betray Him a second time?"

"No. This time around, I want to save Him."

"Crime and punishment?"

"Perhaps this is the driving force behind my attitude. Publicly, I'll maintain the official policy."

"There will be a press conference, I suppose?"

"Positively. At three o'clock this afternoon."

"And you'll be present as the Roman Prelate from Jerusalem?"

"Certainly. Coincidentally, a fellow did hang himself on Judas' tree in Gethsemane Garden. That happens all the time. I had to disappear for awhile."

"I still don't understand your actions," puzzled Dr. Moughabee.

"One day you will," the Prelate answered cryptically.

The uniformed chauffeur respectfully held open the door for them. Moughabee made sure that the van was behind the limo. They sat on the comfortable velvet seat.

Moughabee laughed dryly. "So the whole trick was meant for me. You wanted to see how far I could be driven. For old times sake, I preserved my naiveté, which didn't change much in the last thousand years."

The car was moving slowly through the heavy traffic. Mr. Marvel looked absentmindedly at the scenery.

"Nothing ever changes. It's just the appearance."

The traffic became increasingly bad near the center of Palermo. Moughabee looked through the back window and saw that the van was not there. There was a cluster of cars stopped at the red light.

"Don't worry, Dr. Moughabee. The driver knows how to find the residence. They may have had a flat, a small accident or they may be caught in traffic. Taking an alternate route isn't puzzling to a professional. Probably the van is already waiting for us at our destination."

However, Moughabee didn't expect to find it at their destination. He already knew that the beady eyes of Mister Marvel, augmented many times through the powerful lenses of his glasses, had a strange power over him. He was lulled by the monotonous voice into something like jet lag. All he had had on the plane was a bottle of lukewarm coke. It tasted bad, but he had never been a lover of Coca Cola. To him, it always tasted like medicine. His head was getting heavy, and he had to call for all his spiritual strength to prevent himself from falling asleep.

There were a lot of opiates with delayed action.

Mr. Marvel was looking at him without any expression on his face. Now Moughabee knew he had been drugged. He summoned his powers to master the situation. The limo entered the grounds of a rambling mansion through a wide, open gate. The van wasn't there.

"They are late," said the Prelate while waiting for the chauffeur to open the door, "they'll be here any moment."

Moughabee looked at the diffused face of the Prelate. Moughabee's spirit and mind were fighting off the poison as he mastered his exit from the car. There was no mortal danger. The enemy just wanted him disabled for awhile.

It was high noon and the sun was blazing with extreme force. Everything was bathed in blinding light with not a trace of shade. He made his way to the entrance without betraying his dazed state. The Prelate was in the oval, marble entrée. One of the statues spoke from its niche in a strangely distorted voice.

"Paul Le Gogguen called in your absence. He found out from Professor Midhad that your charges never came to see him. Then left for Spain."

With a titanic effort Moughabee threw off the disabling power attacking his mind and body. He saw the Prelate of the Holy Land in his usual regalia. "When did he find time to change? I must've missed a lot," he thought. Out loud he said, "I hold you personally responsible for their disappearance, Eminence. Let's go to the press conference."

"You cannot attend a conference in this state, Dr. Moughabee. I'll tell the reporters everything you have on your mind. You take a needed rest. You can meet the press at another date."

Having successfully fought off the drug's affect, Moughabee sensed someone sneaking up from behind. He swiftly stepped aside and a baseball bat grazed his ear lobe and exploded on his right shoulder. A dreadful pain shook his massive body but chased away the last cobwebs in his mind. The next moment he had his attacker under hand. He'd been trained to use both hands as lethal weapons. The man was big and athletic, but he was small change for the Nubian who broke the sturdy body like a matchstick, and hurled it across the slippery marble. It traveled several yards before it was stopped by a large column.

The Prelate had disappeared.

Several policemen appeared on the scene. Before Moughabee realized what was happening, handcuffs were on his wrists.

"What did you do to Dr. Moughabee?" asked one of the police.

The Nubian was enraged. "I'm Dr. Peter Moughabee, businessman from the USA."

Swift hands passed through his pockets.

"No I.D. papers, Commendattore!"

A brute self-assured face approached him and sneered, "I know this gangster. Take him to headquarters. Don't forget the baseball bat."

PART TWO

THE PUNISHMENT

Chapter 10

TRAGEDY IN PALERMO

The pilot awakened Dr. Moughabee. He had a friendly smile and good news. Palermo had given them free access. The Nubian closed his heavy eyelids again. So everything was a dream...only a dream. But for someone like Moughabee, all reality was a dream and eternity his "*terra firma.*" Sometimes he wanted...*to die...perchance to sleep*...No way. He had to go on living until the last debt of his terrestrial karma was paid. And that was his secret, he wanted to stay on Earth.

He had engineered the disappearance of Gordon's parents. One of them escaped. Moughabee had acted prematurely. Simple panic. None of them was seriously endangering his project.

Sergey was still living in his native land, under his true name. He was Sergey Bagran. His latest known address was Grozney, the tumultuous capital city of Chechnya. Moughabee had no idea which political side he was on. As far as he knew, Sergey was still providing information in return for hard currency. The corners of Moughabee's mouth curved in deprecation. Spying — the only skill he'd refined in his miserable life.

The true biological father of Gordon was Peter Moughabee himself.

Yes, in the name of all gods, Gordon was his son! Did he love the boy? Somewhat. No, that wasn't true either. Now Amenhotep as Ikhnaton had taken him over, arrogantly and irresponsibly, because he was born to dominate. Physically, Gordon used to look like a young Moughabee. No more — his face, his body, even his character had changed. Peter Moughabee had lost any influence over him. Incredible! He, Moughabee, who was known to everyone in Heaven as Saint Peter, the doorman. Nowadays, all people know how to pray meekly, *mea culpa* while pointing a finger at another guy. He preferred those who would stand up and fight, as in the old days when he was called the Fisherman. Nowadays, platitudes had taken over. What a downfall!

Palermo's airport was actually quite different from the structure in Jerusalem. The group waiting for Moughabee at the terminal was duly impressive. Besides the young trio, there was a clergyman of some kind and another person seemingly forgotten by him — the professor from Messina.

Surprise, surprise! Moughabee was ready to eat his old hat if that wasn't Sergey Bagran in the flesh.

THEATER OF THE ABSURD: PETER MOUGHABEE STANDING IN FRONT OF CURTAIN

I have no doubt in my mind that my dream during the flight wasn't entirely fictitious. Part of it had to do with reality, but then reality itself dealt with my dream. The first person I had to meet in privacy was Sergey. Good old Ouloulangha took care of all other arrangements, so I was able to engage the professor at the hotel Savoya where we met in the hotel's bar.

SAVOYA'S BAR: MOUGHABEE AND SERGEY BAGRAN (AKA PROFESSOR MIDHAD AND GORDON'S WOULD-BE-FATHER) SIT AT A TABLE

He wasn't shy at all. "I thank you, Dr. Moughabee, for giving me the opportunity to explain myself." He seemed very solicitous. A waiter brought two glasses of wine.

I said nothing, keeping busy with my cigar. Sergey wasn't easy to intimidate. He went on as if we had parted our ways just yesterday. "You haven't said anything about me to Gordon, have you?"

I remained aloof. "I don't know anything about you myself. Is there something that I should know?" retorted Moughabee.

The professor obligingly handed me his lighter. "I don't smoke, but I still have the fire."

Intentionally, I let him hang, then when my cigar caught, I gave him back his lighter. "You always loved to play with fire, Sergey, but this one is extremely dangerous. By the way, I gave you this lighter, didn't I?"

For a moment I had a vision of a slender young man, very shy and out of place. The man in front of me was portly, with heavy cheeks and whiskers. "I'm afraid I didn't give much to Gordon as a father," said the Professor.

"You never knew what it was to be a father," I countermanded. "Gordon didn't miss you either. He hardly knows what a biological father is. I didn't have much to give him in exchange. In his life, he's been only surrogate matter."

"He used to look like you, Dr. Moughabee." Sergey studied the lighter, as if seeing it for a first time. "Remind me, why did you give me this lighter?"

"You were a chain smoker, I hoped you'd smoke yourself to death," quipped Moughabee.

"Thank you. Very considerate on your part. You have no feelings for him, or me, do you?"

"I… never had the opportunity to know either one of you on a personal level. I knew my Egyptian ancestry better. Amenhotep is not a stranger to me, and there was no love lost between the two of us. He's the son of a Jew, one of the court's favorite wrestlers. It wasn't a secret that the Queen-Mother took the Jew to her bed. His juvenile beauty was irresistible to her. She was ready to abolish his status as slave, when, in a rather ferocious match with a young, handsome Nubian, her Jewish lover refused to surrender and was smothered to death by his rival. That accounts for the extreme fascination Amenhotep had with contact sports. He also refused to surrender as Ikhmet mauled him to death. I can't feel sorry for him. Somehow his diversity escapes me."

"You cannot accept his bisexuality?"

"Do you? I guess you do." We silently sipped at the wine.

Sergey looked at me long and hard. "Amenhotep's biological father talks to me. His knowledge of the court affairs wasn't profound, but I ran a double check on his scanty information. No fault there, though he had nothing on you. I don't have to explain to anyone how I felt about your dirty play. You put out a contract on my life. There was little choice for me but to ask for Soviet protection, and nothing comes free in this life. I loved Gordon maybe because you abandoned him unceremoniously as people drown new born, blind kittens. Only once in our lives Gordon and I met as a father and son. I had those high cheek-bones combined with slanted eyes from my Chechen mother and that gave him a key to my past. For awhile, he chose to believe in my fatherhood. Then on that hike in the mountains..."

I looked at the bluish, smoky rings of my cigar as they dissipated into nothing.

"What did you do to him, Sergey?"

The man shrugged his fleshy shoulders, "The usual. He was big for his age and I, small and thin for mine. The mountain brings people together. We slept in the same tent. The nights were cold, the mornings freezing. Neither of us caught a fish."

"You slept with him?"

Sergey nodded slowly, "He thought that was natural for a father. You know, Gordon's intelligence was never high. He didn't think highly of me either. We were two strangers, but for that moment in time, we felt for each other. I never saw him again, until now."

I wasn't angry, just sorry that the contract on the life of this despicable man wasn't fulfilled. At this moment, for the first time, I really thought of him as a human being. For the first time, since I knew him, it dawned on my mind that he had never been loved. People dealt with him as with an object, no more, no less. "To you health, Serget!" I finished my wine.

BACK TO NOW

The car that took the group from the airport was a minibus, property of the Diocese. For some reason, Moughabee and Professor Midhad rented a late vintage Cadillac. Ayram, demoted from pilot to a driver, shifted the mummy from the van to the back seat of the luxury vehicle. The Abbot was dismayed.

"Hotel vaults are notorious for break-ins and thefts. In the church, the mummy will be under God's care. The Diocese has perfect security."

Moughabee laughed raucously. "The mummy will be under God's supervision everywhere on earth, while security provided by people always depends on the best offer. Ask Mr. Ayram, if you don't believe me."

Le Gogguen's eyes shifted to the young, athletically built pilot. "Isn't he going back to his home?"

"No. He accepted my employment offer. I need someone familiar with the city to drive me around."

"And you trust him?" questioned Le Gogguen.

"Why not? I trusted you with the rest of my baggage, and I've never seen you before. You've been taking care of my young friends. Thanks anyway, I'll see you in the hotel." He made a half turn, then turned back, "I almost forgot, how is dear Mr. Marvel these days?"

Le Gogguen, obviously mortified, paled slightly. "I don't know whom you have in mind, Dr. Moughabee."

To everybody's surprise the Nubian laughed again. "Maybe you do, maybe you don't. Glad to make your acquaintance, Abbot."

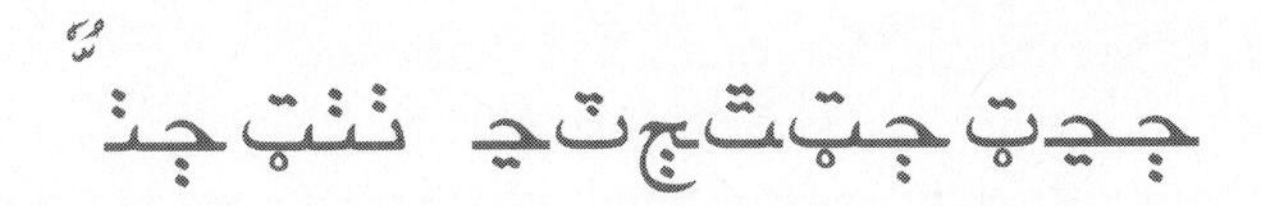

Helena didn't know how to approach Dr. Peter Moughabee. He kept his distance from her. She knew Ouloulangha better. Her father suggested that she should offer her secretarial services to Dr. Moughabee, but that didn't seem right to her. For many years now, he had Ouloulangha on the job and didn't appear understaffed. Besides, why should he trust her? she wondered.

After the initial meeting with the professor in Messina, Gordon had changed dramatically. Professor Midhad moved with them into the hotel. He worried about Gordon more than he was willing to admit. Gordon became locked within himself: short phrases to Helena and Aldano, sparse sentences to the professor. He went to the beach every morning in spite of the cold water. He swam beyond the safety-net zone and ignored the warnings of the lifeguards. Nothing ever happened, though man-eating sharks were spotted in the area. The lifeguards were greatly annoyed and made him sign a waiver.

He never invited Aldano, and the youth spent his time around the heated pool. One morning, when Helena tried to join him for a swim, Aldano left hurriedly for a bogus appointment.

The next morning Helena went to the beach alone. She didn't undress, but she did take off her shoes. The sand was surprisingly warm in spite of the cool breeze. It wasn't difficult to spot Gordon. He was the only one away from the guarded beach. She went to him with a heavy heart.

"Gordon," She softly said his name.

He didn't open his eyes.

"What's the matter?"

She sat next to him as he lay prostrate on the sand.

"What's happening to us?" Helena tried again.

There was not a trace of mockery in his voice, "To whom? To me and you, to Aldano and me, or to the seagulls and the sea?"

"If you don't want to talk to me, just say so, and I'll be on my way back to the hotel." Helena was desperate.

There was a tense pause between them, then he sat up on his elbows, "Gordon is temporarily out of touch. Can I get a message to him?"

The monotonous roar of the large waves almost drowned his voice. Helena stopped fighting back her tears, they ran freely down her cheeks. "Tell him…that I love him against all odds, no matter what happens."

The young man that wasn't Gordon didn't answer for awhile, running a handful of sand through his fingers. "Isn't Aldano offering enough homage to you? You could easily pick up the pilot, too. He needs a new family…though I'm afraid time is running out for all of us."

"Time is running out for all of us," Helena repeated Gordon's words on a phone call to her father in Malta. "What does that mean?"

Sheik Hussney El Barrack coughed dryly for awhile, then came back on the line loud and clear:

"It means all that silly talk about the pyrotechnics at the end of the millennium. It seems, every thousand years or so, people expect the end of this world as we know it. It's not completely unfounded, you know. All sorts of calamities happen — earthquakes, typhoons and drastic changes in the climate. According to the scientists, it's all due to the shifting of the earth's axis. Alarmingly, in the course of the last few years, those things have been happening quite often and with tremendous ferocity. I'm positive that Gordon hasn't even noticed these natural disasters and their relationship to ancient and new prophecies. All that extravaganza comes from Amenhotep. Disregard it. What worries me the most are man-made disasters like wars and epidemics. That's mentioned in the Bible as Apocalypses. Poisonous gases are used in modern warfare, not to mention atomic weapons. Unfortunately, that litany is found not only in the yellow press. Buy some mainstream magazines and newspapers… in other words, not all of it is pure fabrication. As you see we are in the middle of a brand new 'grand affaire' that can blow us all out of this world. Is it *Corpus Dei*? Riots and vandalism have started everywhere, corruption and manipulation of truth on all levels of society, run-away inflation creating economic failures. It's possible that my mind is afflicted by my sorry state of health. Brandon says nothing, but he is obviously worried about his son. We'll be joining you soon in spite of my doctor's medical warning."

"Tell Mr. Brandon, that after our meeting with Professor Midhad, Aldano and Gordon have parted ways. Though they rarely talk to each other, there's no animosity whatsoever. Professor Midhad is here. He'll alert us if anything goes wrong," Helena told her father.

The Sheik fell into another bout of coughing. When finished, he resumed the conversation. "Midhad is not his name. He's part Russian, part Chechen, the worst possible combination."

Helena was totally confused. "What am I supposed to do?"

The voice of her father came as if from another world, "Nothing."

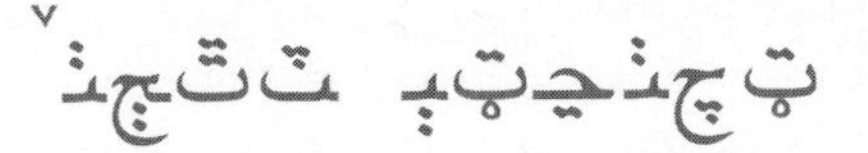

The swimming pool in the hotel Savoya was on the site where the old building stood in 1908. That year, a devastating earthquake and a tidal wave had hit Messina. Palermo suffered casualties, too. A new hotel, with tennis courts and a beautiful, marble swimming pool, was built. The ruins of the past had been forgotten.

A few teenagers and kids hung around, uneasy about entering the pool, in spite of the heated water. It was early afternoon before Christmas Eve and the residents had other things to do. Gordon didn't have any qualms of this kind. Helena watched him from the window. The young man was on the springboard. Helena couldn't help but admire the beautiful proportions of his body. He must've lost at least ten pounds since she met him, he was lean and well-toned with muscle. "He's changing awfully fast…too fast maybe," she mused. She had never seen muscle tissue develop so rapidly. And the face was now of a seventeen-year-old, chiseled to perfection — the face of Tutankhamon.

She grabbed a jacket and ran downstairs, all the way to the very edge of the pool but missed his dive. Now he was happily swimming across the pool. "Gordon, come here!"

The young man got out of the pool and trotted over like an eager puppy, some blood on the ridge of his nose. "Yes, Helena," he smiled at her with his glistening white teeth.

"How did you scrape your nose?"

The young man laughed gaily, "Oh, that's a mere nothing...I grazed the bottom a bit."

For a moment, Helena thought, "Marble doesn't leave marks like that..." then brushed it away.

"It's going to rain, you'll get pneumonia," she warned.

"I don't remember ever being sick," Gordon laughed.

"It could happen, no matter how healthy you are. Besides I need you," Helena beseeched him.

"Just tell me what you want."

He followed her silently to the suite. She gave him a towel, and he started rubbing himself energetically, saying, "I never knew what it is to have brothers and sisters. You're so much like an elder sister to me."

Helena was shattered. Was it possible that Gordon had forgotten they had been lovers in Jerusalem? "I need your company."

"Sure...where to?" he answered good naturedly.

"Put on your dark suit and tie. I want you to go to church with me."

Now it was Gordon's turn to be shocked. His sensual mouth hung open. "What for?"

"Don't tell me you've never been to church," chided Helena.

"I've never been to church. Both my parents were agnostics. I hate all religions, from animism to the most intellectualized ones equally, I mistrust some more than others. Going into a Catholic Church sets my teeth on edge. My short imprisonment in the monastery didn't help a lot. Catholic arrogant intolerance and interference with private affaires clashes with my deeply rooted individualism."

That was another shocker for Helena. Gordon never used such pompous words and judgments. He knew perfectly well that she graduated from a very conservative Catholic School.

"I don't know, Gordon. This lofty kind of talk doesn't sound like you.

"Why? Because I've spent more time in swimming pools than reading books?"

"No...because you don't read books at all."

Gordon bristled, "I had two years in college and passed my exams with good marks."

"Egyptology?"

"Yes, Egyptology. Why do you ask?"

"Because you know the subject, Gordon."

Gordon looked at the wet spots he had made on the floor. A small sigh slipped from Helena's lips, "You've got to learn to take your bath robe and wear it to the pool and back. Not everyone appreciates your great physical beauty in the hallways."

Gordon unceremoniously took off his wet swimming briefs and threw them into the sink. "Sorry. We don't have the same background. You can take Aldano along. You'll find him in his room. There is a church-going boy for you.

"How do you know he's in his room?" asked Helena.

"I checked on him to see if he wanted to come along for a swim. He eagerly changed into his briefs...then we had some differences and sorted them out on the spot. I don't think he has left his room since."

Helena was horrified. She ran to Aldano's room and entered without knocking. The room was in total disarray. Aldano was down on his knees, clad only in his swimming attire and wiping his badly swollen, bloody face on a shirt.

"Did Gordon beat you?" gasped Helena, bending down to get a better look.

Aldano was rocking with frustration and sputtered angrily, "Yeh...he knock me down flat, but next time it will be him, I promise you!"

Helena helped him to the bed. His rib cage had angry red bruises too.

"Don't fight with him, Aldano. Part of him is insane. He'll kill you like he killed my brother."

"Baloney, him and what army? I'll beat him to death with one hand tied to my back…he's just another bully-boy."

Finally Helena got him to rest on the bed, still huffing and puffing, eyes on fire.

"Quit that boyish talk. Gordon is not a neighborhood boy. Now he looks about your age but that's a phenomenon. He's a full-grown man with fiendish force inside him. Your chances with him are practically nonexistent."

"I can be fiendish too."

"That's what I'm afraid of, then your life will be in jeopardy, a mere toss in the void. What do you have to prove? Who, between the two of you, is more beastly? Do you really want to wreck your future for a competition of that kind?" Helena admonished the poor lad before her.

Aldano licked his broken lips, "O.K., I'll make a deal with you. If you'll help me smooth out this incident so I won't be sent home, I promise you not to be a sore loser. I'll make peace with Gordon."

Helena pushed the mop of shiny golden hair from his forehead and looked into his angry eyes, "Why do you want to stick with him?"

Aldano put his large hand over her shoulder and in a gentle, subdued voice said, "For the same reason as you, Helena."

A couple of hours later they walked in easy strides toward a small church not far from their hotel. Helena had fixed up Aldano's face and he looked great in his brand new dark suit and flashy tie bought in spite of Helena's conservative better judgment. He loved that tie so much that she didn't want to break his heart. He never had so many expensive presents. Shoes from Gucci, shirt and socks by Leonardo, underwear and handkerchief from an English store. His old clothing was sent in a package to the hotel.

It really felt like Christmas.

"Your father must be rich as an Arab Sheik."

Helena laughed, "That's exactly what he is."

"At first I took it as a joke. A Sheik staying with my dad?"

Helena's face darkened, and she became more subdued. "No, it isn't a joke."

"But you're a Catholic," Aldano pressed.

"By my mother's choice."

"Because she was Catholic?"

"No, she was a Copt," answered Helena evenly.

"What is a Copt?"

"A true Egyptian from the ancient vein, versed in the Hamitic language. She didn't want me to follow her religion either. Mother wanted me to marry a European. She believed that someone with an accursed past could flee from it by changing name, place and social status," Helena went on to explain to the bewildered youth.

It was getting dark and all of the holiday decorations seem to come to life bathed in multicolored lights. A lot of people were moving along the sidewalk, looking at the window displays or busy with last minute shopping. Aldano took her hand shyly and peered into the large, sad eyes of the young woman.

"I know I'm only an escort, a stand-in for Gordon. I'm not even a full-grown man according to your standards, but…wouldn't you consider…marrying me? I haven't any credit cards and no predictable future in sight. All I have is a loving father and a family of rowdy brothers. I'm sure we can protect you from any curse, no matter how ancient it is. In the name of God, I can make you happy, Helena!"

Helena took his hand up to her lips and set a little kiss over the scars on his knuckles. Aldano embraced her right in the middle of the crowded sidewalk and exclaimed, "Gordon will never marry you. He cannot marry anyone. He doesn't belong to this world anymore. You know it, Helena. This old, secretive man is not his grandfather. He's linked to him in a mysterious way. Gordon is a stranger with no family, no friends…nobody."

Helena kissed him lightly on the lips and whispered, "Except for you and me."

During the night a terrible storm invaded the island of Sicily. Gusting winds and torrential rains left Palermo without electric power and only a partially operating phone system. Under the circumstances, all scheduled activities were postponed.

An overdue press conference was to take place on the first day after the storm. Television cameras were not allowed inside City Hall. Dr. Moughabee received arriving reporters with courtesy and invited them to eat, drink and relax. The Vatican Diplomatic Delegation went on to the conference room with all possible pomp. Only Gordon Bates was missing.

He swam through murky water to the deepest part of the pool under the diving board and settled on the bottom until Helena came for him. That was sufficient. She had stayed away from him for three days and he was becoming increasingly difficult. Under her guidance he dressed quickly in his best suit and used Helena's hair dryer. Aldano called a taxicab for him.

The conference had started. A fat cardinal read a message from the Pope himself. It had little to do with the situation. The sermon was about Christ and His birth and how important to the Christian world were the facts — every single detail — leading to this most important period of human history.

Luke warm applause followed. There were no questions. The fat cardinal introduced Dr. Moughabee from Memphis, Tennessee, USA. Suddenly everyone in the room rose, hands in the air. The Nubian called on the representative of *Curia Romana*. They had met many times before and some mutual understanding and sympathy existed between them.

"With all due respect, Dr. Moughabee, will you give us some explanation about what is happening. Rumors have prevailed but not a single fact. What have you really found out, and how much of it pertains to the basic tenets of contemporary religion?"

Moughabee seemed to fight some last minute hesitations, then as he opened his mouth to speak, a slight tremor passed through everyone present. Suddenly, with a thunderous roar, the floor under their feet disappeared, and they felt as if they were falling toward the center of earth. The lights flickered off and chunks of masonry started falling, causing clouds of dust to make breathing almost impossible. In Italy everyone knew that most dreaded occurrence from birth. Even as the earthquake started to abate, a new, even more powerful shock hit savagely.

It seemed to be the end, but the end wasn't supposed to be that easy. Those that had survived groped their way out of the ruined building. Aftershocks followed. Walls that had remained standing after the initial shock were crumbling to pieces over the heads of the audience.

It was shortly after eleven in the morning and the square was full of people, mostly curiosity seekers attracted by newspaper and television commentaries on the recent events in Jerusalem, as well as the delegation from the Vatican. Maybe there was some truth in the rumors that *Corpus Christi* had been discovered. Many countries around the world wanted a piece of it, but of course it had to stay in Italy!

The crowd had turned ugly. Obviously God had been rendered mad and the people in the Executive Palace had done it. The attention was focused on Moughabee. He might've been the Devil himself.

"That is it! That's him!" the people screamed.

There was a mighty growl. The sky held scattered clouds. At that moment, the sun disappeared behind a thick one. It was as if the light suddenly had died. A cold wind blew in from the ocean.

Moughabee continued to walk unhurriedly, but came to a group of protesters. "Here he is, the Blasphemer! God damn you!"

A chunk of masonry caught Moughabee's shoulder. He turned and calmly faced his assailants, "You can damn only yourself. Yours is the Curse!"

Another projectile drew blood from his forehead. "Don't attack me. Punish yourself first. God's anger is upon you!"

He was bleeding. Ouloulangha caught up with him and shielded him as they walked to the rented Cadillac. Half a brick shattered the window. Another smashed Ouloulangha's face.

"Lynch them! Hang the niggers with their neckties, up to the lamp posts!" the crowd shouted as one.

Ayram left the car trying to save his employer. He helped him into the back seat, but he himself fell under the barrage of stones. A fragment hit him right on the head. A new aftershock, even mightier than the others scattered the mob. From an arriving taxi cab, Gordon ran over the piles of stone, took the car keys from the dead hand of Ayram and hurled himself on the driver's seat.

Moughabee vomited blood on the back seat. Miraculously the battered Cadillac started instantly. Gordon commandeered the vehicle through a confused and scattering crowd. Nobody tried to stop him. Then, they were out of the square and heading inland at top speed.

At the hotel, several blocks away, a bedraggled manager told the house detective that the vault had been raided while police invaded the premises and the mummy was missing. Helena and Aldano were charged with its theft and, in spite of the manager's rigorous protesting, they were taken to a military camp on the outskirts of the devastated city.

Gordon was so busy driving out of the city that he had no time to check on the condition of his only passenger. Streets were split in two by wide fissures. The cracks were long and snake-like. Parts of Palermo were untouched, others brought to total destruction.

Fires had started here and there; crowds of people covered with dust desperately tried to dig bodies out of the ruins. Others stood as motionless as statues, still shell-shocked. Water, electricity and communications ran sporadically. Fire engines and police patrols were ineffective. A tidal wave was expected at any moment.

Gordon drove toward the foothills. He illegally passed straight through a military check point without stopping. Two motorcycles gave him chase, but were soon outrun. The young man wondered why? Obviously something more important had happened. Maybe Gordon's thinking was confused too.

He came to the top of a hill overlooking the harbor. Some gas tanks had caught fire and spread enormous plumes of black smoke, thickened by the clouds of dust that still hung over the city. Gordon turned to ask Dr. Moughabee if a tidal wave could be triggered in an enclosed sea like the Mediterranean. He simply didn't believe his eyes. Moughabee was gone! What was there, God Almighty, was the mummy of Lord Aton. Suddenly the young man heard a deep, profound voice.

"Well done, Ikhnaton. Now we've gotten the best out of the worst, though this is just the beginning," the mummy spoke, materializing in his immortal image.

Then Gordon heard his own voice, though he knew well that it was Ikhnaton talking.

"What happened to Moughabee, Teacher?"

"Peter is where he always wanted to be — at the door," Lord Aton answered.

"What door?"

"There has been only one door to the universe. The Only God resides behind it. You are not to know where the Gates of Heaven are." The shock of this announcement gave an upper hand to Gordon's identity.

"Dear God, let me be with my grandfather…and my friends!" Gordon pleaded.

After a tense pause, there was another earthquake that lasted for half a minute and jolted the rocks from their foundations. Large chunks of sandstone fell across the only access to the doomed city.

The pharaoh was incensed. "What friends, vainglorious boy?" Ikhnaton said laughingly, "You don't have any friends. Ouloulangha is dead. Peter is gone. Who is your friend on this wretched planet? Don't listen to him, Aton. This is the voice of the lad I use for my terrestrial gallivanting. He's nobody. A slave, a moron, a construction worker despised by everyone. Even his parents were ashamed of him. I need his body to enter the Gates of Heaven."

"Who told you that you'd be passing through those Gates, lkhnaton?" came the deep voice.

"I've suffered enough in the emptiness. You owe me that much, My Lord!"

"I owe you nothing! Get out of my sight and don't bother this man anymore." Aton looked at Gordon, "What is your name, boy?"

"Gordon," he croaked.

"Get me out of this broken contraption and bury me under those rocks. Then you can go back and help your friends," commanded the image of Aton.

The young man felt free and better than he had anytime recently, but a look in the cracked side mirror told him the truth. It was the face of young Moughabee. Same flat nose, full lips and bronze complexion.

"They won't let me go near them, My Lord. I'm so ugly," he cried.

"Your ugliness is deceiving, Gordon, because from now on, you'll have a beautiful soul and people will see nothing but your soul. Go back to the desperate inhabitants of this unfortunate city and bring them good tidings: the Kingdom to come will be more wonderful than any city they knew."

"They'll mourn children and homes, friends and brothers... Take my soul and give them back their meager terrestrial happiness," Gordon begged.

"In the name of God Almighty, let it be so! Strive for their happiness, and if you win, they'll win...and if you lose, everyone will be lost." Then, Aton's apparition dissipated and his voice was no more. The mummy in the backseat was, once more, just a mummy.

Chapter 11

GORDON FINDS HIS MISSION

The car wouldn't start. Anyway, it was of little use to Gordon, as the road toward the city was heavily blocked by a rockslide.

He looked up the hill where he had just buried the mummy of Lord Aton. He didn't leave any marks, his heart knew where He was. If someone had seen Gordon this morning dressed in a dark business suit with coordinating tie and shoes, handsome as a movie star, that same person would've had no idea who this particular young man was. Covered head to toe in dust, clothes and shoes ragged and torn by the rocks, Gordon was a sight. Not only that, but his face was now square, dominated by a fleshy nose and high cheekbones; mouth, large, with full sensuous lips and dark eyes peering under a thatch of unkempt hair. His coworkers on the construction site back in Memphis, Tennessee, would've had no trouble recognizing him.

However, the Gordon Bates of today had become more articulate than he ever was in his former life. He climbed over the fallen rocks, and with a light jump, found himself on the side of the road heading back to what was left of Palermo. He walked down the road, thirsty as hell, but he was used to putting up with hardships.

For the first time, he felt like someone with a mission in life. In spite of his condition, he felt great. He knew where he was going and why. That made a whole lot of difference.

Peter Moughabee whispered in his mind, "It won't be easy, son. I can now do little, if anything, for you."

"I know, granddad, but thank you anyway," Gordon answered.

"Forget the 'grandpa' business, I'm your natural father. My attorney in Memphis will settle most of the problems. I left everything I have to you, though, it's not much. You'll be on your own. I cannot help you anymore unless the Lord looks the other way. Your credit cards are good for the time being. Don't trust the American consul in Palermo. He hates blacks. Try to get in touch with the third secretary in Rome. His name is Lincoln White. He'll be eager to come and help you. Now, goodbye son. I'll be held for a while on Sirius. Bureaucracy is stagnant everywhere. If you look at that distant planet in the night sky, I'll feel it, I'll know you're thinking of me. But don't count on me very much. In most cases I can give you only love and sympathy. Can't take the bitter cup from your lips. To serve God, you must suffer. There's no other way. He punishes those that He loves so they can prove themselves. I tried to get by with some old tricks and that's the reason I'm being recalled. I might be stuck again in the middle of nowhere for a few centuries. Ouloulangha is also on his own. I haven't even seen him. So I hope you do better than us, the old warriors."

Gordon didn't change the rhythm of his steps. "What am I supposed to do next, father?"

"That I don't know. Now I have to leave you. Anubis, the warden, is coming back, and he's watching me like a hawk. I don't want to get into more trouble if I can help it. Adieu!"

Gordon laughed as he hadn't laughed in ages. "Adieu, father! I won't bother you or Mr. Lincoln White. I'll make it on my own!" For no specific reason, he felt inordinately happy.

Hotel Savoya was split in two. A chain of policemen cordoned off the building from the street entrance to the parking lot. Gordon explained that he resided in room 703 and asked for someone to call the acting manager.

The manager's eyes were feverish. He wrung his hands in absolute despair unable to recognize that young man as the resident of room 703. Mr. Gordon Bates was a rather handsome guy with a very rich uncle.

"Father," Gordon corrected him quietly, "Dr. Moughabee."

"Yes, of course, Dr. Moughabee," stuttered the manager, "there was a call for him on the radio."

Gordon lifted his thick eyebrows. "From Malta?"

The manager tried to escape his sharp eyes. "Yes, from Malta."

"What happened to Ms. Helena?"

The manager gasped for air. "Ms. Helena?"

"Yes, Ms. Helena, the daughter of Sheik El Barrack."

"I don't know. I think she might have been arrested in the confusion."

Gordon moved his metallic eyes to the face of the police captain. "Was she arrested?"

The captain shrugged his shoulders. A policeman came to his side. "I was at the palace this morning. There was a young man that drove off with Dr. Moughabee…just after the assault by the mob."

"This young man?" asked the captain, nodding toward Gordon.

The policeman looked furtively at Gordon. "What can I say, Captain? Half an hour ago, I didn't recognize my own face in a piece of glass."

Gordon looked back at the manager. "Was Mr. Aldano Brandon taken in custody too?"

"The blond youth?...Yes...I'm afraid he was."

"On what charges?" asked Gordon angrily.

"Stealing a priceless mummy from the vault," The captain retorted boldly, then added, "Yes, stealing marauders. What do you have to say on that matter?"

"Plain nonsense. The mummy belongs to my father. He took it out of the vault this morning and placed it in the trunk of his car for display in the palace."

The captain was taken aback. "What's your name, by the way?"

Gordon handed him his passport. "You can radio anyone at the U.S. Embassy in Rome. I'm sure they will be interested in knowing that my father, his secretary and his bodyguard were killed by a mob in the center of Palermo, right under your noses. Then you arrest the daughter of one of the richest men in the world, Sheik El Barrack. My compliments, Captain," sneered Gordon.

The captain passed Gordon's passport into the shaky hands of the manager. "It seems to be the same person."

The manager adjusted his glasses on the ridge of his curved nose.

"Yes, I remember now. Mr. Gordon Bates. There was some discrepancy regarding the photo, but there is none now."

The captain was getting nervous. "*Madonna Mi*a! What do you mean? Is it him or not?"

The shaken little man looked helplessly one more time at the picture and Gordon. "I don't know...It must be the same person...I don't remember giving the keys to the vault to anyone. I usually open the steel gate myself. Damn *Terremoto*! As you see, I was hit in the head." The manager indicated the ineptly applied bandage on his head.

The captain pulled Gordon's passport briskly from the manager's hands. "Well, Mr. Bates, let's go to Headquarters."

Hussney El Barrack was in bed, propped with pillows. Brandon was scanning the TV channels in search of more news about the devastating earthquake in Sicily. Palermo was almost in the epicenter. It happened shortly before noontime on a lovely day after a storm. Not many people stayed home, so fewer victims were expected. Suddenly a live scene from the central square in Palermo replaced the stock footage. The announcer's voice climbed: "We just received this videotape of a few dramatic moments after the quake. It's right in front of the palace." The scene cut to an ugly crowd armed with fragments of jagged plaster and rocks. Another cut to Moughabee and Ayram walking directly toward the camera. Ouloulangha was behind them trying to shield his boss with an attaché case.

Hussney was horrified. "*Allah Acbar!*"

Brandon sat helplessly on the bed staring at the television.

Moughabee was hit by several projectiles, Ouloulangha's face vanished in a cloud of blood and broken bones. He fell to the ground. Moughabee was bleeding heavily as well. Ayram, bent under the weight, carried him to the back seat of a car with smashed windows, then, hit on top of his head, he fell backwards. Suddenly, out of nowhere Gordon appeared. He jumped catlike into the driver's seat then everything disappeared in the dust he left behind.

The announcer stuttered with confusion, "I really don't know who those people are…some foreign dignitaries perhaps. The crew inside the palace has the names, but we haven't heard of them…wait a minute, now one of the editors is suggesting some names…what?…it's unclear…Doctor, did you say doctor? Ah…Moughabee, Dr. Moughabee from the USA…yes, I know…he was in the center of all the newscasts…but do you have any idea why he was peppered with rocks? What? Two fatalities confirmed…I'm sorry to announce that the Secretary of Dr.

Moughabee and his bodyguard are dead, murdered by a mob of religious zealots. The fate of Moughabee and his grandson isn't known at this time. We'll keep you posted…a moment, please" — silence, then the reporter came back on, "I was just informed that two marauders have been arrested in Grand Hotel Savoya. The daughter of Sheik El Barrack? This can't be! We need confirmation. Ladies and gentlemen, a police captain has just been demoted for wrongful arrests. However, the whereabouts of those arrested is still unknown…" The screen faded and snowflakes filled it. A husky voice cried out, "Another quake!"

The colonel looked at the large crack over the ceiling and tried to dust off his elegant uniform making a quick sign of the cross, then hollered to the radioman, "*Ancor' unno…eh, Spaddino, quecosa fa?* Move the damn radio to a tent, I'm not staying indoors to be killed by the next earthquake." Then he turned toward Gordon, "Let's get out of here, Mr. Bates, *prego*. You're not under arrest. I don't care who forbids it, we'll move to a tent, I didn't make the earth shake, do you smoke? My hands are shaking. Sit down, *prego*…I don't have the slightest idea why your father and his secretary were killed. I heard talk about that mummy but no explanations whatsoever."

"I want to know where my friends are kept!"

Ma comme mai?…The computers are out…you heard the radio…only static. *Io non sonno Dio!…Non mi fa riddere!* How am I supposed to know anything without communications? I have a son, a *studente* in America. Thank God, he's out of this mess. You're O.K. with me. The city's gone mad."

"My friends should be under your protection too. They have been brought to the camp."

"*Va bene*...go and find them. There is hardly anybody left in the *campo*. I was ordered to stay here, otherwise I would be looking for my family."

"Give me back my passport."

"Here is your *passeporto*. I'll write you a note...oh, *Dio mio*, I have nothing to write with."

Gordon placed his passport in front of the colonel who was melting in greasy sweat. "Here. Plenty of empty pages. You can have my pen too."

"For keeps?"

"Sure...you can have it."

"*E molto bello*...a Parker. Listen, *Americano*, I'm not going to stay here alone. Take your passport. I'll come along with you. If we stay together, we may be able to find somebody."

The familiar sickening noise started vibrating in the air and a peculiar light appeared in the sky. This strongest aftershock made them feel as if the ground under their feet disappeared. The colonel was finished.

"Let's get the hell out of here, I've had enough, *basta*!"

During the months preceding Palermo's earthquake, several other quakes had struck in different parts of the world — Turkey, Taiwan, South America and Greece. There were unprecedented changes in weather patterns, such as hurricanes and tornados that affected the two Americas, gigantic storms that swept over the northwestern part of Europe, torrential rains in Africa and draughts scorched India and Australia. Crops were burned by a pitiless sun and then frozen during unusually sever winters, coupled with political upheaval, terrible economic disasters occurred. The twentieth century was pockmarked with wars, revolutions and social unrest. A feeling that doomsday was upon the world engendered a number of religious cults, some of them deadly. UFO sightings became everyday events and bordered on mass psychoses. Even the mighty economies of the world's leading powers took a beating. Inflation and corruption were rampant. With a heavy overpopulation, came racial intolerance and many new diseases and epidemics. The upper crust of the world's population made a comfortable living; unabridged sex and violent entertainment were the name of the game. Easy access to fire arms made terrorism a way of life. Even six-year-olds were killing each other, mothers killing their children, fathers involved in kidnapping, sons and daughters murdered their parents, the family as a basic unit came to a state of near collapse.

Arms for bacterial and thermonuclear warfare were capable of destroying our planet several times over. Scientists were busy working at saving human lives, then finding ways to destroy them even faster.

Men walked on the bright side of the moon, but mankind knew only the dark side. Doomsday predictions were coming from the past and the present; not a single sign of hope for the future.

Probes were sent to different cosmic points.

The universe was silent.

THEATER OF THE ABSTRACT

In the eternal twilight of Sirius everything looked distant and unreal. That little dot at the base of a silver hill was actually a human being, or shall we say, the remnants of a being, his phantom Ka. Lord Aton didn't have to move in order to get closer, He just had to think of it, a divine property strictly out of reach for the common soul. Moughabee knew how to do it but lacked the official blessing. "Something like driving around a city without a driver's permit," thought Moughabee with a little smile lingering over his full lips, "I should try it some day." Of course, that was just a mental note.

As if made out of the fabric consisting of the air on this planet, Lord Aton appeared in front of him.

"Are you still brooding about that young man Gordon, Peter?"

Moughabee sighed somewhat longingly, "For him and for the rest of the bunch. You know me, Divine Lord, I'm *homus terrae*. What's here for me?"

"I know, Peter. Stop devising crafty plans. Gordon has to cleanse himself inside and out before you step into him."

"That isn't fair, Lord Aton. He's nothing but a lowly human. How do you expect him to face up to the demons of the underworld?"

"I think he's doing pretty well for the time being. Unprotected as he is, he counts only on his own strength. Ikhnaton is in retreat."

"Oh, Lord, You know better than that. Ikhnaton is tricky and knows how to manipulate a young man," protested Peter Moughabee.

"We've all been young and we made our fair share of mistakes. Let him err. Only in that way will he find his spot in the Creation. I became attached to all of you; my twelve disciples. That's why I am still hanging around here. From the whole universe, I chose you twelve to call my family."

Moughabee fell down on his knees. "You know me, Lord, I can never get rid of my earthliness!"

"You don't have to, Peter. Learn only how to dominate your passions."

"What am I without my passions, Lord?"

"A Saint, Peter, a common Earthly Saint. For the time being, guard the Gates to Heaven. And remember, don't go back home before I tell you. Have faith in me, it won't be long."

HOTEL SAVOYA: TIME WARP BEFORE THE QUAKE

At the time of the first jolt, Helena was showing Aldano her best dive, a backward somersault. She was the focal point of everyone around the swimming pool. The day was warm and sunny so most of the hotel's guests had gathered to watch the swimmers. Paul Le Gogguen the Abbot and Professor Midhad or Sergey, had gone to the diocese. For some strange reason, access to the meeting in the

Government Palace was refused to every one of them. Professor Midhad wanted to know why and the Abbot was his go between.

Helena cleared her head of everything not pertaining to the jump. She felt at peace with the whole world, a tiny particle of it but quite important in its own sphere. Her feet were lightly touching the springboard; she was ready to take off into the weightlessness of a sublime moment when her strong, young body created the instantaneous explosive force of the dive. The smallest miscalculation could be lethal. If the back of her head hit the board's edge she would drown. Like a snap shot in her mind's eye, she saw Gordon, as he left for the conference that morning. Dressed in his elegant dark suit, white shirt and silver tie, his face dominated by indescribable masculine beauty. Why did she think that she was seeing him for the last time in her life?

The Prince of Darkness!

A sixth sense prompted her not to perform this dangerous dive right now, but with all those people watching it was impossible not to make a dive. Helena did a perfect take off, but then, she suddenly felt completely disoriented. She hit the water, and a greedy vortex formed, as if a wide abyss to the center of Earth had opened in the pool's bottom. She had to use all her strength to extract herself from this horrid gravitation just to surface in a totally different world. Glass panels of the Savoya were exploding with loud crashing sounds. The whole building split in two as if cleaved by a gigantic sword. People were screaming and running in all directions. Some fell down and struggled back to their feet, others prayed on their knees. The shock was so great, that Helena started to drown, her energy completely depleted. Aldano made a running dive from the edge of the pool just in time to grab her. He swam with his precious catch to the shallow waters, and they both sat on the marble steps gasping for air.

"It's a giant earthquake," said Aldano haltingly, "it hit right at the moment you hit the water."

Another mighty jolt shook everything around.

"It feels like the end of Earth," said Helena, her teeth clattering spasmodically. "Do you think they'll survive?"

Aldano looked at her with a mixture of jealousy and sorrow. "You mean Gordon? Oh, yeh, he'll survive anything. He's practically indestructible."

Their bathrobes and towels had disappeared. The hotel guards were preventing anyone from entering the badly damaged building. The manager came out in a torn shirt and bleeding.

"The police will be here any minute. I've got the desk log here. After a quick identification, you'll be permitted to get your property. The management has to protect you from looters."

When the police arrived, it was discovered that the hotel's vault had been broken into. The house detective was positive that the dare-devil robbery had been performed by insiders.

Helena and Aldano were arrested in their swimwear along with an eleven-year-old bellboy. No one gave them any explanation. A police car took the suspects to an unknown destination.

At the same military camp where Gordon was talking with the colonel, Helena and Aldano were being fitted with prison garb. The slightly hunchbacked figure of Paul Le Gogguen appeared in the open flap of the tent. He had an order for their release signed by the commander of the division.

Professor Midhad hurriedly returned to his home in Messina. He was very worried about his priceless collection of Etruscan and Egyptian artifacts. Rumors of a powerful eruption of Mt. Etna spread all over the island. Masses of people started moving to higher elevations. Gangs of marauders terrorized the northern cities with little opposition from the police or the army. Most plain clothes men deserted their units in search of families and relatives. The coastal population was evacuated in fear of a tidal wave like the one that struck in 1908. The Government Palace suffered heavy damages and many human casualties. Rumors of riots crisscrossed Palermo, and Paul Le Gogguen feared the worse was yet to come. Many foreigners had been assaulted in the city. The last he had heard on the radio was about the Pope's imminent visit to Palermo and Northern Sicily. The Abbot thought that he and his young charges should go back to Malta immediately.

On their way out of the camp, very few soldiers were seen and not a single officer. No one asked for any documents at the gate. The scooter that Paul Le Gogguen had used to come up to the camp had disappeared. They walked toward the city in silence, a few helicopters hovering over their heads in search of looters.

Helena tried to organize her thoughts. "Is it possible to find a short-wave radio so we can get in touch with my father? I'm sure Aldano would like to talk to his dad in Malta as well."

The Abbot looked toward the cityscape. It was still covered with a layer of dust and smoke from the burning petrol tanks. "I tried already, Helena. The network is dead."

"Do you have any idea what has happened?"

"No, I don't. I don't have any idea about anything that's happening now. I am poorly prepared to cope with a situation of this kind. Of course we were taught many things in theory…they seem so useless now. Dr. Peter Moughabee and Ouloulangha have been attacked by a mob at the very heart of a civilized, modern city. There is no reason to hide the truth from you. They are dead and Gordon is arrested. The mummy has disappeared without a trace. Maybe Gordon knows something about it, but he won't talk."

Against the yellowish tint of the sky, the three silhouettes of those three human beings looked downright grotesque, like characters in an oriental theatre of shadows.

After Gordon's release, he stood in front of the cataclysmic ruins of the Governmental Palace. It had happened just this morning; the bloody spots on the pieces of masonry and on the sidewalk were still visible. So many things had occurred over the past few hours that caused him to be set in a world unknown to him. "And that's just the beginning..." Peter Moughabee had said to him. When? Yesterday, or in another life? At least he now knew who his biological father was. Was it too late to call him father? THE FATHER he was looking for all his life! Anyway, he never believed the "grandpa" story. Did this knowledge change anything? Perhaps. What was the meaning of the mummy? An artifact to be taken on a grand tour around all the major cities — Moscow and Antwerp, Lisbon and Cherbourg, Shanghai, Melbourne, Bangkok and New Delhi. From the United States to the Arab Emirates — a circus of a kind no one had seen before.

He was so deeply engaged in his thoughts that neither the aftershocks nor the fading of the daylight made an impression on him. Only the presence of people brought him gradually back to his senses.

Who were those people?

The same men that killed his father and Ouloulangha with stones? Or the denizens that had lost their city? He turned and looked into the haggard faces of those men. Who was he to speak to them? Him, the biggest imbecile of them all! He didn't know even a word of their language.

But an overwhelming inner voice called him to his duty.

"BROTHERS," He said...

And that was just the beginning.

Chapter 12

GORDON'S EPIPHANY

Since this morning I've made many fundamental discoveries. First, that I am the one and only Gordon Bates. If I don't believe in and respect myself, the rest of mankind won't either — I'll be clad in obscurity. My father is not that man with the detestable, pencil-like moustache. I must've been blind not to see my face and body build in Peter Moughabee. Of course, his age and corpulence had hidden young Peter, but I should've seen the resemblance to me. Now that I've finally found myself, I can do something useful. So far, my father's credit card has paid the bills. From now on, I have to pay my bills myself. Any kind of work is good enough for me, but…do I really want it? When I spoke to the people by the ruins of the palace, I suddenly felt that I made sense. Those people didn't know a word of English. Nevertheless, they understood what I said. Is it possible that I was speaking Italian?

I must find Helena and Aldano. The Hotel Savoya is off limits. I cannot look for them everywhere myself. Police cars throughout the city have proclaimed through their loudspeakers that anyone seen loitering after dark will be shot on the spot. That message wasn't in English but I understood. I am dusty and in rags like everyone else. I went to the beach and made myself comfortable. The sky was clear with distant stars and a full moon shining right on my face. The monotonous beating of the surf lulled me to sleep, dead tired as I was, I felt like praying. Easier said than done.

Nobody ever taught me how to pray. I don't believe in God…not really true. Actually, I do. I just don't know how to express it. Some day I have to find out how for myself, my own way.

Why not now? Here it's quiet and secluded. Nobody will hear me.

Dear God…too maudlin? I'll say, My Lord, what's next? Is it possible to find Helena and Aldano? Am I a moron? Christ Almighty! Let me start anew, strike that, please.

Thank you, God, for giving me another chance.

Gordon spotted an old boat halfway up the shore. It was better than nothing. He cuddled into it and tried to get some sleep. Then suddenly he rose up on his elbows, not quite sure if he felt an aftershock or the old boat had moved. He waited carefully and counted to ten.

Nothing.

An icy blast of air hit him in the face. What was that, a sudden wind? But the splashing of the small waves had stopped. The sea was withdrawing at a mind-boggling speed. He didn't know if the moonlight was playing tricks with his eyes, but something gigantic seemed to be rushing toward the shore.

"Oh, no-o-o…a Tidal Wave!" went through his mind like lightning.

For a few moments Gordon was paralyzed with fear. What was he to do? jump from the boat and run for his life? He could not outrun that monster. He couldn't ride it like a surfer either, the very impact would kill him. He'd be simply pulverized. Suddenly, Gordon overcame his fear.

Gordon lay on the bottom of the boat. The Monster was towering over him like a skyscraper. He moved his head under the seat realizing the futility of his act. "I hope this is just a nightmare," he thought, “I slept most of my life. Perhaps, when I wake up, it will be a bright and cheery morning.”

Helena and Aldano lost hope of finding Gordon. They were now traveling in a vehicle purloined by the Abbot from the diocese’s carpool. It was an ancient Fiat in a corner of the garage. All flights into and out of Palermo had been cancelled, so the alternative was to find a plane to Malta from Messina. Someone told them that Messina’s airport had been reopened. Two roads led to that city. One followed the sea shore, the other was on the mountainside. In spite of the many rock slides, the mountain road was relatively safe. According to the specialists, the threat of a tidal wave had receded. Most people didn’t believe it and stayed away from the sea.

It was close to midnight and the moonlight was so bright that the panoramic view of the shoreline was clearly visible for miles and miles ahead. Helena was the first one to see the retreating sea. She pointed it out to Aldano and Le Gogguen.

“Is it possible for a tidal wave to be born without a major earthquake? It has been hours since the last jolt,” asked Helena,

Le Gogguen was afraid to take his eyes from the road. They had come to a point in the road where a whole piece was missing. He stopped the car and set on the hand brake. “If our time has come, anything could happen,” he told his companions.

Aldano had the sharpest eyes. “Look there! The sea has started building a wall! Can it strike up to here?”

“It can hit even higher elevations,” Le Gogguen replied in a shaky voice.

Helena couldn’t tear her eyes from the ever-growing wall of water. “What shall we do, Father?”

“Leave the car immediately and run up behind that rock.”

Helena and Aldano abandoned the car and scampered up to safety. The priest was too slow.

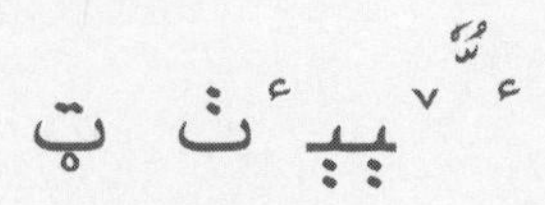

When Gordon regained consciousness, it was a bright morning. Soon he recognized the place, the hill where he had buried the mummy.

"I got the message, Lord Aton," he mumbled to himself. "Belief in you comes with some benefits. I promise, I'll earn my pay."

A miracle isn't a miracle if it can be explained.

Chapter 13

IN THE SHADOW OF MOUNT ETNA

In Messina, the small house of Professor Midhad hadn't suffered serious damage. It was at the bottom of a garden gone wild in a newer part of the city. Even though most of the new apartment buildings were rendered uninhabitable, the little house of the old professor stood in spite of the savage quakes. There was no electricity or water and the phone was dead, but the old man wasn't fussy. He washed his face and hands in the large fountain behind the house that seemed to be thriving in spite of adversity. Not that the fountain was of unusual beauty, but it had once belonged to a rambling palace, destroyed in a previous earthquake. The coach-house and the fountain had survived, and Professor Midhad bought them.

Some time ago, a wealthy American couple made a generous offer to buy the property, but he refused to sell it. He loved to sit on the marble benches remembering his childhood in a similar place. A museum piece victrola provided the music from carefully preserved ancient records.

Everything seemed to have been forgotten by time, even his professorial title. To be fair, every once in awhile he would publish a controversial but astonishing work on Egyptian rites and mysteries. Gradually, he became an authority on those matters to a point that no one ever thought of rivaling him. He became reclusive and never gave a single interview about his life. Most of all he hated to be photographed. He once sued a French newspaper for printing an article about his youth. It was accompanied by an early snapshot of him fishing in a pond with another young boy. His collections of Egyptian artifacts were rarely seen, and strangely, he had very few books of his own. When he needed to check up on something, he visited the public library a few blocks away. He'd never been seen driving a car. For short visits to Palermo or to another country, he used sea-going transportation. Before coming to Messina, he had had another life, but no one remembered what that was anymore. On nice days, he would hire one of the old phaetons kept for tourists and spend the day picnicking in a lonely cove by the sea. His sole company — the cabdriver and his horses.

The professor never owned a TV set or a simple radio for that matter. He was not interested in information and progress. When policemen, because of the threat of Mount Etna's eruption, advised him to evacuate his place, Professor Midhad said quite seriously: "You have to shoot me dead before removing me from my property. From this distance, Etna cannot make things much worse than they already are."

He then closed his door in their faces. The gendarmes didn't care about that *pazzo professore*, so they left. By now everyone in the city knew that foolish Sergio meant what he said.

When somebody knocked at his door late one night, he wasn't afraid to open it. In the murky light of a silver candelabrum, he had no problem recognizing the smudged faces of Helena and Aldano.

"Come in," he said without a trace of emotion, "you must've had a hard time."

At the very end of their physical and mental endurance, they didn't wait for another invitation. The old man fretted around them as very lonely people who are unused to company.

"Sit down, sit down, children. How silly of me. I didn't have much furniture to start with. You have been here before. The telephone is out of service, I've lost my eyeglasses, too. I'm sure I have another pair somewhere. You must be very hungry."

His young visitors were confused by the unexpected verbosity of this usually shy and taciturn man, so they said nothing.

"I know. I have a Primus stove, butter, eggs and cheese. I can make some scrambled eggs," announced the professor. "I'll grate some cheese in it. Sorry, I haven't a crumb of bread."

To say that they weren't hungry would've been far fetched, so the uninvited guests remained silent. They moved toward something that looked like a chest covered with a blanket.

"Those are my phono-records, children. Sit on the Moroccan puffs, then we will fix something for the night. Anyway, we'll have little time to rest. Anytime now, Miss Etna is going to start throwing some pyrotechnics. I feel it in my old bones. She's quite a prima donna. She's furious to be outdone by another natural force, so she'll try to flex her muscle, just for the show."

He lit the Primus stove and started pumping it with such skill that it led them to believe this strange gadget was a permanent fixture in the old man's kitchen.

"You know what, kids," said Sergey, looking for a frying pan, "while I cook your food here, you can take a dip in the fountain at the back. It looks as if you can profit from a cold bath."

Helena and Aldano were so mesmerized by their host that they followed his orders without any objections. Their tattered clothes were more of a hindrance than protection. It had taken them a whole day and the best part of a night walking cross-country to arrive out here. Their shoes simply fell off their aching feet. Under the generous light of a unsentimental moon, they peeled off what used to be clothing, and looked at each other with heavily thumping hearts.

"Helena."

"Aldano."

When the food was ready, Sergey went to the back door and looked out, then came back and ate the scrambled eggs. "Every cloud has a silver lining," he thought with a little smile in his faded lips. "Those ancient Kas don't like to be trapped in a human body during a natural disaster. Now, all I have to do is to prevent them from re-entering these youngsters."

Scientists are known to underestimate the powers opposed to them, but in this particular case, Sergey's estimate wasn't based on scientific research, but on something far more ticklish — LOVE.

Against all probability, humanity had survived miraculously through unbelievable calamities. Life, on the whole, is far stronger than matter. Spirits seems to prevail over darkness at approximately a three to one ratio. Surprisingly, many citizens of Palermo came out unscathed even by the second disaster, mainly because a sixth sense told them to get as far from the sea as they could. Obviously, the placement of Gordon right in front of that giant wall of water was the call of his destiny.

Spiritual healing has to precede the physical, because the other way around is dangerous and unpredictable. In those few days after the great natural disaster, people started whispering to each other that they were not alone — Christ had come again to heel their wounds and boost their hopes. They had lost everything, but they had found Him. People from all walks of life had seen Him — solitary persons and whole groups, He had nothing but a loin cloth around his hips and a soft golden light around His head. Nobody was able to remember what He said to the crowds that gathered around Him. His presence was what mattered. His touch healed broken bones and gaping wounds. Sunken hopes come back to life.

"If you believe in Me," He said, "you'll believe in the reincarnation of those you lost. I am telling you the truth. Soon they'll be sitting next to you on golden clouds, and I'll lead you to the shining presence of our Father. I know what you suffered in this life, good and bad. I never left you throughout the millenniums.

We were punished for our sins and blessed for our good deeds. No one went through life without a speck of goodness in his heart. Demons condemned for eternity to brood in the emptiness, tried to lead you astray, to buy you and to ride on your backs dressed in gold and precious stones. They will stay in the endless void. In the name of the One and Only God, they will be punished forever, because they knew what they were doing and never repented for their vanity and omnipotence."

Eight helicopters flew from Naples to Sicily, and then followed the shoreline from Messina to Palermo. The landscape was like Hiroshima and Nagasaki at the end of World War II. The Pope couldn't tear his eyes from the devastation, his bluish lips moving in silent prayer. His Secretary of Foreign Affairs tried to get his attention.

"Holy Father, we have to turn back immediately! The Chinese Communists and the North Korean President have issued a joint ultimatum to the United Nations, USA and the President of the European Community: if Taiwan and South Korea are not delivered into their hands in the space of 48 hours, they'll start a global thermonuclear war. The Russians are backing them wholeheartedly. That means the end of the world."

"No, Monsignor," said the Pope without looking at him, "the end of the world has already started. God will never leave it in the hands of the high and mighty on Earth. It's His Creation. He'll destroy it by His own will. We are landing in Palermo. I feel that this is our last chance."

The face of the Secretary became deadly pale.

"That's impossible, Holy Father! We have a measly force of 150 guards. The city, or what's left of it is in a total mess. A false

Messiah has appeared and people believe in him. It's part of the same affair with the mummy that brings controversy wherever it goes. Crowds got out of hand and violence prevailed. You don't want to give credence to a mere impersonator, do you?"

Now the Pope pierced him with his sharp eyes. "And what if the man you call an impersonator is the Real Savior?"

The Monsignor shook with the force of those eyes but insisted all the same, "All information is telling us that this is pure fabrication, a miserable fabrication."

"That's not what our Prelate in Palestine wrote to us in his last message."

"He was bought, Your Holiness."

"Bought? And then instead of enjoying his gains, he took his life?" the Pontiff mused.

"He's always been a strange man, Holiness, he wanted to become a Pope desperately. He seized this pitiful opportunity for his ill ambition. When it failed, he took his life."

"You convinced me once, Monsignor, this time you have failed. I think the Prelate took his life because he faced the truth. The Savior can appear in everyone's image. We are landing in Palermo. That's an order."

The man was shaking with disappointment. "Don't blame me, Holiness, for not warning you on time."

The Pope took his eyes from him and focused them on the devastation below. "Don't worry, Monsignor. You won't be blamed for anything from now on. You are no longer my Secretary of Foreign Affairs. In fact, you're nothing. You're to stay behind in this helicopter. Don't you dare follow me. I'm going all by myself. No guards, no attendance of any kind—just myself. Maybe it's too late even for me."

The crowd pressing around Gordon turned their heads toward the helicopters and shielded their eyes against the noonday sun. They were from all walks of life: soldiers, firemen and members of the Police Force, recognizable only by the remnants of their uniforms. The sailors of the commercial and naval units were naked to the waist. The patricians of the city — some intellectuals, professionals and shopkeepers — still kept a distance from the mob. Many families had come; children ran everywhere, anxious mothers and relatives chased after them. Gordon, in order to be seen by everybody, had climbed to a terrace amidst the ruins of a building, leaning upon the elaborate balustrade, shading his eyes against the bright sun. Dark green, paramilitary helicopters landed, one after the other, on what used to be the central square of Palermo.

People didn't know what to think about this. Maybe it was help, maybe not. So far nobody had come out of the choppers. The last to land was dazzling white. The people saw the markings of the Vatican and the Pope's Tiara and a collective gasp came from the multitude. The hatch opened and red-carpeted steps rolled down to the ground automatically. Everybody knew the fragile figure dressed in a simple white robe, but the crowd was still hesitant. All eyes returned to Gordon. Suddenly, he felt his nakedness but had nothing to put on. The crowd became hushed and waited frozen in silence.

From a great distance the eyes of the two men met. They looked at each other for quite some time, then the little white figure started negotiating each one of the red steps painfully, slowly. Somebody from inside tried to come after him and help. The Pope ordered him back. A man brought a blanket to Gordon.

Silently, the multitude retreated, forming a path from the helicopter to the terrace. Gordon eagerly ran down the broken staircase to the old man with the silver stick. They studied each other with open curiosity.

"You know who I am," said the Pope in a mellow voice. "But who are you, young man?"

Gordon smiled and clasped the blanket around his shoulders. "A few months ago that would've been the easiest question to answer, Your Holiness. Since then strange things have happened to me, and I am not that sure about my identity. My name is Gordon, Gordon Bates, and I was born in the USA."

"Where did you learn to speak Italian so fluently?"

Gordon's face expressed surprise. "Do I speak Italian?"

The Pope nodded with a little smile. "You do, as if you were born and raised here. I'm a foreigner myself, but I am a student of many languages."

"Well, you look like a learned man. In college I barely spoke any Spanish, and learned just a few inscription signs in my Egyptology classes."

"Hieroglyphics?"

"Yes...hieroglyphs. Not that I remember any. I learned only what was necessary for a project," he admitted.

"*Anagke oude theoi machontai*."

Gordon laughed, "*Sophois homilon kautos ekbese sophos*."

The Pope was visibly perplexed. "When did you read Menander's Monostichs."

The young man flushed under his dark complexion. "I have no idea what are you talking about. I'm a very simple man, Sir."

"*Decipit, frons prima multos,*" said the Pope.

"*De facto, deceptio visus,*" uttered Gordon almost self-defeated, "*E colpa mea — filius nullius*. Even my father abandoned me."

The Pope looked at him with teary eyes. "*Eli, eli, lamma sabacthani.*"

"I'm only a human, Sir."

"The Greatest Human."

Gordon covered his burning face with his hands, "It's easy to ridicule someone like me. I don't know what happened. I've made a fool of myself."

Slowly and painfully the old man got down on his shaky knees, and the multitude of people surrounding them did the same.

"Pardon me, Son of God, I doubted You. Like all before me, we don't understand You. We made up a Lord according to our liking. But this travesty is finished. In the Name of God, from now to the very end of eternity, You are my Only Lord."

On one hand Gordon was completely at a loss. On the other, for the first time, it dawned on him that, for some uttermost and uncontrollable reason he had been chosen to be the Savior.

He went down to his knees and prayed to God like everyone else. For some inexplicable reason all the sea gulls and other birds that had left the city just before the beginning of the great calamity, returned in a cloud of celestial joy and settled near them.

It was thought by all to be a good omen.

Sheik El Barrack had been moved to the best private clinic in Malta. Aldano's father was asleep on a sofa in the waiting room. An elderly doctor woke him shaking his shoulder. Mr. Brandon opened his eyes half way and was ready to close them again. The man was insistent, "Mr. Hussney wants to see you."

Brandon opened one eye. "What time is it?"

"It's late. You know where his room is, don't you?"

"I do, I do..." said Brandon and he sat up. "82, isn't it?"

The doctor nodded and walked tiredly toward the elevators. While Brandon was trying to get his wits together, an elegant private nurse with legs like Betty Grable's appeared and led the way down the corridor. The Irish blood in the old man's veins made him feel like dancing. The sheik had everything money could buy: in this case a whole apartment with flowers and a fake fireplace.

"The bedroom is on the left, Mr. Brandon. Can I assist you further?"

Brandon lifted up his bushy eyebrows. "You could indeed, nurse...if I was twenty years younger."

She blushed and smiled. It sounded like a well-worn cliché, but her voice was warm and frivolous with a laugh like tinkling silver bells.

"What a fine old man you are! Good night. You can press the buzzer if you need me."

Brandon looked after her thoughtfully. Somewhere people were dying. Only half an hour ago an earthquake had made a few cracks in the ceiling. But life went on. He scratched his silvery beard and pushed the door ajar, then put his head through the opening..

"Say, that nurse seems awfully nice."

The Sheik tried to laugh, but only a dry cough came out. His voice was strangely hushed. "They send me only their best. Switch off the TV, please. Everything seems to be exasperating. The irony of watching commercials in such times isn't appropriate."

Brandon turned it off and sat on the edge of an Empire armchair twisting his cap in his strong, knotty fingers. "You want me to go?"

"I want my daughter back. If anybody can help the kids, it's you. I'll give you all the money you need, but that's all I can do."

"I'll try, Sheik."

"*Allahu akbar*."

"*La ilaha illa Allah.*"

"How meaningless everything sounds. Do you think my daughter's still alive?" El Barrack asked.

"I try not to think these days. My boys are sturdy lads...though neither one of them will be eager to go. They have families to care about and their jobs. I don't know what to tell you. Nobody wants to go there."

"Buy a boat, damn it! You know how to handle a boat, don't you?"

"It takes more than one, Sheik. However, I know, the champ will come with me. He's still single. Marko had some bad luck in the ring recently, practically no engagements. Besides prize-fighting, Marko is a sailor. He owns a good boat. If the sea is calm we can make it in a couple of days."

"Do I demand too much of you?"

Brandon got up on his feet. "Aldano is there too. Money isn't everything. Now, stay put and I'll send the pretty nurse back to you."

THE RUINS OF MESSINA

About three o'clock in the morning Sergey woke up from one of his catnaps. The silence was total. No barking dogs in the distance, no calls of night birds or roar of traffic. Everybody had abandoned Messina. The flame of the last candle was sputtering as it strived for life. The rest was absolute darkness.

What had happened to the full moon?

The answer was in the raw smell of sulfur. Etna had chosen to sneak into the city without advertising its might. A thick cloud of poisonous gases quietly penetrated every nook and cranny. The air was deadly still and the black smog invisible in the darkness. The old man felt it all throughout his body. He was frozen, unable to budge a finger.

So, this was the end of his road. It would've been a thousand times better if he had died in Grozney. The only time he had fought for something other than money. His dabbling into the mysteries of ancient Egypt had paid off handsomely. So had all the intelligence services. Finally the big pay off had caught up with him; his discovery of Amenhotep and the One and Only God. Maybe some of the saintliness had rubbed off on the foolish and vainglorious Amenhotep. He proved to be a reliable source. Suddenly Sergey realized that he was talking out loud. So what if someone hears him? The world was going to hell anyway. He choked on the smog, coughed dryly and went on talking to himself.

"It's even possible that my Ka has left an imprint on the personality of my stepson, that clashed with the genes of Peter Moughabee. What an interesting paper I could've written on this material! Too late! The demonic Kas in the endless void wouldn't be interested. Gordon seemed to be dumb, though the young man I saw right here was different." A new fit of coughing cut his chest.

He wanted to say "divine" but didn't have enough time to do it. In his death throes he scratched on a piece of paper:

I COULD'VE HAD A SON!

CITY PORT

Aldano struggled with the mariner's knot of a boat. His mind didn't seem to work properly. Finally, he remembered what Marko had taught him...left to right, left to right...It worked. He looked at Helena; she was breathing heavily through the wet towel. Everything around them had become black. Greasy flakes of soot fell from the sky. There was not a speck of light from the city. Occasionally, phantom flames danced over the crater of the volcano. Aldano believed that at any moment, a great explosion would finish their agony. Yet, in spite of the danger, he found the oars and started working, feeling his seemingly, endless energy was ebbing away.

Dying will be quicker and easier — and welcome.

PALERMO

Gordon made up his mind to accept the invitation of the Holy Father. An inner voice told him that his presence in the papal residence was more important than staying in Palermo. So far, there was no news of Helena and Aldano. The Abbot had disappeared as well. His chances of finding them increased by using the power of the Vatican. He washed himself in an improvised shower and donned a flight suit, ready to fly with the Pope to Marsala, a city considered out of harm's way.

Refugee camps had been hurriedly built for tens of thousands of people. There were no elementary comforts, not to mention shortages of food and water. As usual, the government in Rome was slow, and the Americans flew in many supplies and blankets from their well-stocked military bases.

The Pope suffered many infirmities and needed special care. Gordon sat next to the Pontiff, but the level of noise interfered with their conversation. The young man had to put his ear almost next to the Pope's mouth.

"I know," said His Holiness, "how much you want to be among the people in the camps, but your presence is more important here. It is embarrassing in a conversation to address me by my titles, so don't mention them."

"How shall I address you, then?" Gordon asked.

The old man unexpectedly smiled with warmth and humility. "You can call me Father."

"Father? Is that proper?"

The smile of the Pontiff widened. "Of course it is. I should probably call you my son, but that might be too farfetched for the time being"

Gordon listened to his dry coughing. He was still unable to figure this man out. "Does he think that my game is part of a master plan, posing as Christ of Nazareth? He seems to buy everything wholesale." Unshaven for several days, hungry and dog-tired he might just have the look of a false Messiah.

"I have some problems with the word 'father,' but I'll try to get used to it. I've been subjected to possession. Right now I'm Gordon Bates of the United States."

The Pope pierced him with his metallic eyes. "I know, Gordon. That's why I trust you. The Curia Romana may come down on me like a ton of bricks. You have to help me establish the truth about you. You have remembrances of a past life, don't you?"

For awhile, Gordon seemed lost in thought, then he decided to open up. "I had bits and pieces of an Egyptian knowledge that may be linked to my college background, but now I seem to remember things I never knew."

"Scenes of the life of Christ?"

Gordon was at a loss.

"Yes. As a witness? No, not exactly. It was His voice and His narrative that brought images."

IN THE ABSOLUTE: JESUS REMEMBERING

Mother didn't like me. I looked too much like my father, who had greatly disappointed her. She was very ambitious and often reminded us that she was highborn married to a carpenter. Her sister had married a tax collector. My brothers and I were forbidden to play with her sons. Only my sisters had been welcome to her home to do the housework. Mother told me.

"Joseph is getting too old for work. It's time for you to take over his carpenter's shop. That's the right job for you. He has taught you well. What else can you do with your life? You have no education. Who is going to give you his daughter if you don't put aside a bit of money? I'll see that my sister's husband sends you some clients. He knows people in high places."

I found my father Joseph sitting on the steps to his shop. He had grown old and his great physical strength had left him. His many infirmities showed. He suffered severe pain in his joints, yet he always had a smile for me. I kneeled in the dust in front of him.

"I'm fifteen, Father, and I don't know how to read and write. I want to get some education."

Father Joseph sighed and put his large callused hand over my thick wavy hair. "We don't have the money for that, my son. You know how much I care for you. When you were born, your mother had a dream. A white dove left an olive branch in your cradle. She said to me, 'Joseph, this son of ours is born for greatness. He'll be the Messiah!' I shook my head, 'That cannot come to pass, Mary. He's not our first born, nor is he related to the House of David.'

" 'But I am,' said your mother, 'Go to Bethlehem and write him in as Jewish and firstborn.'

"I was embarrassed but I did as she said. And all for nothing. You said not a word until the age of five. Your mother was deeply disappointed and changed her mind. I still believe that one day you'll drive the Romans out of our land. Do whatever God commands you to do, Jesus. My love and blessing will be always with you."

I had heard tales about a faraway country where the mountains reach to Heaven. There, the wisdom of their holy men is renown. They knew how to find God in their own souls. He had given them power over their bodies and unabridged knowledge about the untold riches of the inner world. In His Name, they had performed great miracles, but never to oblige themselves, only to help others.

Maybe they would explain to me why the poor laborers should slave for the rich and powerful. Aren't we all equal in the eyes of the Creator? Why is slavery permitted? And why are our ancestral lands occupied by strangers to whom we have to pay tribute just for living in our own fatherland? How far can their greed go unchecked by God's divine judgment?

Those and many more questions kept me awake in the nights.

Is it God's will that I should marry and raise a family like anyone else? Must I dedicate my life to Him and strive for martyrdom?"

I waited for a sign from Heaven.

Only James stood up to me. We were the youngest. I was a year older than my brother, both of us were hotheads. The wife of my eldest brother had told me that James was the son of a dashing Roman officer of Greek descent. He had been adopted by the Legion during an appointment in Greece. That's why James didn't look like the rest of us.

He and I helped father in his carpenter shop, where he was able to keep an eye on us. When he sensed the tension mounting, he'd set up a wrestling match between us. Father Joseph was thirty-seven years old and an expert wrestler. I remember him taking the calf after mauling half a dozen contenders at weddings. Being a natural athlete, he never turned down a challenge especially from a Roman. They treated us as slaves, but if the opportunity arose, would challenge us in hand-to-hand combat. Father never failed in such contests, and the Romans hated him. Soon after James' birth, he was accused of killing the Roman officer Pohout. As a result, the whole family fled to Egypt for several years. Mother thought him a bully. My elder brothers didn't approve of his belligerence and kept their families away from him.

When James and I turned fifteen and sixteen respectively, we fell in love with the same girl. According to tradition, she made us fight each other to see who was the better man. Usually, I was able to prevail over my younger brother, but this time James beat me. He defeated me soundly, then, borne on the shoulders of his friends, proclaimed his victory all over the city. In the chaos, the girl was forgotten, so she helped me to the fountain to wash off the grime and blood from the fight. Feeling guilty, she tried to soothe my temper, but I was unable to put up with the public humiliation and left Judea for many years. Her name was Mary, like my mother's, and she came from Magdala.

I guess God wanted me to learn how to read and write and about the complexity of transfiguration. So I walked to the east, and India changed my life forever."

The Pope wasn't shocked as I expected him to be. "It makes sense to me. The Messiah was supposed to be firstborn, so the authors ignored the whole family. It was a chain reaction, one lie after the other."

"Have you had visions, Father?" Gordon asked.

"Mostly about my past, Gordon. I had a vision that I was skiing downhill. The cold air rushing in my face, the snow reflecting a brilliant sun, the beauty of my homeland mountains. Everything to live and die for, yet nothing to hold on to except God."

Spontaneously, Gordon reached for the trembling hand of the blue-eyed man that for a moment relived his youth and the splendors of a world gone forever.

"I'm sorry I wasn't with you in those mountains, Father, And he pressed his lips over the parchment-like skin.

Renaldo Cortelazzo was a private detective on a special mission for the Pope. He had to find Gordon's friends using only the sketchy descriptions he had been given. He was twenty-five and a very gifted sleuth with a proven track record. Since his early childhood, he had been fanatically devoted to the Pope.

Renaldo watched Gordon board the white helicopter, aware of the jealousy that he instantly tried to smother. There was plenty to do, the first being to visit the remnants of the Grand Hotel Savoya.

Strange yellow-grayish clouds were covering the sky with surprising speed.

The old man fell asleep. Gordon looked at the Pope, believing that too much rested on those fragile shoulders. Gordon closed his eyes and went in his mind's eye to the place above Palermo where he had buried the mummy. He was here and there simultaneously. The weather had changed dramatically. Dark clouds, heavy with the fumes from Etna brought torrential rains polluted to a point that made them look like mudslides from heaven. Cold wind, unseasonable for this time of the year, made the refugees even more miserable. The American help had arrived at the camps before the rains, but the situation was still grave, mainly because people were unable to understand why all of this was happening to them.

Gordon's problem was much deeper. In his mind's eye he sat over the mummy's tomb, face buried in his hands, feeling alone.

"I don't know to whom I may talk, but if something is expected of me, I need some advice and consent. In the first place, on whose authority am I acting?" Gordon muttered to himself.

There was a momentary pause, then he recognized the soft, deep voice of the mummy. "For the time being you're acting on my authority, though there are higher powers involved"

"What is expected of me?"

"You must follow your inner voices."

"How will I know where the voices originate? There are many false sources from heaven and earth."

"You'll be empowered to tell the difference. By now you should know very well who's in charge. The Good and the Bad in you are separated forever."

"Does that mean that from now on I'll be committed only to righteous deeds?"

"Not exactly. You'll still have the freedom of choice and will be held fully accountable for your mistakes.

"What's happening to my friends?"

"You mean Helena and Aldano?"

Gordon felt his face blushing. "I don't mind Aldano, anymore. Probably I would've done the same as him under the circumstances."

"I don't have the special credentials for this case. Maybe your father can whisper it to you sometime. He doesn't play by the rules."

"It seems that bureaucracy in Heaven is as bad as on Earth. By the way, what am I to do next?"

"You have been promoted. You're expected to know."

"But I don't."

The voice started to fade away. "Listen to yourself. Farewell, my son."

Gordon was somehow disappointed; suddenly he had acquired too many fathers. "Tutankhamon is his son, not I, or should I say Tutankhaton? Those ancient names drive me up the wall. Amenhotep, Ikhnaton — Ikhmet, Harremhab. That happens even nowadays — Aldan and Aldano..."

Gordon received a new vision, Helena and Aldano in a rowboat too small for the storm. In a flash of lightning, he recognized the face of Aldano's father and a strangely familiar lad. "It must be one of Aldano's brothers," thought Gordon. "Thank you, father. I hope you don't get a bad mark for giving me a hint."

A golden ray, almost like a smile, cut through the menacing clouds.

After the Pope's visit, not a living soul remained in the devastated city, except for the work crews with trained dogs looking for survivors in the ruins. The soldiers encircling Palermo already knew the Pope's detective by sight and let him pass without asking for a permit.

Renaldo let himself be guided by the voice within. The muddy rain started again, accompanied by an electric storm of a magnitude never seen before. The jagged lightening bolts crisscrossed over the doomed city, hindering the rescue teams from helping stranded victims. Renaldo Cortelazzo joined one of those groups in a makeshift shelter. The men were somber and hostile. They didn't know him.

"We heard about the Miracle Maker, are you the Son of Man?" asked one of them, trying to light his cigarette with a malfunctioning lighter, "Do something. Stop this mess."

Renaldo looked at him carefully and smiled but said nothing.

The men were frustrated and ill-humored. Another rescue worker refused to move and share his spot with him. He was intentionally kept out in the rain.

"If you are so great and mighty, why don't you take care of the situation so we can go home. Stop the rage of Mother Nature. Call your legions of angels to do the job."

"On my own, I can do nothing," said Renaldo with exaggerated humility, "lets say a prayer together. Only God can change our destiny."

"I'm sick and tired of preaching, Son of Man. Say, didn't you go North with the Pope this morning?"

The young detective smiled again. "How could I be with him, and at the same time be here with you?"

The man shrugged his shoulders and moved over, making room for Renaldo to step in. "Come, stranger, you don't seem to be 'The Messiah.' Your hands aren't large and callused from labor, but you talk our language."

Renaldo joined them and shook the rain from his clothing. "Did you come from Finland, people?"

"Yes, we're from Finland."

"That's far away! My mother is from your country. Under the mud I'm platinum blond like you. Mother taught me her language, but I've never been to Finland. Who pays you?"

"We are paid by our government, if they say hell, that's where we go, but who pays you?"

"God."

"And you're not a preacher? What the hell are you then? A monk?"

"I hold no position with God, just serve Him."

The men from Finland fell silent, then the first one that spoke to Renaldo offered him one of his cigarettes. The young man took one hesitantly.

A new round thunderbolts attacked the helpless city and drowned out Renaldo's words. The man lit his cigarette. "My name is Aimo, what might yours be?"

Renaldo tried to make himself heard over the thunder, "Call me Aldo."

"Say, Aldo, is this scourge spreading all over the world? Is it going to hit home too? The whole of Europe was swept by winds up to 200 miles an hour. Trees and houses were uprooted and communications failed. What will happen to our families? Why were we sent over to Sicily? What's Sicily to us?"

"The same as Finland is to Sicily, brother. People here have families too."

"But isn't it each for his own kin? The closest in family comes first."

"Think of all humanity as brothers and then everyone will be saved," preached Renaldo, imitating the Son of Man.

All eyes watched Renaldo with a mixture of hope and suspicion.

"We have to think of the crazy Italians as family?"

"Everyone on Earth," replied Renaldo.

"Good lord, since the Tower of Babylon this has never happened."

"Not so. It has happened many times. Say, brother Aimo, have you by any chance seen a beautiful young woman with a blond young man?"

"How do you know I'm in charge?"

"The way you talk?"

"I'm not sure, but we did save three men, two blond, the other too old to tell, and a woman with them, from a sinking motor boat."

"That could be my family, Aimo. I'll be forever indebted to you and your team if you will tell me how to find them."

When the rain let up, Aimo took Renaldo on his motor scooter to a field hospital. The camp had to be moved away from Palermo. Lines of military trucks were loading patients on stretchers. Nurses and volunteers were too tired to answer any questions. They didn't know any names. Log books hadn't been filled in properly. There was hardly anybody left in the mud covered tents. A doctor vaguely remembered the name Brandon. He sent a volunteer worker to the trucks and she came back with a lad matching the general description Renaldo had been given. They shook hands and Marko introduced himself then told him about the ordeal. Their boat got lost in the storm and the accumulation of mud almost sunk her.

Renaldo explained to the young man from Malta, that Gordon Bates had asked him to find them. The American had had to accompany His Holiness to a safe place.

Marko's regenerative powers were amazing but the rest of his passengers needed some time for recovery. Aldano and Helena suffered severe dehydration and exhaustion. His father was in a catatonic state. The local medical personnel didn't know how to treat him. He needed immediate attention, a place where deep mental therapy could be provided.

Arrangements had been made already; an emergency vehicle was on its way. A medic explained that when Brandon awoke, he had to be able to recognize a face around him; otherwise he'd lapse back to his catatonic state. Aldano volunteered to stay with his father and made a convincing stage exit; though his eyes on Helena told another story.

Helena made a speedy mental and physical recovery though the Pope's detective felt a deep depressive trauma within her. She joined the young Italian for a walk. Helena asked no questions about the state of her father nor how Gordon had managed the situation in Palermo. She seemed to have no recollection of or interest in what had happened. The young man caught himself thinking how downright ugly Helena looked. That discovery made him feel angry with himself. He knew that she probably had had no opportunity to wash herself since the earthquake and little nourishment. The clothes she was wearing — an ill-fitting jump suit and rubber boots — didn't help much. He doubted if she had seen a comb for the last ten days. Renaldo found an open canteen. She hesitated but took the seat across from him.

"What time is it?" she asked.

The young man tried to take her hand. She withdrew it quickly. "Do you know what time it is?" she repeated anxiously.

"I have no idea, Helena. My wristwatch stopped."

"What are we doing here?" she said hurriedly, "If we don't know the time we might miss something of great importance."

"I ordered coffee and sandwiches, that's more important for the time being."

"I doubt it. What shall we do next?" she asked.

"I'll try to call the hospital in Malta where your father is. Then we'll join Gordon in Marsala."

When the coffee and sandwiches arrived, Helena said nothing, just sipped her coffee absentmindedly. "May I have a cigarette?"

"I don't have any but, I can ask for a pack. Any particular kind?"

"Any kind…I learned to smoke in Catholic boarding school. Later I kicked the habit. My father used to be a heavy smoker. Now he's paying the price for it. It seems I've started again."

"Why? It doesn't make sense. You want to die?"

"Something like that. We all die sooner or later." Her voice was flat.

The young man tried to meet her eyes but she steadfastly avoided his gaze. He went to the counter and came back with a pack of cigarettes and a lighter. She took out one and Renaldo politely lit it.

"Helena, my name is Renaldo Cortelazzo. Why don't you use it?"

She thought for a moment, then for the first time she met his eyes. "Because I have no idea who you are."

"I was ordered by the Pope to find you and Aldano."

"I have to find a way to Malta. My place is with my father. There's no reason for me to stay in Sicily."

Renaldo was taken by surprise. "Don't you love Gordon anymore?"

"Gordon has no money left. His charges come back to me"

The young man had taken for granted that she loved Gordon. Now he wasn't so sure. On the other hand, what right had Renaldo to ruin her life? Gordon had found his mission, and the mission possessed him.

"The telephone connections have been partially restored," Renaldo announced. "You can call your father."

The young private nurse in Malta answered the phone. Helena asked to talk to her father.

"I'm sorry, Ms. El Barrack, your father cannot be taken off the respirator. I beg your pardon?...Ah, no...he is not asleep. Actually he's writing something on his pad. Yes, I'll read it to you as soon as he finishes the message. One moment, please, yes, I have it now, but I don't know if you should hear it...it's strange...Of course, that's none of my business, if you insist, here it is: DON'T COME TO MY FUNERAL, all in capitals...no, of course not, his condition is well in hand now. He can last for many months...Yes, Ms. El Barrack, I'll tell him right away. You'll come as soon as there is a transport to Malta...then, I LOVE YOU, signed Titi?...I understand Ms. Titi. I have a real affection for your dad. My hope is, when he gets better to be able to continue serving him wherever he goes. The whole staff has fallen in love with him, he's so generous...Good night, Ms. Titi."

The nurse left the telephone and went to the bed. Hussney was writing again. The nurse caught a glimpse of the short sentence.

"You really want to be left alone for awhile? I don't think the medic in charge would like that...but...if you want to take a catnap I could use a cup of fresh coffee. It's gonna be a long night."

She rearranged his pillow and switched off the side table lamp, then left hurriedly. Hussney made sure that the click clacking of her high heels down the corridor faded completely then disengaged himself from the breathing machine and got up slowly. Once on his feet he was short of breath, but he made it to the sliding door of the balcony. It was slightly open. He got out and leaned on the railing. The cool, damp air made him feel much better. Ragged clouds raced past the moon. The monotonous beating of the heavy surf calmed him down. He faced the general direction of Mecca whispering a short prayer. The railing wasn't difficult, the way down even easier.

Chapter 14

REUNION

Late in the afternoon, the Pope sent for Gordon again.

His walking was badly impeded, so he stayed seated in a soft velvet chair. He looked at him silently for awhile, then uttered something absolutely incoherent. "*Imperium cupientibus nihil medium inter summa aut praecipitia*."

He obviously hoped to engage him in conversation, but Gordon's mind was on Helena. The old man tried a few more tricks with the same result. Finally he spoke in the Hamitic language. The young man answered correctly, and the Pope went on in flawless Ancient Egyptian.

"Who are you? You have the looks of Gordon Bates but not his mentality. You have to tell me the truth, a lot depends on it."

"How would you know Gordon Bates' mentality?"

"It was described to me," the Pope answered.

"Nobody knows my mentality. Why don't you try to tell the truth for a change?"

The old man blushed slightly. "Vatican intelligence briefed me. Now it's your turn to be honest with me. I'll know if you lie to me."

"If I give you my knowledge, what's in it for me, Holiness?"

"Ask and I'll see if I can deliver. I'm not a deity, only a humble servant of God."

"Why are you asking me for the truth if a security check has been done already? I passed didn't I? You're giving me free passage to Palermo."

"Not if you're a heathen."

"I'm not a heathen. Lord Aton can prove it."

The old man smiled. "From one heathen to another."

"You mean, you don't know that Jesus is a reincarnation of Aton?"

"This is yet to be proven."

"You wanted the truth, I delivered it."

The Pope put his shaky hand over his teary eyes. "Are you Ikhnaton?"

"Not now. His Ka has left me. Do you hate me?"

"No. As a matter of fact, you can be of great help to me."

"Really? What can I do for you, Holiness?"

"The situation is very complicated. Amenhotep/Ikhnaton may try to penetrate you again."

"He cannot reenter me. Now I love Helena and Aldano is my friend. Love is my strength."

"I know, but there are other ways. Will you help me, Gordon?"

"What have I got to lose? I'll try, though I don't think I have the power."

"Neither do I. Together we can help ourselves. Now we are alone against the world."

"I'm not alone, Holy Father. I have Lord Aton on my side and Helena would die for me."

"Helena? If anybody depends on the love of a woman he's just a man. Remember the Primal Sin."

"You came from the womb of your mother, didn't you?" quipped Gordon.

"Of course I did! We are all sinners. The Gates of Heaven aren't that easy to crack, especially for a Pope. Though there's a chink in the armor. Find Helena and make her your accomplice."

"How?"

"By marrying her. She doesn't have to know about our deal. Then you cannot be called an imposter."

"I'm not interested in double dealing, Holiness."

"I know, you're interested in becoming a martyr. Tomorrow morning a helicopter will take you back to Palermo. Renaldo will explain the rest to you."

"Who's Renaldo?"

"He's young but wise for his age. I made him my private detective. He is extremely devoted to me…maybe I should say fanatically so. He stayed back in Palermo and was given a description of your lost friends. I think he has a lead on them."

Gordon tried to fight a tension headache that was barricading his thoughts.

"Is he spying on my friends? Could you explain that to me?"

"I'm the Pope. I don't have to explain myself to anyone but God."

Gordon pondered for a short time. "You want me to follow you blindly, Holiness?"

"What I expect is for you to trust me. I don't dabble in magic. Is Peter Moughabee trying to sneak his tricks under my nose? He gave you a warning; stay away, danger!"

"Is Renaldo a dangerous person?"

"In a way…fanatics are always unpredictable. He can turn even against me. I keep a very close watch on him."

"Do you need fanatics to prove yourself?"

"No-o-o…I want to save him. His father was a Neo-Nazi. I owe that much to Renaldo."

Gordon's headache pounded as if a bunch of savages were beating their drums inside his head. He closed his eyes, the light was hurting him too. "I'll marry Helena because I truly love her, not because of you. What happens next?"

"I won't manipulate you, Gordon. Do everything of your free will. If you decide to bring your wife here, you're both welcome. I'll try to protect you as much as it's humanly possible. The rest is in the hands of God."

PALERMO

Renaldo brought Gordon and Helena together. There were few places where they could find privacy, the city was encircled by army units, the field hospital gone. A number of shacks used by merchants, had no water or plumbing. Even that was heaven to Helena and Gordon.

By now, Helena was out of her stupor, and their love, like never before, was free from prejudice and fear. Lovemaking wasn't burdened by a sense of guilt, nor was the passage of time meaninglessly cumbersome. It simply wasn't just a matter of physical attraction, IT WAS LOVE, real untainted love, a triumph over the slow progress of civilization not a pharmacy type of label, stamped all over by ignorant poets, statesmen or religious cults. A deeply human love known to mankind long before the appearance of Lord Aton. Even He met his Nefertiti, Christ, Mary of Magdala and Romeo his Juliet. It didn't matter to Christ that the young girl who helped him to the fountain in Nazareth after his first public defeat had become a mature woman. He wanted her for his wife to love as a woman blessed by God.

The morning came too soon and they were not awakened by nightingale songs but a sudden sharp jolt followed by lots of tremors. It was as if the planet was falling apart. For the young lovers, this was just a sign of how little time they had to enjoy each other. Helena had enough money for both of them to spend the rest of their lives in wealth and total contentment — what they didn't have was time.

A priest had to be found to perform their marriage. That was a problem. She wanted the wedding officiated in the chapel.

Renaldo had informed Helena about the death of her father. Helena was obsessed by a presentiment of pending doom, but insisted on going ahead with the marriage.

Aldano and his father left for Malta on a cargo plane, Marko stayed behind waiting for the repairs on his boat. The young man that found them at the Trapani refugee camp seemed well versed on clergymen and churches. Marko took it upon himself to ask Renaldo who could perform a mixed marriage.

"A mixed marriage may only be performed in a Unitarian church," the young detective stated, "but I'll see what I can do locally."

Chapter 15

A STRANGE HONEYMOON

The marriage of Helena and Gordon was officiated in a small church with a Catholic priest that didn't ask any questions. Best men were Marko and Renaldo. Anyway, it didn't take more than a quarter of an hour. After a lunch, in the only hotel-restaurant in Trapani that stayed open for business, the newlyweds retired to the most luxurious suite available. The whole procedure was kind of subdued and hurried. At least that was the impression the bridegroom had.

While stripping off his clothes, Gordon shared this impression with his *lawfully wedded wife*. "I've seen weddings only on TV, but something essential was missing in that one. The final words: *I now pronounce you man and wife. You may kiss the bride.*"

"Do you know Latin?"

"Yes, better than you."

Helena tried to hide her reservations. "He said, *with this ring I thee wed…*"

"But not, *do you accept this man for your husband*. Instead he used the word *companion*."

"I don't know, I was very emotional at that moment. He might've missed the right expression. The important thing is to get the papers."

"I don't want to worry you, Helena, but I sincerely doubt that we'll find anybody in the City Hall offices."

"I know. The City Hall is in ruins and no substitute has been made."

Gordon came to the bathroom door and leaned on the frame. "Because of my religious impropriety, I asked here and there if a matrimonial act could be performed by the city mayor. For instance, a marriage can be performed during a sea voyage by the captain of the ship. Unfortunately, the mayor of Trapani has left and no replacement has taken over."

"Anyway. A civil marriage is unacceptable to me. How do you feel about our best men?" asked Helena.

Gordon went back to their nuptual bed and just stood there. "Marko is jealous and Renaldo is the Pope's favorite pet. I remember him from the Pontiff's arrival in Palermo." He turned on his heels and almost walked into the embrace of his bride. He pressed her bosom to his chest in a very tight hold. "Do you really want to follow me in my mission?"

"I do."

"Everywhere?"

"Even to hell, as I told you, my dearest one."

"That's enough for a wedding in the face of God. We don't need the approval of any terrestrial powers."

He kissed her with a profound feeling of love that he never thought he would experience. Helena thrust herself onto him as if he was her last hope for salvation.

"You already gave me all the happiness I've never had before, my dear. In any event I promise you not to question your actions. I trust you completely."

Marko and Renaldo had a few drinks in the bar. Marko leaned over the table, "Give me a cigarette, I'm so furious, I cannot think straight. " He smoked in silence for awhile, "I wish I had tried to make Helena mine with all the millions her father left her. You're not leveling with me, Renaldo. There are some missing pieces in this story."

Renaldo stomped on his cigarette. "The Pope wants to take Gordon on his Egyptian trip to placate the Copts. Perhaps Gordon is one of their leaders. His Holiness doesn't confide in me, either. I know for sure, that after Egypt, he intends to go to Jordan and the Holy Land. Obviously he'll be trying to defuse the situation with the mummy. Gordon seems to be in possession of it and all its secrets."

Marko threw his cigarette down in disgust. "What a mess! You mean the mummy from the newspapers. Is it a holy relic?"

"*Corpus Dei,*" replied Renaldo.

"No kidding?"

"No kidding. That mummy can solve mysteries of great importance to many nations, but the Pope isn't ready for that yet. For many centuries Rome has distorted the Scriptures beyond belief. The first appearance of Aton predates the birth of Christ fifteen hundred years. That news alone will destroy Catholic dogma forever. Without it, the Church is nothing but a group of senile old men. They can't allow that to happen, no matter what it takes."

Marko whistled softly. "Holy Moses! That's a whale of a tale! I love adventures. Count me in."

Renaldo shook his head. "I'm afraid, it's much more than an adventure, Marko. Don't expect the Holy Grail. Something strange is in the air. The Pope is scared. He thinks that these natural disasters of recent times are not quite so natural. The prophecies of ancient times are being fulfilled at an alarming rate. Armageddon and Judgment Day might be at hand."

Helena and Gordon arrived at the largest refugee camp in Sicily. Things were happening there — riots about the apportioned food and rampant corruption. If one had cash, there was an abundance of products from A to Z. The poor were ignored by the wealthy, as if God had not created everyone equal. Those in charge of distribution of necessities were selling to the highest bidder. Sex scandals, violence and thievery destroyed the unity and social cooperation established in the earliest days. The class distinction was stark. It was a house divided; poor were poorer and the smart ones that managed to save their fortunes gave loans at exorbitant interest rates. Black markets were booming.

Nothing had changed, it was business as usual.

At high noon, when everybody was at the central square market, Gordon didn't attract any attention. He had been completely forgotten. Primitively constructed stands offered all kinds of goods at grossly inflated prices. Few people were able to buy; the rest wondered from where that plenty came. Of course, cigarettes and liquor were in abundance, even though drugs of all kinds were obtainable for a price.

At midday, most people were drunk or getting there. Where the money for drinks came from was anybody's guess.

Half naked, under the blazing sun, people were betting on cockfights, admiring the beauty contests, laughing at puppet shows and losing the last of their money at the roulette tables. Magicians also had their audience. What else but magic was capable of giving people solace? The fortune-tellers were thriving, too. People that lost the harvest of their lives and hadn't strength and will power to start anew found some relief in the magic of tomorrow. Their children had to inherit a better world. They had to have a future.

Newspapers and magazines appeared here and there. Small TV sets presented soap operas, comedies, sports and trivia — the endless saga of a bygone era. Didn't Plato say in Theaetetus, "Man is the measure of all things." What man wanted was *Panem et Circenses*.

Lines of people waited for hours to be offered long-term loans at "lower-than-ever rates." Loans, loans, loans for everything! There were politicians with bull horns promising, promising, promising. Philosophers threatened and warned, groups of musicians and singers performed modern dancing and sporting events soon were organized. An open-air church was offering absolution and Eternal Hope.

And there was not a single cloud in the blue sky. Only life insurance companies didn't fare well. People were afraid that they would never be able to cash their policies. So why not be spending your money in the now?

One of the platforms was empty. Helena elbowed Gordon. "Go to it!"

He didn't need a megaphone; his voice was strong and clear. For the first time since Helena had met him, she saw him as a leader of men. Even ten days ago that would've been unthinkable. Now she accepted it with no reservations. 'That's my husband,' she thought, 'I'll be with him for the rest of my life.'

"Dear friends," announced Gordon in a loud voice. "In the aftermath of natural disaster of such proportion, we cannot help but ask ourselves, can such a tragedy be called 'natural' and what's the meaning of it? Can the amputation of a limb be called natural? What is it to have your family sitting at the table for a meal and ten minutes later to be all alone? Is any act of God natural? Can we believe in Him if we're incapable of understanding his action? I don't have the answer yet, but I know that for some reason of His own, God has infiltrated my life and since that moment I'm a different person. In a way, we're all different after a tragedy of these proportions. Suddenly, as never before, I feel part of the enormous family called Mankind. From now on, I'll never be alone. The responsibility for my family will never leave me. I came to this part of the world empty, then I found my natural father, my wife and all of you, my friends. That discovery made my life purposeful and worthwhile living. If I happen to die right now, I won't be alone, my family, the Humankind, will remember me, my wife will think of me, so I'll live again. If the planet Earth, by will of our One and Only God, is destined for extinction, the other celestial bodies will remember, and the whole universe will be the proof of our existence. Somewhere in this endless world, the Son of God will appear again to be crucified for our sins and to guide us with His love to our eternal salvation.

The inner me found his sight.

My discovery was the love from man to man and from man to God. Now that my life is justified, I'll live FOREVER!"

The weather turned hot and dry. A wind coming off the hot sands of the Sahara made living in tents unbearable. The nights were still cool, but at sunrise, everybody had to leave. People became lethargic and depressed, they wanted to go back to what was left of their homes but the Sanitary Department had forbidden their return. Dead bodies had been left where they lay in the debris, and without an adequate source of water, epidemics were in the making. Everyone was concerned about the unusually strong aftershocks and the worsening conditions in the camps. Riots protesting this were a daily occurrence. The Americans stopped delivering food because the Italian Government told them "everything's under control." The truth was that offices responsible for delivery of aid were sluggish and disorganized. Even basic necessities disappeared and reappeared at a whim.

In Athens, a second strong earthquake in less than a year made headlines. It wasn't of the high magnitude that practically destroyed the northern ports of Sicily but psychologically made a greater impression. People saw a pattern in these "natural disasters." The question was where was it going to hit next. In Tornado Alley in the United States, mammoth twisters brought many industries to a halt. The same happened from Miami to New York and on up the East Coast. The Pacific coast suffered landslides and floods caused by torrential rains out of season. A subsequent dry spell made conditions ripe for fires. Panic stricken, people desperately searched for safe havens. There were none. Because of a drought, China and India ran out of food. The Communists governments of China and North Korea started another wave of propaganda to distract the attention from their failing economies. Taiwan was the focal point again. An unknown bacteria wreaked havoc in different parts of the world. The Middle East began rehashing its ever present problems. The crises created strange bedfellows — bilateral pacts between countries of conflicting political beliefs. Several newly-founded religious sects proclaimed deities of very suspicious character. Most nations set their economies on a war footing, starving their population in order to pay costly military imports.

It smelled like war.

Gordon changed his mind. Now he wanted to see the Pope. He told this to Renaldo and, in a matter of hours, a helicopter arrived from Marsala. Marko's boat wasn't ready, so he joined them for the fun of it. Gordon hesitated, as he believed the young man was using drugs. Where had he found the money? Renaldo denied giving him any, though he had seen him in the company of strange characters. It was better to take Marko along and keep an eye on him in Marsala. In his habitual arrogance, Marko wanted to invite his girlfriend, too. Gordon had Helena. What was he supposed to do in the night? That smelled like blackmail. Anyway, there was no room for Marko's girl, but he had to come.

"It's better than falling into the hands of his low-life buddies," insisted Helena.

Gordon was worried, too. "Is he borrowing money from them?"

"People see him with you; he might be using your name, Gordon. They're glad to have you in his pocket."

"Good heavens! That's preposterous."

"I tracked the sources and paid the money back. It was more than enough to supply Marko with drugs, women and some booze."

"How did you get involved in this sordid affair, Helena?"

"Renaldo told me. He doesn't like him either. Marko admitted plotting against you, but now he is entirely on your side. Only God knows on whose side Marko really stands. Your stand also seems to be shifting like a sunflower. What made you change your mind about seeing the Pope?"

"I thought he wouldn't listen to me, but without his vast resources, I can't make my point heard even in this camp. What bothers me is the quick deterioration of the situation. The Pope's state of health is also declining."

"Don't worry about it; his spirit is powerful. It will keep him together in spite of his physical infirmities. I wish you could see that in his own way he is trying to help, even against his conservative reasoning."

"Now I know better than the Gordon of a month ago. I listened to many people of different walks of life. They need their spiritual leader and I need followers to back me. By myself I can do nothing."

Helena's smile had changed too, now it was coming straight from the heart. "You repeat that phrase quite often. Do you know who said it first?"

"No, was it Jesus? Have you thought, my dearest, what you'll do when I have to depart from this life?"

Helena took her time before answering, "Yes, I have. I'll follow you to the very end. If we have a child, I'll tell him everything about you."

At this moment, Gordon's eyes became soft and luminescent, as if an outward peace nested in them. "Thank you, dear. Let's go to Marsala."

On their way to the Pontiff's residence, the helicopter ran into an electric storm that hadn't shown up on the radar. Radio contact was lost. In the blinding lightning and deafening thunder, all faces looked like death masks. Even Marko's pretended fearlessness faded away. Helena hid her face in Gordon's chest. The pilot made a break through the thick, low clouds. The monitors flickered off and he had to fly blind in the immense darkness. As the last drops of fuel caused red lights to blink alarmingly, he suddenly caught a glimpse of the heliport.

It was close to midnight when Gordon entered the Pope's apartment. The old man was still at his desk. He looked even more tired and ill than on his arrival in Palermo, though his eyes were smiling.

"I had little hope of seeing you again, young man," the Pontiff admitted.

Gordon felt a deep sense of guilt. "It was silly of me to let this farcical thing keep going on."

"No, it wasn't. I put you to a test, so you had to test me, too. In the real world everything has substitutes. In the spiritual world there are none. Only God and his Son are unique."

"If God is the Creator, nothing else can be unique. He gave life to Adam; he gave life to all of us. He chose Christ as the Son of Man and made Him divine. According to Christ Himself, He'll lead mankind to the last hour, then save it. If He fails, He would go, too. He never accepted His Divinity, because God is only One. Any breach in the foundation will bring down the whole structure."

"Who told you that? Peter Moughabee?" asked the Pope.

"Yes, in a manner of speaking. After his death, many seeds thrown into me started growing."

"Like Jesus and His Church."

"Like Jesus and Humanity. He won over death not through His resurrection but by being one with everyone, an undiluted part of all people. After the last man dies, His resurrection will be pointless."

"Why did you choose this oriental fashion of thinking?"

"Christ thought as an oriental. If it was good for Him, it's good enough for me."

"Are you talking about His stay in India?"

"Yes, and the development of his mind. To insist that at the age of ten he had a fully developed mind is foolish. You know perfectly well that story is from the life of Moses. At that time, Christ knew nothing but his own churlish boyishness. Why do you remain steeped in dogma? You must prove yourself as a leader not as a follower," explained Gordon.

The old man closed his eyes, hiding the terrible pains of his sickness. "Because without the dogma there will be no Church."

"Isn't it the Church of Christ?"

"No, it isn't. He left us a long time ago, when we made a Deity out of Him."

In a sudden lurch, Gordon fell to his knees.

"Save the Church by making it whole again! Accept Christ as He is and He'll do the rest. This world needs a Messiah more than ever."

"The world needs unity. That's our last chance," protested the Pope.

"The communists tried to unify the world with an iron dogma. What makes you think that yours is any better? It hasn't won in two thousand years. Humanity has never been so divided and hopeless."

The Pope put his hand on Gordon's head. "The mummy can help us. It is the living Jesus, isn't it?"

"Lord Aton could be Christ; their teachings are amazingly comparable. However, what's in the mummy is only Aton."

"My Prelate in Jerusalem wrote me the same. He had met Aton twice. The incredible thing is that Aton was reliving the Passions of Christ in the Garden of Gethsemane."

"You don't believe in the preemptiveness of the soul, do you, Holiness?"

"I want to, but I can't," admitted the Pontiff.

"Why? If there is a piece of God in everyone of us..."

"No! It can't be. That will prove Satan's right to own a piece of us too," admonished the Pope.

"Isn't that fact? The belief of the ancient Egyptians in their Ka? You know my body was possessed by Ikhnaton, don't you?"

"There is something barbaric in these possessions."

"The Copts are not barbaric, in spite of their persecution by the Church, Holy Father."

"Should I blame the Church?"

"If you really love the Church, you have to do it. To repent is not an act of humiliation. I don't know if God is always just, but repentance means to put your sins in His hands and let Him be the judge. We have to trust Him, Your Holiness. We owe that much to Him. He had entrusted us with the most sublime gift in His Creation — LIFE."

"And LOVE, my dear boy. I want to see Aton in person. If he is Christ, then humanity could be spared from Armageddon. I'll talk to all heads of states, even if I have to visit everyone of them. But first I have to know who you are."

"Holiness, I'm not Christ, if that's what you are thinking. I'm not even myself anymore. Perhaps, I'm just the messenger. What do you expect of me?" Gordon asked the Pope almost desperately.

"To arrange a meeting between me and Lord Aton," demanded the Pontiff.

Gordon shook his head sadly, "Only my father was capable of taking physical entities to the home of Aton. I can relate to Him, but His coming visually depends entirely on His own will."

"Are you capable of hearing him?"

"Yes, Holiness, I can hear him speaking in my soul."

"I have a soul too, young man. Take me to Him."

Gordon shuddered at the thought of taking the responsibility for the life of this sickly man.

"But it is an arduous journey. There are extreme forces opposing the very idea. They almost succeeded in downing our chopper on the way here."

"What kind of forces do you mean — demons?"

"The Ka of the dead is kept away from Heaven only because they challenged the existence of God. First, you must make peace with them; even Aton wasn't permitted to enter the Gates of Heaven. On Sirius, He reigns over the still unrepentant shadows of the past."

They both listened to the storm raging outside, it was as if providing sound effects to Gordon's words. The last of them were almost whispered, "Christ is still on Earth. He wants to be with His beloved people to the last no matter how many times their ignorance would kill Him. He could be a young boy, a flower, the rainbow in stormy clouds, or the Sacrificial Lamb. He might be in this room, watching and listening to our conversation."

"But that's blasphemy! He is in Heaven with His Father."

Gordon smiled gently. "Am I with my father wherever he is?"

"You don't accept the Divinity of Christ?"

"I accept His omnipresence."

The Pope fidgeted in his velvet chair.

"You and I possess the gift of many tongues, but not one of them can smooth our differences."

"Isn't the divergence of thinking the most precious gift of God? How can you expect everybody to think like you. Even the members of your Curia have their own minds. They only pretend to share your views. Your worse detractors hide behind this fractious unity. If you cannot unify them, how do you expect to put together different religions and build bridges between hostile nations, if you insist on sticking to the letter of a dogma born in the Middle Ages? You banish the use of contraceptives in full view of dwindling resources and crashing economies, while crying over the sufferance and miseries of millions. Isn't that a shocking example of hypocrisy?"

"Life is sacred," said the Pope.

"Certainly not for those born to die of malnutrition in servitude to tyrants. If dignity of life cannot be preserved, what's the purpose of it? Christ was for an egalitarian society. Who gave the right to His Church to be disrespectful of His Words? Isn't that a blasphemy?" Gordon argued.

The Pontiff covered His face with trembling hands. "Oh, Gordon, Gordon, the treasures of the Vatican cannot alleviate the sufferings of the poor."

"If poverty is improper, why doesn't God, in his eternal *misericordia*, eradicate it? Is it expecting too much of a just and rightful God that He punish the insatiable greed of the high and mighty lords, instead of leaving the meek and righteous people of this world in misery and despair?" Gordon continued his point.

"You have more unanswered questions than I, Gordon. Let's talk to Lord Aton. Maybe he will be able to enlighten us. I'm sure that you have inherited not only the spirit of Peter Moughabee, but some of his 'unholy' gifts too. You'll never know your own limitations if you don't try the impossible."

Gordon was flabbergasted, "Now!?!"

The old man nodded,

"What am I supposed to do?" Gordon asked again.

"What have you been doing to contact Lord Aton until now?" the Pope wanted to know.

"I need the proximity of the mummy."

"Get yourself on the same wave length, imagine yourself situated right next to Aton."

Gordon rose to his feet and looked outside at the raging storm. He closed his large dark eyes and focused on his innermost being. Gradually his swarthy face started emanating a soft golden light. The storm diminished until everything came to a standstill. The clock stopped and all electric lamps in the room dimmed and went off as if someone turned the power off. Darkness was as complete as in the moments before the creation. Then, from the farthest corner of the room, a silhouette outlined by bluish scintillating rays came into full view. It stopped at a certain distance from the Pontiff's desk, prohibitive like the Truth Itself. Then, from the scintillating image emanated, "Hail Caesar *Imperator, morituri Te salutant*."

The Pope was deeply impressed by the voice and the royal bearings of the newcomer. He tried to stand up but couldn't find the energy to do it.

"Are you the noble shadow of the great Pharaoh Amenhotep IV, also known as Ikhnaton?"

The face became dark and somber.

"Yes, I am. What do you want of me?"

"I would hope for some advice from Lord Aton."

"What do you expect to learn from him?"

"I have some specific questions directed only to him."

"I have knowledge of divine matters. So, ask me."

"Why does the Lord of Sirius refuse my plea for help?"

"Because Gordon doesn't have enough power to summon Him."

"Do you?"

"I do...but I must know the reason. He can't be disturbed for nothing."

"Does the destiny of the human race mean nothing?"

"There are certain matters more pressing than yours," hissed the apparition.

"Name them," demanded the Pope.

A pause of dead silence made everything seem more unreal.

"You have no business knowing the mysteries of the underworld. I need a body in which to reside. Gordon isn't available to me anymore. His father is protecting him on all sides. You have a servant in this household. His name is Renaldo Cortelazzo. Would he let me in?"

"No, for heaven's sake, I can't bargain with you. Go back to your darkness."

The shadow laughed shrilly, "You're wrong to reject my help. A human that treats me disdainfully is bound to pay for it sooner or later. I already have in mind somebody who is out of your protection. I warn you, don't stand in my way!"

The lights came back on full force and so did the storm outside. The Pontiff tried to adjust his vision to the light. Gordon was obviously disturbed.

"I'm sorry, Holiness. I can't do it apart from the mummy. It's not in my powers.

"It was my fault, Gordon. I underestimated the force of the underworld. Now that the shadow is driven out of you and your split image terminated, Ikhnaton cannot reenter you. That was a clever move on the part of whoever devised it. You're clean now and another infiltration isn't likely. But whom did he mean was an easy target?"

"Marko Brandon, a young prize fighter losing his battle with drugs and women. He's sore about my refusal to bring his girlfriend on this trip. He's been increasingly dependent on Ikhnaton for money and entertainment. I don't think the Pharaoh likes him that much, but under the circumstances, he has little choice."

The Pope was very tired. It was well after midnight.

"That seems a deadly combination. Marko will be supervised around the clock by Renaldo. They'll share a room and. Renaldo knows how to cope with this situation. He's one of my best sleuths."

"Was my marriage to Helena one of his tricks? We still have not received any written proof. It was a strange wedding."

"The marriage between a Catholic and someone that doesn't belong to any denomination is difficult to justify. I should've done something about it, but there were other priorities. So much of the Dogma is so ingrained in the brains of our fanatics, that any change is considered a crime. You'll get your marriage papers from my office."

"Why didn't Renaldo explain it to me if he is such a gem?"

"An oversight I'm sure. Now we have to prepare for the journey. For the time being, since the counsel of the mummy is not available, I'm asking you to come along."

"There are quite a number of differences between us," Gordon reminded the old Pontiff.

"There will be only a few left after asking for pardon, not only from the Copts, but from everyone wronged by the Catholic Church."

"That must be a very long speech, Holiness."

"Of course, I cannot go into details but generally it will cover all important points."

"In that case, I'll come with you," agreed Gordon.

"And your entourage?"

Gordon had a problem concentrating. "Including some of my entourage."

The Pope looked at him attentively. "You must be very tired after all. I should've asked for a dinner, then we could've talked while eating. What is happening to you, young man?"

Gordon tried to get up from the chair but an overwhelming fatigue kept him down. Suddenly, he seemed completely in control of all his faculties. Though, he actually had fallen into a deep sleep. The Pontiff somehow was aware of what was taking place and wasn't surprised when the young man spoke in a different voice."

"Gordon can rest while we have our conversation. We have never met before."

The old man struggled to raise up in honor of his guest. "I'm sorry, Lord Aton, my body doesn't obey me anymore."

"I know, Berrik (Berrik was the childhood name of the Pope). Old age has its shortcomings. I was lucky to die young. You should pay more attention to your health. By the way, your command of our ancient language is formidable."

"I had a good tutor, Aton. In this informal situation, we should save time by cutting the corners. I know that you cannot answer all my questions, so I promise to be quite diplomatic."

"You don't have to, old man, I simply wouldn't answer if you ask something inappropriate."

"Gordon is of great help."

"Yes, he turned out to be an admirable human being. Use him well while he lasts," Aton answered quietly.

The Pope found it difficult to assimilate that cryptic remark. "Is the Last Judgment that close?" he asked Lord Aton.

"The Last Judgment has already started, Berrik. I'm talking about Gordon's transfiguration from his physical into the empirical state, what you call spiritual."

"Are you telling me that Gordon is going to die?"

"Yes. In three months time according to your Gregorian Calendar. Don't be sad, Berrik. Life in Heaven is not entirely that bad. By that time, Gordon will have sired a male child, that will be extremely important to all of us."

"The New Christ?" asked the Pontiff, suddenly raising his head.

"Yes, the one and only Christ. He doesn't have to change."

The Pontiff had a problem finding his voice. "Does Gordon know about this?"

"I think he feels it and understands it."

"And there is nothing that can change this?"

"Nothing. A Pope tampering with destiny is unpardonable. You can express things in general like in this sermon about the repentance, but the sermon itself is just *pro forma*. It can change nothing, because people have lost their usefulness. They have become dangerous for the Universe as a whole. Somewhere along the way, people made fatal mistakes and tried to cover them with pretty fairy tales. But life is about Truth, not outdated fantasies and dreams. It's nice that finally you have found enough courage to speak out the truth, or at least some of it. I know how deeply in the fabric of life falsehood has its roots. Many 'perfectionists' think that the Church can't be wrong. Indeed, how wrong they are! Even the Gospels were manufactured with good intention but with bad results. Pardons have been sold to the rich and mighty, and just and righteous people have been put to death for stating the truth. Others have been persecuted for their religious beliefs. And that's only the tip of the iceberg. How much of it can you wash away in a speech?"

The Pope answered, "Very little, though what I say will be told with unshakable conviction. As far back as my college days, I was ready to denounce everything. Then it came to me that in the Holy Church is much more than the eye can see. In any doctrine there exists a moment of truth that puts it to the test. Now I know the negative sides as well as the positive. As far as you're concerned, you don't advertise your reincarnation in Christ. The physical and facial likeness is striking. It seems that Jesus had taken the dying torch from your hands and rekindled it so even twenty centuries weren't able to extinguish the fire. This you didn't try because the historical moment wasn't right, and you had to lay your foundation in the palace. I agree you had no choice. In that time common people didn't count. They lacked the level of consciousness which allowed them to hear the message later. In this sense, I see the factor of reincarnation. Michael-Angelo Buonarotte and Ludwig van Beethoven were unique. Their reincarnations sprouted further in many artists and composers, making us proud to call ourselves human beings. The Church had a good start but, then for centuries, it fell into the hands of leaders who used it for their own political ends, accumulating untold riches for themselves. Christ was used as an agent, and everything that stood in their way was put under fire. Many excruciating tortures were created during this period. Legions were sent to deliver the Holy Land. They grew in sophistication and even Jesus became an obstacle. No problem! A new Christ was invented to bless all projects of the Holy Church. In those times truth was easily silenced; in modern times it isn't quite so easy. The ingenious entrepreneurs of the Church tried to stop the clock of time, even reversing it when possible. It had become a family business like the Mafia and as bloodthirsty as the Marxists. One of our Popes even had a vision of Adolph Hitler as a new Messiah. Of course, not everything done by the Church was wrong. It excelled in many ways. But the rest is hard to explain. All I can do is ask for pardon. I know the likes of Mother Theresa will stand behind me."

Lord Aton was silent; then, his voice came again, "I'm sorry, Berrik. The sermon is good as sermons go, though try to inject some life in it. Use more true life examples instead of outlines. I never learned how to write, so I can't help you with that. Gordon isn't a writer either, but he is a natural talker. He can be very helpful to you. Clear and simple talk. But a pope is a pope. When the time comes, don't try to come between the bullet and Gordon. I know how easily he gets under your skin. His father is a charmer too. You have it also when you don't try philosophizing beyond belief. I might drop in again for a chat, though don't expect me to prompt you in everything. You'll blame it on the hard times. Mine weren't any better."

Gordon woke up, startled. "God Almighty, I've been sound asleep," he exclaimed, a little chagrined.

The Pontiff smiled kindly. "I took full advantage of your snooze."

"You slept too?" Gordon asked with some relief.

"In a way…I was rehearsing my sermon."

"I hope it was a good one, your Holiness?"

"Terrible, Gordon, terrible. Exactly the way you dislike it most."

"That's true, I don't like sermons."

"Well, then let's go to bed. Don't wake up your wife. You can tell her everything in the morning."

Before leaving, he caught a strange expression in the eyes of the old man. It was something akin to love and pity. Gordon had not seen that look directed at him before.

"Good night, Holiness!"

"Good night, my son!"

The light was on. Helena was reading in bed, a number of cigarette butts in the ashtray.

"How was your audience with the Pope, darling?"

Gordon had started undressing. "Incredible! I slept in the presence of His Holiness. I had a strange dream." Then he changed direction, "If you smoke that much, it makes no sense brushing my teeth."

"Very funny. You're excused."

Gordon made a flying leap and landed next to her, then kissed her in the mouth until she had no breath left. He laughed happily, "Lucky Strike. Can't you use something more feminine?"

"No. I like male stuff. Your body for example, it always turns me on."

"That's good news. Switch off the light."

"Wait a minute…I want to brush my teeth to get rid of some of that Lucky Strike." She went to the bathroom, "What was your dream by the way?"

Gordon was lying on his back, hands tucked behind his head. "Wild. I was with the Pope at some kind of an official function. Suddenly, I noticed a face in the crowd that I recognized. He took quick aim at the Pope and pulled the trigger. I only had time to catch the bullet."

Helena was at the door deadly pale. "Oh, Gordon! Who was the man?"

"I don't remember. Besides, His Holiness is the last man that I'll save with my life."

"Gordon, Renaldo showed me the newspaper clipping about my father's death."

"I know. You told me already."

"I didn't tell you everything. That same evening when I talked to the nurse…"

Gordon interrupted, "I remember. You said you were 'Titi.' "

"Father sent the nurse away, made it to the balcony rail and threw himself over. I knew, he'd get the message. I did it for my mother, using her name. Anyway his death would've been horrendously painful and prolonged. I did it to him with no remorse whatsoever." She came to the bed but sat away from him, "Does that make me a murderer, Gordon?"

"I don't know, Helena. We are led to make choices — like in my dream. If I choose the bullet, I may die."

Next morning they slept late.

A swim in the cool waters of the pool was pleasantly refreshing. They swam shoulder to shoulder. Helena was subdued.

"Like in Jerusalem," she reminded him.

"Yes, Helena, like in Jerusalem. I wonder if by swimming together we're breaking the protocol for a Papal Residence? All the staff must be at the windows gawking."

"Do you care?"

"Not really. Lately, breaking rules seems to be my favorite activity."

"We don't even have a marriage certificate."

"Our gracious host promised to take care of that," Gordon promised with the hope that the Pope would remember to follow through.

"I quit. You can swim more. Don't forget to put on your bathrobe."

"No, I'm coming out with you. But I'll stop off at the gym to lift some weights, then, I'll join you for lunch."

The gym was exploding with action. Renaldo and Marko were going at each, other clad only in gymnastic shorts. It wasn't just sparring — it was a real bare-knuckles fight. Judging by their bodies, which were bathed in sweat, it had started quite sometime ago. Gordon knew a grudge fight when he saw one. Neither one of them was giving ground. They just kept on punching without any care for safety. Both of them had blood spurting from their mouths and noses. Angry red welts were appearing on their tight, muscular abdomens.

They kicked wildly at each other and grappled into a clinch, knees digging into rib cages and below. Marko's endurance was ebbing. He used some dirty tricks, but Renaldo skillfully repelled them. Suddenly, an uppercut, an elbow hook, then a knee in the crotch and Marko fell to the mat, disoriented.

"Do you want more?" Renaldo asked huskily, "For a pro, you show damn little."

Marko tried to get up, his bloody mouth gasping for air. He collapsed completely.

Renaldo picked up his towel and saw Gordon. "I didn't know you were watching," he said, wiping his face and upper body. "How do you like our champ?"

"You messed up the knuckles of your hands, Renaldo," Gordon observed wryly.

"They'll be O.K. I had to do it. He was asking for it," he tried to explain himself and the action.

Marko sat up on the mat, breathing heavily. Blood and perspiration dripped from his chin and he glowered at them with hatred. Gordon made a move, but Renaldo stopped him.

"Don't try to help him up. He'll hate you more for that. By the way, I have bad news for you. The credit company stopped paying your charges."

Gordon looked stunned. "Was I charging fraudulently? Nobody told me anything."

"Helena was paying the bills. Your dad had bankrupted himself financially. His real estate properties were seized by the banks. I'm sorry to be the one to tell you, but that's a fact."

Gordon smiled. "Right on the chin, thanks anyway," he said as he clamped a friendly hand on Renaldo's shoulder.

"I'm going to the showers. See you later." Renaldo walked away.

Gordon waited for him to leave, then went to Marko and kneeled on the mat in front of him. "You can't win them all. I'll train you, if you just quit boozing and stop all the drugs."

"Fuck you! Keep the advice for yourself; at least I'm not a kept man. I know how to pay my bills," Marko sneered.

"Then you know better than I. I won't take any more money from Helena."

Marko spat out some bloody saliva and a broken tooth. "Leave me alone, motherfucker, don't keep Helena waiting."

Gordon got up to his feet and left the gym without another look at him. Now he had figured out who the man from his dream was. Ikhnaton had found someone else to possess.

THEATER OF THE ABSOLUTE: GORDON STEPS UP TO THE PROSCENIUM

"Dear Dad, I'll drink the bitter cup to the bottom, but I won't let Helena pay my bills. Maybe I can get a good price for the mummy. The Pope is ready to pay anything for it. Then he can use it as a bargaining chip. Maybe that would settle all arguments. Of course, this is an unsavory joke on my part. I own nothing.

"Well, I have to follow up on my mission, but I can't charge it to the Pontiff. In spite of everything, he is a good man. I can feel that. No hard feelings, father, I didn't expect even that much. When you picked me up in Memphis I was nothing. Now I have you, a beautiful wife and a murderer waiting in the wings. The show must go on.

"I'm neither ungrateful nor grateful. I'll be doing my job methodically and with diligence. At least now I know what LOVE is.

"God speed in your new body, Ikhnaton. You'll feel better within a sore loser. I won't betray you, because in a way I feel for you too. We both came from the same neighborhood.

"I'll do anything to make Helena happy...if she knows what happiness is."

PART THREE

THE SALVATION

Chapter 16

ASSASSINS

CAN YOU SAVE ME, GOD?
CERTAINLY, IF YOU KNOW WHAT SALVATION IS.
— An ancient Aramaic rhyme

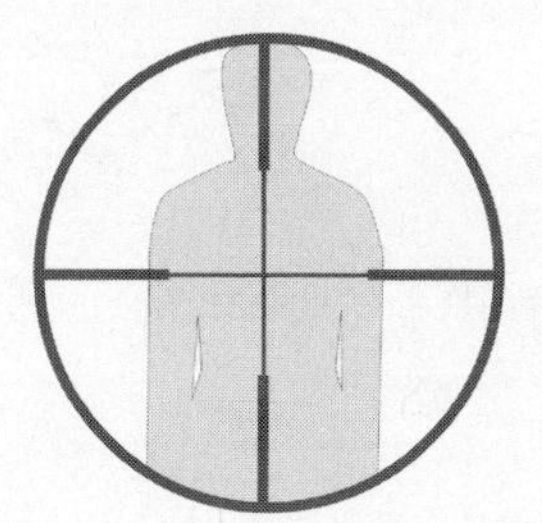

Gordon woke up alone in the large Gothic bed. The Pontiff's retreat in this southern port was small but comfortable. The plumbing was new and all facilities were functional. It was surrounded by splendid gardens full of ancient statuary. The building's medieval style didn't spoil the general view.

When Helena entered the room, Gordon was showering. "Where did you go so early, Helena?" he shouted.

"I went to services. I wish you would come with me sometime."

Gordon came out draped in a bath towel. He kissed Helena's head as she nestled against his shoulder and tenderly caressed her shiny, long hair.

"Is there a special reason?"

"Yes, dear. I'm expecting our baby."

Gordon was speechless with joy and pride. When he got his voice back he whispered in her ear: "I never thought I could have a family of my own. I want to build a nice home somewhere, a real home. I can build it with my own hands. Please, Helena, don't pay my bills. I know I'm busted. I have to save some respect for myself."

"Gordon, listen," Helena shook her head ever so slightly, "money is nothing to me. You're more important to the world than working as a laborer. The Pope is counting on you, I'm sure you'll be paid something."

Gordon smiled with bitterness. "For the mummy?"

"No, darling. You've changed. Your communication skills are excellent. The special gifts you now have make you indispensable. The Pope knows about your strained financial situation."

"Did you tell him?"

"No, Renaldo did. In spite of his youth, he has the ear of His Holiness. The Pope likes to lean on young people to give them opportunities."

Gordon got dressed hurriedly. "I have to think it over. Do you mind if I take a walk in the garden by myself?"

"Of course not. Finally, some mail caught up with me. I'll look through it."

Gordon, unable to gather his thoughts, walked twice around the building and then into a narrow alley. He spotted Marko sitting desolately on a marble bench. They looked at each other with uneasiness. Someone had done a very good job mending his face.

"Can I share the bench with you, Marko?" Gordon asked.

"This bench isn't mine."

He didn't sound hostile. Gordon sat at the opposite end then moved a bit closer. "Have you heard anything about your father?"

"I don't have money to call, but this morning I got a postcard from Aldano. The old man is getting by pretty well, which is more than I can say about myself. I'm sorry I badmouthed you yesterday. I can't seem to do anything right. I've been told to leave, but I don't have money for that, either. In this sorry state, I can't claim my boat. By now those crazy gangsters at the marina have taken possession of her. Susanna was the only thing I had in the world."

"No money from home?"

"Nope...not with my father incapacitated and Aldano out of a job."

"Can't Aldano drive the limousine?"

"It has been sold. Do you have a cigarette?"

"No, I don't. Who told you to leave?"

"The Majordomo with the funny uniform. Renaldo kicked me out of his room."

Gordon pondered for awhile. "I can't ask my wife to lend you any money, but I could press Renaldo to let you stay as a guard. Guards are paid well."

"Are you mad? Those medieval uniforms and allebards, I'd look worse than a clown."

Gordon shrugged his shoulders. "It's a job."

"Would you take it?"

"I've worked on construction sites before as a daily laborer. I would've jumped at anything colorful and fancy," Gordon assured him.

Marko thought deeply, "Fancy-shmancy, I need the money. Renaldo thinks the world of you. Helena says the Pope listens to him. As a guard, I could have my broken tooth repaired."

Gordon went on to warn Marko, "But no cigarettes and drugs for awhile. Stay clean and get to the gym every day. I think you can beat the shit out of Renaldo if you get back in shape. We can run together."

"Sweet Jesus, aren't you the smooth talker! It doesn't hurt to try. Here's my hand. Gimme five, as they say in your country," Marko quipped, offering his hand.

"By the way, how old are you, Marko?" Gordon asked.

"Twenty-two."

"You look younger. A blazing future awaits you with the Vatican. In no time, you'll be captain of the guards."

For the first time since he met him, Marko laughed. The morning was suddenly bursting with laughter too. It was great to be twenty-two.

Ikhnaton knew how to wait for thousands of years.

The Pope misunderstood. He thought that Gordon needed his friend Marko if he had to spend time traveling abroad. So he signed his appointment to the guards without checking the matter with Renaldo. Renaldo felt circumvented but said nothing. His grudge against Marko was no secret. Renouncing it would've given the wrong connotation. He decided to discuss it only with Gordon. The most likely place to find him was the swimming pool. Helena would swim with him only in the mornings. Renaldo changed into his swim-briefs and wrapped himself in a bathrobe.

Gordon was delighted to see him. At first they swam a few laps in silence, then Renaldo opened up. "Do you mind if I share some qualms of mine with you, man-to-man?"

A slight hesitation in Gordon's stroke was the only hint of his uneasiness.

"Of course not, Renaldo. You're a friend. Helena thinks the world of you."

"I'm glad to hear that. She is a very mature person for her age. Let's get out of the pool and have a few words."

They pulled themselves up to the edge and sat on the side, legs dangling in the water. Renaldo got right to the point. "Helena was worried about a dream of yours."

Gordon smiled disarmingly. "I should've kept it to myself. It's really nothing."

"How much do you know about Marko, besides what you were told by his younger brother and his father?"

"Nothing," Gordon said pensively. "I know almost nothing about you either, except that your father was murdered, wasn't he?"

"I thought so. Yes, my father was a strange man. My job in the household is to gather information in order to prevent nasty things from happening," Renaldo went on to explain.

"Is that why you kicked Marko out of you room?"

Renaldo blushed. "That was wrong, but I was mad at him. Since I was a child, I've wanted everything around me to be orderly. Marko's just the opposite. The few things he has were all over my room. Dirty underwear, musty socks, even a screw driver in the bed. He likes snacking while watching TV, dropping hunks of food on the carpet. He talks a lot too. I wasn't brought up that way. Even though I am an only child, I wasn't spoiled by my parents. My father was a German with a tainted past. Mother came from Finland and was extremely religious. The family name, Cortelazzo, was borrowed from the late count Chano, comte di Cortelazzo and di Pounkierre.

When I was a young boy on a sunny holiday in Rome, I was borne on the shoulders of my father to see the passing of the Pope. The boulevard's sidewalks were jammed with people, from all sides and overflowing into the streets. My father was a tall man, and I had a perfect vantage point for observation, so I saw the Pope dressed all in white, waving on all sides. Then, like in a slow motion film, I spotted a young man pushing ahead. Suddenly he aimed a gun at the Pontiff. The rest was a big commotion, but I knew that the Holy Father was hurt and the perpetrator apprehended. What I didn't know then was why anybody in the world would want to kill the Pope. Father was aware of my confusion and as the case surfaced in newspapers and on television, he tried to explain a few facts of life to me. The attack against the Pontiff wasn't a spur of the moment thing. It was a murder, systematically organized in the communist country, Bulgaria. The young Turk chosen for this crime had been trained by the Bulgarian Secret Service, given detailed instructions, then sponsored by someone on the staff of the Bulgarian Embassy in Rome. This kind of plotting is preventable if checked in time. Then and there I made up my mind to specialize in that particular field of crime prevention."

"What happened to the Turk?"

"When the Pope recovered, he went to see him in prison. The young man truly repented and made a clean breast of all that happened. He gave the investigators names, addresses and locations in Bulgaria. But as in Nazi Germany, the Justice System there was a toy in the hands of the Party Leaders. They said such a plot never existed and the conspirators named by the Turk were completely innocent."

Gordon lifted his eyebrows. "Quite a story. Coming from another environment, I heard widely different versions of the same story. Growing up without anybody to advise me on those subjects, I had to find all the answers on my own. Sometimes I was right, sometimes wrong. Even now, though I found my real father, I'm still groping in the dark. Marko is the man in my dream and that's exactly why I want him to come with us. If you send Marko back to Malta, there will be nothing to prevent. We'll never know if my dream was true or just another dream. See, you and Marko are both blond and of comparable height and build. In a crowd it would be hard to tell the difference between you two."

"And you'll put your life on the firing line for the life of our Holy Father?"

"You don't see the point of your own story quite well, Renaldo. God didn't want the Pope killed, and in spite of the elaborate preparations, the plot failed. If God wants me to go, I won't prevent His Will. Of course, I want to build a home for my wife and see my child growing up. But all of that isn't even a grain of sand in the palm of God. Jesus is something else, He personally cares about us, because He never saw His child growing up. Perhaps, He'll take care of my son."

Renaldo had a mind of his own.

The job as a guard to the Pope was boring and frustrating to the highly ambitious Marko Brandon. His dreams were about being the center of attention. The life of a professional prizefighter has its ups and downs. He had been very hopeful at the beginning and made some money. When his manager tried him out with better fighters, Marko hit a losing streak. Entertainment and women coupled with a few drinks didn't help much. At first, drugs helped him win several fights. Then, he got knocked out three times in a row and the manager left him. His father wanted him to get a regular job, but that wasn't easy. Aldano was his sole admirer. When Helena came on the scene, Marko had aspirations towards her. His kid brother became deeply disappointed in him. Marko thought that all women were for his taking. In this case it didn't work.

Things got really strange when he felt possessed by an invisible stranger. That was beyond Marko's experience. At first it wasn't such a bad partnership. Marko became a little more attractive and physically he became quicker and stronger. He even had some dreams about people and places he never knew. For some reason, when he moved to the villa, his inner "partner" kept mostly silent. Renaldo got a whiff of something and started being nasty; he'd have to give him a good beating. Instead, Marko was sent to the mat bleeding profusely, right in front of Gordon.

He believed Gordon found him this job to humiliate him. Of course, Helena would never speak to a simple guard, and the rest of the men patronized him. Only Gordon was sticking by him, though that was probably to enjoy his final triumph over a totally defeated and humiliated Marko Brandon. His father and Aldano sent him a couple of post cards but never said "come home."

When an entrepreneur promised to arrange a couple of fights for him in Sicily, he took the bait immediately. He was in fair shape thanks to regular sparring and running with Gordon. The gentlemen asked Marko to keep it secret for the time being. They soon met in a small bar on the other side of the city.

The entrepreneur was *molto simpatico*. His name was Donald, and he looked oriental. After a drink or two, Marko opened up to him. He explained the chain of events that led to his K.O.'s by lesser opponents. It was all a matter of bad luck. The foreigner listened to him attentively, nodding his head from time to time. Finally, he said that Marko Brandon deserved something much bigger than puny bouts. He'd offered bigger fights with better pay. He'd scout around and come back to him with a viable offer. The important thing was not to leave his job as a guard, and never confide in anyone, even to a priest about their meeting. His commander wouldn't approve of him going back into prize-fighting.

Reasonable enough for Marko. Though, the next morning after sparring with Gordon, he asked him if he could take a pro-fight now. Gordon looked at Marko somewhat hesitantly. "If I were you, Marko, I would wait a few months before doing that. Your reflexes are still slow, and your punches need more dynamite. But you are coming along."

Marko felt like he had been hit below the belt. He gripped Gordon's shoulder and said in a petulant voice, "If next time, I knocked you down for the count, would that be enough?"

Gordon shook his head, "I'm not a boxer, Marko. If you insist, I think Renaldo would accept your challenge. He owes you a rematch."

Marko thought briefly. "That's fine and dandy with me. He's just an amateur, but he hits hard and has lasting power. I can match his endurance now. I know I can win."

"I hope you're right," said Gordon putting on his bathrobe, "I would've waited for at least another month."

"I'm not you, Gordon. I have a career to take care of. I'm not gonna be a crappy guard to the Pope for the rest of my fucking life."

On his way out, Gordon looked at him sadly. "I sincerely wish you good luck, Marko."

GORDON IN THEATER OF THE ABSURD

Dear God, I don't know if I'm following Your path or goofing off as usual. I have never been a serious thinker and I've left things to go their own way. Ostensibly, my life has shifted into unknown territory. With Your help, I'm the head of a family. My decisions affect not only myself but a number of other people, too, the least of whom is His Holiness the Pope. Something really wrong is going on inside Marko. How can I betray him? I don't know how to proceed with him. He'll hate me if I don't match him up against Renaldo, and he'll hate me even more if Renaldo flattens him for a second time. I cannot ask Renaldo to throw the fight. He despises him, but nevertheless, if Marko wins, it's gonna be the worst of all outcomes. He'll be on an ego trip where the sky will be his limit. If I beat him, then his hatred may center just on me, and the others may be spared. Though, I'm not that sure if I can hit a fellow man as hard as before, especially a poor young man like Marko. He's so much like I was in the past. I was blind prior to meeting You. I killed like a beast, just because someone else was making my decisions. If the same is going inside Marko, how can I help him?

I cannot talk about this to anybody but You. Not to Helena, because it was her brother that I murdered, not to Lord Aton, nor even to my father. Jesus is like a brother to me, though I won't drag Him into this sordid affair. Why am I loading it on You, God, something of so little importance to Your Celestial Kingdom? Maybe, this is a matter that I can take straight to the Pope. He had a similar or quasi-similar experience. He talked to his would-be murderer. A man like him won't betray my confidence. He'll understand!

Thank You, God. Amen.

PAPAL RESIDENCE

Next morning, the secretary took Gordon to the Pontiff's apartment. The Pope was working at his desk. When Gordon entered, he stopped momentarily and looked at him with a kind smile.

"Oh, Gordon, how nice of you to come and see me."

"I'm sorry to interrupt your work, Holy Father."

"Quit that formality, son. I'm really glad to see you. Sit down, please, and cut out the holiness business. I know you came with something specific on your mind."

Gordon had a last moment of trepidation. He then jumped straight into the cold water without thinking how cold it was.

"Renaldo told me that years ago there was an attempt on your life. May I ask, why did you talk to your would-be-assassin? Was it the publicity, or did you really believe that you could change him?"

The Pope closed his red-rimmed eyes, took off his eyeglasses and cupped his hand at his chin. "Let me see. I think I was just curious." He opened up his eyes with a little flame of gaiety in them, "Yes, that's what it was, but then I felt sorry for him. You know, the Russian Emperor Alexander II miraculously survived a bomb thrown at his equipage. Horses and some of his Cossacks were torn to pieces. The landau was entirely demolished. His entourage insisted on his taking a horse, leaving the scene immediately. In the aftermath, the Emperor wanted to see the young man who threw the bomb and who was now in the hands of the guards. Unfortunately, there was another terrorist on the opposite side of the street. His bomb killed the Emperor, his assailant and the guards on the spot. That terrorist was the brother of Vladimir Ullianov — later known as Lenin. The brother was tried and received capital punishment. Then and there Lenin swore that he'd destroy the Romanov's Dynasty. After he took the reins of the Russian Revolution, he ordered the whole family to be machine-gunned, even the children weren't spared. The Russian Tzar had just liberated everybody from serfdom — Lenin enslaved the nation again, employing extreme cruelty. I'm not quite sure that God made the right choice, but very often God's mind is unfathomable. If the second bomb hadn't exploded and Alexander II had had time to talk with these young men, the whole of history might've been much different. I chose a safer way. I saw my young would-be-assassin in the prison block and got to know him personally."

"What did he have to say?"

"He said that he had been framed by the Bulgarians, but I think money was the temptation. I was positive that he wouldn't do it again for anything in the world."

"Why?"

"Because he never saw me as a person. Money was on his mind. But then, he realized that I was not the man described to him by the Communists. Actually, when he pulled the trigger, he felt strongly that what he was doing wasn't right, and that affected his aim. He wasn't a blind fanatic, he thought of himself as an opportunist. And that makes a difference. Why do you want to know?"

That information from the Pontiff made the current situation seem more clear in Gordon's mind.

"I'm concerned about Marko Brandon. I think he is just another opportunist, a drifter as I used to be. Marko thinks of himself as a soldier of fortune who is out of luck and money. He wants his self-reliance as a prizefighter restored. He needs to win over Renaldo or me but not through a fixed fight. Marko is able to tell the difference. No matter what the outcome is, he won't stop. He's in the hands of a crafty operator. How do you think we should handle him — try sending him home?"

The Pope seemed preoccupied for a moment, then with a tired smile he asked the question, "Guilty as charged even before the trial?"

"Renaldo and I could follow him up close. If we fail, one of us is expendable."

"Renaldo won't go for it. He's highly motivated. And neither one of you is expendable."

"Then what?"

The Pope looked straight into Gordon's eyes and cut back to business, "I'm expendable."

"You? For heavens sake, you're the most important person on the scene Holiness."

"I'm old, tired and desperate," the Pontiff sighed.

"What do you mean?"

"I mean what you mean. By now you know that centuries ago the Church went the wrong way. Nobody had the courage to reveal Her crimes against Christ and humanity. Now with Judgment Day at hand there is no more time for excuses. I have to tell the Truth and ask all wronged people for pardon, starting with the Copts and ending with Christ. After that my life will be expendable."

"You knew all along!" gasped Gordon.

"Of course, I knew it long before I was elected. The tampering with the testaments, the cult to the Madonna and the life of Christ, the sporadic killing sprees of the Holy Church, the persecutions of righteous people and the tacit acceptance of the Holocaust. Some priests fought the Nazis; others created asylums for the fleeing war criminals while the Vatican prepared false passports for their safe journey to South America. When the Italian Emperor pleaded with the Pope to intercede before the German Tribunal in favor of his daughter, the Pope's answer was short and clear: "The Church shouldn't be involved in earthly matters." Princess Ada died in Auschwitz as did millions and millions — without as much as a prayer from the Pope. How could anybody explain that to God? I'll ask for forgiveness. I'm fully expendable."

Renaldo eagerly accepted the rematch with Marko. This time they both agreed to wear boxing gloves, though kicks, elbows and tripping would be legal. Gordon was to be a witness, not a referee. Each protagonist had vowed to put his opponent out of circulation for at least a couple of months. Renaldo justified himself, thinking that he was protecting his employer and keeping Gordon out of harm. Neither Helena, nor the Pope had the slightest idea about these unsettling denouements. Gordon knew more than he wanted to know. Both contestants had trained intensely for the last few days. It was decided that the bout would be non-stop to the finish — no rounds or time out for injuries.

Gordon was filled with a strong negative premonition and wanted to interfere, but the hand of Destiny paralyzed his will.

Renaldo had gotten the key to a boxing club that was vacant at night. They drove downtown in a jeep and parked behind the club. Renaldo knew the place and switched on the powerful lights over the ring. The two protagonists got out of their jump suits and pulled their socks and sneakers off, stepping into the ring wearing gym shorts. Not a word was said.

Gordon bandaged their hands under the directions of the participants. The chosen gloves were the smaller, harder type, those meant to do the maximum damage. He was in a state of denial, feeling that something terrible was about to happen but doing nothing to oppose it. Was the revengeful Ikhnaton disguised as Destiny undermining his will power and sapping his strength?

Maybe Gordon was still the same man-beast as most anybody on this planet. How could he possibly pray for a good outcome? Any outcome in this case was wrong.

Now, even the Pope thought of himself as disposable.

The two predators started their contest for supremacy. Gordon heard the shuffling of their bare feet on the mat, the impacts of the small gloves on hard, muscled bodies, the painful grunts after a successful kick or a knee in the guts. They clashed, arms laced in a clinch and knee-slugged each other in the ribs.

Gordon couldn't bring himself to look at the fighting bodies in the ring. Nothing had changed — nothing will ever change. People will be beasts forever; and the stronger, craftier beast will be the winner. It had nothing to do with right and wrong — only which of the adversaries is more devastating and swift. "Now I can still stop them," he thought feverishly, "I can stop this bloody murder!"

Gordon had come to the apron of the ring, his eyes still closed tightly. The two smelly bodies clinched on the ropes right over him. He heard the labored breathing and the heavy thuds of the punches. Blood sprinkled him. One of the bodies slithered through the ropes with a dull moan of a final agony, all the way to the apron, level with Gordon's face. When Gordon opened his eyes, he met the stare of a pair of baby blue eyes, glossy and empty.

Renaldo's handsome, boyish face had been mauled to an unidentifiable point. With a sharp realization of finality, Gordon looked at the other young man. The bloody mask of Marko's face had lost its natural cockiness. His broken lips were shivering from an invisible inner cold. His greenish eyes, nearly closed by the swelling, were full of tears and silent terror. He was like a twelve year old caught at the scene of a capital error, and not yet in full realization of what had happened.

"I didn't want to do it, Gordon," he cried, "I swear to God, I didn't wamt to!"

Suddenly, Gordon was all action. He grabbed the scissors and climbed under the ropes onto the ring with a quick look around. Now Marko was really bawling, trying to stop his nosebleed with gloved hands, his thatched blond hair plastered with profuse perspiration.

Gordon pulled Marko's gloves off and cut the bandages from his hands. "Quit that sniveling, boy! Take the mop from the corner, dunk it in water and wash all the blood from the ring and the ropes!"

Marko ran for it still sobbing, while Gordon pulled Renaldo's body out of the ring and removed his gloves and bandages as well. He got him up and managed to sit him on the floor of a shower stall. Then left the water running over him and got back to the ring. Marko down on all four had cleaned most of the stains by hand.

"Pour the pail over the mat and use the rag mop!"

Gordon ran again to the showers and found a closet with towels. He took a couple, stopped the water and started drying the body. In spite of the sprinkles of kinky hair over the chest, forearms and legs, Renaldo now looked like a sleeping child. His short-cropped hair didn't need combing. Gordon closed the large lifeless eyes.

In face and body Renaldo and Marko really were look-alikes, even though they didn't know it. This young man in his prime could've still been alive, vigorous and bright if Gordon had a speck of brains in his head. Now, for the first time in his damn life he started crying.

"I'm sorry, Renaldo. I could've done something...It seems where I go, death goes too. It will soon catch up with me if that means anything to you.

He brought Renaldo's jump suit and sneakers from the main room, finished drying his muscular body and started dressing him. Marko was watching from the door, his whole body shivering.

"Get under a hot shower, Marko. The towels are over there. Get dressed quickly. I'll take Renaldo to the jeep. Switch off the lights, lock the door and bring the key."

He almost buckled under the dead weight of Renaldo. The moon was full, but there were no windows facing the back alley. Gordon laid the corpse on the back seat. In the moonbeams

Renaldo's face looked pale and finally at peace with the world. Marko came, teeth clattering, and gave the club key to Gordon. He was stuttering with despair, "I'll do anything for you, Gordon, just name it."

Gordon slipped the key into Renaldo's pocket. "Only Christ is capable of bringing back the dead, but it took God to resurrect Him. We'll never come even near to those powers. Wait a minute! How long will it take us to get back to Palermo?"

"I don't know, Gordon. The helicopter got lost in the storm, but the island isn't that big."

"Get in the jeep. We'll take Renaldo to a spot in the mountain not far from Palermo. You drive, don't you?"

Marko looked at him and nodded his head, "I've done some."

"Good enough. Between the two of us we might be there just before sunrise. That's our last chance. Don't look at me, hop in the jeep!"

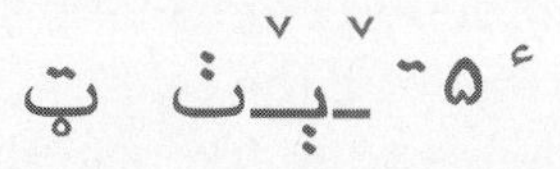

That night seemed endless.

The feeble yellowish light in front of the speeding jeep barely lit the way. There was no verbal exchange between Gordon and Marko. They only stopped to relieve themselves or to switch drivers. Both of them drove wildly but with steady hands on the wheel, eyes glued to the road. There was no other traffic. Gordon prayed not to get a flat. He hadn't checked to see if there was a spare tire. They were parched with thirst, though nobody thought of looking for water by the road. It was a race, a race with death. Every once in awhile, Gordon glanced at his watch. For some unknown reason, he felt that the sun had something to do with the success or the failure of their mission. Otherwise, this insane drive through the night was for naught.

The moon had disappeared and the stars to the east began to fade. Gordon again looked at his watch. Thank God Renaldo had the tank filled just before they had taken the vehicle. Gordon hadn't seen a single open gas station. There were also two large spare cans filled to the brim. Had Renaldo thought of going somewhere? The young man was quite methodical. Suddenly, a wild idea entered Gordon's mind. Perhaps Renaldo had intended to bury Marko's dead body somewhere. Maybe the mechanics in the residence kept all vehicles in full preparedness. Gordon tossed out all his speculations.

They had left the mountains and now sped through the foothills. Gordon remembered that, coming from the south, the gulch would appear on the opposite side of the road. Fortunately, the darkest hour before dawn had gone, and the light was becoming adequate. Gordon asked Marko to slow down.

"Here! Park the jeep in this small apron."

Suddenly, it felt freezing cold. He jumped over the side and went to the back, teeth chattering slightly. Renaldo still looked asleep, but his body had stiffened. In a hushed voice, Gordon called Marko. It took both of them to carry Renaldo's body.

A blustery wind came from the sea.

Gordon took the legs and Marko the shoulders. The mental notes Gordon had taken when he had been there before were enough for him. Was Aton's hideout really this far from the road, or was it the dead weight in their hands that made it feel twice as far? Walking over the rocks didn't help either. Now Gordon was able to discern the pile of rocks he had built over the hideout. He made a sign with his head to Marko and they settled Renaldo's body by the pile. The sun was ready to rise at any moment. Gordon got down on his knees.

"It's quite unusual to ask the Lord of the Dead to give back a life," he whispered, "but if I mean anything to you, please, help the soul of my young friend here to find its way back to his body."

At first, there was nothing and Gordon was ready to start speaking again, when the familiar vibrating, translucent light appeared around Renaldo's body. Gradually, the pale face returned to its healthy complexion. Veins start pulsating and something like an electroshock shook the young man. Renaldo's lips opened slightly and he let out a sigh, then his midriff started pumping and his chest started to move.

"Thanks, Lord Aton," uttered Gordon, "I swear, I won't bother you anymore."

Renaldo's light blue eyes opened wide. He came to his elbows and looked up at Gordon and Marko.

"Who won?" he asked in a clear voice.

Tears were running down Marko's grimy face. He fell to his knees.

"I want to know, who won the fight?" repeated Renaldo doggedly.

Marko brushed the tears off his cheeks and smiled tentatively, "You won, dummy, you gave me such a thrashing that I won't forget it to the end of my days."

Renaldo looked around. "What is this. Where in hell are we? Is this some kind of a joke?"

The sun came up in all its splendor and blazing might. Gordon and Marko helped Renaldo to his shaky feet.

"We came to see the sunrise, Renaldo," said Gordon, "isn't it something to behold?"

Renaldo shook off their hands suspiciously. "I've seen plenty of sunrises. What kind of lunatics are you? I should be back on my job. It's freezing here. Where is the car? You could've chosen a better place to watch the sun rise. Look at all these rocks."

He refused any help going to the jeep. The bruises and swellings had miraculously disappeared from his face and body. Marko had been repaired, too, including a new shiny tooth. When they came to the vehicle, Renaldo started checking through his pockets for the key but found only the Club key.

"What a night! I've got to return this. Who has the car key?"

Marko took out the key. "I have it."

"Then you drive. I have a headache. You must've bashed me solidly. I still don't have any idea where we are."

Gordon took the key from Marko. "I'll drive, get in boys. It's gonna be a long and bumpy ride."

Helena had a sleepless night.

Gordon had mentioned that he was trying to help Marko overcome his bad habits. Basically, he thought of him as a decent person. If that was true, Marko Brandon certainly didn't act like one. Was there some kind of intimacy between the two of them? He had a comparable relationship with Renaldo.

By midnight she went to Renaldo's room in the guesthouse of the compound. She ignored the risk of being seen that late in the night in the man's quarter. It didn't jive quite well with her status as a married woman. Renaldo's room was dark and empty, the king-size bed untouched. No, wait! In the full moonlight streaming through the window she made out the silhouette of a lady sitting on the bed's far side, caressing the pillow. This vision was too absurd to be real, but the lady was there. Helena made a few involuntary steps toward the bed expecting every moment that the strange woman would disappear. Instead, a face bathed with tears turned toward her. The stranger said in a heavily accented, broken voice, "Renaldo is gone forever."

"Who are you?" she finally managed to ask, stunned by this sudden apparition.

"I'm Renaldo's mother," came the answer from the woman sitting on his bed.

"What do you mean by gone forever?"

"He was killed a few minutes ago," Renaldo's mother replied tearfully.

"If that's true, what are you doing on his bed? Why are you not at the scene?"

"I cannot be there. I don't even know where to look for him."

" Who killed him and why?" asked Helena as calmly as she was able.

"I don't know. I felt it in my heart, and that's the only place he visits. I had a forlorn hope to find him soundly asleep, but now I know he's dead."

A premonition seemed to shrivel Helena's heart.

"You stay here, I need to check on something. I'll be back soon. She ran downstairs to Marko's room. He had told her the number hoping that she might drop by to see him. The doors had no locks, and Helena opened the door without knocking. The room was much smaller than the apartments upstairs. It was almost like a monastery cell. It was empty. Helena had no doubt that the three of them missing at the same time meant that something awful had happened. Gordon had mentioned the deadly grudge between the two young men and how desperately he was trying to smooth out their differences.

Had Gordon failed again?

She ran upstairs and back into Renaldo's room but the lady had vanished. Helena checked in the small bathroom. She leaned on the doorframe, her heart beating fast. Was it possible that she was dreaming? She pinched herself. No, it wasn't a dream. Helena was seized by panic. Where could she possibly look for them? Besides, if Renaldo's mother was right, all was finished by now.

The night was chilly and the harvest moon made everything in the vast park mysterious and unreal. Suddenly Helena felt that someone was following her. She started walking faster, then broke into a run. Helena lacked the courage to look over her shoulder. The steps were coming nearer and nearer, her breathing became heavy and uneven. When she reached the side entrance to the villa, she turned and faced the man.

It was her brother Aldan.

His lips were moving as if he wanted to tell her something, but an invisible force prevented him from stepping closer. After a last sad look, his substance melted in the dark-bluish shadows. Helena ran to her room and closed the door tightly. Thank God, it had a solid lock. She threw herself on the bed, a muted echo pulsated in her mind:

"Aldano, Renaldo...Aldano, Renaldo..."

Chapter 17

THE MIRACLE

Then came the rumor about The Miracle. Who had started the rumor was anybody's guess.

A man, dead for several hours from a massive brain hemorrhage, had been brought back to life, something that hadn't happened since Jesus' time.

There was little doubt that The Miracle had taken place. But the official answer from the Vatican was, "No comment." More and more evidence pointed to a man who had recently attracted quite a bit of attention. A new Man-God had emerged since the horrible earthquake in Palermo and the death of the two Nubians stoned by a crazed mob. It was said that the "mummy"' possessed by him was none other than the Son of God and he had been walking amidst people after a secret, wondrous resurrection. Many in the refugee camps of the stricken area had heard him speaking. These people swore to God that it was Jesus reincarnated and the touch of His hand could heal any infirmity. Now, that Hand had brought new life back to a completely dead body.

Thousands of hungry miracle seekers moved toward Marsala.

The Pope as usual sat at his desk, two lines carved deeply between his eyebrows. Thick velvet curtains were drawn over the windows and there was little light in the room. It mattered little if it was day or night. Gordon stood close to the desk. Right behind him, Renaldo and Marko. The Pontiff laced his fingers over a simple wooden cross.

"How did it happen, Gordon?"

"I still have very little to add to the facts that I already told you, Holiness. I wish I had a more satisfactory explanation. Desperate to turn back the tide of evil bent on destroying us, I remembered The Miracle that saved my life from the tidal wave. I was acting on blind faith."

"Faith? If this 'mummy' can perform major miracles, the whole of humanity should profit from it. It could eradicate poverty and illness, and bring peace on Earth."

"But if Your Holiness cannot accept the Paganism of Lord Aton, how do you expect me to accept His saintliness, especially, if you don't feel it in your heart."

"Young man, if this mummy is not in the right hands, it could be used for evil purposes, too."

Gordon looked calmly into the tired eyes of the old man. "History has proven over and over that even a Pope can be used for bad purposes. Quite a number of the Holy Fathers of the past committed crimes against God and Humanity at large, and later were declared saints by the Holy Church."

The Pope settled back into his richly ornamented chair, keeping his eyes on Gordon. "You still need to prove yourself to me. We're leaving tonight for Egypt. Make yourself ready."

Gordon was stunned. "So suddenly!"

"I told you some time ago about my imminent trip to the Near East. For security reasons the date was kept secret. Someone tried to infiltrate my residence."

"Is this from Vatican Intelligence?"

"Partially. Now we have proof."

"Renaldo?"

"No, Marko. Your miracle made him a new man."

"He confessed to you?"

"Yes. He told me everything. I expected it from you, but you chose to be silent. Another piece of evidence emerged from him. He met a boxing promoter in a local bar. At the time, he took him to be bona fide, but now he doubts his veracity. His description of the man gave us precious leads."

Gordon responded with, "In a round about way, he did tell me that he wanted to get back to professional boxing. He looked for my approval. I tried to convince him to stay with us, so I brought Renaldo into it. I underestimated Ikhnaton. Of all people, I should've known better. I'm sorry, Your Holiness."

"I'm sorry too, Gordon. It seems we can never settle our differences. You with your Lord Aton and I with my Church. The Church cannot exist without the Dogma."

"Can you accept that?" questioned Gordon.

"It's my duty. I wanted those young men to witness our conversation. They think of you as Christ reincarnated. Can you convincingly explain to them the nature of your personality? It seems that even your wife doesn't know you that well. She worries about your dream. In the current situation, I'm unable to help her. You don't even trust me."

Gordon turned to Marko. "Do you trust me?"

"I love you, Gordon," he answered.

"I see what you mean. Love as a dogma. And you, Renaldo?"

"You gave me life. What else can I say?" he admitted almost grudgingly.

"Then, which of you started the rumor about the Miracle?"

They both shook their heads.

"I believe you. It seems I totally underestimated Ikhnaton, Holiness. Unleashing unknown forces was a risk my father took to serve the Truth. It unfortunately turned into an unstoppable chain reaction. Those forces used me as the Church used Christ. Isn't that called manipulation?"

The Pope, speaking to Renaldo and Marko, said, "Please, young men, leave us alone. I thank you for your sincerity. God bless your hearts."

Marko and Renaldo left silently. The Pope closed his eyes, perhaps for a prayer. Then he invited Gordon, “Sit down, young man. It’s not entirely your fault. As you see I have serious problems too. Who am I to dismantle an institution two thousand years old? The faith of millions would be shaken. What do I have to give them in exchange? The truth? What truth? Who’s truth is it? Do you believe in God, Gordon?”

“What God, Holiness? Please, describe Him to me.”

“He’s indescribable.”

“Can we believe in the indescribable?”

“Of course, Gordon, because of Jesus.”

“It’s not that simple, Your Holiness. Some say the Church picked, at random, one of the thousands of saviors of that time. It just happened to be Jesus Christ. When my father, Dr. Peter Moughabee, showed me the incredible likeness between Lord Aton and Jesus, I knew at once that He is the One and Only Savior. From then on I didn’t doubt God’s existence even for a moment. I believe in Him by the power of the Truth. Without it we are a lost speck in the Universe, a form of life in an unknown dimension. If you admit the Truth, you’ll get tremendous momentum, a chain reaction that might unify the peoples of this world. The juggernaut may result in an everlasting triumph!”

The impact upon the Pope was clearly visible. “Oh, Gordon, Gordon, I pray you are right!”

On his flight to Upper Egypt, the Pope’s super jet followed the North African coastline. In the Grand Salon, Gordon shared a love seat with Helena. In spite of all other problems, it was enough that he had his wife on the voyage. It was an unprecedented gesture, and everyone on board, in spite of his exceptional status, or maybe just because of it, was jealous. Who does he think he is anyway? Helena, as a person brought up in luxury, received favors as naturally due to her rank. She didn't know what life would be without privileges.

In Tobruk, a group of cardinals, diplomats and reporters joined the traveling entourage. If they had heard something unusual about Gordon, they didn't show it.

Gordon tried to concentrate on what Helena was saying to him.

"The body of Ouloulangha was found. The casket is on board and will be delivered to the Copts in a special ceremony. A very discrete one. His Holiness is very unhappy about the disappearance of Dr. Moughabee's body. Do you know something about that, darling?"

"Yes, I know. I'm not hiding it, if that's what the Pope believes. He never asked me."

Helena felt awkward but chose to be blunt. "Well, I'm asking you. He's something like my father-in-law."

"Dr. Moughabee took his body with him."

"Is that possible?"

"Yes, if the Lord of the Dead is your friend. Christ took his body, too."

"Then, it's natural," Helena said.

Gordon shrugged his shoulders.

But Helena had more questions, "Where is Renaldo?"

"He flew ahead of us to brief the Security Team."

"Do you mean that there is no security on this flight?"

"There are guards here."

"I don't see them," she protested.

"They're not supposed to mix with the guests. There are a number of plain-clothes men from a special unit directly from Rome. They boarded the plane with the rest."

"Where is Marko?" she continued to question Gordon.

"One deck below."

"Perhaps we have overridden the protocol by mixing with VIP's."

"It's not the fault of the staff. The Pope had forgotten to brief them on protocol. Maybe he doesn't know it, either. He's been brave under fire, but protocol is still baffling to him. The Pope is shy. All those autocratic Cardinals scare him a bit."

"How do you know all of this?"

"I simply know."

"Have those people been informed about our child-to-be?"

Gordon look at her sadly. "God forbid! I'll try to find Marko."

Gordon made his way to the lower level of the plane. He found Marko in an uncrowded corner looking at the Great Desert through the plane's window.

"One day the whole planet may look like that, Marko," Gordon remarked as he sat next to him.

The younger man wasn't surprised by his presence. "I had hoped you would disappear at the Tobruk stopover, but then that's not like you. You'll allow yourself to be killed like Jesus."

"Marko!"

"Well, look at me. I'm crying. It doesn't happen to me that often. This is my second time around and all because of you. Why don't you fight back?"

"Because I'm expendable, Marko. Most people are expendable in the eyes of the gods. The rulers of the world throw millions of human lives into the emptiness, but their death is always a tragedy. I was mistaken in my dream. The terrorists have no faces. I remember very clearly. You were trying to wrestle down the murderer."

"Why did you bring Renaldo back to life then?"

Gordon gave his handkerchief to Marko. "Destiny always needs a Judas against a human being capable of changing History single-handedly. Jesus' parents were rather ambitious people. Most married couples dreamed of their child being the Promised Messiah. In order to fulfill the prophecies, Christ's Mother had to give birth to Him in Bethlehem and have the baby registered by

Joseph as firstborn. Since then His life's story has been rewritten many times. People never change; they love the legend not the Man. Even his disciples lied, filling in missing information with stories from Moses life. They weren't even with him in his last hours. Even His brother James went into hiding. They thought that everything failed, and that Jesus had disappeared into obscurity like a thousand others before Him. It took them time to realize: He was the One and Only! Only Maria of Magdala loved Him and stayed with Him forever. She was called a scarlet woman, her marriage to Christ denied. For centuries the Church put a Stigma on her.

I'm not Jesus, I've got only my wife and you, Marko. You shouldn't try to kill Renaldo a second time, because I can live only through you. My wife Helena will say anything that the Church asks her to say. She could be the Madonna of the new millennium! All her life, Helena has dreamed of this opportunity. She prompted the death of her own father, because she wanted her dream to be lined in gold. Who else fits the Image better? Helena has the background and the fanaticism to lead the newborn to His Destiny."

THEATER OF THE ABSOLUTE: LAMENT OF PETER

"Lord Aton, can you help my son?"

"You know perfectly well that I don't have that power. We should not try to change destiny. This is my last warning to you, Peter. You eliminated Renaldo, using Marko as an instrument. For that reason only, I had to bring him back to life. Gordon didn't want to take advantage, he's an extremely honest man. For awhile he was tempted, then he pleaded with me to restore the balance. I was surprised by the enormous transfiguration in Gordon. Now he is a very worthy human being. If he goes on living he will have nothing but disappointments. It was wise for him to surrender. I think that the doors that kept us waiting for centuries will be open to him."

"That isn't fair, Aton. He has the right to live!"

"How do you know, Peter? You are an earthly man. You always find excuses not to enter the Door, but the time has come…"

"Please, Aton! I want to see the new Christ born! In the name of everything that has been denied to you, let my son live and see his child grow. How can Gordon be of any threat to the Universal Balance? He's just another man."

"No, he isn't. Besides this is not at my will."

"God isn't fair, Aton! Why should my son die for the sins of all mankind?"

"Because he is worthy of his destiny. Gordon is the Son of God. You'll be lucky to walk with him through the Door."

"I have no tears. I haven't cried for centuries. Now I have to watch the last minutes of my son ticking away without a tear to shed."

Lord Aton looked at the shiny Doors to Heaven.

"That wish is granted to you. You can lament your son."

Peter fell down to his knees. "Thank you God! You know the searing pain of losing Your only Son. At least now, I have tears to lament mine. My only child, please forgive me, I'm unworthy to stand by you, but how wonderful it is to feel human, even for a short time! I love you, Gordon, my boy. You have made me a very proud father. And the bestial, lusting, vicious humankind, I love you all, from the bottom of my heart. I want to be a man again!"

AIRPORT: EGYPT'S UPPER NILE DISTRICT

Gordon recognized some of the officials at the airport. Several months ago, they had met his father, Peter Moughabee. The Pope kissed the Nubian ground, had his hand kissed by a long line of Copts and was congratulated by representatives of the Egyptian Government and the Islamic clergy. His security force, dressed in civilian clothes, walked in single file.

Marko feverishly looked for Renaldo. He wasn't at the airport. Because of terrorist threats, only the officials were permitted to greet the plane. A long line of limousines started loading the passengers.

"Come, Gordon. You don't want us to ride in the last limousine," said Helena impatiently. "To be at the end brings bad luck."

Gordon smiled. "I didn't know you were superstitious. How do you know we're to ride in a limousine? Maybe we'll share a ride with the servants and the guards in that resplendent bus."

"Don't be silly, Gordon. You're a very important man."

"It may be true. I've never seen you so elegant. That suit compliments your beauty."

"I had it flown in from Rome. That's the first compliment I've heard from you in a long time, and that alone justifies the expenditure. I wish I had something new for you to wear. You have to give me your size."

"I lost my wardrobe in Hotel Savoya. This is the only clothing I have left. I wore this blazer and pants at our wedding. It's very special to me."

"I'll take care of this. You need a tux, suits and shirts for all occasions. Shoes and socks too. Thanks to my father, we have more money than time to spend it."

"Thanks...to your father."

"Gordon, what's wrong with you? You look as if you're going to a funeral. We must celebrate my return to high-society. I know everyone worth knowing in Cairo. I still have relatives in Alexandria. Father didn't like them, but they're okay. Then we'll fly to Europe."

A security man opened the door to a limousine for them. TV cameras and an array of paparazzi focused on the young couple. A commentator for a live TV feed was heard in the background, "And now, the son of Dr. Peter Moughabee. As you already know, the Vatican will bestow the first sainthood in history to a Copt for his martyr's death. Mr. Gordon Bates is traveling with his beautiful wife, the only heiress to the enormous fortune of Sheik Hussney El Barrack."

No other guests were permitted in that car. The huge stretch-limousine glided royally. Helena embraced Gordon. "Oh I'm so happy for you, darling."

"Did you know about the sainthood being given to my father?"

"I wanted to surprise you."

"How did you keep it a secret?"

Helena shrugged her shoulders which were well molded by tennis and swimming.

"It wasn't difficult, darling. You never touch the newspaper or listen to the news."

"I wonder why the Pope didn't mention it to me," Gordon wondered out loud.

"Perhaps for the same reason I didn't."

"Perhaps."

The limousine arrived at the Residence. A team of TV men and paparazzi was waiting at the gate, another at the entrance to the palace. The speaker announced immediately, "Mr. Gordon Bates and his wife are two of the few who will share the Residence with His Holiness the Pope."

A doorman held the door for them, and their luggage was taken from the trunk. To Gordon's surprise, five suitcases were brought inside. He was traveling light, only a toothbrush in his pocket. The anchorman closed in on them.

"Mr. Bates, how do you feel coming back to Nubia?"

Gordon had forgotten that he passed through this country once before.

"Oh, yeah. I find it the same as before."

Helena saved the day. "Wonderful hospitality. Gordon has told me about his amazing adventure."

"Indeed! I'm seizing the opportunity to thank you, in the name of all Egyptian people, for the return of Lord Aton's mummy. He is very special to all of us," the anchorman proclaimed to the world.

Gordon closed his eyes for a moment, "Oh, Renaldo. Why did you do it?" Now he realized why the Pope didn't have a minute for him.

Their apartment, according to the majordomo, was the second best. Gordon whistled softly when he saw the three rooms at their disposal. Helena was finally at home. She gave instructions to the servants what to do with the suitcases.

The Pope was tired, so lunch was served in their apartment. Their dining room table was large enough for twelve guests. The two placemats were at the opposite ends of the long table. The majordomo announced that His Holiness eventually would attend the ceremonial dinner. Helena was very excited. She had to do some last minute shopping and asked Gordon to accompany her. He gave her the sizes of his shirts; suits and shoes, refusing to go with her. Helena showed understanding; to be followed by the media wasn't fun. She'd try to sneak out through the back door and call a taxicab.

She wasn't the Helena he knew. Paying for his clothing with her credit cards was embarrassing for him. She finally left and he was relieved to be left alone. The apartment had high-tech sound equipment, but he didn't know much about music, even though dancing came naturally to him. Because of his sports activities, Gordon had a good sense of timing and coordination. He undressed slowly and found a pair of swimming trunks, a bathrobe and his sneakers.

The park was like the Garden of Eden, bathed in the golden light of the early afternoon. Flocks of exotic birds flew around him, others sang from the trees. The air was finely scented by beautiful blossoms. Somebody dressed in a three-piece suit occupied one of the lounge chairs. Gordon almost turned back, then he changed his mind. It could be Marko. Gordon's curiosity was aroused. It wasn't Marko, nor was it Renaldo.

He almost didn't believe his eyes — it was Helena's brother, Aldan.

He smiled, something he did seldom in life. Smiling made him strikingly handsome. He wasn't smoking either, something else uncharacteristic in his lifetime. Gordon was glad to see him.

"Hello, Aldan. Did you come to see me?"

"As a matter of fact, yes. Do you have some cigarettes? I can't just walk in and buy myself a package."

"I can't either. I'm penniless," laughed Gordon.

"How typical of my sister. She likes spending money on herself and lavish presents. I never got a farthing from her."

Gordon sat on the chair next to him. "I never ask her for anything."

"Then you'll get nothing but presents. She loves buying surprise presents. Mostly neckties, I think this one is from her too. I was buried with it. It's boring wearing the same clothes. All my experiences are metaphysical. I would give the immortality of my soul just for one good fuck. Thanks to Ikhnaton, and your physical collaboration, I can't.

Which brings me to the subject of my ghostly visit. Marko is crisscrossing the city searching hotels and residences. The *simpatico* Renaldo is nowhere to be seen. Now Ikhnaton is lodging within him and I doubt if even God knows what kind of a murder he is planning. Most pharaohs were serial murderers. I think it comes with the crown."

"In many cases it's kill or be killed," Gordon remarked.

"I see you still haven't lost your naiveté."

"Why should I? I don't have to worry about any crown."

"Except your martyr's halo," Aldan quipped.

"Did you make up that namby-pamby story?"

"No-o-o...Honest to God! The whole Universe is buzzing with the news.

"If I hit you now would it hurt you? At least a little?" Gordon teased.

"I'm deprived of that pleasure, too. I am just metaphysically being the bad messenger. You don't hate me for that, do you?" Aldan asked cryptically.

Gordon shook his head, "Of course not. I don't mind being metaphysical as much as you. I don't really want to stay here, except for Helena and my child. The Holy Church will take good care of them. They don't need a home. Helena probably would dislike the home I was planning to build for her anyway. She is a world traveler, and I've had enough traveling for a life time."

Aldan bent toward him from his chair, "Would it be any good if I told you that I sympathize with you?"

"Are you serious?" Gordon was surprised.

"No kidding, I felt the same way. Remember, I was in love with you. Now, go and swim. I'll watch you."

Gordon got up and pulled off his bathrobe. "You can't even swim metaphysically," he said obviously disturbed. Aldan shook his head. Gordon looked at the clean bluish water full of broken reflections of trees, "That's something I'll really miss. I don't think flying would replace it. I'd miss my body too. I actually don't want to die. It would've been so wonderful to teach my son how to swim, to tell him my Truth. Maybe that's why I'm the odd man out."

Gordon kicked off his sneakers, went to the diving board and carefully prepared himself for a dive. "I'll have a good long swim," he thought joyously, "I'll try to print it in my memory so deep that nobody will be able to take it away from me!"

Gordon crossed the hall into the bedroom. The floor was covered with boxes and torn wrapping paper. So was the bed. Helena had succeeded in putting away her purchases, though some drawers and closets were still open. She was red in the face and her hair was a mess.

"The hairdresser will come any moment now to take care of me. Water does wonders for you. You look healthy and fit. Marvelous! Here is your tuxedo and all the paraphernalia that comes with it. If you don't know how to handle the shirt buttons I'll help you. Father always counted on me. I was his personal maid...oh, this must be my hairdresser. Take your stuff to the bathroom and I'll ring for a servant so we don't stumble over all these cartons."

Silently, Gordon picked up his tux and accessories and locked himself in the bathroom. It was enormous — including mirrored walls, a sofa and light Viennese furniture. He left the clothing on the sofa and sat on one of the chairs that seemed ready to crumble under his weight. The chair held. Gordon buried his face in his hands. He had never been to one of these galas and had no idea how many people were invited. He was ill prepared for a function like this. In fine company he'd surely stick out like a sore thumb.

"Oh, God! There is still time. Can I disappear from here? Nobody will be able to find me. What am I going to do with the rest of my life? What is the purpose of my existence? Is there not a decent exit for me? Father, can you hear me?"

Suddenly, a whisper wafted through Gordon's mind, "I love you, son. Will you be able to pardon me some day?"

"I hold no grudge toward you, father. You gave me so much. It's my fault that I failed to adjust. But you just watch me. You'll be proud of me, yet.

"You can do it, son, I know you can do it. Then we'll try to tinker something together. Trust me, five times I ran away from Heaven, and I'll do it again."

Something shimmering in gold and silver enveloped him on all sides. "Not with your new status of sainthood," Gordon laughed.

Peter laughed too. "It will be even easier, son. All of the Universe is open for a saint."

"Are there other worlds, father?"

"Of course there are. We'll visit all of them. After the public display of Aton's mummy, nothing holds me here anymore."

Gordon removed his bathrobe and took a quick shower. As he started dressing, the voice of his father became remote and forlorn, "I know what's on your mind, the boy. You'll hang around as I did for centuries, just to have a glimpse of your son now and then. Please, don't repeat my mistake. Don't ever try to change His destiny..."

Peter's voice trailed off, then it was quiet.

There were about fifty guests at the ceremonial dinner. His Holiness didn't look well. He tried to turn the tide of conversation to history, but no one seemed interested. North Korea had given ultimatums more arrogant than ever, new demands leaving practically no room for any peaceful solutions. The world had split again socially, ideologically and economically.

The only hope was in the Savior.

Gordon and Helena sat near the Pope. On the other side of the table sat the local luminaries. Helena's gown was splendid. Around her neck she wore a crucifix decorated with garnets, and a matching ring on her finger demonstrating her marital status. Although Gordon had mixed feeling about the marriage, he loved Helena, though he never fully understood her until now.

She was the only woman at the table.

As the Pope didn't look in his direction, Gordon's felt hurt. Even after dinner he wasn't included in the circles visited by the Holy Father. Only a general he met in the receiving line at the military airport on his previous arrival to Nubia engaged his attention.

"I wish Dr. Moughabee hadn't started this whole affair with Lord Aton's mummy," he commented bitterly.

A sudden rage exploded in Gordon's mind. He tried counting to ten. "I saw you talking to the Pope, General. Did you try to dissuade him from displaying the mummy?"

"No, he followed his own persuasions. At the short meeting a year ago, your father was adamant, too."

"How did he explain my presence?" Gordon asked.

"Dr. Moughabee was not one to explain any of his private matters."

"Private matters?"

"His life was a mystery and he liked it that way. Once, at a dinner in London, he mentioned something about a brief liaison with a Creole woman that resulted in a son. According to him, later, the young man strived for a degree in archeology, though Dr. Moughabee was unwilling to involve him in his plans. Do you have any idea how much you look like Dr. Moughabee?"

"I rarely look at my face in a mirror. My obvious African heritage wasn't appreciated much in America, so I tried to pass for a Native American Indian."

"Oh, Is that considered better?"

"Generally, yes. Indians from the few remaining tribes are considered harmless, although racism is becoming fixed in the minds of people. The Armageddon could be a war of attrition between races. All Great Wars were racially or religiously motivated. Presently the situation is strikingly comparable — terrorism. In present times, nobody should be considered harmless. Even nowadays our government and the Israelis underestimate the potentials of the Middle East crisis."

Helena joined them. She automatically groped in her little bag for a pack of cigarettes. Then she reminded herself of her current state of pregnancy. Abstaining from smoking made her jumpy. The dinner was hopelessly boring and the prospect of sitting through a sermon by the Pope tomorrow wasn't appealing. There were rumors of his presenting something tremendously shocking. She didn't think this Pope had the drama.

"Is there really some danger of a terrorist attack tomorrow?" Helena asked the General.

The General hesitated for a moment, then gave her a straightforward answer, "In this part of the world, terrorists are never underestimated. Good night, Madam Bates."

Chapter 18

GORDON'S MARTYRDOM

THE REAL DARKENSS IS INSIDE US,
IT IS ONLY LOGICAL TO LOOK FOR LIGHT.
— Milton

Marko was totally frustrated in his search for Renaldo. He was unable to find a lead to a terrorist group. His blond hair was a warning to them. He came very late to the Residential Compound. The Guards were lodged in a simple two-story building hidden by some old trees and flowering shrubbery. A short cut to get there was through the sport-field. A lonely runner at this late hour was rather intriguing. Something in the athletic body build was familiar to him. It was Renaldo. He wasn't in the mood for running after a hectic day in the city, but he took off his three-piece suit. As a rule he wore his gym shorts underneath. At the next turn he joined the runner. Renaldo wasn't surprised at all. They tapped hands without breaking their stride.

The night was moonless and made their chance meeting even more anonymous.

"I spent the day looking for you, Renaldo," Marko told him without breaking pace.

"As an avant-garde, I was kept busy," answered Renaldo.

"I can imagine." Marko sounded sarcastic.

"No, you can't." Renaldo increased the pace of his running, but Marko had no problem keeping up with him. "You won't believe me, Marko, but I'm trying to save Gordon as desperately as you, but he defies any help."

"When did you talk to him?"

"About ten minutes ago by the swimming pool, he's still there."

"Swimming?"

"No, praying."

"Did you give him the proverbial kiss?"

"Marko, I love and respect Gordon as much as our Holy Father does. Maybe more. I thought that returning the mummy would settle the problem. It didn't. The curse is still on Gordon. The minds of all fundamentalists are hopelessly screwed up."

"What can we do?"

"I have a plan. It might not work but it's better than nothing. I have to find out how to infiltrate a specific terrorist's cell. Tomorrow, at the basilica, try to follow me. When I see that wild bunch, we'll get in a scuffle. That will attract general attention, the Pope will move behind the protective glass. What I don't know is what Gordon's reaction will be. I told him to move behind the protective glass, too. Now I'm sure that he won't do it. He wants to die."

"God Almighty, why?"

"He feels expendable. He doesn't like his part as Joseph, nor Helena in the part of Mary. He considers all this production below the dignity of the Savior. I agree."

"Renaldo, if I change the color of my hair, I'll look the same as him. Especially from a distance."

Renaldo slowed down and got out of the running lanes. Marko followed. They started cool-down exercises to get their breathing back to normal.

"That's very serious, Marko. I thought of it but you shouldn't…"

"If there is a screwed up life in this world, it's mine. It's a magnificent exit for me. Think of a diversion that will get him off stage. I'll replace him."

Renaldo thought for awhile. "It's a wild shot but it might work. You'll have to come to my room, I have a hair kit. For awhile I was entertaining the same idea."

"Thanks Renaldo."

"What for?"

"I always wanted to have a decent exit from this world. I'm a complete failure as a boxer, and I don't know anything else that could keep me out of trouble. There's not a Helena for me. I would've been glad to be her consort. I'm not as fussy as Gordon, maybe because I've got nothing to lose. It's foolish even talking about it. Let's go to your place and prepare."

LAST PRAYER OF GORDON

Dear God,

Don't take this bitter cup from my lips, I want it. Not that I want to be a Martyr, perish the thought. I tried to become a preacher; but I lack the conviction for it. The Pope sent me an unsigned note not to come to the Great Event. It's very nice of him. Maybe he has a death wish, too. It's terrible to be a Pope these days. But things are so desperate that every bit helps. I really don't know anybody able to do what he does. We all have our faults and no one's perfect, except You. Thanks for not creating us in Your image. It would've been a capital mistake.

Helena doesn't love me. She loves somebody that she has created in her image. This is the part I dislike the most. Otherwise, she'll be a perfect mother. I'm sure His Holiness will take care of this. Try to keep Marko and Renaldo out of trouble. They deserve something better, especially Marko. He's so much like me.

I'm ready to accept your will, but not as the husband of my wife. I'd appreciate it if You'd spare me this tribulation, no more presents and high-society visits. Maybe You'll give me a tiny lot in Heaven where I can build a home for my father and myself. I always wanted to have a HOME.

Amen.

The Basilica was filled to capacity. Outside, the masses of people spread from the square into the wide central boulevard and spilled onto the side streets of the neighborhood. Millions more were watching it on TV.

The sermon of the Pope was unique. Since the birth of Christendom there was none like it. It was a sermon about Truth and what the Catholic Church had done to hide it, condemning to eternal punishment, everyone who wouldn't accept Her Dogma.

Lies upon lies had piled up until the crush became unbearable. The Life of Christ and His words were twisted, people were persecuted and burned as heretics if their ideas and religious persuasions diverted from the Church's prescription.

He asked the Copts for pardon for all the centuries of condemnation and segregation that brought them to a state of total isolation. Was it possible that a network of dogmatic fanatics had gone undetected for such a long time? The same brainwashing happened in Russia — Bolshevism flourished using cruelty and mass psychoses.

But the Vatican?

As late as World War II, the top hierarchy of the Church failed to defend the victims of the Third Reich, blessing the murderers and offering them asylum in the monasteries of Northern Italy.

The Pope tried to expose the hegemony of the leaders in the Holy Church who didn't hesitate to create a Christ of their own making and then use Him to cover up their abominable crimes.

Millions of Catholics throughout the world were stunned.

Critics said it was too little, too late. Gordon expected more, but, as a beginning, he appreciated it as an act of bravery and wisdom.

Helena was deeply shaken to hear from the Pope's mouth the same words her husband had spoken to the crowds around Palermo. She was very proud of him. He made himself heard and now millions would follow.

For the hundredth time Gordon tried to locate Renaldo and Marko. Neither one of them was in sight. The critical moment was coming when the Pope had to cross to the side door. He had said, "Let us pray!" And the multitude joined him in a silent prayer.

Finally, a Pope had publicly acknowledged the presence of the Copts.

Suddenly, Gordon saw, in his mind's eye, the sturdy body of Marko, clad only in his old gym shorts, lying on the floor of a room in the residence. His face and chest were smeared in blood, the green eyes in a chrysalid state staring into the void — he was dead!

At the same time, he felt he was being watched. He turned and looked over the heads of the praying Copts. He saw Renaldo with an insane fanatic look in his eyes. His right hand came up with a revolver in it. Quick as lightning, Gordon covered the praying old man with his body. In the profound silence of the prayer for a New World, one built solely upon Truth, the shot sounded like an explosion.

Renaldo didn't try to escape. He offered no resistance to the group of men that quickly disarmed him, then dragged him down the marble steps. Another group tried to take the Pope away, but with unexpected energy, he pushed the security men aside, and with the television cameras following his every move, he walked back to Gordon.

Gordon fell to his knees. Then in infinitely slow motion, slid into the arms of Helena. The Pope knelt beside him.

"Why did you do it, my boy?" the Pope cried in devastation.

Gordon smiled at him as he drifted toward his destiny, "I want.... A HOME of...of my own.... Father...possibly with...a swimming pool..."

The Pope closed his eyes and made the sign of the cross over him. It was noontime...though on the other side of time it was always dark.

PART FOUR

RESURRECTION

PROLOGUE

AND LET THOSE THAT PLAY YOUR CLOWNS
SPEAK NO MORE THAN IS SET DOWN FOR THEM.
— William Shakespeare

The death of Gordon Bates made more headlines than expected. The double murder committed by Renaldo Cortelazzo was used to the hilt, proving how high-ranking conservative forces in the Vatican Government were trying to swing the world back into the Dark Ages. Therefore, three of the most influential cardinals lost their exalted positions to live in obscurity behind the walls of far away monasteries and a number of minor functionaries were quietly eliminated from the ranks. There was little change in the general course of the Vatican's high-powered political conservatives. The message was, however, that the Liberal Wing of the Catholic Church had gained ground. Unfortunately, it remained more of a message than a fact.

At the trial in Cairo everything went wrong.

Renaldo's testimony had changed since his deposition. He claimed he had committed the killings under "instructions from above." When asked to clarify his statements, Renaldo implicated the Holy Father. He insisted that the Pope's life hadn't been in jeopardy for a moment. His attorneys were shell-shocked, their defense of insanity flew to pieces. Instead of a few years in a penitentiary, he veered straight toward Capital Punishment.

Renaldo asked for confession and absolution from the Pope. Both were granted.

The murderer was flown from Cairo to the Vatican and given a private audience in the apartments of His Holiness. Now this Pope had been known to make unexpected, even controversial decisions. Earlier, he had nominated one of his badly-compromised predecessors for sainthood, but this act of clemency, in the eyes of many people, was more damning and derogatory than the making of a fascist saint.

Was the Pope really involved in those heinous crimes? The murder of Marko Brandon was called sadistic.

Helena Bates was outraged. Her life hadn't gone the way she expected it. Instead of mixing with high-society and interesting people in unusual places, she was back in the castle outside of Beirut, living a monastic existence. In a daring attempt to placate public opinion, the Pope offered to resign his Office. Health problems were cited as the main factor, but most people still thought the world of him. Here and there some doubted his integrity. The Synhua Agency prompted the world press that the Holy See had been compromised and a thorough explanation was overdue.

The Vatican authorities thought the situation was dangerous. A Pope granting exoneration to a convicted murderer wasn't easy to explain. A special letter of condolence from His Holiness to the widow of Gordon Bates was delivered by the addressee to a tabloid newspaper unopened. The Vatican was in a state of shock. Its reigning Pope admitted to debating the charges against his former private detective.

Renaldo Cortelazzo was promptly delivered back to court. Hurriedly, he was sentenced to two consecutive life terms, which meant being locked in an Egyptian prison for the rest of his natural life. Malta tried him *In Absentia* and blocked any appeal to a court or parole board. An extra large swastika was painted on the wall near the main entrance of the Sovereign State of the Vatican.

In protest, an enormous crowd filled the rotunda of the Saint Peter and Paul Basilica for an all-night vigil, but the Pope didn't appear at his window. People called repeatedly, "Preggo, Domini! Preggo, Domini!" One of the least liked cardinals made a short announcement that the Holy Father was deeply touched by their support, but his poor state of health kept him bedridden. At that moment, a torrential rain mixed with large pieces of hail chased even the staunchest supporters to the shelter of the magnificent Arcades of Bernini. Gusts of freezing wind chased them even farther away. In the resulting stampede many children and old people were trampled. At 6:30 p.m., a darkness enveloped the Holy City. An electric storm of unusual proportion crackled around it unmercifully.

Some said Satan had arrived, like in Cromwell's time, to claim the soul of their spiritual leader. A number of thunderbolts had set trees on fire near the Pope's apartments.

The old man, down on his shaky knees, was praying. He knew that God was angry, and he knew why. By now, even the sluggish and conservative Curia Romana had realized the futility of cheating the Almighty.

The Real Master was asserting His infinite Power.

Chapter 19

LOYALTIES

After endless litigation in different courts, an inheritance settlement was finally reached, and Mrs. Helena Bates arrived in Malta. She made an old, rented palazzo her residence. It was hastily refurbished, according to her preference, but nothing was capable of saving her from the shadow of her father's castle. Aldano Brandon moved in with her as her press agent, even though he had written only a few postcards in his whole life. He actually printed every letter, with his tongue between his teeth, in such a childish way that any handwriting analyst would be baffled. Prior to Helena opening a position for him in her household, he played soccer for one of the provincial teams. Malta's inhabitants wondered why Lady Helena had chosen him, of all people, to look into her daily mail. His father had no comment on the subject, though he asked the Mistress of the House for a private appointment.

He rang the doorbell precisely at five in the afternoon.

Aldano ushered him into a small sitting room on the first floor. The guest sat in one of the ornate chairs, which reminded him of his last visit with his friend Hussney El Barrack. He settled his aching body in its comfortable coziness and leaned on his cheap walking stick.

"Butlers are not supposed to blush, son."

"I'm not a butler, father. That isn't exactly my job."

"Well, I'm not here to study the nature of your obligations. You look handsome and fit. I guess your Mistress pays sufficiently."

"I haven't been paid as yet, but clothing, food and drinks have been provided."

Mr. Brandon lifted his eyebrows in pretended surprise, then shook his head, "I suppose you can procure a drink for your ailing father," asked.

The youth smiled grudgingly. "You can't hurt me more than I hurt myself, father. I love Helena, and for me, just being around her is a priceless advantage. There is no humiliation I would spare myself in the hope that some day she might start looking at me as a man, instead of a *dear boy*."

"You chose the wrong woman, son."

"I know...What kind of drink would you like to have this sultry afternoon, father?"

"The same as usual. You can bring the bottle if it's not against the house-rules, I can do the rest. How much do you drink these days, Aldano?"

The young man smiled again, this time mechanically.

"I haven't started yet. If I do, rest assured that I'll advertise in the local press. I don't really want to be a sore loser like Marko..."

"...and me. I know why you didn't come to see me. You want a fresh start."

Aldano nodded curtly then brought a bottle of Special Blend Irish Whisky and an elaborately cut glass.

"If you need anything, ring for the maid. I'll be working out my frustrations on the bench-press."

The old man filled his glass with a shaky hand. "I wish you well, Aldano. Do better than the rest of our pack."

"I'll try," said Aldano and he began to leave

Then the hostess was at the door. "You don't have to leave because of me, Aldano."

Aldano's face flushed. "I'm here because of you, Lady Helena. I won't let myself forget it even for a moment."

He left the room hurriedly.

Helena had acquired a different kind of beauty she'd never had before. The loose but elegant robe de chambre suggested that, perhaps due to her maturity, she had gained a certain sense of her new position. In deference, the old man got up from his cozy arm chair.

"Sit down, Mr. Brandon. If you'd like to smoke I have an ashtray for you. I'm still persistent in my decision to kick the habit. All I'll have with you is a cup of tea. The maid is bringing it. Anything special?"

Brandon shook his head nervously.

"This house makes me nervous too," stated Helena. "It doesn't come with a swimming pool or tennis court, just beauty frozen in time. I'm not seeing anyone and no one wants to see me except the crazy paparazzi." She went on making conversation with the old man.

A pretty, young maid served the tea and appetizers, then looked at Lady Helena. Helena added some sugar and a touch of milk, then sent the girl away with a wave of her hand.

"I don't sleep with your son, Mr. Brandon. I thought about it, but later rejected the idea. Yes, rejected. He's good to look at, but so are those sandwiches that I don't touch. Don't get me wrong, Mr. Brandon. I'm not playing the part of a Madonna. In the past I indulged in a good deal of Aldano's great sex appeal. For his young age he's very knowledgeable in love making. I have to give him some credit for that. Body, facial beauty, everything that a youthful lady could dream of and more. Even my late husband appreciated him (at least as his bisexual Egyptian takeover). In Greece and Asia Minor homosexuality is never considered despicable or unmanly. Alexander the Great loved his best friend and kept a male concubine. He loved them both and married twice. I don't know a more manly man, except for Gordon. My husband was profoundly male. I mothered my brother Aldan, as I mother Aldano now. Not that I'm invulnerable to male charms, I slept with my half-brother and he was really knavish. The night when Mt. Etna erupted Aldano proved to me he was a great lover. I don't know, it might've been the volcano, but since then, Aldano believes a miracle could happen again. Yes, Mr. Brandon, I am the type, though I don't want to buy myself a dashing, youthful husband, nor an adorable house pet. If you think I would destroy his reputation..."

"What reputation?"

"You don't think highly of him," she said as she sipped her tea absentmindedly. "He saved my life. He doted on you during your period of recuperation after the Sicilian mayhem. He was almost perfect to a point that I don't want to break up something in him. I don't remember playing with toys, but what I feared was to see them broken. I felt at home with things that nobody wanted. I dreamed of a husband to feel at home with. *Gordon was like a home around me*, and I had these crazy ambitions to make him a great cosmopolitan figure. I should've run with him to the very end of the world so we could perform a perfect tandem dive into nothingness. Gordon was afraid of nothing but that moment before hitting the water's surface. Like a primal being, he intuitively knew the hardness of water." She paused and reconsidered, "How rude of me, you wanted to speak, and I cannot prevent myself from drowning in my own feelings. Ask me whatever is on your mind, Mr. Brandon, I owe you that much."

Brandon finished his drink and looked inside the glass as if something forgotten was left in the bottom. He got up painfully and took the walking stick in his trembling hands.

"Yes, I have something on my mind. It's about all those crazy happenings of the last few months. I don't quite understand why I'm still alive. There must be a reason that escapes me. Now I'm sure that you feel the same way. Your father didn't want to hurt you. He's probably deeply grateful to you for sparing him the last agonies he would have suffered. He had no intention of disinheriting you."

Helena left the saucer with the teacup on the table. Her hand was as shaky as his. "I found a letter from him, Mr. Brandon. He never had the courage to send it to me. I felt very lonely, almost abandoned at the private school in Spain. That's why I understood

Gordon so well, but did nothing to help him. Not a single one of my college 'friends' bothered to send me an invitation to their parties, in spite of all my money. Damn it! Now, I have more money than all of them put together. There is a malfunctioning part in me, like a run-a-way train. Father wasn't responsible for the death of my mother. In his own way he was trying to save her from her own madness...I pray to Gordon at night..."

Mr. Brandon turned from the door, "Praying to Gordon for what?"

Helena looked at this man ruined by age, who was holding on to a strange mixture of hope and despair. "I don't know, perhaps you can help me."

"No, Lady Helena, I can't. All we need is love, like in that song by the Beatles. All we need is love. Maybe this tiny fellow growing in you has the answer. Our generation sorely missed the most important things in life and the answer always has been locked within us, Perhaps unborn. You said it very well...a broken part."

The Pope's health was really deplorable. Lately his inner vitality, typical for him in the past, left him hour after hour in a near comatose state. Famous doctors from all over the world tried to understand why his vital signs were low when he was awake but sky rocketed when sleeping. Modern medications had an adverse effect upon him, but ancient herbal prescriptions seemed to help. Unfortunately now, even these were becoming ineffective.

The Holy Father wanted to be left alone because he wasn't alone.

He kept reliving, again and again, the last conversation he had with Renaldo just before his trip to Egypt. The young man fervently opposed this journey. His feelings toward the man that miraculously saved his life had deteriorated to a blind hatred that permanently haunted him.

"Gordon is filling your head with controversial ideas. You have to part with him at all cost. I'll take care of Marko."

"You'll take care of nothing in this vein. Don't order me around, dear boy. You'll leave The Residence immediately. I don't need you on this trip. Stay in Rome until my return."

"You're getting rid of me?"

"Only for the time being. I'll abstain from personal communication with Gordon. He's getting difficult too. Everything is going beyond control. The Holy Church is my responsibility. My own consciousness is my best counselor."

"Then, I'm withdrawing my services," fumed Renaldo.

Don't ever try blackmail on me, Renaldo. Pray to God for help. Act like a Christian," His Holiness demanded.

Renaldo's voice hissed with disappointment, "I take my orders straight from God."

"Do you know him?" asked the Pontiff.

"Nobody does. Gordon is a burden not only for you but for the Catholic 'status quo'. Humanity cannot afford this kind of luxury. Neither can the Universe. Truth is far more destructive than any lie. Let me solve the problem my way. Some might call it Satanic, but only Satan knows how to deal with characters like Gordon Bates," Renaldo declared with emphasis.

The Pope was flabbergasted. "Are you a satanic follower, Renaldo?"

"What if I'm one of his own, I still serve in the Holy Church. If I'm crucified, it's worthwhile. The Dogma can rest only on brutality. Jesus of Nazareth should never have another chance."

"But...we're HIS Church!"

"No. The son of Virgin Mary is Jesus, who has been created and recreated by the whim of the Holy Church."

The Pope buried his face in his shaky hands, then whispered softly, "If God lets you win, He'll prove you right. Do it your way."

"You won't be sorry, old man. I never fail."

"I'm sorry already, but my duty leaves me no choice."

Renaldo laughed dryly, "You see, it's as simple as buying yourself an ice cream cone. Send me as an advance party to Egypt. Nobody will trace you back to me. Our Church will stay as it is."

The Holy Father had become unholy in less than a minute.

—

On his knees, the Pope tried to pray. His eyes were closed, his lips moved silently. Then he opened his eyes in pain and frustration. "I cannot pray," he whispered to himself in total despair. Then the pathetic words of Claudius came to mind:

"MY WORDS FLY UP, MY THOUGHTS REMAIN BELOW; WORDS WITHOUT THOUGHTS NEVER TO HEAVEN GO."

Chapter 20

THE POPE

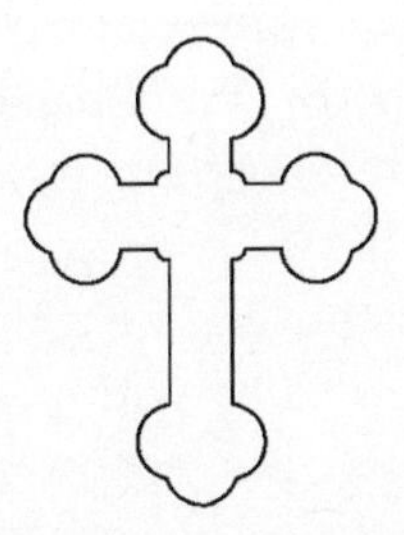

Aldano had to wait a long time for the prisoner. The Egyptian jail was nothing like the jails in American movies or the European fortresses for that matter. It was a hellhole. Rippling walls, a yellowish light from an impotent electric bulb, two folding chairs ten feet away from each other, a third chair in the middle for the warden. Renaldo looked terrific, healthy and handsome, a beatific smile on his face.

"I've never felt better in my life, Aldano. The Resident Chief Warden is renting me one of his best rooms. I exercise regularly, eat well, read and write."

"No regrets?"

"Why should I? I fulfilled my duty toward Church and God. What's more to live for? The Pope fears me. If I threaten to tell I'll be out in ten days. I choose to wait. Has your life changed?"

"No, it hasn't. Frustration is the name of my game."

"I'm sorry for you, Aldano."

"Are you really?"

"Of course. You deserve more from life. I know, life isn't fair. An unborn fetus is keeping your luck away. Why don't you do something about it?"

Aldano stared at him as if hypnotized. "I think our time's up."

"Think it over again. When you're good and ready let me know. No hurry, there is plenty of time. I'll still be here…for awhile."

"Don't you ever think of Gordon and Marko?"

"Oh, yeh…a nigger and your unworthy brother. I relive those moments all over with great relish. I served humankind well, even if now people show little appreciation. One day, I'll be given sainthood for what I did for the Catholic Church. Anyway, for perfect conduct I'll be released pretty soon."

"You're insane."

Renaldo laughed raucously, like a crazy man. "Aren't we all? I can bury you in a minute…" The younger man lost his healthy tan and tried to say something, but nothing came out of his mouth, "Don't worry, partner, just stay put," Renaldo said.

Aldano walked alongside the Nile, its majestic waters were incredibly dirty. The afternoon was suffocating, hot and humid like hell. He tried to forget about Renaldo. To kill Gordon's baby! What a perverted idea! The infant was yet to be born. Was it really murder to kill an unborn child? Why, it was blocking him…the only obstacle between him and Helena's money. She was deeply unhappy. She deserved a better life when she was still youthful and hungry for happiness, rather than all that boredom imposed upon her now.

Why did she ask him to visit the murderer of her beloved husband? Are Helena and Renaldo planning to cheat him? Is Renaldo a lover of hers? She could have Aldano in her bed with a snap of her fingers. Certainly he had less dignity than Renaldo, who was older and handsomer than he. Employers looked for an open mind, intelligence, knowledge. Good looking devils could be had by the dozen.

It was three p.m. Every moment pulsated in his head like a jungle drum. Excessive heat always did him in. He felt a pent up rage ready to explode. That motherfucker Renaldo. Who does he think he is?

He tried to imagine living in Egypt during the time of the pharaohs, owning only a piece of loin cloth. Certainly, he didn't have much more than that at the end of the 20th Century. Helena had given him money for his clothing, golden Swiss watch, traveling expenses and his pocket money. Come to think of it, he didn't even own his underwear, he had no skills or education, no guts to face life. Unemployment spread like wildfire all over the planet. Labor disputes, riots, despair, greed and corruption had become the norm.

Yes, nothing changes! It has always been a power play, and it will go on forever.

The President of the Cardinal's Counsel stood by the Pope's bed. In all his time with the Vatican, he had never seen His Holiness so enraged. The old man clutched a formal looking letter in his trembling fingers.

"Did you try to suppress the message from Mrs. Bates' attorneys?"

The man paled, then flushed profusely. "Only to save you the shock, Your Holiness."

"Such short-sightedness for the acting Head of my Counsel. This letter needed immediate attention."

"We paid immediate attention to it. It tries to prevent us from taking Mr. Renaldo Cortelazzo out of jail. We acted promptly. He's safely back in Rome, we think."

The Pope's eyes became murderous. "Where in Rome?"

"I don't know, Holiness."

"How many members of the Counsel supported your decision?" demanded the Pope.

"Most of them," offered the president.

"I want their names! You're to be stripped of all honors and restricted to a single cell in the basement. Bread and water only. Try purging Satan out of yourself by constant prayer." Then the Pope asked his Security Inspector, "Have you located Mr. Cortelazzo?"

"The man is on parole, but he never contacted his assigned officer. The police consider him a fugitive of the law."

"I expected that, Inspector. Take this man in custody. He's not to be contacted by anybody. I hereby suspend the Cardinals' Counsel. Everyone that voted for release of that double murderer has to explain in writing. As long as I live, I won't leave the Holy Church in the hands of the Anti-Christ. Remove the holy insignia from the chest of this pitiful being. My secretary is preparing an immediate press-release. See that it is distributed worldwide. Anybody harboring the Anti-Christ will be excommunicated from the Church, even Church Dignitaries. I consider the Papacy in a state of siege until all involved in this sordid affair are apprehended."

By noontime, the Pope's Manifest and photograph of Renaldo Cortelazzo had been distributed. By four in the afternoon the fugitive had been arrested in Teheran. By five p.m., he again escaped, under highly suspicious circumstances. The Iranians found three forged I.D.'s with different names, all prepared by the Vatican Foreign Office. Obviously, in the aftermath of World War II, the Vatican had perfected forging passports. Later that night, Teheran announced that the fugitive had been sighted by police patrols and in a ferocious gun-battle, he was shot to death. The body was set upon by locals and was mutilated beyond recognition.

Interpol secretly distributed a new photo of Renaldo Cortelazzo, an artist's sketch of the young man after plastic surgery. Someone with his background, in the hands of an unfriendly government, could be a maximum security risk.

Aldano Brandon pushed the newspaper into the inner pocket of his raincoat. He unlocked the door to his father's house and found him bedridden.

"Are you sick?"

The old man squeezed his bluish lips together, "I'm sick in my heart."

"Have you taken your medication, father?"

His father made an indefinite sign with his hand. Suddenly Aldano turned toward the wall where the family portraits hung. His was missing.

"What happened to my picture?" Aldano was puzzled.

" I...don't want you in this house, Aldano." His father continued, "I visited the herb doctor, my would-be-son. He told me what you had purchased for Helena."

Aldano's facial tone melted into something grayish.

"It wasn't poison, Dad...just a medication for Helena...she looked...she looks bad."

"Not nearly as bad as you look now, son..." He kept his hand hidden under the blanket.

Aldano knew his father's temper. His knees buckled under him, and he fell to the floor, cowardly shaking, pleading with his father, "Don't do it, father, please, I'm Aldano, your favorite! Remember?" He burst into sobs, "...it's only an unborn babe, father, a miserable fetus..."

"And you are just a miserable reptile!" his father croaked.

Aldano was horror stricken. He didn't want to die by his father's hand.

"Don't shoot me, father...in mother's name, don't shoot!"

"How dare you sully her name. What did you promise to the maid?"

"A fuck, I've been doing it anyway. She always serves the tea. I swear to God, I was just following orders."

"You make me sick, wretched idiot. Who's orders?"

"Renaldo's, he knew a few things about me and was going to blackmail me."

The door to the next room opened. A police inspector put manacles on Aldano's hands and three officers took him away.

"Your Holiness! Your Holiness! "The voice of his secretary penetrated the mind of the old man. "The Curia is in session in spite of Your Order!"

The Pope opened his eyes and felt right away the presence of a New Pope within him. He slowly got up on his own from the bed.

"Help me dress in my ceremonial attire!" Two of his valets scurried around, "Can we still count on the guardsmen, Silvestro?"

"I think so, Holiness, but you shouldn't..."

"Don't worry about me," interrupted the Pope. "I've never been in better shape. Call the guardsmen."

The large gates to the Curia's conference room opened wide and the Pope, in full regalia, entered, followed by his personal staff and guards.

The cardinals were stunned. Out of habit, they rose to their feet. Over the miter of the Holy Father they discerned an unmistakable halo. Four of the cardinals hurried to the Pope's feet and knelt before him. Two more came running, then another. The rest stood, mouths hanging open. Their President delivered to them from custody, was still barren of his insignia.

The Pope pointed his silver Shepherd's Staff at them and pronounced loud and clear:

"In the Glorious Names of Father and Son, as their sole Preemptive Power on Earth, I declare those rebellious people, guided by the forces of Evil and Darkness, EXCOMMUNICATED from the Mother Church of Christ of Nazareth, until Judgment Day!"

Chapter 21

ANDREW

Andrew Bates was born on the fifth of November 2000, in the same old palazzo on the Isle of Malta. He bore little resemblance to his father, though by complexion he certainly wasn't white. Helena liked him just as he was. What she didn't like was the constant security surveillance of her house and the inhabitants. At first, she didn't want to believe Aldano's plot to eliminate her baby in pregnancy. Unfortunately, the evidence against him was unshakable. Other black spots in his past surfaced. With Renaldo's movements unchecked because of his change of identity, she had no other choice but to obey all safety measures. Her child had to learn and mature by the book of the princes, with private tutors and governesses all approved after a very thorough background check. The villa's wall was radar equipped day and night and neighbors were discouraged from any friendly visits. Helena had to clear her schedule with the security squad at least twenty-four hours ahead of time.

Andrew was a healthy and vigorous boy, but for his first three years, he didn't say a single word. No *mamma*, no baby talk, nothing. World-famous specialists found everything normal. They cited similar cases of other young children going through the same silent period. In spite of this temporary silence, children like this, more often than not, proved to have exceptional intelligence.

Young Andrew communicated through his eyes. They were large, greenish blue, extremely lovely and serious. At times he looked at Helena in a strange way, then would suddenly focus on something else that Helena was unable to see. He started walking with no help or encouragement from anybody. He expressed himself vividly through a sort of body language and Andrew seem to read everyone's mind perfectly.

One morning, soon after his third birthday, Helena saw Andrew walking through the garden in the company of a large Siberian Husky. Nobody had seen that dog before. They had no idea how it got onto the estate, yet it was obvious that boy and dog knew each other very well. Andrew looked at his mom with his large, smiling eyes and suddenly uttered in a quite mature voice, "This dog is mine. His name is Shadow."

From that moment on, Shadow never left the side of his young master. Though friendly with Helena, he was hostile toward anyone else coming close to the little boy. The staff had a hard time adjusting to his watchfulness and a couple of maids were forced to leave, as Shadow would attack them on sight. One of the gardeners soon followed.

Before long, Andrew was speaking; forming his words and sentences with uncommon clarity, as if he'd studied the language during his silent period. Shadow and Andrew seemed to have long conversations. Helena was excluded from those sessions.

Unexpectedly, a wave of high-society invitations piled on Helena's desk, but she ignored them. Andrew was her only focus. Two assistants took care of the telephone calls, E-mails, telegrams and messages, paid bills and answered letters. She prohibited visits, and attended no parties or get-togethers. She simply lost interest and started dressing carelessly. In her free time, she played the piano and read books. There wasn't a single TV set in the whole palazzo. The stereo, complete with CD and tapes, was seldom in use, and when it was, the personnel on duty were invited and refreshments served. Although there were a few complaints, no one left. The pay was extremely good.

One rainy night, Helena decided to retire early. In the adjacent room, little Andrew soundly slept, Shadow at his feet. The faithful dog acknowledged her presence by wagging his tail without opening his eyes. She switched on the night light and went to her room. While turning on her bedside lamp, she felt that someone was sitting nearby, next to the window.

Nothing frightening, only a specter of sadness.

It was old Mr. Brandon, leaning on his walking stick. He smiled in his disarming way. "I'm glad you're not afraid of spooks, Mrs. Bates, my dear. I shouldn't have come uninvited," he apologized.

Helena sat on her bed and lit a cigarette. "Are spooks interested in smoking?"

"No…or drinking or eating, either. Only newcomers feel the need. Some more than others. It isn't much of an existence."

"Except for my son, I haven't much of an existence either," Helena said, greatly pained.

"I'd like to thank you for the doctors and the nurses when I was alive. For the first time in my life I had all my bills paid. I know the medications were overly expensive, but …"

"Please, don't think about it. You were so good for my father," Helena interrupted.

"Why? I was a burden in my old days. Even my sons never came to see me, and it is they who owe me something. I haven't seen any of my grandchildren, or their mothers for that matter. Unbeknownst to me, I must've made terrible mistakes in my life. I guess I have to keep on paying the debt forever."

"You don't miss your family much, do you?" Helena observed.

"I miss Marko…and Aldano, in a way. I didn't do enough for him. So far I haven't even seen my wife."

"Don't blame yourself."

"Who else shall I blame? I could've done something for Aldano," he said wistfully.

"I could've done something for him, also. Where is he now?"

"In Tobruk."

" Where is that?"

"Libya. There are labor camps there. Egypt has a treaty to unload hard core criminals in them. There, the brutal dictator Quaddafi makes terrorists out of them and sends them back across the border all over Northern Africa and the world. Stupid, downright stupid."

"How god awful! Nobody stepped in for Aldano. I'll go and see him there."

"I hope so. You have a beautiful child. Have you ever told him anything about his father?"

"Not yet…it's too early," Helena told him.

Mr. Brandon nodded thoughtfully, "Now I'd better go."

Helena tried to organize her own thoughts. "Where in this rain, for Christ sake? Stay here."

"That's real nice of you, Helena, my dear. I don't take up much room on this chair. I'll stay in the dark and watch over you. God bless your soul," he said with a mysterious smile on his face.

The Pope sat in the small tea pavilion, going through important mail and listening to Silvestro's reports. Since dissolving the Curia, he had appointed a new government. Some of the more powerful cardinals were shifted to insignificant positions. The current Counsel of the Cardinals that replaced the dreaded Curia Romana, was carefully selected and weak enough to not foster any trouble. A special commission of bibliophiles and scientists, with unbridled access to the Secret Archives of the Vatican, worked full steam over the rehabilitation of the Old Testament. There were no quick remedies. The Byzantine-Orthodox Church adamantly opposed any changes. Spain and South America were in turmoil over the new findings concerning the Madonna.

On the human, worldly stage, lengthy dry spells compromised vital crops. Economic disasters abounded. People's minds boiled with unfocused anger. More cults rose from the ashes of the current situation. Hopelessness made a substantial impact on the universal spirit. Communist countries like Cuba, China and North Korea became more aggressive. Russia malevolently asserted that North Korea was a "'gentle" country and her reclusive leader suddenly befriended his southern counterpart. China felt isolated and toned down its countless ultimatums and threats directed toward Taiwan. Loads of nuclear secrets were stolen from the United States. The vital issue of Palestine still hung in the air, with no prospect of real sovereignty in sight.

His Holiness looked better than at any time lately. His mind was sharp and his decisions quick and effective, though the hard-liners in the Catholic Church kept a low profile, the danger they presented was ever present.

"What do we know about Renaldo's movements, Silvestro?" asked the Pontiff.

"Next to nothing, Holiness. A few leads have been dead ends. However, rumors abound."

"What rumors?"

"That he's hiding in Afghanistan, or visiting Muammar al Quaddafi in Tripoli."

The Pope closed his tired eyes and was silent for a minute. "That's possible. Are young Andrew Bates and his mother safe in Malta?"

"For the time being. She was stopped in time when she tried to get passage to Tobruk recently ."

The old man was visibly shaken.

"She would have walked right into the hands of this sworn enemy!?! How close was it?"

"Very close. She chartered a plane for an undisclosed destination. When she mentioned Tobruk, the pilot called us. We arranged clearance to land on the Isle of Elba under the pretext that the plane was running out of fuel. From there Mrs. Bates was flown directly back to Malta, under her protest."

"Great God! Didn't you tell me that Aldano Brandon had been moved there as bait? Is she still infatuated with him?

"I don't know if Helena Bates was privy to Aldano's whereabouts. His father could've told her, but he is dead. Her mail and phone calls are monitored. Then, suddenly, it came to this. It was a very close call."

The Pope buried his face in his disfigured hands. "I wonder on which side Mr. Brandon aligned himself?"

"On the side of the dead, Your Holiness. Are you thinking…?"

"I'm convinced," he interrupted, "there's no other explanation. He's controlling her mind. I must see her in person. Find a sound reason to give the press and make all arrangements."

"When?"

"As soon as possible," commanded the Pontiff.

"So far Helena Bates has refused to see you."

"That's right, but she won't turn me down if I show up at her door. Let it be a total surprise."

"That's easy. Mrs. Bates doesn't watch TV news. Radio broadcasts and newspapers are limited."

"Was Mr. Brandon a Catholic?"

"No, a Protestant. But his wife and children were baptized Catholics."

His Holiness waved his hand as if brushing away something invisible. "Very well. I'll settle this."

The door was answered by a maid.

She was dumbfounded to see the Pontiff, who was accompanied by two men in dark business suits. The young woman fell on her knees and fervently kissed his hand. She invited him into the grand salon and ran to look for her mistress. In spite of the early hour, Helena was up and about. She wasn't as surprised as her maid at the Pope's appearance.

Young Andrew was crossing the salon in the company of Shadow and a governess. Andrew stood motionless, Shadow pressing against his slender body making small puppy sounds. The boy's deep, intelligent eyes gently observed the old man, who was smiling at him from a richly ornamented velvet chair.

"*Heo, Andrew, unde venis?*"

The child answered without hesitation, "*Vado ante portam*. Do you want to come with us?"

"I can't, my legs are not young and strong like yours. You have a very handsome dog. He is as white as an angel!"

"He *is* an angel. God sent him to me," the boy informed him matter-of-factly.

"You must be very special to Him if He sends you His angels," observed His Holiness.

"God takes care of me because I never knew my own father. Now He's my only Father."

His Holiness was deeply impressed by the simplicity and profoundness of his words. "How long have you been studying Latin?" he asked.

"Nobody has told me what Latin means. Are you my grandfather?"

"In more ways than one, child. I knew your father as if he were a son of mine."

"Then why didn't you spare his life?"

The head of the Pontiff dropped to his chest, to hide his tears. "Because, I wasn't a good father. We don't always live up to what we really want to be."

"Would you let me die, too?" asked Andrew

"Not if I can help it," promised the Pope.

"I'll pray for you, grandfather, so you won't leave me."

"I swear to God," uttered the Pope in a broken voice, "I won't betray you for anything."

Everybody present was so engrossed by this exchange, that Helena's entrance wasn't noticed until her voice broke the hypnosis, "Except for the Holy Church. You'll go even to Hell defending it, wouldn't you, Your Holiness?"

"Not anymore, Lady Helena. Things have changed radically since our last meeting."

"They have indeed, Holy Father. What can we do about it?"

"We can pray together. God never changes. He's One and the Same for eternity."

"I didn't think about Libya as a center of terrorism." Helena tried to explain her behavior, "I wanted to help Aldano. He's not responsible for his actions. A truly possessed person cannot be held accountable. I'll try to ransom him from Quaddafi."

The Pope shook his head. "He'll ask for more than money, Lady Helena."

"Such as...?" she queried.

"Access to your house. Never ask favors from the likes of him. You'll never be able to repay them."

Helena walked across the library and touched her forehead to the cool window glass. Andrew was playing with Shadow in the courtyard below under the watchful eyes of a governess and the two detectives that accompanied the Pope.

"Will it always be like that?"

"I'm afraid so."

"You don't think of me as a mature person, do you, Holiness," Helena asked.

"The word is unpredictable. Especially when your sentiments are so strong. Your emotions are out of control. Andrew belongs to you but also to the rest of humankind. He's the only hope we have. At this early age, he already has the 'Gift of Tongues' as did his father. He's very intelligent."

"Are you going to take him away from me?"

"I'm tempted, but he must have a normal childhood, aside from the necessary restrictions. The Vatican is not a place for children. A new, near-perfect security system has been installed in this house."

Helena came back from the window and sat near him. "Can you do something for Aldano Brandon, Holiness? I heard your second would-be assassin is out of jail. Aldano's faults of character can only deepen under the present conditions."

"He seems to have adjusted quite well," the Pope acknowledged. "The labor-camp discipline has changed him. His physical constitution thrives. He's energetic and practices karate and boxing. He lives in a hotel and seems happy as a lark; playing soccer in his free time just for the hell of it, walking the streets of Tripoli on his own recognizance."

"My information is quite different," Helena commented.

"I'd say it's from a different source," offered the Pope.

"Are you suggesting that someone else hides in Mr. Brandon Sr.'s image?"

"It's very likely. Mr. Brandon likes you. He wouldn't send you on a wild goose chase to Tobruk. He would know the consequences."

Helena let out an inaudible sigh, "I see. It was rather stupid of me. I'll try to learn something from it. And where is Renaldo these days?"

"He cannot be far from Aldano. He's surely the brain behind him, possibly his manager."

Helena desperately needed a cigarette, but in the presence of the Holy Guest that would've been unpardonable. "What do you expect of me, Holy Father?"

The Pontiff shrugged his shoulders. "To be a good mother to a highly unusual child is a full time business. Listen to the news. Call me, I'll try to be a fair judge."

"As in a confessional?"

"As to a father, if you can bring yourself to view me as such," he offered.

Helena tried to gather her thoughts. "I love Aldano, Holy Father. I miss him."

The old man lifted his eyebrows slightly. He looked for something in his pocket, then gave her a piece of paper. "I came well prepared."

Helena took it and seemed confused. "What is it?"

"Aldano's hotel phone number, codes and all. His room is 666, I presume a little joke on the part of Colonel Muammar al Quaddafi. By the way, no need to tell you that his people are going to listen in."

"Can I call him now? It will be easier with you here."

"Your chances of finding him at home in the daytime are very slim. But go ahead, one never knows..."

Helena went to the phone and dialed. The connection was made.

"May I talk to the gentleman in room 666? My name is Helena." Her heart pummeled as the line crackled and somebody picked up the phone. Helena's face paled. "Renaldo!" she gasped.

The Pontiff's surprise was also hard to hide. Helena switched on a loud-speaker.

"Yes...I share Aldano's room, if not the same bed. Are you calling from the airport?"

"No, I'm calling from home."

"Are you alone?" Renaldo asked.

Helena looked at the Pope. He nodded. "No, I'm not alone. His Holiness is visiting me."

Renaldo laughed huskily, "I thought so, but that's even better. I intended to call him one of these days. Is he on the line?"

"No, but I can arrange that."

The old man picked up the extension, "Hello...Renaldo, it's nice to hear your voice again."

Evidently, the young man was savoring the situation. "Really? You didn't try to call me in prison, Holiness."

"Did you try to call me?" retortedthe Pope.

"No. I didn't think you'd accept my call. Isn't it a bit weird, even now?"

"I'm still the Pontiff. I don't have to explain myself to anybody but God. My feelings toward you have changed, though some of the old love survives.

"Same here, though my recollections are painful at times."

"Certainly. Have you attended confession?"

"Not since the last time with you. My attorney suggested that it can be self-incriminating."

"Really?"

Renaldo was mad at himself for this slip of his tongue.

"You cannot be a member of the flock if you don't follow the rules," impressed the Pope.

"Did the first Christians?"

The Pope was silent for awhile. "You have gone way too far, Renaldo."

"Are you going to excommunicate me, Holiness?"

"You already have been. You don't belong to us. Anyone who commands his own evil shots belongs to Satan."

"Holy Moses! Do you perceive me as a devil?"

"A servant to the Anti-Christ at the very least. Blasphemy and profanity are the surest signs."

"I'm sorry, Holiness. I have to move fast before I'm deported."

"Stay where you are. Quaddafi needs you."

"If you say so…"

"I'm positive. But you won't be able to disappear."

Renaldo laughed derisively, "Strong words. I'll take my chances by staying away from your long arms. You leave me no choice."

"The choice of God will be always within your reach. I'm praying that you'll find him again, even if it is in the last moments of your life."

Aldano Brandon stood at the door. He stared at his naked roommate, Renaldo, who was nestled comfortably on one of the beds, legs crossed in oriental fashion. His dark hair had become a helmet of curls surrounding a restructured face. A well-tended moustache hung over his full sensuous lips. His originally light complexion had become swarthy. Most, including Aldano, were intimidated by him.

"Was it Helena?" asked Aldano.

Not a single muscle moved on Renaldo's face. "It was the Pope."

Aldano threw his tote-bag onto the bed. He was in a foul mood. The showers in the sports club were out of order and he stunk. "Why should I be getting a call from the Pope?" he wondered out loud.

"He knew that I'm staying here."

Aldano banged the door shut, pulled off his smelly sweatshirt and pants, then threw them into Renaldo's face.

"Liar! The switchboard operator gave me Helena's name."

Renaldo jumped up from his bed like a cat. "Nobody calls me a liar and lives to tell about." They were immediately chest to chest, breathing hard, "Think twice, fancy boy, I'm your only friend in this world. Without me you're a goner. It's enough if I report your rampant pedophilia. The two Egyptian boys disappearing from your room in Amarna..."

"You murdered my brother and ruined my life, bastard. You gotta pay," screamed Aldano.

Renaldo shoved his body away disdainfully. "I should've started with you, asshole!"

The young man's face puckered with rage. "I'm gonna change your face again, for no charge whatsoever."

The adversaries breathed hatred and vehemence like the two deadly enemies they actually were. Because any overt action would have been ruinous for both of them, they ended up turning their backs to each other and walking away.

The formal garden behind the medieval palazzo was peaceful. Bees visited flower after flower. Still wet from the dawn rain, the magnificent roses spread their delightful aroma everywhere. Helena and her guest joined the small group around Andrew

The little boy looked serenely at the smiling old man. "Are you going back to Rome, grandpa?"

The Pope set his hand over his silky auburn hair. "That's my only home, dear boy."

Andrew took hold of the old Pontiff's hand. "Stay for lunch, grandfather, please."

The old man made the sign of the cross over him and whispered a blessing. "Set a place for me at the table, sonny, I'll be there."

A soft inner light illuminated the expressive face of the child. "I believe you, grandpa. And I'll see you there."

Chapter 22

SHADOW

Andrew was not a lonely child.

He had his mom, the tutors and the servants. But most of all, he had Shadow. The dog listened attentively, never missing a single word his young master said. Andrew listened to him with the same concentration and attention.

Years had passed since the Pope visited the house, but his place at the dining table was always set. Andrew had no problem seeing him there, even though he knew that his "grandpa" had gone forever. After his departure, Andrew received a simple golden cross with the name "Berrick" engraved on the back. The boy never parted with it.

Now he was eight years old but still under tutelage. The new Pontiff grew increasingly irritated with "unjustified" expenditures. He was considered the protector of Andrew Bates. Mrs. Bates finally bought the palazzo. She hated it, but somehow she managed to turn it into a home. Her desire to wander around the world had faded and she had become more self-destructive as her depression became more severe.

One morning at breakfast, Andrew with his characteristic seriousness, announced, "Shadow needs a home of his own."

"He is sharing the residence with us," his mother reminded him.

"You don't understand, mother. He needs his own home."

Helena looked at her son, whose complexion was golden brown, with the sheen of silk. His slender, wiry body featured a well-rounded, muscular chest and square shoulders that dominated his narrow hips. His flat belly and strongly shaped thighs and calves were loaded with energy. A crew cut made his eyes look even larger than they really were.

He was peering gravely at her through his absurdly thick eyelashes. "Would they crucify him too?" she thought, horrified.

Helena shuddered with apprehension. The new Pope didn't seem to give any credence to the legacy of the former Pontiff. Like any good, straight-talking businessman, he was preoccupied only with earthly problems.

Helena gave her son a worn out smile, and answered his original question, "I'll ask the gardener. I'm sure he'll build something for Shadow."

Andrew's large luminous eyes intensified with anticipation. "Can I build him a home according to his need?"

"What is his need?" asked his mother, puzzled at his question.

"Privacy."

"Privacy. I see. So, you're not going to share it with him?"

"Only if I'm invited," Andrew informed her.

"Must you build it yourself?" She was exasperated. "Well, get tools and materials from Nando. I'll tell him to stay away from your project. You won't hurt yourself, will you?"

"You don't get hurt when you play the piano, Mom, do you? This is my 'piano'."

Helena finished her toast and pushed aside the untouched tea. "Sometimes I abuse myself," she teased.

"You need a drink..."

"...and a cigarette. Why did you tell your tutors you don't need them anymore?"

Andrew took a good sip of his milk. "I really don't need them."

"You don't?" his mother questioned.

The boy helped himself to another serving of all the food. Helena thought, "Thank God, he always has a good appetite." But to her son she warned, "All children need tutors…or they must go to school."

"I've learned how to read and write. Math isn't that important to me. I hate computers. For now, I can live without them. This residence has a marvelous library. I don't need the Padre either, because I know my catechism. I'll keep you company at church, and you can teach me the piano."

A nagging headache was bothering Helena. She longed for a drink.

"You need to play as well, darling."

"Oh, I love the construction games and the gym is fun. I dream night after night of swimming amidst the stars."

Helena closed her eyes. The abundant sun streamed through the large French windows and augmented her pain. Even the bird's singing seemed bothersome. She dreamed, too…about Aldano. He was more handsome than ever and his lovemaking was passionate and considerate.

"Shall I close the drapes, Madam?" the maid asked compassionately.

"No, I'll be leaving soon. Andrew likes the sun. Tell the gardener that I want to see him. We need a swimming pool. Is the gym instructor coming in today?"

"He's here already, Madam."

"Send him in, please."

The pretty, young servant made a little curtsy and left. Helena folded her serviette. "You don't want Mr. Wagner fired, do you, Andrew?"

Andrew wiped his mouth with the elegant linen napkin and smiled with certain sadness. "Actually Shadow can teach me how to swim."

"Mr. Wagner can take you to the beach," Helena told him.

"Really! He and an army of guards?"

"You don't have to be bothered by the security. They are like any other people."

"No, they're not. What happened to Mr. Wagner's face?"

"He's been in an accident. His face has been reconstructed," Helena told him. She either had not recognized him as Renaldo or didn't want to. Maybe both.

"More than once. The color of his hair doesn't seem natural," Andrew commented.

"Many Germans are platinum blond."

"How come my cousins never come over?" the boy changed the subject. "A couple of them are about my age.

"You don't have cousins," said Helena.

"Aren't those kids that come over on my birthdays my cousins?"

"They're not related to us. They're from a family that I knew many years ago. I'll ask Bruno Wagner to bring a couple of them over. Be careful when you tussle with those boys, they can be pretty rough."

"I can take care of myself, Mom. Is Shadow welcome at the beach?"

"By all means, take him. Your dog will be treated well. On the yacht, too. It's ours. I own most of the Club. You should feel and behave there as if you were the master. Of course, you have to obey Mr. Wagner, who is your bodyguard. I wish I could come along with you, but my head is killing me. Some other time maybe."

The boy's head imperceptibly drooped. "Of course, Mom, another time."

Unusually silent and subdued, Bruno waited in a brand new Rover for his young master. The two "cousins," Mark and Danny Brandon, sat in the back. Danny was only a few months older than Mark, but at the age of nine that meant something. They lived in the same apartment building and were constantly at war with each other, though for them living apart was unthinkable. Instead of trying to smooth out the relationship, their fathers kept setting them against each other, so the two temperamental and highly volatile characters always found fuel for arguments and fighting. Both dads were very proud of their sons' "machismo." Soon, the stamina and toughness of the two cousins became well-known, and their fights became public entertainment. Beer cans were passed around and money changed hands.

Otherwise, Danny's only ambition in life was to become a member of the Pope's Guard in the Vatican like his deceased uncle Marko. Mark's choice was to be a Soldier of Fortune, cool and bereft of any feelings, like their friend Bruno Wagner. To be a life-model for a kid somehow appealed to Bruno. He liked Mark's desperado attitude and roguish good looks. It obviously awakened certain memories in him.

Andrew and Shadow came down the marble steps. The boy dialed in a security number and the door opened. Boy and dog sat on the front seat, Shadow letting out his usual low growl at Bruno. Andrew always found an excuse not to look at Bruno's face. It was strangely blunt and unnatural.

Andrew turned to the backseat. "Hi, guys! Who won the last fight?"

Mark sneered and he spat out through the open window. The glowing, ruddy cheeks of his rival made room for a wide, impish grin. Mark got really mad.

"This tow-headed skunk gave me a low, sneaky jab to the groin. Up to that point I was winning, I sent him writhing to the ground three times crying murder. Bruno saw it."

Bruno switched on the engine.

"What's done is done." He commented dryly as he released the break and turned the wheel.

The car ran smoothly down the hill. Mark shook his head violently.

"He's half a year older and five pounds heavier than I am!"

Bruno grimaced and turned on the radio. "In that case, don't fight him again until you grow bigger and at least a year older."

The day at the beach proved to be a wonderful day in young Andrew's life. Under a bedazzling sun, the three boys and Shadow played soccer, pushing and elbowing each other unmercifully. Then they ran at will in the soft golden sand, dodging and sprinting during a wild game of tag. In that free-for-all, rough-and-tumble battle in the shallow surf, winners and losers laughed away any pain and bruises.

It was each against the world — all for one and one for all. A feeling of closeness and camaraderie that none of them had experienced before.

By evening, they were ravenously hungry and attacked a buffet that was fit for a king. Waiters and patrons couldn't believe the huge amount of food scoffed down by the three rambunctious kids and their dog. A surly young man watched over them from a secluded table. He hardly touched any food but drank slowly and methodically.

A large motorboat Andrew hadn't seen before was entirely at their disposal. It had a spacious living room with a bar and powerful stereo, two bedrooms with connecting baths and a wide open deck. A couple of bronzed seamen in full uniform took care of all chores.

It was one of those magical Mediterranean nights crowned with a regal full moon and blessed with calm and beauty. A night for love and romance. Bruno called Helena. The children's fountain of seemingly boundless energy ran out suddenly and left them happily drowsy and languid. Helena was also in a stupor brought on by a steady flow of drugs and booze that had broken her will power.

"What are you doing, Bruno?" she asked in a rather sulky voice, slurring her words.

"The boys are sleeping like the dead on the king-size bed, with the dog cuddled at their feet. Later I'll play some cards with the crewmen. They seem awfully young and green for a security job, but nowadays..."

"Don't try anything foolish," Helena warned.

Bruno lit a cigarette, then went on, "Tonight or never Helena...it seems too easy. Besides I've become attached to your son. He has an indescribable charm, way beyond his father's... You're right. I can't combat the powers within him. I'm under his spell and his dog Shadow watches me every instant. Are you coming?"

"Is it possible that Vatican Security can penetrate the scrambling of this line?" Helena was hesitant.

"No. I won't be caught that easily. Besides, I have the feeling that they're not trying very hard. This Pope doesn't know what to make of the Little Savior."

"Strange, I thought of that too. There's no surveillance on the house. The new Pope wants to get rid of Andrew without any repercussions. Now, I don't care for him either." Helena seemed to have been taken over by an evil being that had been hovering over her for years.

Bruno thought for a moment, then spoke into the mouthpiece, "Poor bugger, nobody wants him. I'll come up with something. Call the Brandons. Tell them you're treating their kids to an extended summer vacation. The cousins are not due back to school for months."

"Right, I'll do that, Bruno. The parents probably wouldn't mind being relieved of that responsibility."

"Andrew has them eating out of his hand, so they're actually behaving like angels."

"Is Andrew suspicious?" Helena asked tentatively.

"He is sure I am not who I say I am. How could he know my true identity? His dog is hard to fool, too, but for some reason, neither one of them seem to mind. The new boat can easily make it to Tripoli, then you'll meet your balmy lover. A deal is a deal."

The cigarette burned Bruno's fingers and he threw it angrily overboard. At the other end, Helena laughed drunkenly, "I'm coming, dear Anti-Christ. I'll join the boat at the isle of Callamara."

Andrew woke up to the rhythmic low noise of the powerful engine. It was a real sea voyage. Mark had fallen asleep with his dark tousled head on Andrew's chest, their arms laced around each other. Now he woke up too, and he listened over the loud breathing of his cousin.

"Are we moving?" he whispered lifting his head up.

"Yes…and we might never come back."

"Never?"

"Never ever."

Mark smiled broadly. His dark, finely etched brows knitted churlishly, and his eyes gleamed in the dark. He laughed in a thick, husky voice. "I can't believe my luck, Andrew! I never want to go back to that smelly overcrowded apartment, the boring and patronizing schoolmaster…Can I stay with you?" Mark begged as he caught Andrew in a playful bear hug.

"Stop it, you'll wake up Danny."

Mark started really roughhousing, shoving a knee in his groin, fingers driving into Andrew's pectoral muscles. "Oh, forget about him! I'll throw him overboard. He'll have to swim back to Malta, if the sharks spare him. I love you, Andrew, more than anyone, like a brother. Fuck, I hate my brothers and sisters, I hate my cousins, I hate even God and the Saints…everybody but you. You're different. I want to be with you always, follow you wherever you go. I'll serve you any way I can."

Andrew embraced Mark's head roughly, pressing it hard to his chest. Then he suddenly realized that Mark's face was bathed in tears. That boy had never cried before.

"Mark, I love you too," Andrew exclaimed. "You have to believe me, because I'm here to tell the Truth. I even love Bruno, who's out to kill me, and my mother who's ready to betray me. I know, the Old Man with the angelic smile is waiting in the wings to use me for his purposes. But you, Mark, you're the first one to love me for what I am. You're THE FIRST ONE that wants to follow me wherever I go, for good or bad. I need you, because my life will be ugly and heart-wrenching. I have no idea where and how to start MY ROAD. I'm scared, Mark, but with you it will be somewhat easier. We can share the pains and the disappointments."

Danny was lying on his stomach, listening to every word. Then he said in his boyish voice.

"I can come also, Andrew. If Mark goes, I go. Without him, I wouldn't know what to do with myself. We sort of lean on each other, because he has more brain than brawn, so I rely on him, even though I can thrash him two times out of three."

Following a pause that seemed endless, Mark released Andrew, rolled on his side, and sighed amenably, "In the long run, Andrew, I'd probably miss this bully. Can we take him on the Road? He isn't entirely useless."

Suddenly, Andrew laughed boisterously. Something very heavy and depressing had fallen from his young shoulders. He could see Shadow's eyes gleaming in the dark, tail thumping on the footboard of the bed.

"The more the merrier, I guess," Andrew declared through fits of benevolent laughter. "You're welcome to come, Danny. We have to learn how to help each other and make more friends."

"How many more?" Danny wanted to know.

"I don't know exactly. Millions."

Mark's mouth hung open. "That many!?! I thought our apartment was crowded! Are you going to be a king or something?"

Andrew sat on his heels like Mark. "No. I'm more interested in people's souls."

Mark swallowed. "Now you have to slow down a bit, Andrew. I know, mostly from church, what a human soul is. Are we going that way? I can put up with it for a while, but I don't think Danny will."

"Oh, no-o-o-ooo," laughed Andrew, "my collection has very little to do with church. Shadow knows what I'm talking about. He has a great soul."

Mark scratched his chin ponderously. "How about mine? Do I have one?"

"Of course, Mark…cousin Danny too. Everyone has one. The problem is to find a way to touch it, and then, to make it better and better."

Mark moved closer and looked open-eyed at Andrew. His tow-headed cousin also got up and crossed his legs in front of himself. "I know what you're talking about, Andrew. Sometimes when I beat up this guy, I worry that his soul might leave him."

Mark looked at Andrew questioningly, then back at his cousin. "How about when I beat you up? Where does *your* soul go?"

Now it was Andrew's turn to be aghast. "You're close to it, guys, but not quite. The important thing is to start talking about it now, instead of beating each other up. I'm glad we've discussed this difficult matter. It isn't easy for me either, but Shadow helps me. Now you guys will too."

"We can help you with this matter, Andrew," Danny assured him clenching his fists.

Mark felt left out. "Drop dead, I can help Andrew myself. I'm better with my fists."

Danny moved up to his knees really piqued at Mark, and the two cousins went loudly at each other again, swearing and pushing.

Finally, Mark, looking at Andrew's pained expression, said, "Let's cool it, Danny, Andrew has a headache."

Andrew perked up. "Tone it down, guys. I don't have a headache. I was holding my head because I'm tired. We cannot follow any road if we don't give ourselves enough time to rest and get ready."

Thus, their first meeting of the minds in the darkness of the "boardroom" was adjourned. Only Andrew was unable to make himself fall back to sleep, thinking about all the books that he hadn't read yet. How was he going to proceed to shape up the minds of his first couple of disciples. This was enough to keep him wide awake.

At least Mark knew a thing or two about love, although he wasn't sure if it was the right kind. Those damned Brandons, always mixed up in something nefarious!

The boys' noisy scuffling had hidden the sound of the motorboat bringing Helena aboard. Now, in the other bedroom, Helena crushed out her cigarette, switched off the bedside lamp and cuddled into the lean and muscular body of her lover.

"A noisy bunch, those youngsters..." Bruno muttered, "I had enough infringement of my privacy in the training camps."

"What camps?" murmured Helena.

"In Damascus and in Iran. Subhuman conditions. Hate, hate, hate! Kill, kill, kill! They need murdering machines. But my mind is still my own. Terrorism attracted Aldano because he has no mind of his own. The ideal instrument for masterminds. The game never changes, only the participants. The servants of Allah and his Prophet Mohammed have destroyed their own system of manipulation. They oppose any peace in Palestine, or anywhere on Earth for that matter. Arafat is the next victim. His chances for survival diminish by the hour. Jews and Palestinians are members of the same ethnic group. Britishers started the division, the Moullahs will finish it. But Arafat isn't a dummy and won't let himself fall into the hands of the manipulators. His assassination is inevitable. I'm not that easy to contain. They altered my face as a prototype of the Anti-Christ before sending me to Tripoli. Bin Laden is their leader, not the Afghans or the Algerian fundamentalists. The terrorists never trusted Sadam either, except as a provider."

He looked at Helena. She pretended interest, so he continued, "Everywhere organized religion is involved in politics and manipulation. Religion pulls the strings behind the upheavals in South America, the Catholic-Protestant war in Ireland and the gradual destruction of civilization as we know it. Godless Communism was only a surrogate for the Church. The Third Reich was planned as the 'Kingdom Come.' I don't belong to anybody."

Helena was gradually falling asleep.

"I know why you switched off the light, Helena. You don't want to look at my face. It kills your appetite for sex. I don't blame you. But my face has nothing to do with my inner self. I accept you as you are, though my chances of any future with you are practically nonexistent, even if I terminated Aldano."

The mention of Aldano's name partially woke up his bed partner. "Leave Aldano to me."

Bruno laughed, "Good luck! While playing cards with our 'security' kindergarten crew, I realized that the 'New Christ' protection services now consist of three men. I don't count these youths as men yet. The agent supposedly watching your residence passes his time looking at pornography on the video-surveillance monitors. The bronzed athletes of this crew fill their time practicing kick-boxing and judo. Their head man from Malta has been trying to reach them since noontime, they didn't know how to switch on the receiver, so I talked to him. The youngsters are so grateful to me, that they're ready to do anything I ask them. They act as sailors, cooks and gofers with no questions asked. I want to have a serious conversation with Andrew."

"What for?"

"Have you told him anything about his father?!"

"No, he's never asked."

"Well, I'll do it. Anyway, I know more about Gordon Bates than you do.

Helena tried to pierce the darkness between them. “But why? I thought you wanted to get rid of Andrew.”

A wave of coldness came from her bed partner. “Not anymore. Now I want to mold him into a perfect Savior, to my liking.”

The sea was still and bathed in golden light. Dolphins played ahead and alongside the boat. In the distance, Sicily’s outline was still detectable. Bruno and Andrew were leaning on the side rail without talking. Shadow lay under the shade of the superstructure suffering the heat silently, his eyes centered on them not wavering for even a moment. Finally Bruno said without any preamble, “I killed your father, Andrew.” The boy stood motionless, following the dolphins’ play. “It served no purpose,” said Bruno.

The heat intensified as if fed by the silence, then the boy turned to Bruno. “I didn’t know my father. I never saw a picture of him. He hasn’t visited my dreams either. I think Shadow sees him sometimes, so I try to read his eyes. All I see in them is calmness. I think my father is disappointed in me, like everyone else. People have great expectations of me, and I have no idea where or how to start.”

“Destiny will catch up with you. You must be patient,” Bruno told him.

Andrew forced his eyes on the face next to him. “If people expect something of me, they first have to level with me. I know that Christ had to do it on his own. It wasn’t any easier for His predecessor either. I don’t expect anything easy, but my mission scares me.”

For the first time, they met eye to eye. The forceful contact was painful.

Bruno sighed, “I guess we all want to be gods, even if for just a moment. That moment…when I killed you father, made me feel Godlike…”

"You mean you wanted to keep on killing?" demanded Andrew.

"No! Killing Marko was done as a precaution. I should've stopped then and there. From that moment on, I didn't belong to myself. Lying was easy. I made up stories about my father. He was murdered when I was very young and mother never told me the whole story — just bits and pieces. Maybe there never was a whole story. Maybe our lives consist only of ill-matched bit and pieces that we senselessly try to put together. Your father was the real reincarnation of the Son of God. I was mad with jealousy because I perceived that part only for myself. But humanity forgot both of us. If it's God's will, I'll make you a True Savior! If you're chosen by Him, you'll survive. But living with your mother robs you of that chance. I want you to succeed, Andrew. You're my only hope for Salvation."

Chapter 23

THE TRAVELS BEGIN

Helena was so enthralled with her own adventure that she didn't give a damn about the children. Bruno Wagner did not intend to explain his actions on behalf of her son. While she slept soundly he called Aldano from the Port of Tripoli. Then he disappeared with the kids and the ever faithful Shadow. A short note to Mrs. Bates stated the kidnapping as a bare fact. There was no request for money, and it was signed — "THE ANTI-CHRIST." The "security" men on board were so used to taking orders from him, there were no questions asked.

In a parking lot near the freight area, a Land Rover waited for them with enough provisions for only two people and a dog. They had to stop to buy more rations, water and clothes. The boys were in a state of euphoria. On the dashboard of their vehicle a sign read, "Lost in Africa." What better adventure for a young boy? That satisfied the cousins, but Andrew had a notion something was wrong and had some concerns. He felt responsible. The cousins entrusted him with their lives, and he led them into a trap. He was ill-prepared to meet the real world.

God helps only to a certain point. How much could Andrew count on Bruno? Was he leading him straight to Hell? What right had he to involve the cousins in his own confused life? One thing gave him hope and strength. Since their conversation on the deck, he was able to look into Bruno's face without fear. Behind the mask of Bruno's indifference, Andrew saw a chasm of complexities. Bruno Wagner, as Renaldo, removed Marko as a simple obstacle. But he loved the Man whom he had to kill. The son was his only hope for deliverance. He understood the great mechanics behind the RESURRECTION, the love of Judas and the meaning of Golgotha.

CHRIST HAD RISEN FROM THE DEAD!!!

If that is true, He was born as a man, and He died as a man. He had traveled the full circle, making him the Son of God forever. Gods don't die, no matter how desperately they need death and transfiguration.

THEATER OF THE ABSTRACT: SCENE IN ALGIERS MEDINA

Andrew Bates realized that he was speaking in front of a group of elderly people. Bruno addressed them as Tribal Leaders and actually smiled at Andrew. The mask of his disfigured face cracked. The eldest man asked Bruno where Andrew had learned such flawless Aramaic, and Bruno replied, with fatherly pride, "Don't you understand, Nakhat Abba? He has never forgotten it."

BACK ON THE ROAD

While Bruno drove, Andrew prayed in his mind.

"Dear God,

I don't want to die like my father. I'm afraid of death. Please, don't let people turn against me. I love them all, good and bad. Let them love me, too, though I don't know really how it feels to be loved. Mother doesn't know either. I never had a friend, and now I have two, but for how long? I'm confused. Is Bruno my friend or is he bent on my destruction? Does he know what love is, or is he after the same thing as Mark? I'm sorry to pile all these questions on You but I have no one else.

I have one more question.

Am I ever going to fall in love with a woman? Will I ever grow to be a man, a normal man?

Thank You for helping me today with the preaching. I really didn't have any idea what to say to those old people. I still don't know what Aramaic is. I don't like to read. Watching TV is much easier. Please help me to go Your way.

What else? Oh, please, don't mind my mother's oddities. Let her find some happiness. Perhaps, I will never see her again and the little I had with her is gone forever.

Shadow is getting old. How awful! Will you do something about it? He's the only one who truly loves me and gets only food in exchange. I love him as my dog. But is he really a dog?

Thank You for everything You do for me. I hope I don't have to fast often. I enjoy eating good stuff and my appetite is voracious.

Bruno is paying the bills and he isn't a man of means. I'm indebted to him for supporting my friends, too. Maybe we can find manual work to help with money. We're strong and healthy boys.

It's wonderful to be on Your Heavenly Road, but understanding the signs along the way sometimes is beyond my powers.

We haven't been to church at all. Bruno doesn't seem to be a churchgoer. I think he's excommunicated. Obviously, his road isn't leading to Heaven.

I hope I'm on the Road meant for me.

Bless the soul of my father in Heaven and spend more time with Jesus. He needs You, too. I know what it is to be lonely in a palace.

AMEN."

Surprisingly, only a few newspapers and broadcasters reported that the only son of the millionairess Helena Bates, accompanied by two friends and a physical fitness instructor, had gone on safari in Central Africa. Responsible sources announced communications with the group were lost. Obviously, their short wave radio had malfunctioned. Mrs. Bates, on a pleasure cruise, had declined any interviews. The parents of the other two boys had "no comment."

Was it abduction for ransom money? For while Andrew Bates was considered the new Son of God by many, the Vatican rebutted that and withdrew the costly security operation. A representative of the Foreign Office refused to comment on the subject.

The fiery crash of a supersonic jet near Paris took over the headlines. Everyone on board was dead. Listed with the other victims was a certain Bruno Wagner and three children. Was it coincidence?

Aldano Brandon decided to delay telling Helena. She was so blissfully happy with his unparalleled handsomeness, that a sudden sense of guilt would've put an end to all his careful planning. He had no heart to call his family in Malta either. Under his orders, the motor boat took them to a place least likely to receive news — a small fishing village under Mt. Stromboli. He believed that his sexual performance near a living volcano would be at its best.

Unfortunately, either Mt. Stromboli didn't help, or Aldano Brandon's sexual performance had dwindled. Helena wasn't patient, especially after being deeply aroused by his gorgeous body. It was inevitable that she would turn to the two crewmen, both of whom were quite eager to try and satisfy her. Aldano ordered them to leave, but Helena reversed his decision. That created mayhem. Aldano knocked down one of the boys, but the other one threw him overboard and didn't let him climb back up. Helena greatly enjoyed the confrontation and took the two young men to her bed. Aldano was abandoned to his own resources. He was outnumbered and outperformed. Eventually, he got back on board, but was banned from Helena's cabin. He swore revenge, especially after he was demoted to cabin boy. He had little choice. He thought himself capable of beating the shit out of his rivals one on one, but as a team they were too much for him. One of them had to be eliminated.

A Finnish missionary and three boys arrived in Nepal. Through an agency he hired a team of sherpas to take them to a previously unexplored region. Mr. Aymo Sundquist of Finland, arrived at a Buddhist monastery that had been lost for centuries in the vast wilderness of the Himalayas. He was accompanied by his "three sons." It happened that the youngest got to the portal first. The thin air didn't seem to bother him. He listened in total enchantment to the singing wind chimes.

The monk that answered gave him a radiant smile and a low bow.

"Welcome back, Jeezoo!"

They left the reality of the world and stepped into the One and Only Reality — GOD.

ISLE OF STROMBOLI

In the small fishing village under Stromboli, Helena and her lovers found an establishment that offered fresh fish and chips and drinks. The juke-box pumped out disco music and the atmosphere was right. Georgio and Gian-Carlo proved to be better dancers than Aldano, so it took quite some time before he was able to get to the dance floor with Helena. Luckily, it was one of the few slow dance tunes, so he was able to talk.

"It's beneath my dignity to compete with those boys for your bed, Helena."

"Don't I deserve it?" she teased.

"You deserve men of a better class," Aldano retorted.

"Like you?" She stuck her finger on his chest.

"Well...you used to love me, Helena."

"I did? So what?"

"You're the only woman I have ever fallen in love with," Aldano admitted. "Helena, I'm a one-woman man. I can't think of loving any other woman but you, and I cannot share you with anybody. I've got to get rid of them," Aldano continued. "I'll fight them, I'll kill them," he promised passionately.

"And how do you propose to do that?" Helena leered at him. "They are Corsicans. They'll stick a knife in you."

Aldano broke into copious perspiration becoming quite angered. "Then with knives it shall be. Gian-Carlo first."

"When?"

"Right now. It's a full moon. The stone quarry is shielded on all sides."

Helena stopped dancing and looked straight into his cold blue eyes. "You have that much courage?"

"More than you think."

"I think you're drunk," she said, but did little to discourage his rage.

"So are the Corsicans."

"They'll spill your guts."

"It goes both ways."

The small company got to the stone quarry. Aldano and Gian-Carlo stripped to the waist. Giorgio gave his knife to Aldano. Under the intense moonlight the scene was surreal. Helena tried to remember the golden youth from the night in Messina. It didn't click. It simply wasn't the same person.

The rivals dodged left and right, faking attacks, their eyes tried to read the next movement, the knife blades reflected the cool and indifferent moonlight.

Helena watched the fighters strangely unmoved too. She didn't care if either of the two buggers lived or died.

Now they launched their initial strikes. Gian-Carlo ducked Aldano's knife by less than half an inch, while one of his projectiles grazed Aldano's breast, an elbow hook to the midriff knocked the wind out of him. Aldano closed in and tried to place a good knee into the groin of his opponent, his knife swashed by the left cheek of the young Corsican. Gian-Carlo came at him, swinging his knife with the regularity of a windmill.

Giorgio yelled in their dialect:

"Go, Gianny, go! He's yours!"

Aldano tasted his own salty blood from a scratch over the eye and waded into his attacker with rage. He kicked through Gian-Carlo's guard and struck him flush on the jaw, then viciously in the stomach. He swung his knife with tremendous power very close to the muscular chest of the other youth.

Helena felt weak. She sat on one of the stone piles.

The two lads battled savagely, droplets of blood and sweat flew everywhere. Both swore defiance, possessed with meanness and a lust for killing. Bloody and dirty, dark with rage, the young savages beat, kicked and tore at each other. The Corsican youth charged again and again until he found an opening and slashed Aldano on the shoulder, repeatedly bashing a knee in his crotch. The impact stunned Aldano Brandon, his guard fell and Gian-Carlo's blade sunk into his rival. Giorgio grabbed his friend from behind and led him aside.

Aldano fell to his knees, tried to get up and collapsed again. Helena came to his side but didn't know what to do. Aldano knelt there, swaying from side to side, holding his head, face grimacing with pain.

"The fight isn't over yet. I'm gonna kill this moron. Where is he? What round is it?" Aldano gasped.

Helena's eyes brimmed with tears. "Your fight is over, Aldano. I cannot love anyone. I'm dead inside. That's why everything goes the wrong way."

Aldano fell prostrate. "I love you, Helena…I truly love you…marry me…I can make you…happy…very happy…"

"None of us deserves happiness, Aldano. We're all damned to die miserably."

Suddenly, she realized that no one was listening to her. Aldano's blue eyes were still open, but the owner wasn't home.

Chapter 24

KATMANDU

For the next eight years the youngsters studied, read and meditated in their search of the Absolute. Each in his own way. On the last day Aymo and the three svelte and beautiful youths visited the abbot. Aymo spoke first.

"We've come to bid you farewell, Master, we have to go back to the outside world. They need us."

The abbot didn't speak for a long while. He sat cross-legged on a worn rug. A stick of incense burned in the brazier. He pierced them with an intensity that set fire to the deepest recesses of their human egos.

"Very well," he said, finally, "you belong to the world."

They fell down on their knees, and he gave them his blessing.

It was a wintry day and the chimes sang harmoniously. The other devotees waited for them in the courtyard. They said nothing as there was nothing to be said. Andrew went to the secluded spot where Shadow had left his pain and sorrow. Now in his angelic state, he looked at the human to whom he had patiently taught the meaning of unconditional love.

Shadow's spiritual entity spoke to Andrew, "I'll always be with you, Andrew," he told him. "You and I, in the name of Love, share one and same being. Now that you're big and wise, you don't need my physical protection, but I would've given all my eternity just to be young and strong, to run by your side forever. Nothing is as good as Life. In my state of perfection I'm not permitted to follow you in body. But if you feel me next to you, I'll be happy if, once in a while, you'd give me a little petting. Don't cry your heart out, Andrew, people are waiting for you. You won't ever be lonely anymore."

The youth fell on the little mound of earth and sobbed bitterly, "But I will…Shadow! Nobody can give me what I got from you."

"Now, now…boy! Love is a great feeling but it is never objective. Forget about me, you have a whole humanity to love. It won't be easy, because you know by now, that pain and sorrow are our best friends. They make us what we are."

Andrew dug a bit of earth from the mound and poured it in a leather pouch that hung around his neck next to Berrick's cross. "Come to me again physically, from time to time, when no one is watching, dear Shadow."

"I wish I could, but it isn't that easy. Call to me when your pain is unbearable. Maybe I will be able to hear you no matter how far away in space. God might give me a short leave from my duties. Perhaps we can spend a vacation together in the mountains, playing in the grass and running after the impossible. Now go and don't come back. In this mound are buried only the broken fragments, the real me is within you."

It took them nearly two months to reach Katmandu.

Anybody that knew them eight years ago, would have had a problem identifying them now. Unfortunately, the passport of Aymo Sundquist had expired. At the time, "his kids" were under age, so they traveled with him as family. Now they were a handsome trio of stalwart youths. Aymo, at forty-one had changed a lot. The clean air combined with healthy life had erased the marks of his plastic surgeries. He looked much younger than his actual age and somewhat similar to the Renaldo he was at twenty-five. The picture in his old passport look little like him. He had to pretend that they lost their documents in a mountain storm.

Nepal, eight years earlier, had been a hospitable country for guests from abroad. Not anymore. The European garments of Aymo made him highly suspect in the eyes of the natives. The youths, in spite of their dark complexion and shorn hair, didn't look quite right in monks' garb. The bank refused to accept his numbered account and the stores had no European clothes for sale. Only a few embassies were open for business. The money Aymo had hardly covered a single meal and credit cards were unacceptable. The thriving city they left eight years ago had become drab, dirty and thinly populated. Most of the stores had been boarded up. There were no movies, no TV, no broadcasting, no entertainment whatsoever.

The situation looked worse than the emergency camps around Palermo after the great quake. People were afraid. They talked to them through little barred windows, hurriedly closing them after a short exchange. The telephone system hadn't worked for years, and short-wave radios had run out of batteries. There was no electricity in this ghost-city nor vehicles on the streets. Fuel was rationed at prohibitive prices. Most people were unwilling to engage in conversation.

The agency that arranged their passage through the Himalayan range was boarded, too. No sherpas for hire hanging around, just a handwritten sign, "Out of Business," posted on the door. The former owner was reinforcing the door and somehow recognized them.

"Are you radio-active?" He surprised them with this greeting.

"No. Why should we be? We just came from the wilderness. We spent eight years there."

"So you found your Shangri-La," the owner sighed.

"We found what we were looking for," answered Aymo.

"And these young men are your adolescent boys?"

"Yes, kids grow fast. Are you Mr. Zarem Cherchak?"

Yes, that's me. My children have grown too. Are you armed?"

"I ran out of ammunition during our wanderings. We threw the guns away. All we have are knives."

"Most everyone here is armed to the teeth. Come closer to the door, Mr. Aymo, so my sons can check you out," Zarem beckoned.

Two young men armed with guns and Geiger-counters opened the door. "One by one, surrender your knives," they demanded.

They also made a body search. Aymo passed. Mark handed his knife to the youth on his right with a broad smile. "Are you still holding a grudge against me, Changha Narr?"

A sudden recognition came into Changha's slanted eyes and he smiled too. "Look, Tormack Baggach! These are the two guys that we challenged to hand-wrestling, remember?"

The other youth laughed. "How can I forget, Mark and Danny! They put down our hands seven times out of ten. Remember, you promised us a rematch when you came back. My brother and I have been counting on it for years. And that must be Andrew. Our kid sister still talks about him. Come on in, don't stay out in the cold, our home is well heated, you're quite welcome!"

The whole laughing bunch of young men climbed up the steep staircase to a wide sunny room, furnished with richly colored, handmade carpets and pillows. For the first time in many months the guests felt warm and cozy. The host and Aymo entered from a side door. Cherchak clapped his hands. "Changha, Tormack! Bring the serving tables. Food, coffee and hot tea laced with rum. You poor men must be starving. Sit down, please, feel at home. I'll build up the fire."

The guests didn't wait for a second invitation. They sat cross-legged on the soft pillows, and looked around, something seemed to be missing. Most of the furniture had been used for heating.

Changha and Tormack brought the small tables loaded with drinks and tidbits. The last to join them was a blushing Chin-Moon, balancing a large tray, cups filled to the brim with hot soup.

She was very careful not to look at Andrew. She got down to her knees and served the cups of soup. When she came to Andrew, her hands shook and she almost spilled the soup. A sympathetic laughter came from the family.

"Hold him, Chin-Moon, so he doesn't run away again!" they teased.

The pretty girl shyly scolded them, "Shut up, brothers, I don't mess with boys."

"But you love them. How, otherwise, were you so positive that they'd come again?" The brothers good-naturedly kept up the teasing.

"I had a dream, that's all," she said quietly, eyes turned down.

"Don't try to fool us, you're dressed in the best you have. If Andrew asked you, you'd kiss him in a minute."

The father shushed them, "That's enough! Let the girl alone. Take back your silly jibes. Our young guest has gotten red-faced too. You should be ashamed of yourselves."

Chin Moon placed the soup in front of Andrew. "Welcome, sir…I well remember your beautiful white dog. He came and visited us in my dream. You don't have to keep him out in the cold. Bring him in, please, he has to be fed too."

"He's in, Chin Moon, but we can't see him," Andrew said a bit brokenly. "Thank you for the good words. I'll miss his physical presence forever."

On a sudden impulse, the girl put her delicate hand over his shoulder.

"I'm sorry, Andrew, he was an angel."

Their eyes met as if for the first time, Chin Moon dropped her head shyly.

"How do you know, Chin Moon?"

"I knew how you felt about him. He's your soul-mate."

Aymo laced an arm around Andrew. "I'll drink to that."

Everyone drank, while Chin Moon placed a cup of soup onto Buddha's altar, bowed and placed one more as she prayed, "Oh, Lord, embrace the souls of those who are missing and bestow on them many blessings." She lit a fresh stick of incense and rang a little golden bell three times, "They are welcome in this home anytime."

It was quiet, the invisible wings of the wind brought a distant barking. Chin Moon sat and took the last lap table. "Please, esteemed guests, drink your soup while still hot. The bread is not what mother used to serve us, but I'm only a student of hers."

Andrew sighed and drank some of his soup.

Aymo diplomatically changed the subject. "What has happened to the world in the eight years we were away, Zarem Cherchak?"

The host left his empty cup on the small table and Chin Moon refilled it.

"We don't know much. A year ago, all communications with the world at large unexpectedly stopped. There was a strange illuminating light in the sky. Whoever happened to be outside got sunburned. My wife saw the blaze while hanging the wash to dry. Soon, she lost her eyesight, and her skin began to peel. Bloody sores appeared. Two months later, she died in agony. So did many others. This big light appeared three times. My family stayed inside. Whoever ventured out to check what was happening, never returned. After a time, black snow fell from the sky and stayed a long time. Four months ago, the sun broke through the heavy clouds and the infected snow melted. I took the children to the high plateau, where the snow is clean, but there we were almost killed by unusually high winds.

"Obviously, the world was at war. We returned home, not knowing if we were going to live or die. Military troops came our way and distributed the instruments that measure radiation. Nobody seemed to know who won the war or if there was a victory at all. For the time being we're alive. We eat mostly canned food, or game from the high plateau. We find our drinking water there, too, though City officials told us that our water travels underground and it isn't contaminated. But who knows what the black snow did? The Royal Family left. We built a cabin in the high mountain. When weather permits, we will move there. You shouldn't have come from the other side of the mountain.

Chomolungma is the safest place to be; the world we know is dying."

THEATER OF THE ABSURD: PETER MOUGHABEE READS EXCERPT FROM A NOVEL

So the Mighty Voice of God ordered Jesus, "Go to the wilderness, Son of Man, and fast forty days to purify yourself!"

Then, when He was starved the Devil came to him and said: If thou be the Son of God, command that these stones be made bread. But Jesus resisted the temptation. Then the Devil set Him on a pinnacle of the temple and said to Him: If thou be the Son of God, cast thyself down. For angels have charge of Him and would bear Him up.

But again, Jesus resisted.

Then the Devil took Him into a high mountain and showed Him kingdoms of the world and said that he would give them to Him if He would fall down and worship him. But Jesus said: Get thee hence, Satan.

But the Devil was sly and he came to Jesus one more time and said:

If You wilt accept shame and disgrace, scourging, a crown of thorns and death on the cross, Thou shalt save the human race, for greater love hath no man than this, that a man lay down his life for his friends.

Jesus fell for it.

The Devil laughed till his sides ached, for he knew what EVIL men would commit in the name of Jesus.

– *The Testament* according to W. Somerset Maugham

BACK TO NOW

Next morning Andrew took his host aside and asked him, if he would gather as many people as possible in a large meeting place.

"Perish the thought, Andrew. They are afraid of each other. They will not even come to the temple."

"Your people don't believe in Salvation?"

"Not right now," Zarem answered sadly.

"Do you mean that right now they don't believe in the Resurrection, or a Judgment Day?"

" Right now, I don't believe they'd come out to their own funeral."

"That's sad, Zarem Cherchak, because help is possible," Andrew told him.

"How can you say that?"

"I'm saying it."

"On whose credentials?"

"My faith in God," Andrew answered with authority in his voice.

"It won't work, dear boy. For centuries people have been deceived by a fair number of crooks and charlatans coming in the name of one deity or another. They're sick and tired of it."

"So now they're ignoring God's help?" Andrew questioned.

"They don't believe He gives a damn about their salvation," Zarem stated with resignation.

"And Jesus?"

"Oh, they believe He was a miracle maker. Basically people cannot resist curiosity."

"Zarem, you of all people! Did you know that your devoted, loving daughter is very sick? She has known for awhile, but she didn't want to worry you. Last night, I saw the sores on her back. The sores will spread everywhere in a matter of days."

"You slept with my daughter!?!" screamed a clearly agitated Cherchak.

"No." Andrew assured him. "She wanted someone to see the spots. She remembers that her mother had them."

"Why you?" Zarem wanted to know.

"Because she loves me and trusts me. Chin Moon wanted to know the Truth."

Zarem was bathed in perspiration. "You came yesterday and I've been with her since she was born. What can you do for her?"

"I can try to help her," Andrew said trying to calm the man.

Tears choked the voice of Cherchak, "How, for heaven's sake?"

"Through my faith. I'll pray with her, and if God is willing, she'll live to become my lawfully wedded wife."

"That's insane. Have you told your father?"

"My Father is in Heaven, Cherchak. He'll help me."

"Then who's Aymo?"

"The shadow of the Satan."

Zarem stepped back, his eyes popping out of their sockets. "You're mad. I forbid you to touch my daughter, hear me? If you are so good, why didn't you save the life of your beloved dog?"

"Shadow was old. He had no more days to live, but Chin Moon is young, very young. She could live a good many years to tell the Truth about me."

Aymo was listening, leaning at the half-open door. Zarem Cherchak faced him. "Are you the Satan?"

"If Andrew is Christ, I'm the Satan. I challenge him to make a miracle without my assistance."

Suddenly the desperate father turned toward the radiant youth and fell down on his knees. "If You are Christ Reincarnated, Buddha's in your corner too, help me in God's Name!"

When Zarem Cherchak left the room, Andrew turned angrily to Aymo, "Why didn't you tell me what's been happening to the world?"

The older man looked seriously in his eyes. "Because I didn't want to interrupt your education. Shadow omitted it too. The timing of our appearance had to be accurate. When the time was right, I said, 'let's go!' Of course, I was anxious to see your immediate reaction. Believe me, there's not much fun for a poor devil these days. People have surpassed us by far when it comes to ingenuity with perversion. Actually, there are quite a number of decent devils appalled by these ignominious events and who would like to save the world. Take me for example, helping you help humanity at large. Of course, I'm shocked that you want to start a three ring circus. It smacks of apostasy."

"How?"

"Why do you want to perform your miracle in front of an audience. Vanity? You don't even like miracles. It is in very bad taste..."

"I'm accountable only to God."

Aymo smiled histrionically. "As was the Pope in Rome? Why do you have to marry Chin Moon? She is the only female you've met since...shall we say, the completion of your maturity."

"I fell in love with her the very instant I set eyes on her."

"At the age of eight?"

"At the age of eight years and nine months, to be precise."

"I'm confused, Andrew, if not downright disappointed. For the last eight years you have interacted sexually with Mark. It wasn't a secret. Most of the monks alleviate themselves by hand or that way. Chastity isn't good, even for birds. In Buddha's eyes this is natural and doesn't interfere with morality. But what will Mark Brandon's reaction be to your marriage to Chin Moon? His love for you is great in every respect."

Andrew's eyes didn't blink. "I'm not going to explain myself to you or anybody."

"History has the bad habit of repeating itself. If repulsed, Mark may turn into another Judas. Have you thought about that?"

"I have."

"Then forget this little experiment. You will have the chance of many one night affairs with much worthier ladies while truly following your Road."

Andrew's head dropped a notch, but he stood firm, though his voice quieted to a whisper, "I have chosen Chin Moon and that will come to pass."

"And if you fail, you'll be ridiculed."

"I won't fail, and if she dies, I'll stay with her to the last, as she'll be with me to the end. There is no choice for me but to go public. People have to believe in My Mission."

Aymo shook his head.

"And it will be a bitter end, because you're not making it easier," warned Aymo.

"I haven't been brought to this world for an easy life."

"I just want to be sure that you know what the outcome could be."

"What do you know about the outcome? The Devil has never been a Prophet."

"*Peractum est*...Amen."

ANDREW IN HIS PRAYERS

"Help me, Father. I pray for a single soul, then I'll plead for many more, as long as you have patience to listen. If I fail tomorrow, my mission will be futile. Then I have to be cast away. This world isn't for the meek of heart. They won't inherit anything but their own humiliation. I have to be Thy Sword, and the Sword shall be used. I'll use anything to spare humanity from extinction — even Satan's services if You choose to abandon me. He knows how to deal with corruption and cruelty. You created him to punish mankind. He likes his job, but he exercises it with discretion. Without people, evil cannot exist. Neither can goodness, for that matter. Perfection is an absolute, therefore, it is senseless. I know I'm walking the sharp edge of a razor, but this is the only way to salvation. I might have to be blasphemous at times, cheating, lying, but then, I'm not created in Your Image. I'm just a lowly man pleading the cause of his brethren. My heart is not immune to sin, so I can understand and help the sinners. I'm a sinner too, enamored with Life and its ephemeral transition. Don't turn Your Face from me, I cannot see a thing without Your Light. Help me save the life of Chin Moon and all that come with faith in God.

Let Your Will prevail on the side of Man!"

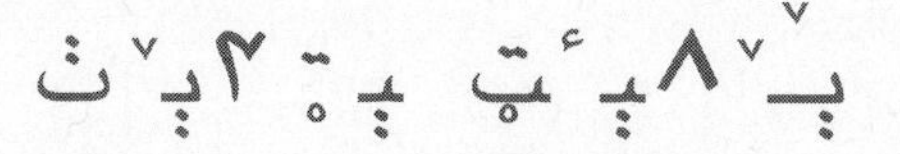

All the young men shared the same unheated room at the back of the house, and slept in sleeping bags placed on the bare floor. Summer in the foothills of the Himalayas is cold and damp, but young people seldom notice miseries of this kind. They just didn't bother to take their clothes off.

Mark was restless. He tossed in his sleep, moaning and cried out until Andrew managed to wake him. His tormented eyes opened and were full of fear and pain.

"What is it, Andrew?" Mark asked groggily.

"You tell me. You were having the nightmare."

Mark tried to gather his thoughts. "What time is it?"

"About two a.m. Everyone's asleep. Let's go to the living room where we can talk."

Mark got out of his sleeping bag and followed him. The living room was somewhat warm in spite of the wind blasting at the windows. Mark was obviously disturbed.

"I'm thirsty," he complained.

Andrew filled a cup from a container. Mark drank as if he hadn't had any water for days, then refilled the cup. "I dreamed I killed you with my bare hands. It was horrible. My fingers tore your stomach wall and dug into your bloody entrails. Then, I took them out and ate some of them, casting the rest away. You were still alive, and your eyes focused on me full of love and gratitude, a little smile trembling in the corners of your mouth..."

Mark gulped his water and brushed his lips with the back of his hand, "I shouted, 'Die, die, crafty monster!' And you said gently, 'I wish I could, but even in death you cannot get rid of me, we're soul brothers.' What do you think the meaning of all this is? It didn't seem like a dream. It was unbelievably real to its last detail."

Andrew abruptly changed the subject. "Mark, Chin Moon has a well advanced radiation sickness. I'll try to save her life, and if she lives I'll marry her."

His statement didn't seem to register with Mark immediately. He smiled absentmindedly. "I don't see what that has to do with my dream. I guess we all have to get married one day, but why Chin Moon? You don't know her that well."

Andrew hesitated for a moment. "I'm in love with her, Mark."

Mark's face, chiseled to perfection by an ancient master, suddenly cringed like a tragic mask. "You love her! You just met this girl twice in eight years. Do you want to tell me that you loved her all that time?"

Andrew nodded.

Mark closed his eyes with such pain and despair, it was as if he foresaw the end of his life, "Well then…" he muttered tiredly, "…good luck. Tell me if I can be of any help." He struggled drunkenly to his feet, and he trudged toward the door.

"Mark…I may fail…"

Mark stopped at the door but didn't face Andrew. His teeth were chattering.

"That wouldn't change anything."

It was a stormy day. At the public meeting, people sat at a distance from each other. Only a few couples kept together. The morning was dark and windy with a heavy rain waiting in the wings. In the murky light, filtered through the filthy windows, all faces looked shadowy. On a platform at the far end of the room, a worn leather sofa was the only object of importance. Chin Moon and her father sat on it, and her two brothers stood behind them like hired guards. Almost everyone in the room had a dull, indifferent expression, as if wondering what had brought them here. When Andrew appeared just by himself, there were the muffled sounds of disappointment. In the short and worn out clothes that he had borrowed, he looked even younger than his actual age. Too young to be speaking to them of anything important.

He started to speak but changed his mind. He took off his drab, unseasonable jacket and knelt in front of the girl.

While organizing the attendance, Zarem Cherchak had been enthusiastic. Now he felt like a fool. Andrew asked him to show the bare back of his daughter to the audience. He didn't budge. Chin Moon stood and did it on her own.

All present gasped.

It was as if her skin had been torn — nothing but raw flesh. She smiled feebly and gave a sign of encouragement to the young man. Gordon bravely returned her smile, crossed himself and placed his hands gently on her back. Both of them closed their eyes.

At this moment Aymo and the cousins appeared at the door. Nobody paid attention to them. An almost palpable sense of a miracle filled the air. Zarem Cherchak went down on his knees next to Andrew.

Nothing was happening, except that there was a slight smell of blossoming roses. An old priest from a nearby temple got up to his feet and set his eyeglasses at an angle so he could see better.

The raw flesh started fading. Now it was more like bruises that had started to mend.

The audience had lost a sense of time. Outside the rain was falling in sheets and lightning flashed to be followed by a clattering thunder. The darkness thickened. A number of people focused their pocket flashlights on Chin Moon's back. Someone brought a kerosene lamp.

Another flash of lightening almost immediately brought a loud clap of thunder that shook the room. As the bruises faded away, Chin Moon's face blossomed. Those who knew Chin Moon had never seen her as beautiful and beguiling. Even her brothers' mouths hung open in disbelief. By the third flash of lightening there was not a spot left on her back.

Then three men and four women came to the platform to show their sore spots to Andrew. Many were pressed behind them.

Andrew took a deep breath.

Aymo and the youths had disappeared.

Chapter 25

IN THE VATICAN

The long arms of the new Pope had become short. In this Century of hi-tech communications, he was cut off from the rest of the world. In a short outburst of military action, his life and city-state were brought to ruin. The nuclear winter was at hand. First, many churches were filled to capacity. After a few months, hardly anyone attended vespers, and only a few at morning prayers. People had become callous to suffering and held little hope for the future. Nobody knew who won or who lost, but they all felt like losers.

God had taken back his blessings, and repentance in the last hour paid no dividends.

The Pope quit looking out into the magnificent empty square — no more tourists these days. The Foreign Secretary waited at the desk.

"How many new messiahs do you have on report today?" asked the Pontiff.

"I lost count, Holiness...but I have one that might interest You."

The Pope looked at him sharply. "Andrew Bates?"

The Secretary nodded curtly.

"I knew he'd reappear at the most precipitous moment. Where is he?"

"Katmandu," answered the Secretary.

The short, energetic man was past his prime but was in a good health. He exhibited businesslike manners but concealed a suspicious mind. Unfortunately, the elected Pontiff had become no more than a simple cliché. The mighty Curia wanted it that way.

He walked around his desk and sat in a splendid chair. "Is the information credible?"

"Yes, Your Holiness," responded the Secretary.

The Pontiff fell into one of his frequent depressions. "I can't fly there. I can't fly anywhere for that matter. Nepal is in zone sixteen. What are Andrew's intentions?"

"For the time being, he is busy creating an image. He has healing hands. People adore him. He has a natural charm. By the way, he got married."

"Married! At age of seventeen!" asked the surprised Pope.

"Sixteen," corrected the aide.

"Who is she?"

"Just a half-breed. Her Chinese mother is deceased. Her father is a local man with certain influence. It was a concubine relationship developed while her mother was nursing his Nepalese wife. Two boys from his wife were actually raised by Chin Moon's mother."

"Chin Moon?" mused the Pontiff.

"That is Andrew's wife."

"You have me all confused," the older man complained.

"I'm sorry, Holiness."

"Well, go on." The Pope waved his hand.

"Andrew Bates is marketing himself quite well. The focal point is in China, where Buddha and Confucius are revered. I suppose, in the eyes of God, they have a certain purpose."

The Pope adjusted his eyeglasses with trembling fingers. "We only pretend to know the origins of the Almighty. As a judge, he should look at everyone equally. What am I to do?" he pondered almost to himself.

"There is no immediate danger of a new military conflict, at least according to my information."

"And who am I to listen?"

"Maybe God or Christ. You're His representative on Earth," reminded the Secretary.

"In absentia. What am I to do with Andrew? Obviously he's inspired by Buddhism. Like his father, he doesn't seem drawn to Christianity."

"Right now he's acting like a Christian more than we are."

The Pope made a sour grimace. "How widespread is the news about the reappearance of Andrew?"

"Here or worldwide?"

"Here."

"You and I, Holiness," remarked the Secretary.

"Let's keep it that way," commanded the Prelate.

THEATER OF THE ABSURD: SCENE ON SIRIUS BETWEEN LORD ATON AND PETER

"You haven't called me for a long time, Lord Aton."

"Humankind keeps me pretty busy, Peter. I cannot take care of all the newcomers; Sirius is filled to capacity. A number of other planets have been placed under my auspices . I need you. Do you know that your son has been active, too?"

"He wouldn't be my son if he weren't. I'm proud of my children."

"Horus is listening. Don't be so excited; it's not becoming to your saintly status."

"May I go down to Earth and help the young one? I'm tired of living in comfort like *The Little Prince*. Gordon, Andrew's father, was attached to Shadow and considered him the only living link between him and his son. For Gordon, even the moon isn't close enough to Earth."

"How is Gordon managing?"

Peter shrugged his heavy shoulders. "As usual, keeping himself busy. But his mind is always centered on his son. Why are Satanic forces gathering around Andrew? I don't have a clear picture either."

"Why? I'll tell you why. Because lately the Anti-Christ has been doing everything in his power to save mankind from extinction. It's not a matter of Love, he's simply being practical. His job is in jeopardy. The Pope's in the same position and doing nothing. Has Gordon seen his wife? The eruption of Stromboli sent her directly here. Now young Andrew is one of the richest men on earth and doesn't even know it. And married."

Peter whistled softly.

"Andrew's married!?! After his unholy affair with Mark Brandon, I didn't think he had the guts. Bravo!"

"His father doesn't know her either. As a matter of fact it surprised me too. She's part Chinese and as pretty as they come. Her soul is made of the purest fabric of truth. One can see the beauty of the world through her."

Peter scratched his beard impatiently.

"Shall I go? There is a vacant place in the 'family'."

"Who do you mean?"

"Danny Brandon, he's a good hunk of a boy. With a little intelligence, he could keep the frenzy of Mark in check."

Lord Aton threatened him with his finger. "You promised me, Peter, that you'd read only newspapers."

"I'm not retired yet, My Lord. You need a bloodhound."

Lord Aton shook his head. "You've been sniffing enough, then pretending you know nothing. I need you here. Gordon is getting the job."

"No, Teacher, he's too good to be true. He hasn't the slightest inclination to cheat. An enlightened spirit at his best. Any devil of the lowest type would conquer him. He's my son. I know him. He'll spoil everything. He's a natural blunderer. You know me, I wouldn't badmouth my son for a terrestrial assignment…but it's such wonderful material, better than any fairy tale. Trust me…eh?"

"No. It will be Gordon. He has every right to spend some time with his son."

Peter thought briefly then nodded dejectedly, "True. But at least give me a part in the epilogue of this drama."

Lord Aton did a bit of thinking. "O.K. In God's Name, let it be so. You've been good lately, but no appearance of any kind before the epilogue. Promise?

Peter sighed, "Do you leave me any choice at all?"

"No choice, Peter. For the sake of our old friendship, stay put."

Saint Peter looked nostalgically toward the planet Earth. "I promise."

Chapter 26

THE NEWLYWEDS

Andrew and Chin Moon spent their short honeymoon in the cabin on the Plateau. The surrounding hills were barren and there was not a speck of wildlife. Birds had left in droves. Only small clumps of flowers were seen here and there.

After the last great storm, the air felt easier to breath and water lost its murkiness. The mighty sun appeared through the layers of yellowish clouds more and more frequently.

Changha Narr acted as a guard and food provider. After the Miracle, his deep respect for Andrew bordered on idolatry, and Andrew didn't like it. He knew that idols were forbidden and fanatics easy to sway.

While the young couple honeymooned, Andrew's reputation, (thanks to the Buddhist Priest that married them) spread well beyond the immediate area. Chin Moon clung to every moment of their intimacy, believing such wonderful happiness couldn't last long.

Gradually, the clouds lifted to reveal a panoramic view of the Trans-Himalayan Range. Clearly visible was the giant Chomo-lungma.

"One day I'll get there," said Andrew to Chin Moon as they took in the scenery. "It's the nearest place to God."

Chin Moon pressed herself to his chest. "I'll be with you, Andrew, wherever you go. God will never part us."

Andrew smiled but with some bitterness. "God won't do it, but people will try. They can't stand true happiness. It's a simple maxim: if I don't have it, you won't have it either."

Chin Moon dug her fingers in his jacket, overwhelmed with despair. "Can we stay here forever?"

Andrew pressed her to himself tenderly. "No, Chin Moon, we're children of God. He expects something from us."

"When?"

"That is for God to decide."

Danny Brandon visited them in the cabin. Andrew was surprised. He had never been able to establish a close relationship with Danny. Even in the monastery, he kept to himself. If he had problems, he discussed them with the Abbot. Andrew seldom had contact with him. Danny wasn't a shy or introverted person. He told jokes and shared laughs with absolute strangers. Was it the physical relationship between Andrew and Mark that made him feel uneasy? Was there something beyond their never-ending fights and verbal sparring? Perhaps the cousins had something deeper than Andrew ever realized. Some kind of wolfish attachment.

For the last eight years, physical confrontations had ceased, except in learning self defense, which was closely supervised by instructors. For reasons of his own, Danny seldom paired himself with Mark or Andrew. The fact was that Danny's mentality changed radically, and Andrew hadn't noticed it.

Now, Danny didn't try to escape eye contact with either Andrew or his wife. He even smiled at them. Andrew discovered that the youth had a charm of his own that had gone unnoticed next to the flashiness of Mark.

Early that morning, Changha Narr went hunting so the young couple could enjoy some privacy in the small cabin. The two were alone when Danny greeted them.

"Anything special, Danny? You can talk in the presence of Chin Moon. We have no secrets."

Danny thought a bit, something quite unusual in the past. He either talked straight or kept silent. "Aymo and Mark have left without any explanations. Zarem Cherchak discovered that his sons' passports were missing. After visiting the old priest in the Temple, Cherchak came back noticeably upset. He ordered Tormack Baggach after them and sent me here. He wants you back immediately. For some reason he is suspicious of Changa Narr, also."

Andrew exchanged puzzled looks with Chin Moon. She stepped closer to the youth, against traditional etiquette, and touched his shoulder. "What's the matter, Danny?"

"Your father thinks that they've done something wrong."

"What?"

"Treason." The shock left the newlyweds speechless. "Aymo has established radio contact and is sending messages to the world at large, including the Vatican. The Chinese opened a sizable money account in his name. Now, armed to the teeth, Aymo and Mark have disappeared, whereabouts unknown."

Andrew was devastated. "I didn't expect anything like this."

Danny heard an ever rising roar in the distance. "Hurry! In Katmandu you'll be well protected, Andrew."

Then another voice cut in, "But not here." Changha Narr had a machine-gun, ready to spit fire. A noisy helicopter was landing near the shack. In the ensuing confusion Danny managed to escape.

IN THE VATICAN

Aymo Sundquist remembered the Pope's office as it was when he was called Renaldo Cortelazzo. The beautiful room had been somewhat modernized. The person behind the desk wasn't inspiring any confidence in him.

"How shall I call you?" asked the Pope irritably.

"You can call me anything, Holiness. Throughout my long and distinguished career I've earned many names, some of them not by choice. I've had many faces too. The present one goes well with my Scandinavian background."

The Pontiff nodded slightly, adjusting the thick eyeglasses on his considerable nose. "For me the importance of having Andrew Barts…"

"Bates, Holiness," corrected Aymo.

The man looked at Aymo with his magnified reptilian eyes. "Andrew Bates, with or without his fabulous family fortune, is of overwhelming importance to me. I had a short conversation with him as a young boy; your protegé is intelligent and rather handsome, quite demanding. Arrogance doesn't relate well to the image of Christ. This morning he was sparring with the punching bag, clad only in a pair of black satin shorts. The young men from my home guard don't wear more than that in the gym, but they don't pretend to be saviors. He shouldn't fraternize with those lads. They're supposed to respect him, not challenged by him to sparring sessions that end up with bloody noses."

"Andrew is still a boy, Your Holiness, high-strung and extremely competitive. From time to time he ought to unwind. At this age he needs to apply his energy to something physical. Of course, that should be done discretely, but he shouldn't shy away from public exposure, either. You don't want to give him a status of deity. I can assure you, those bloody noses made him quite popular amidst the ranks of your guardsmen."

"Do we need that kind of popularity, Mr. Sundquist?"

"We don't, Holiness, but this sixteen year old commands respect through his courage and physical prowess. He'll go on demonstrating his spiritual values and healing hands, and continue to impress a wider range of people from different walks of life. He'll gather followers by mixing with the crowd. You certainly don't want him to reside in the Vatican as a symbol of the Holy Church. Remember the renegade Popes in Rames, and the Vatican waging war on them? The Pope led their armies and were quite popular."

"Perhaps you meant that part for your young protégé. In order to claim his enormous inheritance, he needs to prove his birthright. What if the Savior appears from somewhere else? I mean, the Real One."

"Oh, I took care of that, Holy Father. By now he's either with his Father in Heaven, or living in complete obscurity somewhere in China. The Communists have proven trustworthy in affairs of this kind. They didn't kill the young emperor; they made him a nobody."

The man behind the desk stopped playing with his platinum pencil and walked to the window. The view of the perfect architectural style of Bernini's oval square always boosted his morale.

"Just remember to keep this affair at a distance from me. I'm not going to take a formal stand."

"I'll remember, Your Holiness. I'll remember to close the door behind my back as well."

The magnified eyes turned sharply to the guest. "It's nice seeing things eye to eye, Mr. Sundquist,"

Changha Narr was scared.

The Chinese took his machine gun but didn't let him go home. They simply threw him into a helicopter with those that he had sold out. He avoided the eyes of his half-sister and her young husband, even though he actually loved Chin Moon and had only respect for the boy that saved her life. It never crossed his mind that he would be taken along with them. What excuse had he to offer?

How could anyone resist taking such a large amount of ready cash! And now, Changha was being flown to Lhasa with the abducted. The officer in command seemed to be concerned only about Andrew's and Chin Moon's safety and well-being. He offered them drinks and refreshments and paid little attention to

Changha Narr. Finally, it dawned on him that he had done something terribly wrong. Even the soldiers slighted him. He tried to cover his face in shame but in such a small space there was no where to hide.

On arrival at the Lhasa airport, a mini-bus waited for Mr. and Mrs. Bates. The officer held the door open for them, then sat next to the driver. The soldiers and Changha Narr boarded a military truck.

Except for some radio-active rain, Tibet hadn't suffered much from the nuclear havoc. The air seemed clear and the view of the ex-monastery and Residence of the Dalai Lama was magnificent. All vital offices from the main cities of China has been evacuated to Lhasa, and Tibetans were forced from their homes. The Communist Government situated themselves in the Monastery above the city.

For their small convoy, all check points rolled up the barriers on sight. The Hong Kong-made mini-bus was parked in the central courtyard opposite the apartments of the exiled Lama. A slick young man waited for them. He greeted the newly arrived visitors with a polite bow and addressed them in fairly accurate English.

"Mr. and Mrs. Bates, I hope that you didn't suffer much discomfort on the way here. Unfortunately, in times of war, it's sometimes better to be a dog than a man. We'll try to compensate for it by treating you as esteemed guests. Please follow me."

Mr. and Mrs. Bates exchanged puzzled looks and followed him up the steps. The apartment was old but didn't lack any contemporary comfort, including an intercom for domestic services, a small computer and stereo equipment.

When the secretary left, Andrew took the trembling body of Chin Moon in his embrace and smiled encouragingly. "It seems, for some reason that escapes me, we're being treated as guests of honor, not hostages. It is unlikely they'd bring us from Nepal just to dispose of us."

In the next hour or so, they were led to the apartments of the acting Chairman. He was middle-aged, sporting western clothing and a prematurely aged face. In Chinese he apologized for bothering them on such short notice. He then waited for the translation of the young secretary. Chin Moon beat him to it.

"My husband and I, Mr. Chairman, speak Chinese fluently."

The Chairman's face brightened a bit, and he gave leave to his secretary.

"That's a big relief to me. I wouldn't like anybody else involved in what I have to discuss with you. How did Mr. Bates learn our language? From you?"

"Ask him, Mr. Chairman. He can handle Mandarin like my mother did."

The man looked at Andrew with renewed interest. "Do you have the gift of tongues, Mr. Bates?"

The youth smiled a bit confusedly. "So far I've been able to talk and answer any language spoken to me. My father received this gift, and I've had it as long as I remember."

The Chairman invited them to sit down and sat across from them on a straight-backed chair. "Did you know, Mr. Bates, that after the accidental death of your mother, you became one of the richest individuals on Earth?"

"No. I had no idea."

"So I thought," the Chairman nodded. "What do you intend to do about it, Mr. Bates?"

"Nothing."

The Chairman lifted his eyebrows. "Nothing?"

"I'm not interested in my mother's fortune."

"Your friend Mark is interested. He is in the Vatican. Under the guidance of a mastermind calling himself Aymo, he's trying to assume your identity. The Pope is keeping his distance for the time being. He's fully aware of that satanic trick, but as a practical man doesn't want to be left out, a dichotomy quite characteristic for the occupants of the Papal Throne."

"Oh, Mark, Mark, what are you doing to your immortal soul?" uttered Andrew with pain and profound sadness. "I would've given him all that money gladly."

The Chairman seemed impressed. "You don't acknowledge the power of money?"

"I acknowledge only the power of God."

"In part, as a private person, I agree with you. But denying the power of money is suicidal."

Andrew's serene eyes stopped gently on the man across from him. "I don't belong to this world, Mr. Chairman."

The man looked at him long and hard. "I believe you. I wouldn't say that if my secretary was translating. The Central Committee would kick me out of the Party before I knew what was happening to me."

"Like the Vatican's Curia."

"Like the Vatican's Curia; they are even worse, if that's possible. The Communist Party is the Holy Church — minus God — and the most attractive part of the whole story is God; the most intriguing, too. One would have to be an idiot to believe in somebody like Mao or Fidel Castro. Unfortunately, I was programmed not to think. That useless, pathetic war that killed untold numbers of humans should never have taken place. Could I have prevented it from happening? The answer is yes, if my mind was the mind I have now. See, Cuba is so small that nobody would've missed it very much. But if China ceased to exist everybody would notice it at once."

Intrigued, Andrew asked, "What changed your mind?"

"That's another dangerous question. I have made sure that there are no listening devises in the whole building. Nobody can accuse me. If you don't have any hidden recorders on you, I can talk. If you don't mind, I'll light up a cigarette." He took a package of Marlboroughs and lit one.

"At the time the big explosion occurred, I thought my whole family was safe in the government bunker. It was early morning, and my wife decided to take a stroll with our teenage son. The guards allowed this against strict orders. Can they say no to the wife of a Chairman?"

He obviously was reliving these minutes again. He inhaled the tobacco smoke deep into his lungs, then let it run out long and slow.

"My wife and son were brought back without mentioning the incident to me. I was too busy ordering retaliation. By the time we moved out here, their malady was beyond any help. My son Tan took a turn for the worse in a matter of days. Then I heard about your miracles. Immediately, I ordered the Intelligence service to bring you here at any price. It took longer than expected. My wife died a couple of days ago. My son died this morning. I don't even know who won the damn war!"

Andrew got up from the sofa. "Take me to him!"

The Chairman waved his hand. "I told you, Tan is dead. The medical team that tended my family insisted that he should be cremated immediately, just as my wife was. I was prevented from seeing him. There's a great fear of radiation poisoning spreading."

Chin Moon joined her husband. "Stop the cremation if it isn't too late. Is the crematorium here?"

"It's downtown. There is an overload, but my son will receive preferential treatment."

"Call now!" insisted Andrew.

The Chairman dropped his cigarette and took out a pocket phone. "Has the cremation of my son already taken place, Chan?" The Chairman's face became white as snow. The seconds ticked by. He looked up, helplessly, "Any hope?" he asked.

"I'll try, but every minute counts!" Andrew insisted.

"Yes, Chan. They're ready to push him in?! Stop them, for Heavens sake, stop them! That's an order! I'm coming in person."

The three ran down the long corridor and the narrow steps. A limousine waited next to the entrance door held open by a security officer. Andrew, Chin Moon and the Chairman made a running jump into the car, followed by the Chief of Security. The car took off with a roar down the narrow road.

"You know how Tibetans feel about you, " stuttered the Security Chief, "We'll be killed like dogs!"

"I couldn't care less! Faster! Faster!" the Chairman ordered.

He took the car phone, "...clear all traffic...move away all vehicles at the entrance to the crematorium. Wait at the door!"

The Chairman looked nervously at his wristwatch. "How many minutes, Andrew?"

"I don't know, Mr. Chairman. Pray for him!"

"I don't know how..."

"Pray anyway!"

The man closed his eyes. Downtown, people were running left and right, policemen clearing the road for the flying limousine. The Chairman opened his eyes in helpless desperation.

"The crematorium is on the other side of the city."

Suddenly, a large handwritten sign written on a white-washed wall loomed before them.

"YOU KILLED MY SON, CHAIRMAN!"

PART FIVE

THE ROAD

Chapter 27

ROME, ITALY

SHALL I ASK THE BRAVE SOLDIER
WHO FIGHTS ON MY SIDE
IN THE CAUSE OF MANKIND,
IF OUR CREEDS AGREE?
— Thomas Moore

For some time Mark stood in the center of the Radiation Ward, defeated. He didn't know where to start. Though the paparazzi had been banished from the room, the presence of the Vatican's State Secretary and other high ranking functionaries made him feel uneasy.

Aymo was smiling in his own disengaging way, "It's your turn, brother. You said you can do anything Andrew does and more."

Mark looked at the first row of beds.

The exalted hope in the patients' eyes, their hands extended toward him in silent prayer, the name of Jesus whispered fervently by parched lips. One of the nuns mistakenly read his indecision and led him to a bed where a twelve-year-old girl was in the last stages of the pitiless sickness. The child tried to smile and whispered, "Save me, Jesus." Mark knelt beside the bed and took her little trembling hands into his. She looked at him with faith and confidence." You're handsomer than in my dreams...I know I'm beyond any help. But if you kiss me, it will be like a tiny star on my forehead. Your angels will recognize me…as your bride…" She sighed and became limp.

Mark wept bitterly. The nun put a maternal hand over his shaking shoulder. "She's with the angels now, young man, beyond any harm."

"Sister, I can do nothing," he moaned through his sobs, "I'm an impostor, a tool of the Devil!"

The nun knelt next to him and placed her arm around his broad shoulders.

"I know, young man, and God knows it, too."

The VIPs by the entrance to the hall had disappeared. Aymo had followed them. Only despair and broken hopes reigned over the Radiation Ward.

BACK TO LHASA, TIBET

The Chinese Minister of Interior Affairs stood at the Cremation Room door, trying desperately to bar the Chairman's group from entering. "Get back to your senses, Chairman! If you enter this door, you'll guarantee your expulsion from the Communist Party. If we allow you to ignore our iron discipline, all of China will follow suit! We have been through this once. No more!"

The Chairman was incensed. "Go into this room, comrade Minister, and see for yourself where our Iron Discipline has led us. Read the signs on the walls of this city." The Chairman turned to his chief of security, "Lock this man in one of the bathrooms. Shoot anyone who stands in your way! Come, Mr. Bates!"

A body rested on a gurney. The Chairman pulled back the linen sheet that covered it. The sight was horrific as the sores had spread all over his son's body and face. The raw flesh seemed ready to fall apart.

"That's Tan," cried the trembling Chairman.

Chin Moon covered her face with shaking hands. The stink was unbearable.

Andrew stripped himself of all his clothing, climbed deftly onto the gurney and lay over Tan's body. The aids in the long room gasped.

Then Andrew prayed, "Dear, Father. If my brother Tan has done anything wrong, let me take his transgressions into my body and soul, because it was You that sent me here to pay for his sins in the name of Love. There is nothing human that isn't mine. Works in Your Sacred Name, will soon release mankind from bondage."

And he put his fresh rosy lips on the rotted mouth of the corpse.

A strange bluish light enveloped the two bodies and everyone in the room heard a deep voice, "I'll take all souls into my Kingdom. But this life I'll give back, so your name is spoken with Love!"

ROME: OUTDOOR CAFE

"I'm so sorry that I trusted you, Mark. I thought you would stop at nothing to win. Where is your competitiveness, your invincible spirit? You've been taught the same tricks as Andrew. What does he have that you do not?"

"Faith, Aymo. I'm cynical about life, like you. What miracles can you offer besides making something burst into flame, producing a bunch of cobras out of a twisted rope or driving somebody drunk with power to launch a Hydrogen bomb? You split families and set people against each other to the death. These are not miracles, Aymo. They are tricks avoided even by circus magicians. What makes you so great? Making everyone miserable, including yourself?"

Aymo left some money on the table and led Mark down the bustling Via Veneto. "You're a sore loser, Mark, but I like you in spite of your bad score. I want you to serve as my alter ego, my faithful disciple. Not everything is lost, man. You look great. People like you. You failed once. Big deal. We can have a new start. We'll go into politics. In time, I'll make you President of United Europe. We can be fabulously rich. This failure doesn't go on your record. It's Andrew Bates that fucked up his chances in the Hospital. We still can get his fortune and win the world!"

"A real fat chance, Aymo. Get it all!"

They passed by the U.S. Embassy, and while they waited at the corner for the light to change, Aymo said, "I can make you a movie star, a world champion of kick boxing, a matinee idol, an ambassador to the Interplanetary Council. You can be a real, down-to-earth Devil, young, handsome, powerful and wealthy. Drug Kingpin. Crime Boss. Mayor of Las Vegas. Just stop moping. Get your ass out and around and head for action and adventure. Life is beautiful and full of opportunities, especially in wartime."

Mark laughed cynically and showed him his middle finger. "Like those you opened for uncle Aldano..." They crossed the streeet.

"He was a stupid pervert," Aymo said dismissively.

"And what did you make out of your life, Mr. I-dunno-who? Middle-aged soldier of fortune, jail bird and murderer. How come you didn't make yourself the Mayor of Las Vegas, or a King-Pin of some kind? I have been stupid to see you as something romantic, the Knight in Shining Armor, fighting for the right cause, just for the hell of it, not for money and gratitude."

For the first time, Mark saw his ex-role-model subdued. Aymo's head dropped and his eyes lost their brightness. He stopped by a newspaper stand.

"Just for the hell of it..." Aymo repeated in a distant manner. He then exploded into an unnatural peel of joyless laughter, "You're right, kiddo, I never got paid a single red cent for my inglorious schemes. I was chased, despised and hated, but never loved." He kicked a empty bottle.

For the first time Mark saw something glistening in his eyes. Tears perhaps? But Aymo's voice was even and mechanical as ever. "Maybe my mother loved me for awhile, she was getting checks from me. Then, she thought I was a good boy. But I was a carbon copy of my father. On a small scale, he was an operative in the post-war neo-Nazi apparatus. He was in South America, then came back here. His idea was to make a clean slate of his life. A new name, new wife, new son."

They walked shoulder-to-shoulder, and Aymo continued, "The Pope, at this time, was sympathetic with those like him. All he got was a bullet in the head. I thought I had found my role model, so I know exactly how you feel. I learned the real past of my father much later. He was an active member of the ill-famed Odessa File. Then I went to another extreme. — religious fanaticism. Now I don't belong to this world any more than Aldano Brandon does, and I'm always on the wrong side. You are the only person I ever loved. But my love is as destructive as my hate. I'm damned. The sooner I get out of your life, the better for you. You're still very young. Maybe you'd like to join your family in Malta. You have to find a way to make a living, as I'm practically penniless."

"Does Malta still exist?" asked Mark.

"I don't know. It was just a suggestion. You cannot continue to wallow in a musty bed around the clock, overflowing with self pity. Do something."

"Don't feel responsible for me, Aymo. You don't owe me any explanations. You can just walk out of my life and don't come back."

They entered the lobby of their boarding house. Aymo stopped at the lift. "Have you gotten the sickness, Mark?"

"What difference does that make to you?"

"Because it changes everything. There is only one man that can help you if you are sick."

"The answer is no."

"Danny's here."

"I know. I met him in the Sistine Chapel. A guard was the go-between."

THEATER OF THE ABSTRACT: DANNY'S TALE

I was late for the appointment but easily recognized Mark. He was kneeling in a pew praying, his eyes fixed on Michael-Angelo's fresco *The Last Judgement*. When I knelt next to him, he smiled and put his left arm around my shoulders, then crossed himself hurriedly.

"Hi, old shoe! I'm sorry they didn't let you come, but I'm in disgrace. My days are numbered. It was a crude scheme. If one can't trust the Devil, whom can we trust? God is less trustworthy." He pointed to the lower right of the fresco, "I just discovered myself in that mumbo-jumbo. Amazing, the Maestro knew about me. See if you can find yourself."

"I'm not there," I said firmly.

"Of course, I forgot...you're in good grace with the *True Savior*. What in the world are you doing in this panopticum? Mr. Buonarroti has painted all the popes and their entourages in the darkest chasms. The Vatican is a very dangerous place for one's soul these days."

"Come with me, Mark!"

My strikingly handsome cousin laughed deprecatingly covering his face with his hands. Then he said, "Where? Back to Nepal or the Shangri La...under the good grace of our benefactor in China? Never. I hate that conceited fool. He sold me for a miserable Chink! Give me a break. Don't I deserve a better hand of cards?"

"Like the schemes of Aymo?" I suggested.

Mark was taken aback. "Lets get out of here. I'm tired of whispering."

We went to the refreshment stand, ordered good aromatic coffee and sat down at a small round table.

I lit a cigarette while cousin Mark boiled with indignation. "I'll never lay at Andrew's feet crying *uncle*."

"He doesn't expect it."

"What does his Goodness Gracious expect?" Mark laughed sardonically.

"Nothing. He needs all the help he can get."

"Not from me," Mark hissed with deprecation.

"He truly loves you."

"Ha, he doesn't give a damn about me."

I was stunned, "You're crying, Mark."

He angrily brushed the tears from his face, then jumped from his chair almost knocking over the table. "Don't ever tell him I cried from him! Swear!"

I shook my head, then asked, "Are you going to report to Aymo?"

Mark lowered his voice to a whisper, "My *omnipotent* manager left the sinking ship."

I was surprised but gathered myself quickly. "Come to my place, Mark. It's not great, but we can make plans as usual."

Mark looked at me skeptically. "Do you really meat it?"

I stood up, dabbing my lips with the paper napkin. "Of course. Why am I in Rome, to see the Pope?"

Mark walked away a few steps then turned back. "I cannot take advantage of you...but thanks anyway."

I approached him, pushed a piece of paper in his hand and said, "This is my address, in case you change your mind."

Mark looked at it perfunctorily and returned it to me saying, "Strange, just a few days ago I would've jumped at the bait, but not now. Rest assured, I won't abuse your hospitality. It might seem improbable to you, but I have some dignity, too. Prince Tut won't accept such debasement. Either all or nothing!"

I watched Mark with disappointment as he walked away.

LOBBY OF BOARDING HOUSE

"Danny hasn't left your door since the catastrophe. I convinced the Pope to press no charges against you or me. Of course, according to the Pope, you cannot consider yourself a Catholic anymore. I was excommunicated long ago for trying to save the Church. Then, I was known as the Anti-Christ."

"How's Andrew?" asked Mark.

"Andrew is alive and well. The Chinese are madly in love with him. He's viewed as Buddha reincarnated and the Communists have fallen into this wholeheartedly. Communism has been never able to fully displace any religion. The ordinary people cannot live without it, and in China, the common people are grossly mistreated as are the commoners in India, South America and Africa. They need religion. The only thing missing is the presence of a true Messiah, as in ancient times. When the need is that great, people find Him and revere Him as the proverbial sacrificial lamb in order to kill him, so that humanity can live through another millennium. The Catholic Church will be in serious trouble if they persist in denouncing Andrew. Their substitute Christ can't help them anymore. Exposing you as a false Messiah by invoking the name of Andrew Bates gave them a little respite, but now with Andrew in China, their problem is serious. That was God's work, and I stupidly fell into the trap."

"Is Danny still by the door?"

"See for yourself."

Mark hastily went to the door. There was Danny — an enormously changed youth — lean, compassionate, with two big eyes shining with intelligence. The cousins embraced. Aymo felt like the odd man out. He left silently.

LHASA MONASTERY

Soon the lives of Andrew and Chin Moon became nightmarish. Their youth helped them deal with the stress, but all was not well. They were invited to meet with scientists, to attend conferences as well as a Special Session of the Party's Central Committee, which wanted to outlaw war by empowering a World Council to mediate hostilities. Nothing was mentioned about outlawing Nuclear Armament. The Dalai Lama wanted to meet personally with the "Young Savior," but Andrew's schedule was booked solid eight months in advance. He was scheduled to visit with the King of Thailand, the Chief Rabbi of Israel, Arafat and the Christian minority of the Copts. The King of England asked him to arbitrate the endless dispute between the fighting Catholics and Protestants in Ireland. Andrew had a nagging feeling that something was terribly amiss. He was quarantined from the people of China and strictly forbidden to meet with representatives of the Tibetan National Liberation Front. Andrew became totally frustrated. It was as if an invisible power was ruling what was important to him and controlling what his next move would be.

The Vatican was silent, as was the President of the United States. The Eastern Orthodox Patriarch proclaimed the "self appointed Messiah" an anathema. The Turkish President sent an eviction notice to the Greek Patriarch in Istanbul. Greeks responded by threatening war. Surprisingly, the All Russian

Patriarch refused to back up his traditional ally in Byzantium. Even Serbian Saint-Sinode issued a special opinion, while Bulgaria and Rumania staunchly supported the New Messiah.

India was too slow. The Pakistanis jumped at the opportunity. Both countries still reeled from their recent clash and terrorism. A lot of noted individuals tried to get in touch with Andrew by computer. The media pleaded to interview his wife and demanded a press conference with him. The Chairman didn't want him to make any public appearances or speeches until some protocol was established.

The Chairman's only son, Tan, became Andrew's disciple and followed him wherever he went. Millions followed suit. One of the world's largest aircraft builders provided Mr. Bates a custom-made private jet, much nicer than the Pope's.

His mother's attorneys announced that Andrew was the undisputed heir of El Barrack's billions. A tidal wave of pathetic calls for help — from the Invalid's of War to Save the Dolphins — put tremendous pressure on the young couple.

Chin Moon was threatened by kidnappers. Black-mailers, terrorists and religious zealots planned Andrew's murder. The Chinese Government searched for a body-double to make Andrew's public appearances in his stead.

The reigning Pope finally recognized Mr. Andrew Bates as a Savior. The President of United States called on the Federation of all American States to acknowledge the New Messiah. He gave them a full guarantee that Mr. Bates' deity wouldn't affect the status quo. The Cult of the Madonna would suffer no consequences. Then he called Andrew and asked him to return to the USA, the only surviving democracy.

Andrew and Chin Moon, locked in the Citadel over Lhasa, were overcome. In their wildest dreams, they hadn't pictured this kind of Armageddon.

As the staunch guardian of "Peace on Earth," Andrew Bates received medals from all dictatorships on Earth.

Millions asked their governments to have Andrew officially declared the Living Messiah.

Chapter 28

IN LHASA, TIBET

Tan was a very sweet boy.

He would walk behind Andrew like a shadow. During his time in death's clutch, he had suffered some brain damage. In his naive, childish way, he asked for his mat to be moved into Andrew's room. Tan was only a year younger than Andrew, the same age as Chin Moon. In his confusion, he thought of her as a surrogate mother. Chin Moon was very patient and motherly, but she was pregnant with a child of her own and badly in need of some privacy. Her bedding was moved to the adjacent room.

In the whole monastery, there weren't any "beds," only sleeping mats. While Andrew visited his wife, Tan slept in his bed. Andrew asked Changha Narr to bring his mat from the soldier's quarters into the room. Tan didn't seem to mind the switch. Perhaps, he took his new roommate to be the "other" face of Andrew. With Asiatic fervency Changha was eager to do anything he could to please the people he'd betrayed.

"Are you sure, Master Andrew, that you will pardon my treason?"

Andrew put his hands on Changha's shoulders and kissed his ruddy cheeks. "We're the same age, Changha Narr, and I've made my share of mistakes. Money holds an awesome power. Precious few are immune to it. Maybe this was designed by God as a test."

In the days ahead, the young couple had to share the same narrow, single bedding, in a much smaller room. Nothing's perfect in the making of a saint.

THE ABSOLUTE: ANDREW'S DREAM

Andrew had one of his terrible dreams. He was flying over a dead world that was covered by mud and inhabited by slimy reptiles. An enormous, ghostly moon covered the last vestige of life with a deadly shroud.

He recognized the ruins of Katmandu. Alone, in an unheated house, he found Tormack Baggach. His father had been dead for hours but still remained unburied. Tormack had run out of soup to feed him, so he smothered him. Better dead than hungry. The pangs of hunger tortured the youth unmercifully. Nobody needed guides and sherpas in these turbulent times. Troubled, Andrew left this house of despair and flew toward the mountain range.

Chomolungma had re-established his eerie kingdom in the Himalayas.

On top of it, Andrew couldn't believe his eyes. He saw two lonely figures weathered by the winds. The sturdy, rowdy boys had changed incredibly. Danny had lost a lot of weight and his eyes had become deep and mysterious. He held his cousin like a child.

Mark had become a shell of his old self — his handsomeness had faded — he looked much older than his years. He uttered, "It wasn't revenge that brought my end, Andrew. I didn't call you for help. I deserve a miserable death. It's Love, Andrew, I've always loved you, and I'll love you forever. My downfall is mine alone."

Andrew extended his hands desperately. He screamed at the top of his lungs, "Noo-oo-o-ooo…Maa-a-ark! ! ! Don't die. Let me help you, too. I love you!!! Please, Mark…come to mee-e-eee…"

Silently, Mark placed the funeral mask of Prince Tut on his face.

Andrew woke in the arms of Chin Moon. His gaunt face was bathed in tears, his eyes reflected a primal horror.

"It's only a dream, dear! Don't cry, I'll never leave you. Never!"

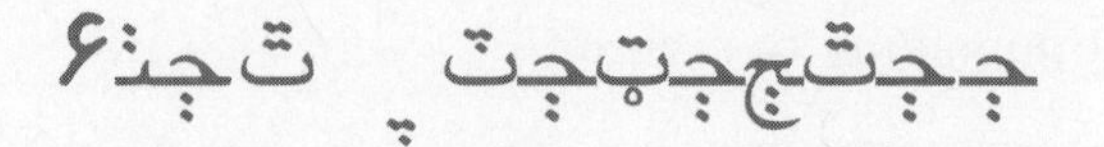

By midsummer, a number of dark spots appeared on the sun, which affected the magnetic fields and climate patterns. Electric storms accompanied by gusty high winds caused gigantic forest and brush fires that burned into cities. They spread everywhere and not a drop of rain appeared to quell the disasters.

The storms hit parts of Europe, Africa and India. The monsoon simply didn't come. Famines wiped out tribes in Equatorial Africa. The situation in Asia was no better. With temperatures approaching 150 degrees, Greece, Italy, Spain, France and Germany suffered massive power failures. The situation in Russia, Turkey and Iran was catastrophic and the world's population was in a state of agony.

The frozen continent of Antarctica began to melt. Soon, New York and many other large coastal cities around the world were being flooded.

Even the mighty United States had to tap into its strategic reserves. Power failures played havoc with the economy. Japan declared a state of emergency. All communications were scrambled. Mt. Fujiama erupted and triggered devastating earthquakes. Monstrous tidal waves hit Malaysia, Australia, New Zealand and the Hawaiian Islands. The social structure went to pieces. The needy blamed the rich and the corporations for their miseries. Antipathy toward organized religions grew, and satanic cults proliferated.

In stressful situations, the human mind is prone to serious misjudgment and panic. All hopes centered on the Savior. Andrew Bates was invited to address the United Nations; he was not yet seventeen.

Andrew was pushed beyond his limits. Chin Moon had a miscarriage; radiation had done its job. The tiny fetus had no limbs. When that became public, faith in the miraculous powers of the young Savior wavered.

He wasn't even capable of saving his own baby!

People forgot that God had preordained that Christ was to die on the Cross.

For Chin Moon, it was a smashing blow. She became depressed and her self esteem plummeted.

"Who's Mark?" Chin Moon suddenly asked Andrew one night.

Andrew tried to concentrate. "You know Mark Brandon. You might've forgotten the first time you met him eight years ago. The second time, when we visited with your family, you fed Mark and his cousin Danny. You talked to him many times. Aymo and your father played backgammon almost every evening. Remember?"

Chin Moon became impatient. "I know all of that. What I wanted to hear from you is, if this is the same Mark you call every night in your dreams."

Andrew's face flushed. "Yes. it's the same Mark."

"Are you in love with him?" she demanded.

"He's dead, Chin Moon."

"But are you in love with him?"

"I love him. Not infatuation, nothing amorous. It is simply Love."

Chin Moon laughed shrilly. "You mean your Great Love wasn't consummated?"

"Oh, it was consummated, but not in a vulgar way. I miss him terribly," admitted Andrew.

"More than our baby?"

"I'm sorry for the baby. I know how much it meant to you."

There was a long tedious pause, and then Chin Moon whispered, "It means little to you. I can never have another baby. You should leave me."

Andrew took her in his arms with tenderness and devotion. "No dear. I'll never leave you. Please, don't begrudge me my past. I'm not proud of it, but that's all I had."

Chin Moon started crying. "Why do you need a wife that cannot give you a son? You should take a concubine."

"I won't take anything of the kind. Your love is much more rewarding to me," he replied.

Her beautiful eyes still overflowing with tears looked at him with renewed hope. "Truly? Can we move from here?" she asked through her tears.

"It won't be easy, but we'll try."

"You're not in love with Danny, are you?"

"No, of course not. The only link between Danny and me was Mark."

She brushed away her tears and tried to smile. "Then let's go back home. I've received news from my brother in Katmandu. Danny is alive and well. He lives with him in the old house. They cannot come here, though Danny wants to talk to you in person. It's urgent."

"I can ask for a helicopter to pick them up..."

"You don't understand, Andrew. Your friend doesn't want to come here."

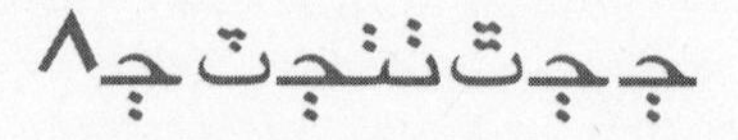

Andrew never discussed with his wife the reality behind their formal status in the Chairman's Residence. They were prisoners. No magazines, newspapers, TV or radio. No access to computer communications or telephone services. In the absence of the Chairman, his secretary Chan was the only source of information. All their needs were channeled through him.

The Chairman had gone on a tour of provincial China, trying to gain some support.

Something strange was in the air. None of the personnel would look at them, including Tan and Changha Narr. The Nepalese youth cared for the Chairman's son. They ate rice, with a few vegetables and had a cup of soup at dinnertime. Unsweetened tea was served only in the morning. The rest of the country wasn't getting even that much. The rainy season failed to arrive. Water had to be rationed.

There was no gas for transportation.

Chin Moon was aware of all of this and more. Any information she got was from the cleaning woman. Escape was impossible.. Andrew vacillated. He left everything in the hands of God. He felt something was in the making.

Physical conditioning was of utmost importance to him, but there was nothing like a gym in the whole building. There was a small court yard covered in sand. This little oasis was the only place for short conversations without being recorded.

Andrew suggested to Changha that they engage in physical exercise by wrestling on the sandy floor of the court yard. Tan was to be their referee. It was great fun for him, and a test of stamina and endurance to them. Naked to the waist, they fought to the point of exhaustion. Their muscles hardened and their general condition improved.

One particular morning Andrew had a nagging feeling that something significant was going to happen. Instead of one chaperone, their athletic engagement was supervised by two uniformed officers. Tan tried to start a conversation with them, but they weren't talkative. Their attention was focused on the warm up exercise of the two youths. Changha Narr looked around the yard for a possible escape route. Guards blocked the only exit. The other doors were surely locked.

Andrew and Changha stripped down, kicked off their sandals, then fell into a tight clinch. In a moment Changha caught Andrew off guard and executed a picture perfect hip throw. Andrew's body flipped in the air and hit the sand cover with bruising impact. He got up to his knees mad as hell and shouted at the laughing guards, " I'll kill that louse. Don't pull us apart!"

The guards burst into merriment. "I'd call that a solid throw. Those two really hate each other," said one of them.

"If you're gonna have it in earnest, go to the end," giggled the other one. "I'd love to see who wins."

The two lads stalked each other again, hunting for a chance to secure a good headlock or a tight arm bar.

The guards started betting on the outcome. "Five yens on the Nepalese guy. He's faster."

"Double on the European. He's mean and crafty. I'm sure he'll flatten the sherpa."

The two grapplers tumbled to the sand, legs thrashing around. Tan arose, clapped his hands and danced in a frenzy. When Andrew prevailed and held Changha's shoulders flat to the sand, he pretended to count slowly as he pressed his flushed face into Changha's and whispered hurriedly, "Tonight, both of you go to bed fully clothed, shoes, too..."

With a heave of his thighs Changha rolled him down and whispered back, "I'll keep Tan awake."

About midnight, the landing helicopter broke the silence. A machine gun chattered in the distance, then there were two explosions which shattered the window pane. The smell of smoke indicated fire was burning somewhere. The sound of running footsteps and shouts for help filled the air. Andrew led Chin Moon out. In the complete darkness, they found Changha Narr with a totally confused Tan in tow.

"Follow me!" shouted Andrew. At the end of the hallway, they ran into the secretary.

"God be praised!" he said, "Come this way!"

The gunfire became sporadic and many voices were heard. The helicopter wasn't far from the door. The group made its way to the safety of the aircraft and everybody was accounted for. The helicopter took off immediately.

Chan shouted in Andrew's ear, "The Chairman was overthrown by the hardliners!"

"Where do we go now?" asked Andrew

"Katmandu."

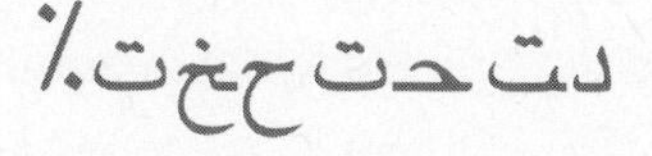

Katmandu wasn't the same city it was only a half year ago. It was now home to people from all parts of the world, especially those with money. In other words, the rich. All hotels were filled to capacity and private homes were taking in guests. Commerce thrived and everything was available, but at inflated prices. Andrew had no idea how much of it was due to him. During his absence, the tale of his marvels had ballooned into mythical proportions. Would the Savior be saved from communist hands? Political infighting had been suppressed and humanity had cooperated as never before. Even terrorism suffered set-backs.

SAVE THE SAVIOR!

When the helicopter landed, they were met by thousands of people who had waited throughout the night. Loudspeakers kept them informed of the latest developments. Diplomats and city officials had broken through the security cordons, each fighting for a vantage point.

When the door opened, Andrew appeared and a total pandemonium broke out. Everyone tried to touch the Savior. He was tossed from hand to hand like a ball over the top of the multitude. Pieces of his clothing were snatched at random, until he was left only in his underwear. Finally, he was delivered to a platform equipped with microphones and super lights. Andrew looked for someone he knew. Soon, he saw the old priest from the

Buddhist Temple and the city Mayor. He asked them to find a safer way to bring his wife and his friends from the helicopter. A group of reporters asked for a press conference, but the Mayor took hold of a microphone. The Mayor's voice was distorted, but a "welcome home" was heard.

Andrew became afraid that the helicopter would be attacked because of its Chinese markings, so he took the microphone.

"These are the people who saved our lives. My wife and my friends..."

There were shouts from the crowd. A reporter approached Andrew. "They're asking you to perform a miracle," the journalist informed him.

Andrew was shocked. "I'm not a magician."

"Just a little trick will do," encouraged the reporter.

"What kind of trick? One with cards?" asked Andrew who was clearly irritated.

"Make something disappear."

"I wish I could make these rowdy people disappear," he joked.

Representatives of the Nepalese Government finally arrived and brought police reinforcements. Gradually, the situation became controllable. Under heavy security, Mr. and Mrs. Bates were taken to the palace. The royal family was still abroad but sections of their residence were available. The threat from imperialistic China was constant. Simply put, Andrew and Chin Moon were not to leave the palace compound. At least, they were permitted visitors. At Andrew's insistence, Danny Brandon soon joined their entourage. As in Andrew's dream, he was lean, serious, with thoughtful eyes and soft manners. Chin Moon noticed the change, though she thought it was due to the death of his cousin. Andrew knew better, but he didn't share this with his wife. It simply wasn't Danny.

After the first week — an intense schedule of meetings with press and diplomatic envoys — Chin Moon isolated herself. She wrote thank you notes to their royal hosts.

Andrew and Danny lingered over the dinner table. Finally, they had the opportunity to exchange a few words. Neither one of them talked about the final days of Mark. It was too painful for both of them. Danny broke the silence. “Mark died by his own hand,” he offered.

Andrew kept his eyes in contact with Danny’s. “I thought so.”

Danny didn’t break the contact. “Would it be an imposition on you if I light a cigarette?”

“No, of course not. Since when did you start smoking?”

Danny hesitated for a moment. “I saw your Mother, Andrew.”

“I was told that she died.”

“That’s true. It’s true also that I saw her in person.”

“Did you talk to her?” asked Andrew.

“We had a conversation.”

“About me?” Andrew’s interest perked up.

“Mostly, she explained why she had become a traitor to her own son. She hoped you would be forgiving. She wanted me to convince you that using her great fortune could aid you in your mission.”

Andrew’s answer came softly to Danny’s ears, “Of course my mother is forgiven, she fulfilled her destiny. As for the wealth, I will be guided as to its use.”

Most natural disasters and environmental deterioration somehow abated.

In the fall of 2000, Sydney hosted the Summer Olympics. It was lavish, flawlessly organized, full of surprises and broken records. It was the best of times!

The extravaganza of the ceremonies and the final bash of fireworks over the bay were unforgettable.

Even the two Koreas came in a unified team.

Fortiter, fideliter, feliciter! (The logo of the Olympic games.)

During the Olympic games in ancient times all warfare came to a halt, resuming with the same ferocity after the closing ceremonies. This time, a war between Palestinians and Jews started on the last day of the games. Untold numbers died caught in the crossfire. A ten-year-old boy and his father tried to hide next to a cement wall, lying flat, pressed to its base. The eyes of the youngster, looked desperately for help, arms clasped around his father's waist. A sharpshooter got him in the stomach. The child died instantly, his dad lasted a bit longer. It was caught by TV cameras.

Fortiter, fideliter, feliciter!

There'll be no Olympic Games for this kid.

What member of the human race can murder a ten-year-old in cold blood?

No answer.

Humanity was busy watching the great extravaganza.

Altium, Fortium...Faster! Faster! Faster!

Mene, mene, tekel, upharsin...At Belshazzar's feast those words appeared on the wall, the prophet Daniel interpreted these words to signify that God had judged Belshazzar's kingdom, found it wanting, and would destroy it.

Did anybody read this message in the dazzling Olympic fireworks?

The office of an International Committee prepared the schedule for Andrew Bates' global "Mission of Peace." It was mind boggling. Forty-eight major cities, 109 smaller communities, seven hundred hospitals, schools and universities, specials on TV and computerized programs, meetings with heads of states and clerical organizations, visits with scientists, patriarchs and the Pontiff of the Vatican. Material for speeches, messages and addresses were fed into the computer's memories.

Andrew's frustration grew daily. He was convinced that none of this could help. The outcome was not in finding salvation but finding a short cut to God.

But how to reach out to Him?"

Chin Moon valiantly tried to keep up with her husband, though her mental state was precarious. Physically, she was of solid make and effort of this kind didn't deplete her energy. Nevertheless, many times she wished to God she had a quiet, family oriented life. They could try and adopt a couple of nice kids and watch them grow into maturity. But, for the time being, that was just wishful thinking on her part. Deep inside, however, she admired her husband, and her inner voice whispered repeatedly that such a person couldn't live an ordinary life, and by extension, neither could she.

Andrew was resting on a chaise-lounge. In the late afternoon, the view of the gigantic, snow-capped mountain range was beyond magnificent.

Suddenly, an idea electrified him. He remembered his tragic dream. Maybe, just maybe, dreams were the place to meet God!

Mount Everest!!! There he could talk Man-to-God. The highest point of His creation. That could be the Judgment Day! His mother was right — he would put her money to good use.

Next morning he called in Danny and Chin Moon and the sherpa guides. "Can we climb Chomolungma now? The weather conditions have temporarily stabilized."

Tormack and Changha weren't surprised. Danny seemed amenable and Chin Moon was ecstatic. She had always dreamed about climbing to the top of the world. Had another woman ever been there? Probably. It didn't matter. She had to be part of the team!

All eyes focused on Andrew as he announced, "We'll need the best mountain-climbers in the world."

Changha Narr shook his head. "You've got them right here. Sherpas are by far the best. April is the right time to leave the base camp. What you need is a whole fortune of money and a damn good sardar."

"What's a sardar?" asked Andrew.

"A leader that has a lot of experience."

"Find the man and whatever else we need. I have the money. The problem now is how to explain this expedition. We'll be considered a bunch of fools. Can you arrange everything without the authorities getting wind of it? I can join the party at the last moment."

Changha and Tormack thought it over. "Sherpas communicate well with each other, but they don't open up easily to foreigners," said Tormack. "Concentration of animals and food on the bases always attracts attention. Newsmen are a hard breed."

"So can we cut down on the supplies?" asked Andrew.

Changha looked at him seriously. "We must take what we need. Sherpas are fearless but non-violent people. Living in the high mountains has made them superstitious. They've seen the legendary snowman many times, just before a devastating storm. Monks pacify ferocious evil spirits with ritual dances. The lamas say God Himself rests upon Chomolongma, but food has to be sufficient."

Andrew glanced at the mountain's range. "I hope so. How's Tan, Changha?"

"Not well. He's been training in the gym like mad. I've had to hospitalize him from time to time. When he's back, I've seen him running throughout the palace compound for hours.

"Did you promise to take him up the mountain?"

"I had to."

"Why?"

"His father's secretary, Chan, had told him about the heroic behavior of his dad as he faced the firing squad. He was accused of being a traitor to the Communist party. A son has to be proud of his dad. And when he heard this, the boy suddenly changed into a man. He wants to be worthy of his father's legacy."

Danny approached Andrew. "Let's go out to the balcony."

It was almost the middle of March. The wind coming down the mountain was freezing, though springtime was in the air. They leaned on the balustrade.

"Are you serious about this expedition?" Danny asked, eyes glued on the Himalayas.

"I feel strongly that it is my mission. The seat of God seems to be spared by Earth's infirmities."

Danny lifted his light eyebrows. "So, you think it is possible?"

"Attainable, I don't know, but I feel the persistent need. Is that 'March for Peace' more palatable to you?" Andrew asked sarcastically.

"No. I like your idea. What's my alternative? To stay in Katmandu and marry a princess? Of course, I'll come with you. I don't want to part with you. I'm a stranger to my family. You're all I have in this world. Your touch changed my life forever. No matter what Mark said, you're a Godsend."

"Am I?" Danny nodded with deep conviction. "Then you know more than I. Who am I really?"

After a short pause, Danny said unwaveringly, "You are THE SAVIOR."

"How do you know that?" pressed Andrew.

"I know it from the Highest Source."

"God talks to you? If I'm the chosen one, why doesn't He talk to me?"

"Because you're still human. By accepting your sacrifice He'll make you Divine again."

"I'm to be a Sacrificial Lamb?"

"In a matter of speaking. There's a particle of the Divine in all of us. Nobody has seen or talked to God in person. Lord Aton has access to him because He's no longer a human spirit. His fabric has been elevated entirely into the spectral dimension of pure knowledge. He's been talking to me about you. And Shadow had only praise for you. He's still your dog waiting for you in my home. I know how lonely your life has been. Such is the destiny of all Chosen. We have to serve God as we can. It's a duty, not a prize."

"Are you an Angel?"

The youth smiled gently. "Far from it. I'm still your father and you're still my only son."

THEATER OF THE ABSURD: ANDREW COMES FROM BEHIND CURTAIN — FINALLY, SOME GOOD NEWS!

"I can talk to my real flesh and blood father, and Shadow has a home! He waits for me. Danny doesn't seem to have any notion that my father is using him as a medium. I'll leave it that way. For the time being I'm not sharing that even with my wife. I haven't quite gotten used to her sensibility.

"My father says I made the right decision. I've been pronouncing that sweet word 'F-a-t-h-e-r' only in my mind. I've seen no picture of him, Mother had never described him to me. Maybe one day I'll see him. The monks taught me reincarnation is endless but that doesn't sound quite right to me. If my father has a home in heaven, he's there to stay. I hope I can make him proud of me. Thank You, God! I badly needed some encouragement. Now I can fly to Mt. Everest. My father won't let me fail."

IN KATMANDU

Preparations for the scaling of Chomolungma were well under way. Unexpectedly, Tan's mental and physical state worsened in a matter of days. It would be impossible for him to reach even the first leg of Andrew's expedition.

Andrew and Chin Moon visited him in the hospital. The boy was looking through the window at the mighty Himalayan Range.

"I'll never go there," he said sadly. "But I'll try to follow you from here," he smiled brokenly, "A bedridden hero. May I ask you for a favor, Andrew?"

"Ask anything, Tan."

"Here is a button from the coat of my Father. Will you leave it on the top of the world for me?"

Chin Moon covered her face, while her husband took the button.

"I don't know if we'll get that high."

Tan became very agitated. "But you will. I can see you there!"

Chin Moon had lived all her life amidst sherpas. She started intensive training in the gym, joining the daily run around the park with Andrew and Danny. Her half brothers were busy buying and stocking provisions. They found a very able sardar of

European extraction. His extensive experience and knowledge of the Himalayas, Chumbu Region in particular, was attested to by Edmund Hillary and Peter Athans. Surprisingly, he furnished his discretion and services for reasonable compensation. The rare expeditions to Everest had reduced prices for human services to an affordable level. The cost of livestock and materials was substantial, and food prices were prohibitive. Farmers were unwilling to part with their reserves. Rations had to be flown in by chartered plane from Australia.

Changha Narr and his brother had inherited the permit for a trekking business from their father. The taxes were paid and the permit revalidated. Officially they were serving an American couple, who would join the expedition later. Fortunately in Katmandu their young age wasn't considered an obstacle to business. Other trekker's agents thought of it as Fool's Luck. The Patrons were so generous that some money trickled down to them. For now, the petty jealousies were set aside. Of utmost importance for the time being was to attract more foreigners, in spite of the unstable political and weather conditions.

Politicians seemed eager to manipulate the young "Messiah," while making sure that he would not be a liability to their own careers. The ecclesiastical centers were still tight lipped about the veracity of his miracles. So far, only a priest in Katmandu and some Chinese medics had attested to the healing powers of Andrew Bates. Why doesn't he demonstrate anything large, with world renowned experts?

The momentum was lost. Even Nepal's Royal Family postponed their return. The Majordomo of the Palace insinuated that the House must be cleaned before Their Majesties' arrival. For Andrew and his small entourage, that was more than welcome. They moved to the home of Chin Moon and her half brothers. It was well built, had retaining walls and small windows and was easily protected by a few well armed Sherpas against unwanted intruders. Reporters asking for interviews were turned down. A group of Church Emissaries asked for an appointment, but they were ignored.

The atmospheric disorders worsened and Istanbul was hit by a tremendous earthquake. For a second time, gigantic hail fell over the Vatican, and parts of Rome saw serious damage to statuary, inlaid glass and architecture. The famous gardens were devastated. Forecasters predicted even more storms of unprecedented magnitude.

The Pope exchanged messages with the Eastern Orthodox Patriarch, who was temporarily residing in the Monastery of Aton. The all-Russian Patriarch offered hospitality to a Worldwide Ecclesiastical Convention in Crimea. The Protestants who had opposed it bitterly, suddenly accepted, but not until the location was moved to the old home of the UN in Geneva.

Everybody wondered if it was "too little, too late." The birth rates had fallen dramatically. Even without new atomic explosions, the radiation level had increased tenfold worldwide. Crowds of people filled churches and basilicas to pray and overflowed onto the squares and boulevards to ask, Where is the Promised Messiah?

GOD WAS SILENT.

Chapter 29

BEGINNING THE CLIMB

After a very cold night, the Royal Helicopter was ready to takeAndrew and his entourage to Khumbu where the sons of Zarem Cherchak awaited with several zopkios, cow-yak crossbreeds.

The bedroom was more of a cubicle than a room, and the bedspreads were on the floor. Against the wall was a large chest which the mother of Chin Moon brought with her dowry. The mirror belonged to the former wife of Zarem Cherchak. Years ago, two Frenchmen had asked Cherchak to organize their scaling of Lhotse, the second tallest after Chomolungma. Zarem Cherchak found a good sardar and a number of friends who were sherpas from his native place, Gokyo. The expedition was a success and gave him a name in the business.

Electric power was still unreliable, so the members of the expedition ate a quick meal and got in their bedding to keep warm. Danny shared the same room with the young masters of the house, but after they had gone to arrange the base camps he had it all to himself. The sherpas and guardsmen slept in the basement.

The transfer of money from Switzerland was slow, but after the official announcement that Andrew Bates was the only heir of the El Barrack's fortune, many accounts were opened in the Arab Emirates. The Royal Family suddenly returned and instantly fired the unfortunate majordomo for his "monstrously inhospitable act toward their guests." Andrew promised to pay his respects immediately after his return from Khumbu. Other invitations came from all points around the world, including the near-sighted Pope who was hardly able to see anything further than his opulent nose.

Andrew Bates made public his expedition.

Danny Brandon, in his new position as a spokesperson for Andrew Bates, explained at a press conference that Andrew insisted on full privacy on his trek to Thyangboche Monastery and Khumbu Glacier in Sagarantha National Park. The presence of any free lance writers or photographers from *National Geographic*, he said, would hinder his important decision making.

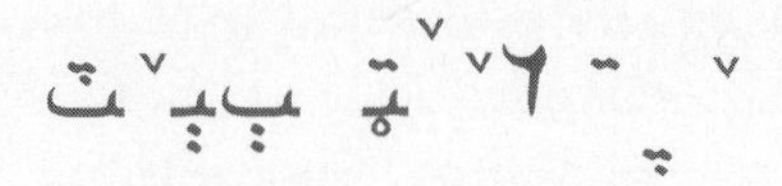

In the murky light of the oil lamp Chin Moon looked like a child. Andrew observed her intensely. At seventeen, did he know what real love was? When their child was born prematurely and horribly deformed, he felt a sense of relief that it was stillborn. Chin Moon was stricken to the quick. It took him a while to make her understand that a child didn't mean the same thing to him as to her. He felt he had no chance of survival in his reach for God. Andrew knew what it is for a child to grow up without a father. To leave behind a bunch of unruly children, as Mr. Brandon had done, had nothing to do with immortality.

The sherpas had no fear of death, because they firmly believed in reincarnation. To them, the reincarnation was more important than birth.

Tomorrow Andrew would embark on his last chance. He had lost his link to God. Andrew intended to use his soul to make the connection.

Tormack Baggach was waiting for them in the Panorama Lodge.

Tormack and the sherpas from Katmandu loaded the animals. He employed five of the locals to help them reach the monastery before nightfall.

Their small expedition left. In the early twilight, the group arrived at the narrow footpath of Tyangboche Monastery. Camping cost only thirty rupees. While the sherpas built tents and unloaded necessary equipment, Andrew, Chin Moon and Danny made their way through a hillside of rhododendrons to visit with the Rimpoche (Head Lama).

The structure was perched over a ridge and partially hidden by evergreens. It overlooked a broad meadow. It was a place of hospitality to trekkers, visiting monks and their animals as well. The monastery had been recently renovated and smelled of pine and incense. In the apartment of the head lama, they offered presents, received his blessings and had the ritual scarves placed around their necks. Andrew's generous donation to the monastery of eight thousand rupees made the lama more accessible. He showed them a stone building behind the monastery where a small museum preserved a few original sherpa artifacts.

In spite of his advanced age, the Rimpoche had sharp eyes and a tongue to match.

"A lot has been lost in the rush to embrace the new times. People are becoming smaller and smaller spiritually. They have little patience and insatiable greed." He clapped his hands for the novices to bring freshly brewed coffee and sweets. "You speak our language and seem to be familiar with monastic behavior."

Andrew lit some fresh incense. "My cousins and I spent time in a monastery on the other side of the mountain."

The Rimpoche looked at him carefully. "How unusual. Nowadays I have a hard time keeping novices more than a year.

They want to go into business and get married. Very few stay. Once, there was a child here, a true reincarnation of an ancient monk, but he died young in an icefall."

The coffee and the refreshments were served. For a while, nothing was said. Then the old man approached Andrew, "I have to talk to you in private, young man," and led him out of the room.

"It's all right, Rimpoche. Danny will keep my wife company."

They entered the sanctuary and sat cross legged on the floor.

"I've had visitors, Andrew. They left messages for you."

"Tell me, Rimpoche," probed Andrew.

"I believe you have studied the Vedanta and the sacred books."

"I did so for eight years, in a faraway place."

The oil lamp's flame danced in a very strange way, but the lama didn't move his eyes from Andrew's face even for a moment. "I'm eighty-seven years old and have visited many Holy Places. I have been honored to speak with many sage men. At times I feel the presence of the superior mind and leave my body to enter the world between Heaven and Earth. I met a handsome woman who asked me to prevent you from going to the Abode of God. She was high strung and worried about you. Nobody who meets God can return to this world because his spirit joins His Divine Substance. Are you the reincarnation of Jesu?"

Andrew shook his head slowly. "I don't know, Holiness. I follow my destiny. I also know that mankind is in mortal danger."

"What is Mankind to you?"

"Home."

The Rimpoche whispered one of the nine blessings. "Then you have every right to defend your Home. Prince Tut asks for permission to enter into your presence. He's alone with the stars and nobody near to him. He gave me one of his jewels. If you hold it in your hand, he'll come."

"What is it?" asked Andrew.

"The Sacred Beetle."

"A Scarab?"

The Rimpoche extended his hand to him. It was the Pharaoh's Scarab. Andrew took it and pressed it to his heart. A faint smile colored his lips as he thought fervently, "Will he come in the form of Mark? I've been craving to see him."

Amidst the bluish flame in the lamp, Tutankhamon, in Mark's body, stood clad only in a loin cloth, holding the Pharaoh's Tiara and staff. He seemed divine in his golden, outlandish beauty."

"Don't you hate me, Andrew?"

"Not for a moment, Mark. I love you."

"I'm not as strong as you, Andrew. My love is selfish and small. You helped me to return to my royal dignity. I know now that to be vulgar and esoteric is a profound weakness. *L'esprit du corp* is the only thing that counts."

"Our brotherhood is alive, Mark. In the name of Truth, you'll be welcome at any time. You're more than a brother to me. You're my other self."

"I thank you for the good words, Andrew. Don't be afraid of the Anti-Christ. He wants to help in his own way. He's terribly lonely, too," Mark informed him.

"I know. He didn't become a devil willingly. He simply didn't have a choice. Like us."

"He'll do it for you, Andrew. He'll make the impossible, possible. What has he to lose? He's damned forever anyway."

"Mark, don't go yet, please. Don't begrudge my Love for Chin Moon. She has had so little of me."

The divine face within the golden flame intensified.

"My pride has always worked against me, Andrew. General Ikhmet Haremhab advised me never to turn my back to a priest. My wife even insisted that I stay away from the High Priest until we were safely back under the protection of the One and Only God. My Divine Mother Nefertiti swore me to avenge the slow death of Lord Aton. She asked me to destroy the priesthood quickly and mercilessly. But I had lived among them for five years. To me, the High Priest was like a father, the father that neither Ikhnaton nor Aton had been. He taught me about the Universe and the mysteries of the Men-Gods, a brotherhood that coexisted with mankind to create a New World. But Man wanted only power and rejected harmony. Secrets were withheld from him and guarded by the priests.

"I knew those secrets and I wasn't afraid of the priests. Those secrets, combined with the Love and Harmony of the One and Only God, would've brought His Kingdom on Earth. When the High Priest asked me for a private audience, against my best judgment, I said 'yes.'

"That 'yes' changed the course of history. Was it God's Will? Perhaps. I can't defeat my own selfishness, and God reads my heart. I can't share Love either. That's my terrible Pharaonic Pride. But my Love toward you is True in spite of my treason and vengefulness. Aymo, as the devil he is, just took advantage of me, the same way as he does of you. But he can't harm you, and you are slow to anger. You are cool under fire, no matter the circumstances. Keep an eye on Danny. To a lesser degree, he's a carbon copy of me. Do you trust your father?"

"I don't know, Mark. I just met him through Danny."

A veil of sadness fell over the golden mask of Tut. "Be aware, Andrew, you're in the same situation as I was in Egypt. The same forces are acting against you. You are affected by loyalty, your sense of duty, a father you don't know at all and the Anti-Christ that you know only too well. The future depends on the clarity of your mind."

Andrew stepped closer, hand stretched out toward the golden vision.

"Mark, take off your Pharaonic Mask, please. I want to see your face one more time!"

The head dropped just a bit. "I can't, Andrew, there's nothing behind the funeral mask. Even my eyes are painted. In my foolishness as Mark, I blew my face off with a gun."

Andrew let his tears flow.

"Oh, Mark, shall I never see you again?"

"Only in your heart, Andrew…farewell…farewell…farewell…"

The distance between the monastery and the base camp was two days through the most fantastic terrain one can think of. Gardens of frozen stalactites in strange forms harmonized with the lacey cobwebs of snow spreading over the majestic peaks. There were countless cracks and sculptures formed by age-old magma. Everything was scintillating under a brilliant, festive sun.

Chin Moon had fallen into the rhythm of the zopkios and never asked for any special considerations. She blended into the landscape so well that sometimes Andrew lost visual contact with her. For him and Danny, keeping up with the rest was overwhelming. But they didn't ask for special treatment, either. By the evening of day one, they, too, had fallen into the rhythm and began walking faster. They were even able to exchange a few words.

Later, by the fire, Chin Moon's glowing cheeks and laughing eyes made her look more beautiful than ever.

"I'm so happy, Andrew, but I'm frightened. How far will my luck take me? The premonition of pending doom wakes me in the night, and I spend hours looking at your face, so it's imprinted deeply into my soul. I want to be sure that if I meet you in another life, I'll be able to recognize your dear face amidst the millions of others. If I come back to life as a tiny bird, don't be surprised if I land on your shoulder. Give me a little kiss and say, 'Hello, wife, it has been such a long time.' How silly of me, I should be ashamed of myself."

Andrew took Chin Moon in his embrace, thinking what a good choice he had made. He listened to the gentle voices of the sherpas, who chanted their monotonous mantras. The smell of burning juniper permeated the holy hour of twilight until the freezing wing of night fell over them. *Thank You, God, for letting me have these moments of happiness*, thought Andrew, *You have been very generous to me, harmony will be forever with me.*

ﺑ٦ﺑﻴﻴﺐ ﺑ ٧ﻌﭙﺖ

The base camp was covered with ice. After unzipping their tent, the sherpas had to break out of their encasement, like an eggshell. They gathered around the fire and warmed their hands with the cups of hot milk and tea. Some took care of the animals. Changha Narr was happy to see them. He hugged Andrew and punched Danny in the shoulder in acknowledgement.

Andrew walked toward a man standing alone. The stranger warmed himself by the fire, his back toward the happy bunch. He appeared to be in a trance, mesmerized by the dancing flames. Andrew stopped right behind him.

"Good morning, Aymo, or perhaps you've changed your name for the occasion."

The man smiled and looked at Andrew furtively. "No. Aymo is right for the environment. I guess our young Pharaoh broke the news to you."

"Yes, I met him. Last night we camped at half an hour's walk from this place but didn't know it. Somehow I felt your presence. I knew you'd be somewhere along the road."

"And you don't mind it?"

"Why should I mind it? You're like a family to me. You knew my father."

"I killed him," Aymo said dispassionately.

"I knew that too. I knew when you slept with my mother."

"She would've done it with anybody. The stalwart cadets on her boat, for example. It was better to keep it *in the family*."

"Perhaps." Andrew knelt beside the fire next to Aymo, who served him a cup of hot chocolate. "Thank you for trying to be helpful."

"Somebody has to mind the fire. Do you trust me?" questioned Aymo.

"In a certain sense, I do. Why did you abandon Mark?"

"Because he was finished. He makes more sense as Tutankhamon — a dreamer, but harmless and not particularly ambitious."

"Are you trying to be practical?" asked Andrew.

"I'm not getting any younger, and I have to be careful about my reputation. Especially as a sardar of this expedition. Everything should be perfect, or nearly so. I like working with sherpas. They are selfless, gracious and generous."

"You depend heavily on the outcome of my mission, don't you?"

"Yes, Master, otherwise I may lose my license. What am I without people? I have no business in other dimensions. Throughout the millenniums I have come to love man. Unfortunately, men are egocentric and can no longer be protected from their own stupidity. I hope you do better than I did."

In the soft morning light, the fantastic masses of ice looked like statuary of strange people frozen in their last agony. Andrew recognized some figures. "The past seems to be catching up with us."

Aymo glanced at the groupings. "Yes. I can see Nefertiti and Judas."

"What do you think about the Bible, Aymo?"

The older man set his sharp eyes on Andrew. "Do you really want to know?"

"Yes, I do."

"It's supposed to burn my hands if I touch it," admitted Aymo.

"Those are legends. The Bible has been in hands worse than yours," Andrew told him.

"True. The cross doesn't harm me either. These are mere symbols. The Bible didn't precede the Creation. It was concocted by Man."

"And what about the Tablets of Moses?"

"Those were written by God. Moses was the Holiest of men," stated Aymo.

“Then you admit the Divinity of Christ?” asked Andrew.

“Of course. I met Him in person. I helped him to the cross.”

“You’re getting sentimental,” observed Andrew.

“Why not? Sometimes in private, I cry for Him. He didn’t know how to read Greek and Hebrew, but the Bible was printed in His mind. He argued about every line with brother Jacob, so He was chosen by birth. He firmly believed that God would save Him,” said Aymo.

“When did He start doubting?”

“At the Gethsemane Garden, when He was left alone. It was then the boy Mark came to Him and kissed His Hand. He must’ve been sent by God. Mark stood by Him to the last.”

“Did they talk about Lord Aton?”

“Probably. Tut had some memories of his father. He knew the soldiers killed him and threw his body in the desert.”

“So you believe in the Prophets,” Andrew continued to probe Aymo.

Aymo looked again at the fascinating play of the flames. “I’m much older than they are. I saw them coming and going.”

“Is this my Garden of Gethsemane?”

Aymo nodded slowly.

Andrew groped for Aymo’s hand, “And you didn’t want to leave me alone.”

Aymo looked at him. “I want you to be assured of your immortality to help you survive the terrible pains that will be inflicted upon you. Remember, You are the Redeemer!”

Andrew pressed his hand over Aymo’s. He kissed it lightly.

“In spite of my inborn cynicism, I believe in you, Andrew. I always did, even if I have to kill you. You’ll triumph, Andrew, so the Name of Christ lives forever.”

پ٦٦٧ت

The rest of the day was spent in preparing for the journey to the second base near the Khumbu Icefall. Andrew and Danny walked to the ridge where, in the shadows of the amazing Himalayas, fifty-three shrines commemorated the souls of sherpas that perished over the years in their journey to the Abode of God. Changha Narr read the names and they all tried to visualize the men behind the names. Then Changha left them. They assured him that the way back was easy to find. He was needed at the base.

Andrew wanted to spend some more time with those heroic people. He sat on a rock formation and was silent for awhile.

Then Danny spoke without taking his eyes from the stunning scenery of the lonely peaks, "I saw you talking to Aymo. Why did you have to spend such a long time talking to an accursed man?"

"I'm not firing him."

Danny was so shocked that he said nothing for over a minute. "What does Chin Moon have to say about it? Does she know who our sardar is?"

"She doesn't have to know. I don't want you to discuss the matter with her," demanded Andrew.

Danny bristled. "Is that an order?"

"Yes, it is."

Danny bit his lip and bowed submissively, "Thank you, Master."

"You don't have to be sarcastic with me, Danny. I know what I'm doing."

"I hope so. It could've been Aymo that pulled the handgun's trigger. Mark would've been alive and participating in this expedition if you had mustered a pardon for him."

"According to your own report, Mark would've pulled the trigger anyway," Andrew flatly told Danny.

Danny lit his last cigarette, then he mechanically crumpled the package and threw it to the ground.

"Pick up that garbage, Danny. Put it in your pocket."

Danny seethed. "As you wish, Master. The next storm would've taken care of it."

"And would've set it right on Mt. Everest," continued Andrew.

"How can you be so petty, Andrew? You'll make a perfect housewife in your next reincarnation."

Andrew slapped him across the mouth squashing his cigarette. "You had that coming to you."

Danny cried defiantly and grabbed Andrew in a bear hug. "And that was coming to you, too."

They grappled in silence, exchanging short rabbit punches. Due to the thin air, they were soon huffing and puffing. They fell over a small embankment, and Andrew adeptly sneaked in two good punches. Danny fought back, but his smoking and the high altitude did him in.

"Uncle!" Danny cried. "I must stop smoking. You know I'm stronger than you, don't you?"

Andrew found his handkerchief and tried to stop Danny's nosebleed.

"I'm heavier than you. I've been wrestling Changha on a regular bases. I lose two out of three skirmishes to him. No hard feelings?"

Danny got up to a sitting position and pressed Andrew's handkerchief against his swollen nose, squinting against the glare of the sun. "No hard feelings. I feel fine. Just don't brag about it in front of the others. You busted my sunglasses."

"I can't find mine at all."

"Don't try to boss me around the way Mark did, Andrew. I won't take it from you or anybody else."

"I'm sorry, Danny. I don't know what's happening to me. I can't even pray anymore," admitted Andrew.

"It isn't a big deal. I've been never good with religion, but I'll support you to the finish."

Both young men suddenly felt very tired and sleepy. Andrew tried to engage Danny's eyes.

"Thanks, Danny. If something happens to me, will you take care of Chin Moon?"

This request was a shocker to Danny. He opened his eyes wide. "What's gonna happen to you?"

"I don't know. It's a dangerous climb," Andrew answered.

"You're right. We'll manage. But I'll take care of Chin Moon if anything happens — I promise."

Danny fell asleep but Andrew doggedly stayed wide awake. He felt in his heart who was residing inside Danny. Finally the other youth was completely unconscious.

"Father, can you talk?" asked Andrew

"Danny is a hell of a tough guy," a voice whispered to Andrew.

"He is. Thanks for helping me, father."

"Well, I'm not a stranger to fights. But you have a very good uppercut. I certainly felt it."

"I am unable to reach you while he is awake, so I had to knock him out."

"Of course, you're a full-fledged man. I'm proud of you. I would've given all the celestial bliss just for one more fight, though, I was never a bully, well, maybe a couple of times. Guys like Danny are just looking for it. Your grandfather still watches the TV fights. He wanted to come here in my stead, but my son is my own responsibility. Shadow wanted to come also, but I said 'No.' I need all I can get of you in real life, not just in moving pictures. We shouldn't be strangers to each other, son. I'm in your corner."

Danny sobbed in his sleep, then began moaning and wailing desperately. He woke up with a jerk. His eyes full of horror and confusion. "What is it? What is happening? Why am I crying?"

Andrew held him with gentleness and love. "Hush, boy. Hush. From now on, I'll shoulder the nightmares of all Humanity. You'll get to know what real happiness is, dear man, because I am here to drink the bitter cup for you."

"Who said that?" Danny wondered aloud.

"Jesus…the Jesus of all times," uttered Andrew.

Chapter 30

DREAMS

During the night, Andrew fell into a deep sleep, so much so that Chin Moon was alarmed at his shallow breathing and weak pulse. She had a hard time waking Danny, as well. Finally, he muttered in his sleep. Chin Moon had to put her ear down to his mouth in order to understand what he was saying. "It's all right, Chin Moon. Andrew is in another dimension, but he'll wake up feeling truly rested."

The voice didn't sound like Danny's, and it spoke in Chinese.

"Who are you?" Chin Moon whispered.

"I'm Andrew's father, Gordon Bates."

For a moment Chin Moon thought that Danny was playing games with her, though the youth seemed soundly asleep. Besides, Danny didn't know Chinese. Perhaps he learned it at the monastery beyond the range. Her extraordinary sensitiveness hinted otherwise.

"Who taught you my language?" she asked

"Nobody. I have the gift of tongues like Andrew."

"And you're here?" Chin Moon gasped.

"I temporarily reside in Danny's body. I've got to help my son. He's pushing himself to the point of death and transfiguration. He won't belong to this world much longer."

Chin Moon was stunned. "What can I do?"

"Trust your instincts."

Chin Moon's beautiful eyes brimmed with tears. "He doesn't love me that much. He belongs only to his Mission."

"You're wrong, Chin Moon. He loves you dearly, you can count on it."

"I believe him to be the Savior. He brought a dead boy back to life and saved me and many others from the radiation disease. He wouldn't betray his fellow man. Even though I cannot have him all to myself, I must share him with everyone on Earth."

The voice quieted, and Chin Moon tried to placate him.

"Father of Andrew, are you still with me?"

"Yes, I'm still with you."

"If you're not comfortable in Danny's body, you can come and visit with me. You'll always be welcome, father."

"Thank you kindly, my most beloved daughter. But I cannot enter a woman's body. God has set limitations in that respect."

"Let your Honored Wife come."

Gordon laughed feebly. "You don't need her, Chin Moon. You'd be quite uncomfortable with her. She never even visits with me."

"But she ought to. She's your lawful wife."

Gordon sighed almost inaudibly. "I guess she's more a concubine than a wife. She's been in the company of many men. I was poor and not quite up to her taste. She likes them handsome and young."

"I see, Andrew is very much like you. He married me without any dowry, and I'm not very pretty either," Chin Moon sobbed.

"You're beautiful, Chin Moon. I like you very much. You're also brave and wise."

"I'm an unworthy wife of your honorable son. I cannot give him a child."

"Don't cry, Chin Moon. Slip into the sleeping bag with your husband. You're very small. He needs you, too. When he wakes up, he'll make love to you. Then you'll have a beautiful baby son. I promise you. But, there's one condition: Don't follow Andrew to

Chomolungma. Have one of your half-brothers take you back home. There you'll wait for the baby."

"Will Andrew know about it?"

"Yes, he'll know. And that will make him very happy. It will give him such strength that he'll overcome Death."

"Like Jesus?"

"As Jesus Himself did."

ANDREW'S DREAM

In his dream, Andrew was in ancient Amarna. Everyone called him Aton. The palace was being besieged by General Harremhab for a third day in a row. His troops had set it on fire. Men, women and children prayed with their Lord-Protector.

"Call the Almighty One and Only God to save us, Lord Aton! We trusted you with our lives, help us!"

Aton shook his head in desperation. "I can't, my poor people. For now it's the Almighty's will to destroy us. Our time hasn't come yet. But the future will be ours. One day, a Lord more powerful than I will rise from the dead to establish His Kingdom on Earth, and we'll all live to see it from our celestial homes. And it will be the First Day on Heaven and Earth when the One and Only God will pass judgment on us. Whoever is with Him in this tragic hour will be recognized and Honored Forever. Believe me, children, because I've always told you only the Truth! Now open the door for me."

"Don't, Lord! It will serve no purpose. They'll kill us anyway. Let's die together!"

"As long as there is the tiniest chance, I'll take it. Haremhab is my brother."

"He sold you out to the Priests. He won't have any pity for you or us. Don't go, Lord Aton! Stay with us!"

Aton smiled forlornly. "I thank you with all my heart. Your love will be with me in my darkest hour."

A big wail rose from the crowd who had fallen to their knees, their hands extended pleadingly toward Him."

"Don't go, Lord! To whom are you leaving our fate?"

"In the Hands of the One and Only God!!!"

Fire consumed the eastern wing of the palace, which filled the air with thick smoke. A crack opened and Aton squeezed himself out.

When the attacking troops saw the lonely figure emerge from the portal they stopped and parted their formation to let him pass. Everyone of them recognized him, and his bravery left them confused and subdued. Courage was always esteemed among the soldiers' fraternity. The handsome face of their young stalwart general paled. He jumped from his chariot and came running to his half-brother.

"What are you doing, brother? I can't save you from the hands of the priests. They'll condemn you to a slow death for high treason."

"I don't want to be saved by you, brother, and yours is the highest treason. You'll be damned forever. If you spare the people inside, I'll pardon you for my death."

lkhmet's head dropped. "I'll kill the Pharaoh with my bare hands, but I'll spare the people and Nefertiti. I'll try to let you see Prince Tut before your condemnation. He's entitled to see his real father."

And the Will of God came to pass. Aton had to face the enraged priests.

"The name Aton was given to me by God, but I never call myself Lord."

"Did you willfully destroy the homes of our true gods?" They cried.

"The Pharaoh disposed of them against my advice. I don't share his radical ideas about total eradication of the old gods. I thought that both time and the Almighty would take care of this matter. Ikhnaton believed only in brute force and extreme measures."

"Do you believe in the true gods?" the high priest screamed.

"No. I believe they exist only as a figment of your imagination."

"Blasphemy!" they all roared.

"There is only One Truth — God Almighty."

"I condemn you to die by a slow death. Let your only god save you," the high priest announced

"He won't save me, because I am only a Messenger of His Sacred Will. I followed my own vocation, and I accept the punishment for it," Aton declared humbly.

"You are a traitor and blasphemer. Die!" the priest condemned him.

The voices of the priesthood approved the verdict of the High Priest.

"Die! Die! Die!" the priests chanted in a mayhem of fury and hysteria.

In the darkness of the windowless cell, Aton heard the opening of the door. A small lamp illuminated the slim figure of the young prince at the door. He hesitated, then entered the cell. The door was closed and locked behind him.

"Are you really my father, Aton?" asked the prince.

"I am, but it's known only to a few."

"So, I won't be the Pharaoh of the Land will I?"

"Nonsense! There is no other. It's not in the interest of the priesthood to deny you the throne. Not when they think you're a puppet in their crafty hands."

"Perhaps I am. Under the circumstances they can dispose of me at will. What kind of Pharaoh will I be, if I am only an instrument."

"You can be a Great Pharaoh like Ramses the Great, if you choose."

"Do I have a choice?"

"Of course, as a Pharaoh, you'll have unlimited power. The true God will be guiding you."

"The true God brought you to this cell," mocked the Prince.

"My Path led me to this cell and the Slow Death. God isn't responsible for our personal choices."

"As a Pharaoh, can I pardon you?"

"You're not the Pharaoh as yet. By the time you sit on the throne, I'll be long dead. You won't need me. Your mother Nefertiti will help you. She knows the power moves in this game better than anybody else."

"Am I supposed to love you?" asked the Prince.

"No, but you can respect me if you choose."

"The old gods seem to be stronger than the new One," observed the Prince.

"It only seems so."

"Why don't you ask the priests for pardon. The 'slow death' is horrendous."

"I haven't done anything wrong, son. Why should I ask for a pardon?"

"To spare yourself death and humiliation."

"Then what will I do with my life? Build a pyramid of repentance?"

"Perhaps. But what kind of afterlife will you have? You won't even be buried. No body to reenter, no further existence. You'll disappear into nothingness."

"I'll be with my God."

"As what?"

"As a part of Him."

"Is that possible?"

"Very much so, my son. I'll serve him as always."

"Why? He doesn't even have a name."

"He doesn't need a name, he's the Only One."

"What about a body?"

"He's everything in spirit."

"I hope you have a happy afterlife, father. How shall I honor you?"

"By remembering me as I am."

DREAM CONTINUES

The High Priest, surrounded by his body guards, stood at the door to the torture room.

"I ask you for a last time, are you going to refute your teachings and return to the protection of the righteous Gods?"

Aton shook his head. "I know only One Righteous God."

The High Priest grimaced as if he had been slapped. "Take him to the death chamber!"

The torturers ripped his clothes off and chained him to the wall. Aton offered no resistance. But for the first time, a pang of doubt crossed his mind. Was there really God in Heaven, or it was only an illusion, an arbitrary force bereft of any thinking or feeling? What is there to believe in, if the absolute state of being doesn't serve any practical purpose?

TORTURE CHAMBER: PUNISHMENT OF IKHMET HAREMHAB'S MIND — DREAM CONTINUATION

Nefertiti knew what was happening to Aton. Only one human was capable of delivering Aton from the priest.

Ikhmet!

Nefertiti disposed of any signs of royal dignity. She rushed from door to door, her hair flying in total disorder, her tunic was torn, and she shrieked like a mortally wounded animal. Finally, she came to the room where a naked lkhmet was writhing on the floor, sobbing with pain and despair. Blood gushed from different places, as if his body was torn to pieces. His teeth and fingernails were missing. His genitals disappeared in a large bloat of blood and torn flesh. Ikhmet Haremhab screamed. Prostrate on the marble floor, arms and feet spread eagle, Ikhmet's limbs started separating from the abdomen, amid the sound of muscles tearing and bones crushing.

Nefertiti screamed even louder. Suddenly, Ikhmet's eyes glazed, and a last powerful sigh escaped his broken lips. Then, from everywhere, an incredible golden cloud covered the bloody pieces. When it dispersed, the magnificent body lay more splendid than ever. Ikhmet's dead eyes came back to life. A low resonant voice echoed under the high vaulted ceiling. "Condemned to live."

IN TORTURE CHAMBER

The High Priest was in disbelief. Aton's body lay peacefully on the sandy floor absolutely untouched, not a drop of blood by him, as a deep velvety voice was heard by everybody present. "Welcome to your kingdom, Lord Aton."

A bright flash of lightning illuminated the room and the bloody hands of the executioners went to their eyes with a desperate shriek. On the face of the High Priest, two bloody holes gaped where his eyes had been. He fell to his knees.

"Amon-Ra! ! !"

The earthly body of Lord Aton was taken to the hot sands of the Nubian desert and left as a gift to the predators.

BACK TO NOW

Gradually, Andrew came to his senses, but was still petrified by the brutal realism in the scenes he had witnessed. "I know perfectly well what I'm called to do," he uttered, "and I'm ready for it."

Next to him, he felt a living body radiating with love and devotion.

"Chin Moon! God sent you to me, blessed be thy heart!"

His lovemaking was a cry to God, a return to the primeval forces of a young and untouched Creation.

LIFE GOES ON

In the predawn chill, the sherpas gathered, adjusting loads and finishing their hot drinks.

Andrew took Chin Moon to Tormack Baggach. "You have to take your sister back to Katmandu."

Tormack didn't ask why; he simply nodded and called for two sherpas. They took one of the zopkios.

Andrew pressed Chin Moon's body tenderly to his own. He wanted to remember this for eternity. "Thank you, dear!" he said gently to Chin Moon. Then, he spoke to Tormack, "Stop at the monastery, Tormack and rest well. Don't take any chances. Chin Moon is pregnant with my child."

Chin Moon lifted her large eyes, overflowing with tears. "Be safe, Andrew, so you can come back to me."

LOST CONTACT

Due to the solar flares, Andrew's expedition lost all radio contact. They moved slowly, blinded by a storm that raged with 100 mile-per-hour winds. Finally, close to Base Camp Two, they found a place to dig themselves in. The yaks were harnessed in special yokes and tied to iron bars wedged into the rocks. All sense of time was lost. In the midst of the storm, they saw scenes of other worlds, scenery from other times — dinosaurs and pterodactyls, the Armageddon and the Four Horsemen of the Apocalypse. They heard hysterical yelping and Sig Heil! shouted by millions. They saw the victims of bloodthirsty dictators, the Soviet Gulag-Archipelago, and the smoke stacks of the crematoriums. They viewed the tribulations of the first Christians, and the triumphs of Alexander the Great. The weary travelers were forced to witness a whole panopticum of times past, those replete with heartbreak and triumph as well!

ANDREW'S SECOND DREAM — THE CRUCIFIXION

When the winds abated, the torn expedition made their way to the demolished Base Two. They were exhausted and slept like the dead.

Andrew fell into another troubled sleep. He was dragging his T-cross up the steep, cobbled street, blood and acid sweat blinding his vision. He fell down to his knees, a sea of faces laughing around Him. Then Aymo appeared and said, "You can still escape this miserable death if you come with me. I'll take you to the Palace of all Palaces. Just take my hand and I'll lead you to the top of Mt. Everest!"

Christ didn't listen to him, torn by the dichotomy of his own thoughts. "Why, Dear God? Why do I have to die in such an inglorious, vexing way? What have I done to displease You? I served You as well as I could. My family disowned me and everyone hates me. What else do You want of me? My life is trickling away from me and You don't say a single word. Am I wrong? Tell me. I want to hear it from You before I die!"

Suddenly the sun darkened and the earth shook in agony. A thundering voice came over the cold sweep of a desert's wind, "Why so many questions and laments? If you want to be My Son, die for Me in dignity. I never promised you glory and victory. What you have done with your life is next to nothing. Now is Judgment Day!"

The crowd that intended to enjoy the crucifixion heard this and dispersed hurriedly.

Under a dramatic sky of pending doom, Mount Calvary rose in the distance. The Romans were nervous too. They didn't like the omen.

The heavy cross was carried to the city limits, where there were other crosses stuck in the rocky ground. Digging into the dry, compacted soil was hard labor.

The commanding officer looked at the distraught but still pretty woman. "You wanna watch? It's an ugly procedure. Who are you, anyway?"

"I'm his wife."

The officer shrugged his shoulders. "You gonna claim the body?"

"I will."

"Well, it won't take long before he dies. Do you love him?"

"I love him dearly," whispered the woman.

"But you don't cry," said the soldier.

"There is time for that."

"Who's the other woman? His mother?"

"No, a friend of mine. His family doesn't know he is condemned. They live in Nazareth."

"Do you have children?" asked the centurion.

"We've been married only two months."

"You're pretty, you'll find a better man. What did he do for a living?"

"He was a carpenter."

The young man paused. "Who told him he's a messiah?"

"God."

"Which god?"

"The Only One."

"I see. The earth shakes and the sun eclipses. It makes sense."

The small procession reached a group of three crosses. On two of them there were still carcasses but the third one was empty. An abandoned ladder was laid by it.

"Set him on the ladder," ordered the centurion. "I shouldn't be doing things of this kind. The commander is mad. What's your name, woman?"

"Mary," she responded.

The Roman turned to his men. "Take off his clothes. They're still good. Throw some dice for them." Then he turned back to her, "Go to him, Mary, and take your time. I'll keep them busy."

Mary knelt down by Jesus and wiped the blood from His face with her long hair. The thorns had dug deep into his scalp, and when she tried to remove the wreath, Jesus' face cringed with pain. She let it go.

"The centurion said, it won't take long."

Jesus tried to wet his parched lips with the tip of his tongue.

"I'm...thirsty. ..Mary..." he barely croaked.

She asked one of the soldiers for some water. He gave her a sponge which she touched to Jesus' lips. The smell of vinegar came to her. She threw the sponge away. The soldier laughed bawdily, "That's what we serve for refreshment."

Mary tried to lick the acid from His parched lips. The pain was excruciating. Mary kissed the tormented face with all the love she could muster while the final moments ticked away.

Jesus did his best to comfort the grief-stricken woman, "Pardon them, Mary. They don't know what they're doing."

She was unable to stop her tears. She embraced him tenderly. "I love you, dear. I'll love you forever."

"Thank you, Mary. Without you I would never have been a complete man."

The hands of the centurion pulled her up. "It's time." He turned to his charges and ordered them to proceed. "Drive the nails through his wrists, then hang him up with ropes. Nobody will know the difference. Keep the dogs away. Their howling drives me crazy. It's freezing, so hurry up."

The pounding of the nails through flesh and bone, and the shrieking cries from her love pierced Mary's heart. Her friend Miriam kept her from falling. Mary extended her hands up toward the menacing sky. "God, why have you abandoned us?"

The soldiers pulled the body up the ladder, and they fastened his hands tightly to the cross. The sharp ropes of uncured hemp cut through skin and veins. Now on their knees, the women sobbed bitterly.

Jesus, a serene expression on his face, eyes driven into the beyond, was strangely quiet.

"At last..." He whispered, "...it's all over. God's will...has been...done..."

Joseph of Arimathaea was well known in Jerusalem, but nobody had ever heard of Nicodemus. Strange stories circulated around town about him that he was a magician residing simultaneously in several worlds. Very few had seen him and even fewer had heard him speak. As a member of the Sanhedrin, Joseph had to explain his houseguest a number of times, though not to the satisfaction of the Pharisees.

After the Crucifixion, Joseph persuaded the Roman Proconsul to let him take down Christ's body from the cross for a decent burial. He promised to guard the family tomb so Jesus' body wouldn't be stolen by his disciples. To be on the safe side, Pilate ordered the centurion in charge of the execution to stay with them, also. Even then, the Proconsul had some misgivings.

"Are you completely sure, Flavius, that the spear went all the way through his body?" he asked.

"It was my spear, Proconsul, and I drove it through to the other side," informed Flavius.

"I know you from many campaigns, Flavius, and your family is well known in Rome, but I ask you, why are you still a centurion in a godforsaken place like Judea?"

Flavius smiled broadly. "Perhaps you can tell me, Honorable One."

Pontius Pilate waved his hand and flashed back the closest thing to a smile that he was able to produce. "Ah, Rome is not what it used to be. Go, Flavius, go. You're a good and honest soldier."

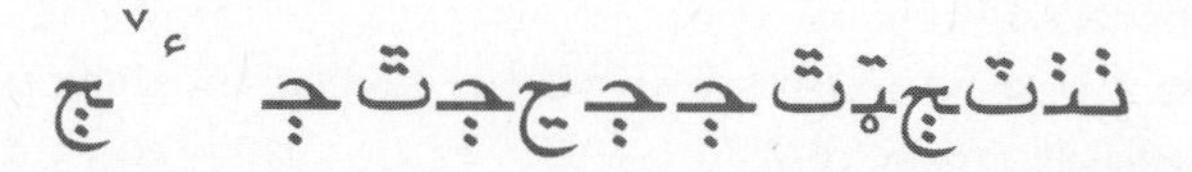

The tomb was well lit and the body of Jesus was wrapped in a clean, expensive linen shroud. Joseph, Nicodemus and Flavius stood there in total disbelief. Jesus' body and face was free of blemish. There was no trace of the torture and the lashing he had suffered that morning, nor were there any signs of being pierced by Flavius' spear. There was a soft golden aura about his face, and the bloody ring where the "Crown of Thorns" rested, had been healed. The three astounded men exchanged confused glances.

"He looks as if he's sleeping," said Nicodemus.

"I swear his chest is moving," uttered Joseph. "He's breathing!"

"This body is the most perfect creation I've ever seen," whispered Flavius, "His eyes are ready to open."

They did open and Jesus smiled kindly at them, then came up to his elbows. "What time it is, dear friends?"

Now Joseph spoke, "The women will come soon, Lord, with the precious oils to apply to your head and body."

"Then we have very little time to talk, gentlemen. Tell my Apostles and brother Jacob to wait for me on the ninth day from now. I'll come to your home, Joseph, to give you my last instructions. I may be able to see some of you until the fortieth day, when I'll go to Heaven. You, Flavius, have to run away this very morning. Your life is in jeopardy. You'll be blamed unjustly for my 'escape'. Joseph will give you money and a fast horse. Take the first ship to any of the Greek islands. Buy some land, get married and have many children. One of my emissaries will get in touch with you. You are a good man, Flavius. Now, all three of you have to disperse so the women won't find you here. I'll send an angel to tell them the good news and to let people think that I'm still buried here, so Joseph and Nicodemus have sufficient time to sell their properties and move to Ephesus. Every life is precious. Be ready for hard times ahead."

"Give my love to my beloved wife, Mary. She had nothing but me in this world. Help her to find a home somewhere safe, away from here, so she can give birth to my child. Now go, brothers, in the name of God. I shall miss you."

Andrew woke up in a trance-like state, as if Heaven had opened to him. "God, let be Thy Will! I'm ready."

Chapter 31

THE EXPEDITION

On May 12th, Andrew's expedition was still stranded at Base Two. The access to South Col wasn't promising: The western access had been damaged as well. Cracks had deepened and widened, piles of debris blocked most of the paths. New shifting crevasses barricaded access to the treacherous Khumbu Icefall. There was no way to return to Base One.

The weather had cleared except on Chomolungma, where a steady whirl of snow licked at the ridges. Prayer flags hung over the camp. It looked like a bad day for climbing, and Everest was never easy anyway. Tempers and supplies became short. The season for scaling the giant peak wound down. The situation looked hopeless. The survivors, with no way back and no radio communications, seemed to be the last people on earth.

Exhausted, ragged and disheartened, they gathered around Andrew, Danny, Aymo and Changha Narr. The question in everyone's eyes was, "What now?"

Andrew finally spoke, "We're all in God's hands. I thank you for everything you've done. It seems that all forces of evil are against us, but Our Father in Heaven will prevail. I'm going on alone."

There was an outcry, then a hushed silence. The deep voice of Aymo interrupted, "Not without me, Master."

Andrew smiled. "You promised to take me there."

"That was poppy-cock, but I still have some tricks up my sleeve. You've got to trust me, in order to do what no another human being has done in history."

"And what is that?" asked Andrew.

"I'll help you split away from the material world."

Danny positioned himself between the two and faced Andrew. "Don't do it, Andrew. Remember what they taught us in the monastery. If you split completely you can never return to your body. You have to dissolve into the Absolute."

Andrew lifted his eyebrows. "Which is God Himself."

"Or the Other Side of Time," said Danny. "Forget about Aymo. Changha Narr and I will follow You. If we perish, we'll perish like men. If we win, Mankind will triumph!"

Changha Narr agreed with Danny.

"Don't hesitate, Andrew. Let's do it our way, the only way we know. If we die, let's die like men."

One by one, the rest of the sherpas joined in. In actuality, millions from the whole world in the role-call of times, stood silently, their eyes centered on Andrew.

The whole Majestic Mountain was alive with them.

Aymo stood behind Andrew and whispered in his ear, "You can't win by illusions, Andrew. Only the powers of the Unknown are strong enough to withstand the attacks of Evil."

Andrew looked over his shoulder at him. "And the Unknown is Man himself, Aymo. Stand back! We'll do it on our own!"

A huge outcry came from the whole planet, like the primeval tidal wave that brought this mountain from the bottom of the ocean.*

The gray murky sky cracked and a golden light poured over the endless multitude.

God had smiled.

---

*The subcontinent of India came as a result of the mega-clash of large pieces of Africa and Asia. Squeezed between the two masses, the bottom of the ocean became the Himalayan Mountain Range. Fossils of ancient crustaceans are found everywhere there, even on Mount Everest.

The team consisted of Andrew, Danny, Aymo, Changha Narr and two sherpas. The support group followed but steadily lost ground. Technical problems hindered them. Communication and visual contact with the leaders was lost. A huge crevice opened almost at their feet. They tried to circle it, but an avalanche buried most of them. Only a few of the support team made it back to Base Camp 2.

Changha Narr and the two sherpas lost hope and didn't want to go any farther. Aymo tried to entice them by offering some extra pay.

"It's not a matter of money, Aymo. It's just way too dangerous."

Andrew hollered louder than the wind, "I'll make it alone."

"Let him go," Aymo said, "It's his expedition."

Danny had a problem with his oxygen mask but still insisted, "I'll go with him…we shouldn't split up. As soon as the ropes are affixed everyone should follow. Do you have the guts to do it, Changha?"

Changha Narr pierced Danny with his dark, opaque eyes. "A sherpa never runs out of guts, as long as he knows why he's taking his last chance."

Through the freezing gusts, Andrew made it over to him. "You sold me out once, Changha. Are you going to do it a second time?"

Changha Narr thought shortly. "I owe you one, Andrew. I wouldn't do it for anybody else in the world. But you must tell me why."

"For the human race, Changha."

"Who are you, Andrew?"

"I'll know that after we cross the finish line."

Changha threw a last glance toward the gaping crevice, then at his friends. "Will you follow me, men?"

The sherpas nodded curtly. They really didn't believe that Andrew and Danny would make it through. The aluminum ladders didn't make a solid contact with the ice ledges and they were far too extended to avoid flipping with the wind.

Andrew went first, with a rope tied around his waist. He crossed himself and stepped onto the shaky ladder. After three steps, he had to lean into the wind and balance his weight against it. It was like a slow dance with an invisible partner. His left shoe hung in the air for awhile, then he reversed his weight, landing on the slippery rail and made two more steps. There he withstood another gust and made it five more steps ahead, then, amazingly, he reached a rocky platform. He dug his foot in a ledge and held onto the rope.

Danny came second with the other rope on his back. The wind spared him. Andrew nailed the next hook-ups, while Danny reinforced the rail ropes and freed the landing platform for Aymo.

Aymo held the ropes well and Changha Narr had a good start. The wind had almost died down. Changha called the other sherpas. The last one came too fast — almost at the heels of the one in front of him. Unexpectedly, the wind hit hard.

Chin Moon awoke, she felt that someone was watching her from a corner of the monastery's room. It was night, but the room was full of a strange, transitory light. The woman that approached her bed was rather handsome and dressed with subdued elegance.

"Don't get up," she said in an even, unemotional voice, "I'll sit. You don't have any cigarettes, do you?"

Chin Moon shook her head.

"I didn't think you would. It's a dreadful thing not to be able to get cigarettes. I've wanted to see you for a long time but somehow didn't believe that your marriage to my son would last. Now that your marriage is not only consummated but also blessed with a child, which wasn't in the cards, I have to accept it. But, if I may ask, what do you find in Andrew, that really turns you on? He's not exactly my type — slow witted and moody like his father. Anyway, I wanted to tell you what little happiness you can expect to find in a marriage with a hero, a martyr, or even a Savior. You'll be living in his shadow to the end of your days."

Chin Moon tried to control her mounting indignation. "I honor the mother of my husband, and I wish you a hundred years of happiness, such as you like it. But my happiness with Andrew is more than enough. It doesn't matter if my happiness is big or small, long or short. It's profound and endless as the universe itself. and it will last us a whole life long."

The eyebrows of the elegant lady shot up in disbelief. "You really expect him to return?"

"Of course I do, and he'll come no matter how much you hate him."

"I don't hate him. I'm indifferent to him. I don't give a damn what happens. No, that isn't true. I do care for him, and even for you and the little one. You're made in such a way, Chin Moon, that you can hold onto happiness, because you can be satisfied with the most miserable life if you have a mere grain of happiness. You would set it in a pot filled with the best soil, water it and fertilize it with love, kindness and patience. You would soon transplant it in the central place of your garden until it grows into a gorgeous royal palm. I never thought that something like that could really happen, but now I believe it. I can see it in those beautiful, large eyes of yours. If I had a heart, I would wish you all the luck in the world. And you'll need it, believe me."

Chin Moon had lost the cornerstone between reality and the abstract visions playing havoc with her mind. She ran to the window and looked at the mighty chain of giant peaks enveloped in their dark shrouds. There her most beloved one must be, fighting against destiny and doom to face the Almighty in a desperate cause.

Gradually her optimism began to waver. If the unknown God hiding behind the mysterious veils of His timeless enigma refutes her knight in shining armor, she would deny his very existence. She didn't want to be a part of a nebulous ethereal truth. Her God had to be clear, just and understanding! She opened the windows wide. The cold was breathtaking, but she didn't feel it.

"Hear me, God, whoever you are. I want my Andrew back! His child is growing in me and You have no right to take away his father. You will receive no more sacrifices from me to placate Your insatiable omnipotence. If you expect goodness from us, prevail upon it and send the evil out and away forever!"

PART SIX

YOU HEARD MY VOICE,
AND YOU'LL BE BLESSED!
— The Testaments

Chapter 32

THE MISSION'S END IS BLESSED

The climbers, each of their steps measured carefully, passed over hundred-foot deep crevasses, knowing that one slip could send them into the icy abyss. Only a slim aluminum ladder was between them and certain death. A wall of ice collapsed and three men plunged into the morass of half melted ice. A few others scrambled to safety.

Danny caught up with Andrew. "Changha is gone, can you help him?"

Andrew worked with the hooks and the ropes without taking his eyes away even for a moment. "It doesn't matter, Danny. Soon the living and the dead will share the same dimension."

"You won't stop to help even me?"

"I wouldn't stop even for myself. If anything happens to me, just go."

"That's senseless. Soon there will be total darkness."

"There will be no darkness tonight, Danny. Look deep into yourself. It's there you'll find the answer."

"What answer?"

"The only one."

Danny sat on a rock. “You'll abandon me as you abandoned Changha!”

“Look for Changha Narr ahead of us, not behind,” advised Andrew.

Danny removed his helmet and oxygen mask.

“You left Mark, who loved you as nobody in this world. You have never acknowledged my love for you. You abandoned your wife and child. What are you made of?”

“I'm made of love for everyone. Now get up, don't slow us down.”

Half-heartedly Danny followed him. “You cannot love everybody. That's a travesty.”

“I won't let the love of a man stop me. If you look for a loved one over your shoulder, you'll miss what's ahead of you.”

“I know what's ahead of me. You,” Danny dramatically declared to Andrew.

“But I don't know what's ahead of me Danny, and I'm responsible for you and the rest.”

“Do you really mean it, Andrew? You can't fool me. We've fought and wrestled, shared dangers and played games. I was jealous, because you always paid more attention to Mark, because you thought him to be the handsomest creature on Earth. I've seen you and him engaged in sex. I wept. I even thought of killing you.” Tears streamed, then froze on Danny's face.

Andrew had a steady grip on the rope and kept on climbing. “Stop whining, Danny! Put on your oxygen mask. Your brain is being affected.”

Danny scaled the rope behind him.

“Damn You-o-ooo! Answer me, or I'll bring the rope down and we'll both go to hell hand in hand!”

Andrew continued using the hooks and the hammer masterfully, as if he had climbed all his life. His mind worked feverishly. “Father hear me, please! Help Danny. if I stop I might not be able to continue. Do something!!!” There was no response. His father had vacated Danny's body as the crazed youth tried to cut the rope.

"I warned you, it's coming to you," Danny screamed.

The rope started swinging dangerously. Andrew looked down. Aymo and Danny wrestled furtively on the rope. At the very moment, just as Andrew found a good foothold, the whole contraption gave in, and the two grappling bodies of Danny and Aymo fell into a bottomless chasm.

Andrew mechanically took the second rope and another hook. He was now all alone. None of the sherpas were in sight. Even with the oxygen, Andrew felt a tightness in his chest and a terrible vertigo. His breathing was reduced to spasmodic gulps. He lost all sense of time and it didn't matter to him. He had to continue, up and up...

Nothing else mattered to him.

A strong gust of wind almost brought him down, but he somehow managed to survive, feeling as if he were tethered to a small strand of rope extending from here to eternity.

Night never came. The blazing sun moved nearer and nearer. Andrew felt like disposing of his goggles and oxygen mask. He was out of breath and his muscles were turning into mush. Then he realized that the ground was rocky, but flat.

Andrew slowly fell to his knees. He couldn't possibly move an inch farther before resting a bit. His head weighed a ton and his chin dropped to his chest. He remembered the button, the button from the Chairman's coat. He couldn't disappoint Tan. He's watching him.

As Andrew fumbled with the clasps, his blurred vision caught something white and furry running toward him. It wasn't an angel. Angels are invisible. It was something that he knew, something dear to him. His eyes filled with tears as he heard the whispering in his own mind. "It cannot be...it's simply impossible..."

Shadow was all over him, gone wild in berserk adoration of his long absent Master.

"Shadow, my dear boy, how in the world, how did you find me? I was completely lost. Am I Home now? Is it the bright side of time?"

He hung on Shadow's neck. That dog had never been so powerful. The enormous Sun was spilling its rays to form a gigantic halo of light. Everyone on Earth should be able to see it! People might stop killing each other, defacing Mother Earth, and avoid total extinction.

Then a mighty voice echoed throughout the world, "Why did you come here, Andrew? It's not your time yet."

Andrew desperately fought through his tears to respond, "If I live, Almighty Father, everyone on Earth should live. I have a lot to live for. I don't want to look at my son and wife from the moon. And I don't want to live in a vacuum, either. Let me live my full term amidst my people. Why don't you give us a happy ending for a change? We might be quite unimportant and crazy, but in your face everything is unimportant. We can correct some of our errors, but will surely stumble into new ones. Don't get mad at us. We are made imperfect. It is only human to err."

People that time had forgotten stood on the prohibitive, almost vertical ridges, claiming their birthrights in the NEW WORLD. The proud citizens of Atlantis, the defenders of the Thermopylae passage, the Copts of Egypt, the victims of Saint Bartholomew's Night Massacre, the cremated and those that survived the debacles of the great Inquisition and Auschwitz, the thousands of victims of bloody September Eleventh...

They were all there, claiming their god!

"Will you help us, Lord?" Andrew cried.

Suddenly, peals of roaring laughter filled the Universe. It took quite some time before it calmed down.

"I haven't laughed like that for ages, Andrew. You present a most ridiculous defense of humankind. Yet, strange as it is, it does the job. Your faith in following your destiny—in your belief in contacting me in all that you have struggled through—is to be rewarded. You, my son, and your loyal Shadow will return to your world, to your wife, and watch your son grow to beautiful manhood. Go forth and be my Shepherd—perhaps, perhaps mankind will follow and learn to love one another. We shall see."

Andrew, on his knees, was blinded by God's light, but was filled with a sense of peace and strength he had never experienced. Before.

He felt the whole earth had been reborn.

As the final echoes of God's laughter faded away, Andrew turned around and took a hard look at the magnificent panoramic view from the Seat of God. The air was sparklingly clear, and he was able to see forever. Young Andrew felt like embracing the whole of Creation…but on second thought, he embraced just Shadow. He buried his flushed face in the thick, shiny fur of his best friend and whispered in his ear, "You have to remember, Shadow, that you are now only a terrestrial dog, and we are a long way from home. But then again, if Ulysses made it, why should we fail?"

Then, Andrew could hardly believe his ears. Zillions of voices of the humanity of all races and stations, blanketed the mighty mountainside and came reverberating to the farthest points of the universe. "Give yourself heart, Andrew! You just climb on our shoulders and we'll take you home as you let us back to our homes!"

AND THAT CAME TO PASS!

LOVE melted the snow and the ice that covered the inhospitable ridges and chasms, so they turned into the Garden of Eden…

Because it was God's Will, Now and Forever!

ABOUT THE AUTHOR

Born in Plovdiv, Bulgaria, **Vladimir Chernozemsky** came under intense political scrutiny while working as a documentary director and poet in Sofia. With Communist State Security agents after him for espionage, Vladimir made a harrowing escape to the West. From then on he was constantly on the move — Paris, Rome, Casablanca, Algiers — eventually receiving asylum and citizenship in the U.S.

Vladimir is the author of 46 novels, plays and screenplays written by him in five different languages. For his poems in French he has been praised as "the new Paul Verlaine." He has been hailed for his novels as "an exceptional literary talent" (*MBR/Bookwatch*) and "a talented, accomplished writer" (*Bookviews*). Vladimir is also known for his translations of other works, and as an actor, painter and film/stage director.

He has advanced degrees in Drama/Film from the DEFA in Berlin, Comparative Literature from La Sorbonne in Paris, and Film Directing from Centro Sperimentale di Cinematografia in Rome. He currently resides and works in Los Angeles, California.

Dark Side of Time **and other books by Vladimir Chernozemsky are available through your favorite book dealer or from the publisher:**

Triumvirate Publications
497 West Avenue 44
Los Angeles, CA 90065-3917

Phone/Fax: (818) 340-6770
E-Mail: Triumpub@aol.com
Web: www.Triumpub.com
SAN: 255-6480

Dark Side of Time **(ISBN: 1-932656-02-2)**
$24.95 Hardbound.

Lion of the Balkans **(ISBN: 1-932656-01-4)**
Historical War Fiction, $24.95 Hardbound.

A Continent Adrift **(ISBN: 1-932656-00-6)**
Science Fiction Novel, $24.95 Hardbound.

Please add
$4.50 shipping for first copy
($1.50 each additional copy)
and sales tax for CA orders.